SERAFIM
AND
CLAIRE

SERAFIM
AND
CLAIRE

MARK LAVORATO

ANANSI

This edition published in 2014 by
House of Anansi Press Inc.
110 Spadina Avenue, Suite 801
Toronto, ON, M5V 2K4
Tel. 416-363-4343
Fax 416-363-1017
www.houseofanansi.com

Distributed in Canada by
HarperCollins Canada Ltd.
1995 Markham Road
Scarborough, ON, M1B 5M8
Toll free tel. 1-800-387-0117

House of Anansi Press is committed to protecting our natural environment.
As part of our efforts, the interior of this book is printed on paper that contains
100% post-consumer recycled fibres, is acid-free, and is processed chlorine-free.

18 17 16 15 14 1 2 3 4 5

Library and Archives Canada Cataloguing in Publication

Lavorato, Mark, 1975–, author
Serafim and Claire / Mark Lavorato.

Issued in print and electronic formats.
ISBN 978-1-77089-365-8 (pbk.).—ISBN 978-1-77089-366-5 (html)

I. Title.

PS8623.A866S47 2014   C813'.6   C2013-904539-2
                                               C2013-904540-6

Cover design: Alysia Shewchuk
Text design and typesetting: Marijke Friesen

*We acknowledge for their financial support of our publishing program
the Canada Council for the Arts, the Ontario Arts Council, and the Government of Canada
through the Canada Book Fund.*

Printed and bound in Canada

For Montreal
And for my family of friends there

[ONE]
BURNING-IN

Ville de Québec, le 23 janvier 1928

Ma chère petite sœur,

It must be said that your last letter troubles me. I know you very well, Claire; well enough to understand when you're keeping something from me. It pains me to think of you in some kind of adversity, while having convinced yourself, in that blindingly stubborn way of yours, that you must face whatever it is alone.

I need not remind you of the things (and one set of precarious details in particular) that I bared to you, trusting, knowing, that you would not judge me. True to your word, I believe you never have. Is it so absurd to think I could reciprocate such clemency? As sisters, we share a bond that other members of a family can never know, a closeness in which only you and I can trust.

You should know that I bring you up as an unruly topic every time I visit or write Maman and Papa. They came to spend Christmas here with Gilles and I last month, and I must report that they are, sadly, as traditionalist and pious as always. On a walk we took alone, Papa asked for news of you.

At any rate, please, know that I am here if you need me, Claire. Montreal is only a brief train ride from Quebec City, and I would be on the next itinerary out should you wish it.

Avec toute ma chaleureuse affection,
Cécile

1

It was madness, and she knew it. Yet Claire Audette could not help needing to hear the song on the phonograph again, one last time, before she picked up the telephone. She watched the device (a second-hand Victrola) from her bed, where she shivered under a pile of duvets and blankets that she had wrapped tightly around herself, shuddering uncontrollably, her teeth clacking in her cheeks, a deafening woodpecker in a forest of dark thoughts. Thoughts, she was aware, that were drifting helplessly towards delirium. Her fever was on the rise; and she could be sure of this by the way the coldness in her muscles was sinking, deeper, into her bones, into the marrow beneath them, turning the jelly there into grating grains of frost. She felt like, even if the fever were to pass, she would never *really* warm up again. Not fully.

But the record on the gramophone had come to its end, and was now blankly rising and falling as it spun, the needle tirelessly tracing the contours, seesawing with the wobble of its vinyl orbit. The single speaker awash with a scratching sea song, the record's dust and blemishes lapping predictable waves against the shores of her tiny room. Claire drifted through it.

Until, shaking her head in a sudden snap of clarity, she realized that she had to formulate some kind of plan before her faculty to do so had entirely slipped away. With great focus she managed to think of what she would do next, but the undertaking took its toll, and her eyes began to close. She struggled to hold them open, fought the growing urge to just succumb. It was as if her body were quicksilver, a dense weight flattening itself out, chrome puddles coagulating into her mattress, sinking, heavy, through the cushion of its fabric.

Time passed — anywhere between a couple of seconds and a few hours — and she started awake, this time quickly rolling herself off the bed, where she called out from a pain that clenched her stomach. As it receded, she squatted, shivering over the bedpan with her skirts hiked up, finished urinating, replaced her Kotex from a box under the bed, and stood to make her way to the gramophone. She was stopped by another pain in her abdomen, which had her anchored there, motionless, until it passed. She was weaker than she'd been only hours ago, her legs fatigued and shaky. But she could still move them, thankfully, could still walk herself out of the apartment. She made it to the Victrola, replaced the needle, clutched the heavy phone, and sat on the floor, her back against the pot belly of the stove in the centre of the room, a bit of warmth already beginning to seep through the layers of blankets as the song, every note memorized, wound up into its first verse.

Claire closed her eyes, picturing each movement, each spin and swirl that she had recently been choreographing to the music. She could see the dancers she'd envisioned on either side of her, supporting her at centre stage in the brighter light. The crescendo, two more dancers joining in from either side, the orchestra swelling, hands pointing in to Claire, her arms outstretched in return. The unpredictable dénouement, slow, subtle, the other dancers retreating, vanishing into the unlit extremities of the stage. Her graceful bow. The deafening applause. The flowers bouncing at her feet. She straightens, beaming, blows a kiss, another, just before bowing a final time.

Claire opened her eyes to her cold, claustrophobic apartment. A phone stood erect beside her. In front of her, a yellow water stain leafed along the wall, sprouting down from the ceiling and fanning out like lichen. The snow-choked wind scratched at the window. All while the Victrola washed its static waves through the quiet once more.

Endeavouring not to fall asleep again, Claire reached for the phone. She had prepared a nuanced, underhanded threat for her family doctor, but exactly how she'd worded it, rehearsing it in her mind for what felt like days, was gone. She was far too exhausted to make another plan, so she drunkenly lifted the receiver, held the candlestick stand.

She heard a woman's voice, anonymous, abrupt. "Code and number, please."

"Uhm ... Lorimier. Zero. Five. One-seven."

On the fourth ring, and likely just before the operator would have cut in to say there wasn't anyone home, Dr. Bertrand answered. Claire slowly gave her name, and her old family doctor recognized her voice immediately. She told him that she was very, very ill, and needed to see him right away. The doctor, wasting no time, had grabbed a pencil and paper and asked for her address, promising that he would be over directly.

"No," she said, "no. I will come to your office instead."

"Unthinkable," he replied, citing the snow, the storm, the high banks that were clogging the streets around the city, the fact that it was well after midnight, "absolutely not."

"Please," she insisted, "you don't understand. Be ready. I am coming immediately." She hung up.

Claire stood, and was temporarily paralyzed with another spasm of pain. It occurred to her that she didn't have it in her to get properly dressed, that she was about to go out in public in a way that might very well see her committed. She shuffled towards her front door with no other choice, wrestled her boots on, then a woollen toque (the kind only children wore), switched off the lights, and paused at the humming of the wind in the porch, where a letter from her sister still lay on the floorboards, unread. Being committed, going to jail, even dying in the storm before making it there — they were all just as likely, really. She felt herself begin to cry, half-heartedly, and heaving open the door, she stepped out into the blizzard. The storm hungrily pulled her forward and slammed the door behind her.

Down the stairs, her blankets flapping, and out onto the snow-drifted sidewalk. The high banks rising to the road obscured both the street and the row of houses on the other side. It would not be possible to see carriages or vehicles as they passed. Above her, wild flakes swarmed the street lights like disturbed hives of albino wasps. The footprints of one or two previous pedestrians plodded out into the distance in front of her, soon vanishing into the abandoned night. She lumbered forward, following them, re-stamping them with her own wobbling footfalls.

At the first intersection, she climbed instinctively over the bank and into the middle of the street, to the centre of the X, where a pain in her stomach suddenly brought her to her knees then eased her to the icy ground. She huddled there, buried in her blankets, convulsing with shivers. The wind moaned through the wires above the intersection, a low, haunting, apathetic hymn.

After some time, she had the vague feeling of being lifted, carried, and placed into a small bit of warmth. The smell of animal furs. A man's voice, asking her something. Claire answering weakly, a name and intersection — Dr. Bertrand, Mont-Royal and Chambord — sure that she couldn't be heard above the wind. The weight of more furs, heavy on top of her, a horse snorting, nickering, movement, sleigh bells. Another man's voice. The sensation of being carried again. A door being shut. Then, for some time, quiet.

The next thing Claire remembered was the feeling of warm hands placing a cool circle onto her chest, fingers pressing at her breasts then her stomach, which had her biting her lip and wincing. The feeling of cold metal between her legs, questions from the doctor about when the fever began, what kind of pain she felt, where, for how long — none of which she could summon the energy to answer.

After some time floating between awareness and a peaceful lack of consciousness, Claire sensed a bustle of irritated movement: drawers slamming, whispered curses, a teakettle squealing to a boil, a table shoved closer, tinkling instruments laid out on a cloth at her side. She realized that her clothes had somehow been removed, and felt soapy water and a sponge scrubbing at her belly, streams of water dripping around her waist and thighs. Then a high lamp with a harsh white light was adjusted over the centre of her body, a glass bottle and some gauze placed beside her right ear.

Finally, there was a hand on her forehead. "Can you hear me, Claire?"

Claire could only produce a weak hum before turning her head away.

"Claire, I cannot actually see what is wrong. But it is clear that you have a very serious infection. To know more, to . . . find out what's causing it, I will have to open you up."

Claire gave another meagre hum, slothful blink.

The doctor let out a sigh, opened the bottle, and poured a cloyingly sweet liquid onto a square of gauze. He placed it over her mouth, where the tincture clung cold against her lips.

Claire stared at the light bulb above her. A faint buzzing in her head began to grow louder, distending, lifting her, as if she were as weightless as the light in the bulb. Then darkness encroached, shadows tightening along the periphery of her vision, a blackness engulfing everything. Until only the bulb was left fighting it, stark and strident, a tiny coil of wire holding tight to its own heat, its light still managing to burn through the black, even through her eyelids. The light was hers now. The light was her. In the way it had always been. All her life. And she could feel it, still, burning in, searing through the dark.

Medium: Gelatin silver print
Description: Women loading boat with stores
Location: Oporto, Portugal
Date: c. 1919

❧

The ship in focus is in the foreground and mid-sized, having both a diesel engine and masts to sail by, from which rigging droops like barbwire against the sheen of the river behind. A thin gangplank stretches up from the bow and reaches the heights of a rocky shore, where seven women have stepped onto it, and are now carrying their loads of foodstuffs and provisions in large wicker baskets, balanced, with the help of one casual hand each, on top of their heads.

There are other boats in the frame, both larger and smaller (and slightly out of focus), anchored along the opposite bank in the background, in front of the cellars of the English-run port wine industry, likely being stocked with crates and bottles for transport that same moment.

A sturdy cable, bolted to a slab of rock, extends its rusty yarn out to another unseen vessel on the left.

The blurry dots of two seabirds perforate the sky at the top.

The women loading the boat are almost certainly the wives of the fishermen, or of the merchants — seamen — who earn their living from its deck. The delicate balance of the heavy baskets on their heads, as they walk along a teetering slat of wood onto a listing ship, which chances the temperamental seas daily, is so practised that it appears ordinary, sure, unprecarious.

Yet one can feel, in their posture and resolve, that they understand, and better than most, that this is not the case.

2

Serafim Vieira stepped hesitantly from the glaring sun of the street and into a doorway that was dark with musty shade. He took off his hat, hung it on one of the pegs at the entrance, and peered into the gloom until his eyes adjusted, revealing that there was indeed a barman inside. The barman was standing behind a zinc counter, either drying a glass or running a grey rag over its milky sides as a means of cleaning it. Considering the type of establishment this was, a commoners' *tasco*, Serafim assumed it to be the latter. He advanced, surveying the murky interior as he walked, wooden tables arranged without any order, some without chairs, their surfaces pitted and stained. It would suit his purposes just fine. The barman turned his back to Serafim and placed the glass on a shelf, mumbling, *"Boa-tarde."*

He stepped meekly up to the bar, but didn't know what to do with the hand that wasn't holding his camera, experimenting with putting it in his pocket then resting it on the counter, and finally just letting it hang at his side. There was a leg of *presunto* on the bar, dry-cured ham, elevated on a wooden crutch, which had already been shaven down to the pink of its bone. A fly was sponging up the rind of its gristle.

"I would" — Serafim cleared his throat — "like a glass of *bagaço*. Please."

The barman reached for the bottle with automated efficiency, then paused, looking Serafim over for a moment, his eyes resting on his stylish vest and jacket, his beige tie in a Windsor knot, his well-trimmed moustache. Serafim feared the barman would ask if he was *sure* he wanted such a hard, unrefined, workingman's drink. But the barkeeper said nothing.

Shot glass poured to the rim, Serafim took it, watching it in his hand as he walked lest it spill over and make a mess, and sat at a table near the doorway, adjusting his uneven chair so he could look out into the bright afternoon street.

The taste was sharp, stung his eyes, scorched his gullet. He put the glass down, surprised to see it empty. Noticing that he'd placed his camera on some crumbs of bread that had been spilled during someone's slapdash breakfast, he lifted it, wiped the morsels away, and placed it gently back onto the wood again. As he did so, and out of nowhere, a swell of tears surged into the back of his throat and he had to lean forward, fighting to swallow them down. When he regained his composure, he lifted the glass to the barman behind him. "Sir?"

The second glass went down more easily. Serafim relaxed in his chair as it click-clacked between two of its legs. Across the narrow street, there was a corridor entrance to a set of apartments, shafting deep into the building, ceramic tiles woven together with azure and yellow designs that faded down the hallway into an aquamarine dark. Eventually a woman in the frills of a white dress emerged from it, her hemline dangerously close to the ground, sleeves to her wrists, a satin ruffled hat. Holding a black umbrella to guard against the sun, she stepped down into the street, tussled gauchely to open it, and strode away with all the grace of a peacock.

Once she was out of sight, Serafim turned around abruptly, lifted his glass. "Sir?"

When the barman filled it this time, the meniscus mushrooming from the rim of the shooter like bread dough after the second kneading, he placed the bottle onto the table in front of Serafim and returned to the bar. It then occurred to Serafim that the barman might already know. Though, if he didn't, he would soon enough. Oporto was a small, staunchly conservative city that festered in the rumours of its own crestfallen inhabitants. He would be made to live out his humiliation gradually, stoically, wearing it off in piecemeal degrees; the painstaking attrition of disgrace.

Serafim downed the glass, poured another, and listened to an ox cart approach from the right. You could always hear the sounds of an ox cart before you saw it: the huffs and grunts of the bulls, the sluggish wooden wheels slipping on the paving stones. A boy in threadbare pants and an oversized leather hat was leading the team, walking them as slowly as he could in order to keep the stacks of rusty terracotta bowls, separated by tufts of grass, from breaking. It reminded him of the child labour restrictions the anarchists were trying to establish; which of course made him think of Álvaro. Serafim wondered where his closest friend was at that moment. Far away and happily engaged in his work, no doubt. In the hills with the libertarian syndicalists, or in Lisbon, taking photos of every rally and protest, recording history so it *would* be history.

He threw back another shot and poured another, spilling some.

When an aged and sun-creased woman passed the doorway with three pigs on a hemp leash, he realized that this was one of the thoroughfares to the river, where people from the morning markets ferried themselves and their goods back to their homes in Gaia, on the other side. One of Serafim's favourite photos ever taken in Oporto was on that river, the Douro. The shot, by an amateur photographer, had been well ahead of its time, and featured a line of women loading a merchant boat, balancing baskets on their heads. He had been down to the loading docks countless times since first seeing the print, trying to catch something like it; but he just didn't have the luck of being in the right place at the right time. Though, he reasoned, luck was a strange thing. And maybe with the luck in his life turning sour in every way it possibly could today, the luck of a perfect exposure might just coast his way. Sure, he nodded to himself, that was as good an idea as any.

He emptied his glass one last time and stood up, feeling a wave of welcome nullity as the alcohol washed over him, pooling at his dizzy feet. Not wanting to speak to the barman, he tossed more escudos onto the table than the bottle of *bagaço* could possibly be worth, and watched as one slow coin rolled along the uneven surface as languid as an ox cart's wheel then jingled onto the floor. He didn't care. It would give the barman something more to talk about, add some flavour to the story, to the pathetic sight of him, Serafim Vieira, the laughingstock.

Out into the squinting light, he lumbered down the lane, which followed the lay of the land that drained every street in the city onto the banks of the Douro. He cupped his tiny camera, a Leica, against his chest; no model name or number, just solid German quality, which had been mailed to him directly from the factory a little under a year ago, only a few months after it was released onto the market. He'd been awaiting its invention for four long years. Finally, a sophisticated camera small enough that it wouldn't be noticed by the people it captured, that could be taken straight into the heart of a dynamic street scene and remain overlooked by its subjects.

Now he could see the water, smell the soap from all the women doing their washing on the banks and in the tributaries. He stopped to take a wobbly picture of a boy climbing to the top of a hoist that angled up over the river. The boy's friends, swimming below, cheered him on as he dove flaccidly into the brown water. Serafim took another shot of the group of them, bobbing around in the filthy river, their heads wading through orange peels and cigarette butts, skimming prisms of oil, the pale of their skinny legs disappearing into a sienna fog.

Serafim noticed that a ship was being loaded a little farther down the quay, and headed towards the commotion, thinking of its potential as a photograph. Longshoremen with square burlap sacks, swollen pillows stuffed to near bursting, were muscling into a tight queue and climbing onto the ship, while another gangplank of them, empty-handed and quick on their toes, filed out of the boat and towards the next parcels for loading.

From where he was standing, it would have been a poorly composed shot, but Serafim had lifted his camera anyway, when he heard his name being called out above the noise and bustle. He turned around to see an old acquaintance from grade school, who'd since taken over his father's merchant business, casually leaning in a doorway with his legs crossed. His friend was standing with another man, who was holding a leather-bound notebook and presumably overseeing the order being loaded.

Serafim approached them, distantly aware that he was visibly drunk, his steps unbalanced against the uneven of the cobblestones. Abandon spilled from his swinging gestures. He was quite unsure what he would do next, feeling, for the first time in his quiet and reserved life, reckless. Just before he'd reached the doorway, the man with the ledger mumbled something into his acquaintance's ear, who then nodded, smiling.

"Mr. Vieira. It's been months, has it not? I trust that you've been well?"

Serafim stopped, and for some reason held his tongue like a barkeeper in a commoners' *tasco*, casting a glance back at the ship being loaded. He swayed slightly, a thin tree in the breeze.

The man with the ledger, apparently discomfited by Serafim's lack of response and drunkenness, excused himself and left to supervise the loading lines.

"Listen." His friend uncrossed his legs. "Why don't you come out of the sun. Step inside for a few minutes, have a drink. I've got a proposition for you."

Serafim turned back, levelled his gaze, considering this, then stepped through the doorway.

Three shot glasses later, sitting on an even-legged steel chair, Serafim found himself laughing for the first time in what felt like weeks. Drinking *aguardente*, an incremental step up from his previous choice, Serafim and his friend butted out cigarette after cigarette, threads of smoke sculpting ever-changing horizons in the room. At first Serafim had scoffed at his acquaintance's offer, but then a hazy conviction began to rise, swarming between the two men and their fervent conversation, plunging through its fateful undercurrents. And when his old friend stood and told him he had to tend to the ship, but suggested Serafim sleep off the drink on the sofa in the next room and think about it, Serafim went there immediately, curling onto the red cushions and unbuttoning his vest and jacket. He glided into an afternoon sleep, convinced that this chance meeting was no chance at all; that it was fortuitous, ordained. Just think of it! That a man of the sea — and a merchant, no less — might hold the solution to his, an artist's, every problem. Serafim smiled to himself as he closed his eyes. Yes, luck was a strange thing.

Ville de Québec, le 2 février 1928

Ma très chère Claire,

I must confess how worried I am becoming. I have telephoned your apartment several times, pleading with the operator to let it ring just a little longer. Would you believe that I've been distraught enough to have even telephoned the only two hospitals I could imagine you in? Where are you, Claire?

The only thing stopping me from catching a train to Montreal is that you mentioned there were auditions coming up and you may've gone out of town. This, at least, is my hope; that you are safe and well, on a stage in another city, impressing some new agent, or maybe even trying for one of those Russian ballets that are passing through New York or Boston. And I hope this while fighting the idea that this letter is just another in a bundle crammed inside your mailbox, while you are somewhere else, in trouble.

Things here are frustrating as always. We're preparing for the suffragist delegation coming to the city for the annual march on the Legislative Assembly. I wish you would come to it one of these years, Claire, join the struggle. Or even just visit.

Please, the moment you get this letter, please telephone me. I desperately need reassurance that you are well, and that I am worrying for no reason at all.

Je pense à toi,
Cécile

3

Claire's memory worked like a radio station: memories that were pleasant and popular were repeated again and again. And with each reminiscence, Claire found that she could discover something new, some hidden timbre or cadence that she hadn't quite appreciated before. And like a radio station, the selection of her memories changed with the times. A popular recollection one year might become forgotten or outmoded the next. Recently, it had been playing a countdown of her all-time favourite moments, the ones that had set her and her career on its bold trajectory.

One particular memory she'd been recalling was an underhanded threat she had been prepared to make to Dr. Bertrand. It was a threat she had rehearsed but couldn't quite remember if she'd delivered. It was a sly implication of how she knew exactly what he'd done for her brother; and how he could go to prison for it. Other doctors certainly had, while Dr. Bertrand remained a free man, untarnished and unapologetic.

She could remember perfectly the feeling in the city that day. Music, the mayhem of mass celebration, the streets of Montreal roiling in dance, bells, singing, the clatter of pots and pans, horns, comet-like streamers tailing through the air above the streetcar wires and landing amid a brass-band frenzy.

For Claire, dancing with Dr. Bertrand the day of the false armistice was only the end of this memory song. The beginning, like most controversial things, featured her grandmother.

Claire's paternal grandmother was an eccentric. She had been widowed early, and had raised Claire's father by scraping by on what little money her husband had left behind. She read voraciously, blasphemed at will, and every year she lived she'd become less and less of a believer, first renouncing the sacraments. By the time she'd come to live with her son, his strait-laced wife, and their three children, Claire, Cécile, and Daniel, she had stopped going to church altogether.

Instead, on the Sabbath, with no one else home, she would shuffle over to the neighbours' apartment — immigrants from France, and non-believers as well — where she would sip cognac on their terrace, discussing books, news, and politics. It was unheard of, scandalous even. But what tipped her scale into the realm of eccentricity was how unashamed she was. "*Je m'en fous,*" she would say, whenever Claire's father or mother challenged her to consider what other people might say about the things she did or didn't do. "If you do come across someone who has issue with me," her grandmother would calmly say, "tell them that I am always right here. They are more than welcome to discuss their qualms, with me, to my face." At which point she would retire to her boudoir, and close the door conclusively behind her.

Her grandmother's boudoir was a tiny room filled with sofas, as well as a rocking chair and an anniversary clock that didn't keep time so well. Several small paintings — rollingly idyllic Quebec landscapes — adorned the walls, interrupted by a window that looked out onto the dreary brick partition of the next apartment. It was a room designated for the women in the house to sit in quietly with their needlework, but it was really only used by Claire's grandmother for reading, and for "poisoning her granddaughters," as Claire's mother liked to say, "with her audacious ideas."

Claire and Cécile adored their grandmother. Once the door to the boudoir was closed, she was easily distracted from her reading and took a genuine interest in the girls and their fantastical whims and play worlds. She would gently clap and hum a tune and Claire would dance and spin on the rectangle of a second-hand rug in the centre of the room, which acted as a padded stage. She would endlessly reread the same fairy tales and stories to Cécile, who learned the words by heart and would mouth them as they were being read, her legs draped over her grandmother's lap, enveloped by her large arms, as a wrinkled hand was lifted to lick a finger for turning the page.

When Claire's grandmother first moved into their apartment, in 1910, Claire was seven, Cécile ten, and Daniel fourteen. That same year, a man named Henri Bourassa started up the newspaper *Le Devoir*, which had a liberal, anti-imperialist, intellectual tilt, and of which Claire's grandmother became an instant disciple. Its daily reading was the only thing she did religiously. But the next two years saw her sight, already feeble, begin to fail, until it was so much work to squint and decipher — hunched-over, magnifying-glass cryptology — that she began asking Cécile to read certain passages aloud to her, to give her eyes some needed rest. She would insist, however, after Cécile had painstakingly sounded out each word individually, that the girl reread the words as a coherent sentence, and once she had, she would get her to repeat it — without its sounding so wooden this time, she would say factually, without malice. Then the entire paragraph again, only with inflection and confidence, like an adult. When she was finally satisfied, she would murmur, *"Excellent, ma petite fille — impeccable. On continue,"* and on it was to the next paragraph, the next page.

Soon enough, Cécile was charged with reading the entire journal, from cover to cover. As she got older, she was asked her opinion on what she was reading. Did she agree that the ruling class was grossly neglecting the rights of the working class? Did she agree that Canada's responsibility began and ended with the defence of its own terrain, that it had no business sending troops to fight in British wars, as it had done in South Africa only a few years ago and seemed itching to do again? For her part, Cécile wasn't exactly sure how one formed an opinion, though she became increasingly certain that an opinion was an important thing to have.

She hadn't quite gotten around to choosing her position on Canada's involvement in British wars before troops were being sent in throngs to fight in Europe. At the outbreak of the Great War, Daniel was eighteen, and by the time he was twenty, several of his friends had either signed up or quietly moved out of the city to relatives' homes in the country, where the army officers who patrolled the cities could be more easily evaded. Officers stopped young men at will on the streets, and handed them papers with instructions to receive a physical and report for service immediately. One spring day, Daniel, who stayed in Montreal throughout the war, working as a shop assistant for a grocer — and who was devout in his boycott of beer as a patriotic gesture, saving on grain while withdrawing his support of the German-dominated brewery sector — was stopped by one such officer and handed his fateful papers. He brought them home shrugging, a sheeplike grin on his face, obedient and oblivious to the danger he faced.

He hadn't taken his hat off at the door before his grandmother doggedly limped towards him, snatched him by the wrist, and dragged him back outside, down the steps, and up the street. They didn't return to the apartment for hours, and when they did, it was with a note from Dr. Bertrand, with the somewhat shocking news that Daniel was suddenly found to have a rare, though minor, heart condition. Daniel moped around for weeks afterwards, sure he was going to be called a coward, insisting in a whisper that he'd even *wanted* to go and fight. Not die, of course, but fight. His mother, lowering her voice as well, would tell him, behind closed doors, that he could just tell the truth. "It was your grandmother's doing. Her fault. Everyone knows what kind of woman she is, anyway. Now, stop fretting about it and set off for work. You're needed here more than there . . ." Her words broke up as she smoothed the collar of her twenty-year-old son and pulled his jacket down straight.

In Claire's family, each child was, in a way, a favourite. Daniel was clearly their mother's, while Cécile always had her grandmother and Claire her father. During the five years of the Great War, when Montreal was the scene of national turmoil and heated polemics, of economic hardship and individual sacrifice, Claire's father was eager to keep her unconcerned and sheltered from it all. Despite being a luxury that the family could ill afford, he somehow found a way to pay for her weekly dance classes at the École de Danse Lacasse-Morenoff, and attended every recital to clap as loudly as he could. He was also the only parent who would whistle, piercingly, with his thumb and forefinger in his mouth. Whenever talk in their house, especially with visitors from church, began to seethe about the gravest of issues — infant mortality among francophones reaching the highest in the Western world, the patent dismissal of their every concern by Ottawa, or the grisly scene of a horse-drawn trolley carting away corpses of those who had succumbed to the Spanish influenza, with one or two of the bodies still in their death throes — Claire's father would pull her close to keep her from hearing any more, asking her about the dances she was rehearsing, or even taking her to another room, where he would wind up the gramophone and close the door behind him, leaving her to practise in peace.

Claire was fifteen years old and in her last year of school when, on a mild day in November, the news rippled through the city like a tsunami of cheers: the war was over. The school bells were suddenly ringing continuously, following the students out into the streets, where the chimes spread into the urban distance, infectiously, to church bells, firemen's sirens, the klaxons of vehicles, descending all the way to the St. Lawrence and the harbour, where ship horns could be heard yawning and bellowing above the boom of cannon fire. Claire, thinking of her father, headed to St. James Street, where he was a lowly record keeper for a small accounting firm. Along the way, the traffic at intersections was sometimes clogged and stagnant, people in the crossroads playing instruments, groups of singers and dancers flocking around them, and annoyed drivers leaving their vehicles only to join in the revelry a few minutes later, clapping their hands with their heads thrown back. The war was really over.

Claire bumped into her father as he was heading towards his favourite tavern. Upon seeing her, he picked her up, swung her in a circle, and kissed her cheeks ecstatically before leading her by the arm through the crowd that was amassing in ever-greater numbers. Inside the tavern, an accordion player stood on a table, his back to the wall to make room for a few more people to dance, while a fiddle player carefully stepped onto another tabletop to do the same. Two navy men, bristling with elation, swung each other by the arms in the centre of the room. The circle of people closest to them, mostly men in straw hats, clapped in unison, cigarettes clamped between their lips. Claire's father ordered drinks, a whiskey for himself and a cocktail for her, and they had just clinked glasses and taken a sip when Claire's father straightened up and exclaimed, "Why, Dr. Bertrand!" and hailed the man to come over.

Dr. Bertrand was a much-respected physician who, everyone knew, had gone to London and Paris just before war had broken out, where he had learned to perform surgical operations. His status in the francophone community was of the highest, and the Audettes were among the few lucky enough to be able to call him their family doctor. Claire's father vigorously shook his hand, clasping the man's shoulder as if to steady him, a dribble of whiskey spilling from the glass in the doctor's left hand. He kissed Claire hello, and all three of them clanked glasses, drinking to the end of all wars.

The two men exchanged small talk for a few minutes, watching the sailors dance. Then, looking into his glass, and half under his breath, Claire's father uttered, "You know, about Daniel, I have never thanked you."

Dr. Bertrand, draining the last thimble of whiskey from his tumbler, continued looking out into the tavern. "With much respect, Mr. Audette, I didn't do it for your gratitude, or anyone else's for that matter. I was just staying true to my own code of conduct. There are things that, unfortunately, we must pay for out of our souls, and I am not a man who is rich in that currency. Brave acts, Mr. Audette, are at times done merely out of weakness."

Claire's father chuckled uncomfortably, threw back the rest of his glass, and shouldered his way closer to the bar. "Of course, of course. Which I imagine is another way of saying I should buy you another whiskey."

Dr. Bertrand turned to him, gave him a hearty slap on the back. "And yourself one too, I hope."

But before the glasses could be poured, the song ended and another began, this one more upbeat, pulsing wildly, and Claire's father was suddenly shooing his daughter and the doctor out into the centre of the room. "*Allez! Dansez, dansez!*" Claire, who had listened hungrily to the conversation, was now seeing the doctor, for the first time, in a duller, more human light; made even more so by his awkward dancing, his lack of rhythm and musicality. Claire soon stepped back from him, lifted one of his hands and passed beneath it, twirling, swaying, swinging her body gracefully around the dance floor. She was young and beautiful, and her dancing held the attention of the room. As the navy men clapped and whistled around her, Claire reached back and let her hair down, where it splashed over her shoulders with every spin, an auburn aura.

As she danced, conversations stopped, sentences hovered, hanging adrift in the smoke, then dissipated, until the words were forgotten entirely.

After an hour of dancing on and off, Claire sensed something troubling passing through the room. She saw her father and Dr. Bertrand exchange a few quick words, followed by a strained return to their previous jovial state. Not wanting to interrupt the two men, she asked one of the naval ratings what was wrong, and he told her that the war, in fact, had not ended. It was a mistake. No armistice had been signed, nor had negotiations even begun. Casualties were still being reported on the Western Front. Yet — and this was the strangest part for Claire — the dancing hadn't stopped. Out in the street, where everyone had doubtlessly heard the news, people were still celebrating, and were now clearing the way for a float to pass. The float — a giant papier mâché Canadian soldier with his bayonet to the throat of a kneeling kaiser — had been prepared for the Victory Bond parade that was scheduled for the following Monday. Claire watched as two men jumped onto the float and began the process of cutting off the kaiser's head.

Patrons streamed out of the bar to watch the feigned execution, and in the flux, Claire found her father. "Papa" — she tapped him on the shoulder — "do you know that none of this is true? The war isn't over."

He appeared unperturbed. "You're right, it isn't. But . . . can't you *feel* how much everyone here wishes it were? We *wish* it. And sometimes that's more important than what actually is. Can you see? Does that make sense?"

And to Claire, it did. Perfectly. Though she had never told anyone about it, this was what she felt when she danced. It was as if there were some fragmented part of her that was perfect, sublime. It was that same part of her, the one that she constantly *wished* she was, that indeed she could become — though for only the most fleeting of moments — in the act of dancing. When the music and her movements lined up flaw-lessly, Claire experienced moments of divinity, glimpses where what she wished she was and what she actually was (even if only for seconds) became one. And for the first time in her life it occurred to her that this might also hold true for the world.

Four days later, on November 11, 1918, when the real armistice was signed and the last war the earth would ever see ended, Claire realized that the collective wish of people could, perhaps, attain the hoped-for result. Human beings seemed to have (and Claire certainly more than most) a hidden ability to will change, to shift things — slightly, and for only short-lived instants — to their advantage. It was an astounding realization, and one that filled her fifteen-year-old mind with drunken promise.

Having recalled this memory through to its end, each detail still as vivid as the day it unfolded, Claire remembered with a measured degree of certainty that she had not gotten around to uttering her delicate threat to Dr. Bertrand the other night. She began to remember other things too — how he'd said she had a serious infection, and that he would have to operate on her to find out more. What did that mean, exactly?

Claire fought towards consciousness, a battle, she found, that wasn't all that easy to win. There was no "waking up" to be had. Instead, she was stuck in a hazy confusion of sounds and images, intermittent sensations swinging in and out of a white-edged awareness. There were brief interruptions of touch and smell — being washed with a harsh soap, turned over, propped up, the bitter rod of a thermometer speared under her tongue — but the rest of the time Claire simply felt adrift in a limbo of her memories, the journey exhausting; though in some far-off and urgent way, she understood that she must not, could not, settle by the wayside to rest.

She felt a sudden hand behind her neck, then the feeling of water in her mouth, washing down the pinching taste of copper that seemed to have coated her palate for an eternity, making her tongue clammy. She opened her eyes for the first time to see a middle-aged nun, her habit framing Claire's focus on her face, constricting it, sharpening the woman's frown, the wrinkles around her lips creasing deeper. "Mademoiselle O'Callaghan?" asked the nun. Claire, whose last name was not O'Callaghan but Audette, felt the need to process this contradiction with a blink, though she never quite got around to lifting her eyelids again. Instead, she slid back into an echoing darkness, while the nun, her voice increasingly distant, called after her.

Some time later, Claire tried to move the dead-stone weight of her limbs, and managed to flex her fingers, then her right hand, and, with this, was soon rushing forward into consciousness. Her eyes slowly opened to a bright, blinding light. She began to stretch herself out, and was instantly met with a shooting pain at the bottom of her stomach.

Seeing her distressed expression and open eyes, a nun appeared at the foot of her bed, stern and indifferent. "Mademoiselle O'Callaghan. How feel you this morning?" she asked, struggling to speak English.

Claire, finding that her pain was not subsiding but increasing, arched her back and sank her head into her pillow, her hands rising to her stomach, where she felt, to her horror, filaments of thread, like grotesque insect legs, protruding from her skin, skittering down a thick scar that made a ridge from below her navel to her pubic bone. She relaxed her muscles and remained breathlessly still, until the pain gradually unclenched its fist.

The nun continued to speak in her broken English, explaining how, several days ago, Claire had been brought in just before dawn and left in the entry hall, with a note from a certain Dr. Reilly, who explained that he was a visiting doctor to Montreal, on his way back to Europe. Just prior to his leaving, however, he was called in to perform an emergency appendix operation on you. With this note and his apologies, he left sufficient funds for your care, estimating your stay to be two to three weeks. You are in the Hôtel-Dieu. This is your fourth day. Can I get you anything? Do you need to use the bedpan?

Claire slowly shook her head, then eyed the nun as she walked away to tend to another patient. The nun, however, kept looking back at her suspiciously.

Claire looked up at the ceiling and thought of Cécile. With a false name, her sister would have no chance at all of tracking her down, or of even knowing that she was ill and had had an operation. Claire knew that the moment she had the energy, she would have to write to her sister. She hoped Cécile wasn't worrying, though she understood her sister well enough to know that, by now, there were likely a number of letters from Quebec City stuffed into her mailbox, urging Claire to send news that she was safe and sound.

The nun gave Claire another sidelong glance as she brusquely tucked a sheet under a mattress. Claire realized that (contrary to what she would be writing to Cécile) she was not at all out of danger. Not yet.

Medium: Wet plate; albumen silver print
Description: Maria Antónia da Silva (carte de visite)
Location: Penafiel, Portugal
Date: 1903

ॐ

A vignette portrait of a girl, just on the cusp of being considered a young woman. Her hair is dark, thick, and heavy, its weight sagging down on all sides from a point high in the back where it has been clasped. Her jawline ascends into milky shadows to meet the lowest drape of her mane, where a single strand can also be seen, having strayed from her barrette, reaching down to touch the tight neckline of her white dress.

She is clearly handsome, her expression at once self-conscious and unassuming. She is also fighting back a smile, her lips pressed tight, laughter mischievous in her eyes. One gets the feeling that she finds the entire portrait-taking ordeal somewhat ridiculous. One also senses that the photographer does not share this amusement; which has only managed to increase it twofold for the young woman.

The portrait, measuring only five by nine centimetres, is bordered with a frosty halo, drawing the eye helplessly in to the young woman's high cheekbones. It is as if she is sitting in a tubular oval of light. And as if this bright tunnel is irrevocably closing in around her.

4

Serafim's long-term memory was terrible. He noticed that when other people reconstructed their pasts, the access they had to previous moments in their lives seemed to be much like looking through a kaleidoscope, in that each infinitesimal compartment glowed just as brightly as the next, and merely by focusing on one particular chamber they could almost transport themselves to that place, to feel its textures, hold up its velvet tastes and sounds, and feel the air as crisp as the day they'd lived it. Whereas for Serafim it was more like looking back onto a grey beach, where a long, twig-scratched line in the sand gradually vanished into the sea haze of the distance. Squint as he might, the farther away it was, the less he could see.

He believed his earliest memory was of standing in a court-yard, being scolded by his father for appearing shy, if not fright-ened, of a new maid who had come to live and work in their house. He realized now that the maid before this — though there might have been several — had likely been employed as his wet nurse, as well as his nanny. But this nanny, arguably the most important one in his rearing, had no image or name to go with her; nor a reason for her disappearance, in the same way that the constant coming and going of other maids in the years that followed transpired without explanation. Between all the nannies, there were also discrepancies regarding how a well-raised young man was supposed to act.

He was taught never to speak in adult company, then to speak only when addressed, though not very much — a "yes, sir" or "no, ma'am" would suffice. Some told him not to slouch when he sat, or to fold his hands on his lap, or to scrunch his hat like a peasant; while others didn't mind any of these things at all. He was taught to eat with his fork and knife, never switching hands, which was consistent enough; but he also remembered a new maid arriving one day, horrified at the way he soaked up his winter stew with a piece of bread, spoon in one hand, crust in the other. She'd slapped the top of his head and pried the bread from his fingers, disgustedly throwing the soggy dough into a slop bucket.

"*Virgem Maria*, child, you're not a barbarian. No reason to eat like one."

"Oh," Serafim said, flattening his bread hand onto the table. "What is a barbarian?"

"The sort of person who soaks up their food with bread." Then, as an afterthought, "Besides Italians."

"Oh."

Serafim's father's room was a place with even more mystery. Sometimes, at night, he would steal through the halls and stand outside the door, listening to the strange struggling sounds that the voices of his father and the current maid were making on the other side. But what really drew him to his father's room was the photo on his escritoire.

Serafim couldn't remember when he first sat on the edge of his father's bed and studied it, he only knew that at some point it had become a fixation. What he did remember was the day one of the maids told him it was his mother. Tidying his hair, she said, "She died two years after this picture was taken, in 1905. And do you know the very last thing she did?" A soft arm wrapped around Serafim's shoulders, her lips speaking half pressed against his head. "She delivered you, Serafim, into this world. She was very brave. She was fifteen."

The photo held her stories in the worst way it could — by hiding them. Serafim had never seen women — in the streets, sitting at café tables with their tall and elaborate hats, washing clothes in the river, filling wooden buckets from the city's foun-tains, removing steaming pots from a range — staring fixedly forward in such a way. The only life that could be derived from the photo was in the painful restraint of her smile, and the faint sepia blush of her cheeks. And what could that possibly tell Serafim? He was at a loss. Hungry for intimacy, for famil-iarity, and the still, brown-scale portrait offered nothing in the way of sustenance.

When his father would catch him sitting in his room with the picture, he would instantly seem tired, sure that Serafim had yet another question for him. Did she like oranges? Could she sing? Was she afraid of heights? What was her favourite bird? And when she wasn't paying attention to what her hands were doing, would she sometimes crumple her hat like a peas-ant? But even more disappointing for Serafim was the fact that, most of the time, his father didn't know the answers. He'd proposed by letter, spent six months getting acquainted with her in public places and in the company of a chaperone, and was only married to her for eleven months before she passed away.

Well, did he have any other photos of her, Serafim wanted to know, pictures where, maybe, she was doing something? No. None. Serafim's uncle, a not exactly successful photographer in Oporto, took a picture of the couple on their wedding day, but, in some kind of bungling chemical mistake in the darkroom, he'd ruined it. "Soon after that," his father said, "she was with child, which is rather unsightly, to say the least. So, no. Only one photo of her was ever taken. Which is why we should put it back on the escritoire where it belongs."

One of the other things Serafim remembered well was how he met his friend Álvaro. It was during their lunch break at school, in the playground. Children were running maniacally in circles, hollering and bellowing, their golden minutes of unrestrained conduct, raising dust from the sandy ground, lines of boys chasing each other, girls skipping rope in song. Serafim, too subdued to run amok with the screaming droves, came across Álvaro crouched near one of the few bushes in the schoolyard. His hat was off and he was reaching as far as he could into the shrub, burying his face in the leaves.

"What are you doing?" Serafim pulled his shorts up higher onto his belly.

Álvaro answered quietly, and in a tone that suggested Serafim would likely not understand. "I'm trying to catch a long green beetle."

Serafim bent down and parted some of the leaves. "Oh. He's nice. Can I help?"

"No," Álvaro said impatiently. "You don't — I don't want to kill him. Just catch him."

"Yes. Me too."

"Well. Okay, then."

It began simply enough, but when the beetle kept crawling farther into the centre of the shrub, adeptly evading the boys' hands and hats that crunched through the twigs and snagged on branches, neither of them stopped. Their arms became scratched, their white shirts — sleeves folded up to the elbows — grass-stained and soiled, their hats sullied. Still they didn't give up. A teacher shook his deafening handbell to summon the children back into class, but neither of them listened, or even seemed to care. They were so close to catching the beetle, Serafim's hat perfectly poised below the insect, deep in the inner branches, Álvaro's extended fingers centimetres away from tipping it into a cloth trap, alive.

Finally, the insect expanded with sudden wings and flew off, bouncing between several branchlets and landing some- where else in the shrub. They tried to locate it again, for sev- eral minutes, exchanging glances that spoke of the trouble they would have to face. At last they gave up and ran into the school, where, hanging their hats up in the cloakroom, they endeavoured to sneak into the class. Serafim went first, slip- ping behind his desk almost unnoticed. But the movement caught the corner of the teacher's eye, and he turned just in time to see Álvaro tiptoeing down an aisle to his seat. Álvaro had to sit at the front of the class for an hour, cowering on a stool taller than he was, wearing a pair of donkey's ears fash- ioned out of folded newspaper. When he'd first put them on, the class erupted in laughter, some pointing, the girls covering their mouths. The teacher slapped a ruler onto his desk, and the classroom fell silent again.

Over the next hour, the boys swapped impish grins, Serafim admiring the scratches on both of their arms, the smudges of green on their sleeves. They had recognized a certain tendency in one another, a kind of obsessiveness, and they understood that what had once been a personal solitude would now be a sovereign country, whose border would redraw itself wherever they chose to walk together. They were inseparable for the next thirteen years, until 1926, when Álvaro moved to Lisbon to follow the anarchists.

While they were thirteen years of resolute friendship for the two boys, they were not easy years for their homeland. The already indelibly serious Portuguese adults were given increasingly grave things to discuss and fret about. There was constant talk of the failing republic, of economic crisis after crisis, political catastrophes, strikes, protests, uprisings, and, when both of them were nine, something called the Great War.

When it began, the Great War hadn't really concerned Portugal, which was officially calling itself neutral. But there was an age-old alliance and interdependence between Portugal and Britain, and when the Germans were seen to be using Portuguese waters undeterred, and even mooring in the country's protected harbours, Britain tapped an admonitory finger on their ancient treaty of allegiance, which had been upheld more or less consistently since the Middle Ages. Portugal kicked the dirt at its feet and reluctantly stepped forth.

Serafim's father had been the owner of a small barrel-making business — his callused hands smelling of oak and pungent shavings, sawdust frosting the hair of his arms — and he filled orders that came almost exclusively from England. With Portugal entering the war, merchant ships became susceptible to

U-boat attacks. Exports all but froze. Serafim's father found himself out of work, and brooded over his financial situation for a month before he made a decision. He rented out their home, joined the army, and sent Serafim to live with his aunt and uncle, the floundering photographer. There were, his father argued, far-reaching benefits to this decision. Besides, he said on the day he left, the Great War couldn't hold ground for eternity.

It would, however, for him. The Portuguese divisions were soon spent and exhausted on the Western Front, desperately holding a position that was precisely at the point where the Germans believed they could breach the line. The Huns gathered their troops for a concerted effort, then, on a clear day with a gentle breeze in April 1918, barraged the Portuguese with heavy artillery and lethal gas, and ploughed through and over them with a troop count that was fivefold that of the Portuguese divisions.

The news of the cataclysmic Battle of the Lys was headlined in bold letters across all of Portugal's newspapers, and was read aloud in cafés in exceedingly quiet tones. The wounded returned equally hushed, in crutches or slings, with wide patches over their eyes, or as *gaseados*, men who wheezed and gurgled as they laboured to breathe. The dead, including Serafim's father, were buried in the hills where they fell.

Serafim was thirteen, and now a de facto adoptee of his aunt and uncle, living at their house, where he spent much of his time sitting on the tiny balcony that overlooked one of Oporto's busiest streets, holding the portrait of his mother as if to compare it to the animate people who passed below. It was an unsettling habit, and one his uncle had stepped out onto the balcony to address on a dreary winter afternoon. He stood for a moment, looking at the laundry that hung from the balcony above, bed linen billowing in the smoky air. A large white sheet heaved a world-weary sigh. No, he couldn't bring himself to reprimand the boy for being so understandably odd. Instead, at a loss for words, and seeing the portrait in Serafim's hand, he scratched the back of his neck. "Would you, perhaps, like to give me a hand today, in the studio? I've got a lot of darkroom work. I could use your help."

Serafim stared listlessly into the street then at the portrait, straightening up in his chair, which was positioned sideways and exactly the width of the balcony. "Making pictures?"

"Developing them, yes."

Serafim struggled to stand up. There was barely enough room for the two of them on the terrace, and he had to half lean out over the wrought-iron railing. "Yes," he said. "Yes, please. Teach me."

Montréal, le 11 mai 1915
À Monsieur le Directeur de l'École Frontenac de St-Eusèbe

Monsieur,

I would like to request your understanding, sir, that both my daughters, Claire and Cécile Audette, are excused from their studies the entirety of the day tomorrow.

This is necessary for private and grave family matters. I thank you to your discretion and of your understanding.

Veuillez agrée, Monsieur, l'expression de nos sentiments distinguées.

Madame Marie Audette

5

As a child, when Claire went out in public, it was often alone with her father. At the youngest age, her parents could see that she loved, even needed, to be the centre of attention, wedging her way through the tall forest of adult legs wherever they had planted themselves, clearing herself a space at their centre, and proceeding to put on some kind of a show. It often involved spinning, singing, running on the spot, madly fanning her skirts up and down, and ended with her hands stretched high, waiting, fingers splayed. The adults knew to clap, and Claire knew to bow. For precisely this reason, her mother, who hated drawing undue notice to herself, chose (at least whenever she had to run errands with the children in tow) to take Cécile and Daniel with her, passing Claire off to her father, who had no problem whatsoever with her madcap scenes and charades.

Claire's father even encouraged her wild antics, doting on her shamelessly; pulling her along on a sled in the winter, the metal runners grating on patches of asphalt as they crossed the streets, sometimes stopping to carry both her and the sled across, just to ease her pristine ears; taking her to Parc

Sohmer — an American-style open-air amusement park for the working class in the east end — lifting her on and off five or six animals on the carousel until she'd found just the right one for her; or propping her up at the window of every vehicle they travelled in, allowing her to point and exclaim and squeal at the ecstatic world she always seemed to see passing by like a parade on display just for her.

On this particular day, they were on St. Lawrence Boulevard (*la Main* as it was known) with the aim of going to a nickelodeon, which always proved to be a hit with Claire, who adored the moving pictures. She would sit with her hands on the seat in front of her, rapt by the music of the piano player stationed only two rows away, who interpreted the tension or glee of each scene as it rolled through, with his eyes on the screen instead of the keys. They'd already chosen which nickelodeon, and what they wanted to see, but were forced to wait fifteen minutes outside before the next showing. It was August 1912, Claire was nine, and the street was teeming with life. Men in straw hats and jackets and women in large and convoluted dresses walked arm in arm along the sidewalks. The grunt and wheeze of an organ grinder cranked out a jumpy tune. Carriages and buggies passed between the streetcars. A group of adolescent boys scurried by, fleeing from some random act of mischief.

Claire's father caught the sound of a handbell from a corn vendor across the street. *"Blé d'Inde! Blé d'Inde!"* called out the vendor, directly at them, having apparently read their minds. It was the poor man's version of sweets for his children, a few pennies getting you an ear of corn, buttered, salted, and wrapped in grease-resistant paper, which folded in wrinkles that soon looked like tiny mouths watering delectably.

"Tu veux du blé d'Inde?" her father asked. And with her elated nod he was off, gesturing for her to stay put as he threaded his way across the street, through the clopping carriages and grumbling trams.

On Claire's left, a young woman squeaked with laughter, while a group of men postured in a tight circle around her. Claire stepped towards them, unconsciously, as if they were gathered there for her arrival. But before she could make her entrance, a door swung open to a theatre beside her, and out of it spilled the musical sounds of horns, drums, and cymbals. As the door began shutting on its slow hinges, Claire moved towards the sounds and soon found herself in a dark lobby, where she passed unknowingly beneath a ticket window, undetected. She approached two ushers, who were so engrossed in their conversation that she passed behind them, unseen. Then, still following the music, she pried her way between two slats of a heavy black curtain and stepped into the theatre.

That was when Claire saw her. A young woman on the stage, alone, dancing, a delicate cane in her hand, waving and tipping it like a scale in perfect equilibrium. The stage was dark, a bright orb of light following the dancer like an eye of blinding intensity. She was wearing a low-cut orange dress with lace straps that bared much of her torso. Ruffles and pleats billowed out from her narrow waist, ending just above her slender, cream-white calves. The music she was dancing to was light and cheerful, but her movements were not. She was lagging to the music, tugging a kind of melancholic tension through her steps and sways. The audience was silent, intent, captivated. Claire, entranced, wanted to be closer to her, and continued down the aisle, stopping periodically to watch what the dancer might do next. It was then that the vaudevillian did something shocking.

She noticed Claire beyond the beam of her spotlight, a nine-year-old girl standing in the passageway, a rogue element, an escapee, and locked eyes with her. The young woman was now dancing *for* her, smiling sadly, all while she possessed the entire theatre, holding the audience's concentration, their wonder, their reverence. Holding it all, holding the world, in balance, on the tip of her cane, the slanting shaft rolling it around playfully, assertively. She could do no wrong. She had even earned their forgiveness.

The mesmeric act finally came to an end, the abrupt lights that blanketed the stage seeming to scare up a flock of countless birds, everyone clapping, frantic, like innumerable sets of wings lifting every patron to their feet, chirping and whistling out. The woman blushed with false modesty, and exited stage left.

Out of nowhere, Claire felt a pair of hands on her shoulders, and turned around to a bombardment of questions. Where are your parents? Do you know someone here? How did you get into the theatre? But Claire didn't want this. What she wanted was for the music to go on, and for the young woman to come out and dance again, then again after that. She wanted her to dance forever. A group of people had now gathered around, crouching on their knees, pressing her for answers. She covered her ears and began to cry.

By the time it became clear that Claire had wandered in off the street, the ushers were sent (after a firm reprimand) out onto the Main to look for a panicked parent of some kind. It took them quite a while to locate her father, as he had been dashing in and out of stores and restaurants, unnerved and flustered, searching with crazed inefficiency, until finally asking a policeman to dismount and help him out. Claire hadn't been reunited with her father for more than thirty seconds before she started rambling on excitedly about what she'd seen. Her father, however, didn't quite seem to comprehend her excitement. What concerned him was that this entire incident be kept, at all costs, from Claire's mother. Claire agreed to keep her visit to the theatre a secret. She could keep a secret, she promised. Then she asked him about dance classes.

There was another time in Claire's life when she was lost, another event that proved how the world was an uncomplicated, glorious place; a place that brimmed with marvel and awe; with splendour that blossomed like weeds, unexpectedly, from the most unlikely cracks and corners.

When she was twelve and Cécile was fifteen and in her last year of school, they took the tram together in the mornings and evenings, sitting as close to each other as they could, though Cécile would jostle with her nose in a book while Claire would make her way to an open window and stick her face out, the city wind blowing the dark of her hair into elated wisps.

It was spring, almost a year into the Great War, and Claire was tapping her feet at the corner of the schoolyard where she and Cécile met every day before heading home together. On this day, however, something was awry, and Claire watched Cécile as she marched towards her through the schoolyard, cutting a straight line between the dispersing students, livid. She stomped to a halt and explained how one of her teachers had kept her after class, and had severely scolded her for speaking out in a "deviant way."

Cécile had had the gall to ask the teacher about a scandal that had erupted a year earlier, when the daughter of a prominent citizen had ridden a horse *astride* on Sherbrooke Street — which, at the time, had caused more of a sensation than the assassination of the archduke in Sarajevo. In response, the teacher calmly asserted that it was a scandal because part of a woman's important role in the home was to uphold that which was proper and right, and to be an inspiration, a living example of a model citizen, when she was in public. Cécile then raised her hand to point out that this didn't seem very "emancipated." (This was a word her grandmother had been throwing around with great vigour at the time, and Cécile was glad finally to be able to use it.) The teacher demanded that Cécile stay after class.

When the other students had cleared out, Cécile was chastised for her impudence. The teacher told her that she, Mademoiselle Audette, appeared to think of herself as a scholar of some sort, a woman of letters, an authority. Which, the teacher had said, was not only an untoward image, but an unlikely one — laughable even. True, Cécile wrote compositions with enthusiasm and intensity, but she was overconfident as to their worth. All the scribblings in the world, if written by an insolent girl, would have no bearing on anything, would bring about no change, not even the slightest. "Now, Mademoiselle Audette," the teacher had said, "I advise you to remember your place. You are excused."

Cécile borrowed a pencil and a piece of paper from Claire's school bag and sat down on the curb. "Don't you see? She's stupid. And wrong. I will write a letter that proves it. It will change things for us. Slightly. Would you like to take the day off with me tomorrow, go and get lost somewhere, do whatever we want?"

Claire bit her lip to hold back a smile that threatened to unbutton her cheeks. Without answering, she began to skip in circles around her sister, while Cécile began her letter. When she was finished, she went back into the school, handed the forged note to the principal with submissiveness and gratitude for his understanding, and walked back out, swaggering, a vindicated heroine. Linking arms with Claire, they headed towards their tram stop. "I think, tomorrow, we should find a place down by the river, in the morning sun. You?"

Claire threw back her head and laughed.

The next day, a Wednesday, turned out to be the warmest day of the month. They rode their usual tram, toting their usual bookbags, and then watched as their usual stop for school lurched past, shrinking in size and importance behind them. Smiling uncontrollably, they got off the tram and descended the cobblestone slope towards the river, and stepped into the liveliness and commotion of the port. The girls walked past elephantine ships, giggling at the famously blasphemous *débardeurs* — the seasonal boat loaders and freight handlers — their every word either a Québécois vulgarity or the English terminology used in their métier: winch, sling, cable, shed. *"Câlice de crisse de tabarnak. C'est un job tough aujourd'hui, hein!"* One of them paused, straightened, whistling a wave at Cécile, who, on that day anyway, waved back with a shy smile.

The two sisters soon made their way far enough past the port that they could hear only its loudest noises: a locomotive colliding into a set of railway cars to link them together, a massive crate being dropped a foot from the ground. They found a patch of yellow grass on the bank of the St. Lawrence that was just beginning to blush with the green of springtime. They lay down, crossed their feet, put their hands behind their heads, and looked up at the clear concave sky above them, which appeared to flex and strain against the walls of its own shell until it seemed ready to crack.

As the day dawdled along, Cécile read her books, mostly novels from France, which thankfully had nothing to do with Catholic morality, in the way that almost all Quebec literature did; while Claire danced to the music in her head, practising a discipline that the nuns in her elementary school, which she'd thankfully left behind the previous year, detested, grumbling that dance was the only art in history that had — and *could* have — nothing at all to do with Catholic morality.

The girls were both unquestionably free. Both magnificently lost.

Claire spun in circles, listening to the notes of songbirds that were amassing in the shrubs around them, their archaic orchestra, a springtime crescendo of new and verdant voices. Looking up, she noticed a few flocks of geese returning in alphabetical formations up the seaway. Claire held her breath, faced the zenith of birds, her arms out wide, and jumped, straight up, as high as she could.

Claire couldn't help but smile while recalling these two childhood episodes from her hospital bed. A nun at the far side of the room glanced over at her, and Claire's smile faded.

Feigning an inability to understand one's mother tongue presented a lot of problems for Claire in the hospital. She had to be constantly on her guard, especially as the nuns at the Hôtel-Dieu instinctively (or maybe just because they suspected something wasn't quite right with her) asked her questions in French first. Claire perfectly understood their requests and queries but pretended she hadn't, grimacing as if she were hard of hearing, shaking her head, and pointing into her ear as if to imply that it was a physical phenomenon, that, sadly, only English words could filter through to register on her eardrums. It was an unconvincing act, and one the nuns had just enough patience to tolerate.

Claire realized that Dr. Bertrand had certainly been thinking on his toes when he made up the story of her being Irish. She could appreciate the way this fallacy automatically explained any discrepancies that might come up, at the same time keeping the nuns' questions plain and direct, so they were unable to pry into her life. She was grateful for what the doctor had done for her, and in more than a few ways.

Later that afternoon, one of the nuns walked past Claire with a pitcher of water. Striding briskly, she pointed at the carafe and offered to top up Claire's glass. *"Plus d'eau?"* she asked, hesitating at the foot of the bed.

"Non, merci, j'ai —" Claire cut herself off, shook her head. "No," she repeated, still frozen. The nun continued through the ward as if nothing out of place had happened.

Medium:	Wet plate; albumen silver print
Description:	Álvaro de Sousa, age thirteen
Location:	Oporto, Portugal
Date:	1918

ॐ

A boy stands on a doorstep. There is an empty pot on the ground beside him, where a flower might have grown at some point but has since withered into a dry curl, a woody, arthritic finger pointing back on itself.

His skin has seen a great deal of sun, looks coarser than it should for his age, wind-dry, dust-furrowed. Eyes pearls inlaid on bronze. A wisp of hair has fallen limply onto the mud beach of his forehead and hangs there forgotten, marooned.

He is wearing pants that might be brown, and a darker vest, presumably black, that contrasts with his off-white shirt. The shirt has distinctive rounded collars, which appear refined. And while his lips are pressed together into a line that should further support this notion of gentility, his expression is one of wild, disquieting focus, his concentration bent entirely on the obscurity of the lens.

His arms dangle at his sides, while the fingers of his right hand are spread open and seem tense with the want of something, as if unconsciously reaching out for it.

One is given the distinct impression that, whatever the object of this unnameable want, this boy will find a way to get it.

6

Serafim and Álvaro first lived at opposite ends of the same neighbourhood, but when Serafim moved to his uncle's house, they found themselves sleeping under roofs that sloped to the south on the very same block. They spent every waking hour they could together, their fixations transforming into what would later be seen as a kind of logical progression, though at the time (at least to the adults in their lives) they appeared as abnormal preoccupations that had no relation to each other whatsoever. They never played with any kind of ball or sought out other boyhood competition; instead, they focused all their energy on catching things. What began with exotic and colourful insects moved to the most venomous — spiders, wasps, centipedes, scorpions — and eventually to birds. They killed none of them.

Hours were spent in Álvaro's tiny treed courtyard, coaxing passerines from the branches onto the ground, a trail of seeds leading them with inching hops towards a down-turned basket propped up with a stick on a string. What adults found unsettling about this was the way two young boys could demonstrate such resolute patience, both of them crouching against a wall, still, silent, waiting, a sundial slat of daylight scanning their faces, making them appear like a pair of pink-marble statues perched on the edge of some plaza fountain, holding a yarn of stone.

What was even more peculiar was what they would do with a bird when they actually caught one. Exploding in gesticulations of success, jumping around in circles, they would descend to lean on the wicker of the basket and peer through the slats of its bottom, taking in every detail of the terrified creature, excitedly pointing out its colours, the tiny talons of its four toes, the kink of its neck that cocked as if the bird were listening to its commentators above. Then, resting their heads on the ground to peer underneath, they would slowly lift the basket, until the bird could finally duck out of the gap. Then they would roll onto their backs to watch it fly straight up, out of the atrium, with a flash and flutter against the blue sky, before disappearing over the red-tiled roof. Álvaro's father would sometimes come out and offer to find them a cage, but they always declined with a kind of condescension, as if the poor man just wasn't quite of the age to get it, and maybe, just maybe, never would be.

Their next preoccupation was flying machines. They'd both been too young to appreciate the significance when the first plane had flown over their heads — a crowd of men with their oiled moustaches curled up at the ends passing around cut-out rectangular shapes to shield their eyes from the glare of the sun, their brass monoculars extended, followed by guffaws of amazement as the skeletal contrivance trailed its buzz out over the wobbly horizon. The Great War brought military aircraft into the skies above Oporto in significant numbers, and Álvaro and Serafim were fascinated by them. They made wooden models out of the thin pine of fig crates, and ran up to the railway tracks where they could fly them at the ends of their outstretched arms, alongside the real ones floating in the sky. When the flying machines had disappeared, they would slow to a huffing stop and hold their models tall in the air, freezing them at the most dramatic angle, then they compared each other's display and pose, each walking thoughtfully around the other's pinched fingers, squinting, inspecting.

On the way home one day, Álvaro suggested they fly their planes back on different routes, meeting up like a military rendezvous. The railway tracks splayed out in two directions, one they knew and one they didn't. They flipped a centavo, Serafim calling it in the air, and soon he was sprinting off into unfamiliar territory, where he would eventually get lost, pacing up and down a net of tight streets and walkways, looking everywhere for the river he knew so well. It grew dark, and Serafim grew hungry. Not knowing what else to do, he finally found a policeman walking his beat, eyeing everyone who passed, not, it seemed, with suspicion, but to inspire subordination. Serafim stood small beside the man and explained his plight. The policeman laughed with a hoarse voice, then coughed. "Lost over the flip of a coin! Not a lucky toss, was it, boy?" The officer escorted him to a tram station and informed the driver that this young man would be riding to the end of the line today, without a ticket. Luck, Serafim was beginning to learn, was a strange thing.

When his father died in the war, Serafim lost interest in playing for a long while. He withdrew from Álvaro's company, and became despondent and reclusive. They might even have drifted apart had Serafim not shown up on his doorstep one Saturday morning, lugging an old, outmoded view camera that belonged to his uncle. He extended the wooden tripod in front of the door, buried himself under the dark cloth that draped over his back like a cape, and looked at the piece of glass, focusing the upside-down and backwards image of his best friend, waiting for the right moment to take a shot. After he'd secured the large-format exposure the way his uncle had shown him, Álvaro was free to give the camera a thorough inspection, both of them trying every dial and adjustment — tilts, shifts, swings, and shutter release — watching what each one did inside the camera whenever possible. When Serafim returned the following day with the print and the news that his uncle would allow them to take up to four such exposures a week, they swapped a look and a smile, understanding how this fixation might take up a lifetime.

Serafim's uncle was used to the boys being inseparable, so it was natural enough to have both of them crammed into the darkroom with him in the evenings and on weekends. They watched everything he did, sometimes asking questions, but mostly they just sat behind him on tall stools, craning around his body to observe his hands with the disconcerting patience and silence that was their custom. At fourteen, Serafim could proudly call himself a darkroom apprentice, with paid work that he received from his uncle. Álvaro, refusing to be outdone, and realizing the potential in the knowledge he'd already picked up, began volunteering his time and services with another photographer in Oporto, and by the time he was sixteen he too was getting a small stipend as a darkroom apprentice.

Finally, one could just about refer to both of them as young men, their voices rupturing low, new-found hair under their arms and in their nether regions; and already between them they had an arsenal of camera types at their disposal, from which they developed know-how in a variety of formats and processes, as well as enough photographic paper, developer, and fixer to explore any avenue of photography they desired.

This exploration began in whatever photographic journals, periodicals, and enthusiast magazines they could lay their hands on, including the *Encyclopedia Photographica*, published in Lisbon in 1906, which had selections and adaptations from foreign manuals, the avant-garde world (or so it always seemed) that existed on the other side of Portugal's borders. It was true that all the abstract discussions and debates on the various isms proved difficult for them to grasp — Naturalism, Symbolism, Pictorialism, Modernism — so instead they focused on the technical details, as well as the sense of aesthetic that was gradually developing between them, fostered by their tactful two-way critiques and solid friendship.

They found themselves drawn away from the studio and out into the streets, but were met there by a public that reacted to them, quite understandably, the way the previous several decades had taught them to. Every photographer before these two eager young men had obstinately required one thing from his subjects: for them to pose deliberately, everyone's face to the camera, standing still for what felt like minutes, staring into some cumbersome device with all the docile sincerity of a herd of cattle. Not surprisingly, their initial photos looked much like those taken in a controlled setting, only with streetscapes giving them an outdoor (and for some reason often outlandish) context. Their technical skills at both taking and developing their exposures were good and getting better, but they found the pictures themselves, at best, uninspiring.

It was Álvaro who hit upon a solution, after seeing an amateur photographer in the street one day with a hand-held box camera, a Kodak Brownie, taking a picture of a birthday celebration as it trickled out into the street, people milling around a doorway, drinks in their hands, backs to the photographer, completely unaware. The following weekend Álvaro borrowed a Vest Pocket Kodak and sat for hours in cafés trying it out, having already set the distance, speed, and aperture, and only slipping it from his jacket when something interesting transpired at the tables nearby. No one caught on. Álvaro and Serafim developed the film together — a massive format, no enlarging necessary — and hung the images up to dry on the loop of string they usually used. Only on this particular day something seemed very different in the deep-sea-green murk of the darkroom. The boys were speechless with excitement, with having stumbled upon a discovery: while a traditional, straight-faced portrait tended to take the personality away from subjects, plucking out whatever vivacity they held and systematically killing it, a picture of people taken when they were unaware somehow managed to retain their animation, their humanness. Caught it, alive.

Both of them painstakingly saved up for, then bought, increasingly smaller cameras and took candid pictures in whatever free time they had. They also came to terms with the fact that no one, not a single person, organization, or institute, would ever pay them to do so. In Portugal, there were only a tiny handful of photographers who had ever managed to sell a candid shot, one of them being Joshua Benoliel, a man whose work they followed with great admiration. He was a "photographer-reporter" who took occasional pictures for one of the country's leading newspapers, *O Século*, a journal that would print one candid shot, perhaps, every two or three months, as if by accident. Serafim and Álvaro had to face the fact that if they wanted to make a living in photography, it would have to be done in a studio, with portrait work. This would have to be the staple, cash crop, the means to their end.

When Serafim had finished school, his uncle requested that he make a more meaningful contribution to the studio — in which he was sure to become a partner one day — instead of just putting in the minimum amount of work required to pay for his own photography projects. Serafim dutifully acquiesced, and enrolled in English courses during the week, as his uncle aspired to break into the market of the British gentry and expats who lived in and around Oporto. Serafim had always had a knack for languages. He had done well in his French studies in grade school and could get the gist when reading Italian and Spanish without too much difficulty.

Serafim wasn't sure what he thought of the English themselves. Besides the fact that his father had died for them — just another piece of fodder for the Crown — in Oporto itself the English were known for being extremely insular, refusing to budge from their deeply set colonialist mentality. The English expats, their pale cheeks rouged with pompous pride, appeared to have set up, in their infamous way, a self-replicating monopoly within the city, tapping into the riches of Portugal only to pipe the money back to their rain-dreary isle. Nevertheless, judge them as he might, they were the ones with all the money; and in that respect Serafim's English lessons paid off. His uncle was soon the only Oporto photographer to get any business from the English. Serafim's lessons also led him and Álvaro to their first, and only, commission for a candid shot they would create together.

It was spring, and both of them were nineteen and proudly sporting downy moustaches. Serafim's uncle was laid up with the flu, and had asked him to take over the studio and deal with the clientele for the week. An Englishman, for whose family Serafim had done a first-rate portrait, came in with a friend from London who had holdings in Oporto and a holiday home in the nearby picturesque village of Lamego. The man from London would only be in Portugal for a month, during which time his daughter would be turning four. She was a very, very special child, he said, and he wanted a very special picture of her on her birthday, one that would do justice to her remarkable character. Serafim asked him what he had in mind. The man shrugged and said he simply wanted a photograph that was unique. He slapped a date and address on the studio's counter, bade Serafim good day, and the two men walked out. Serafim watched the door close behind them, his face sinking into a devilish grin.

He and Álvaro went by train to the village for the birthday party, made giddy by the fact that they had left behind all their cumbersome tripods and view cameras — the kind exclusively used for portraits. They brought with them only two hand-helds each, a modus operandi that was nothing short of daring. They arrived at the house and, after recovering from the sight of the massive English-preened gardens, explained that they had no equipment to set up, that they needed only to spend time near the girl while she was merrymaking. The gentleman certainly thought the approach unconventional, but he took it to be the way things were done in Portugal. Serafim and Álvaro shot a myriad of exposures, but agreed that the best shot was taken when the girl was participating in a scavenger hunt. The two young men were crouched down next to her as she searched a massive planter. Tiptoeing up and reaching inside, the young girl patted around in the underbrush, and just as she found something, she turned her head in excitement. Serafim and Álvaro captured the moment perfectly. The man was so pleased with the final photograph that he made a great scene of giving Serafim and Álvaro a meagre bonus. For Serafim, that small amount was what tipped the scale in the savings for his Leica, which he could now send away for.

A few months later, Álvaro received an offer to fill in as a darkroom apprentice for one of the more prestigious photography studios in Lisbon. For his career, it was great news, though it meant a long and lonely season in Oporto for Serafim. They wrote each other weekly letters, sent contact prints of the films they were developing, independent of each other's influence for the first time. While their photos remained similar, by the end of August the tone in Álvaro's writing had become markedly more political, filled with topics neither of them had ever discussed before.

When he returned to Oporto, Serafim was astounded by the sudden change in Álvaro. He had transformed himself entirely: he was more confident, much louder, and he marched through the streets larger than life. For the first time in their kinship, Serafim felt lesser. Smoking cigarettes in cafés together, Álvaro's colours were as florid as a macaw's, while

Serafim sat beside him in the mist, a drab sparrow, dull and tatty. When Álvaro leaned over the table to sermonize on the current political situation (a subject that always meandered back to the floundering republic), all Serafim could do was listen. He could offer nothing — he believed nothing. He wasn't a republican, or a monarchist, unionist, labour syndicalist; he was a photographer. What he felt, more than anything else, was quiet. Subtle as the sound of advancing film.

That was, until he met Inês Sá. Then everything changed for him as well. He crossed paths with her at the end of October that same year, and as the winter wore on he became even *less* interested in the world outside the tight walls of his own reality. At the same time, Álvaro was ploughing forth in the opposite direction. Then, in February 1926, Álvaro knocked on the door of Serafim's darkroom as if he were sounding the alarm of a fire, the heel of his hand causing the wood at the centre to cough and flex. Serafim was busy developing an image of Inês Sá that he'd taken four months earlier, and had been working on covetously almost every day since.

Serafim hadn't even shut the darkroom door behind him before Álvaro blurted out, "I'm leaving for Lisbon, or maybe somewhere else, tomorrow. Will you come?"

"What?"

"I was speaking with an anarchist today, whom I met in the capital last summer, and he assured me that everything's about to come undone. Big change is on the way, Serafim. The republic is crumbling and something is going to have to replace it when it falls. The libertarian syndicalists have the biggest following they've had since 1914. Don't you see? This is history in the making, right before our eyes. And it is history that has to be recorded. Can you imagine a photographer being given that charge? Can you? That's the offer on the table for me, Serafim, and I'm going to take it. So can you. We'll leave tomorrow, follow them wherever they go, every protest and rally. When they come into power, our photos will be remembered for all time. What do you think?"

Serafim shook his head. It was a notion impossible even to entertain. "Do you know that I was just invited to a dinner party at the Sá residence? I am afraid not. I'm not going any-where. I'm ... going to get married, Álvaro. I plan to take over my uncle's studio, live an easy, quiet life, here in Oporto. I am sorry."

Álvaro walked to the centre of the studio and hesitated before speaking, as if trying to find the correct letter with which to begin his first word, mouthing soundless vowels until, with a loaded chuckle, he gave up and relaxed. Then he strode over to Serafim, grabbed his shoulders, and smiled wide. "I shall write you, dear friend."

Serafim flinched at the intimacy, looking down at the leather of his shoes, "And I you. Of course."

Álvaro, letting go, stamped audibly towards the door, turned, and gave the door frame a solid slap. "I wish you the best of luck, Serafim." Then he gave a single, stout wave, "*Adeus!*" and disappeared.

Salutations précieuse petite sœur,

I must be the first person in history to be elated about an appendix operation! I just received your letter (on which, I might add, the hospital forgot to write a return address, and anglicized my name, of all things) and am so glad to hear that this unforeseen procedure went well, and that you are now in good care, good spirits, and improving rapidly. As an aside, I wonder if it was your illness, just before your diagnosis, that I sensed in your previous letter.

At any rate, I thought to come and visit you. I telephoned the hospital, but they told me they couldn't find your name on the list, so I am assuming you have just been released, and are now, perhaps, staying with a friend who will, hopefully, look after you for a few days? I must admit that I do wish, at times, I had never moved from Montreal, and could be there for you now.

In the same breath, however, I certainly don't miss that city's exclusive form of philanthropy: Catholics strictly for Catholics, Protestant for Protestant, etc. Here, in such a small city, the corrupt factions have no choice but to work together, just to achieve any kind of effect at all. It's oddly refreshing.

In other news, Papa took a ship downriver this weekend, to lend Gilles a hand with our renovations. When I told him about your operation, he insisted on sending you a cheque, which I've enclosed, to tide you over, he said, until you are well enough to perform again. I do hope you take it, Claire.

Au plaisir de te lire bientôt,
Cécile

7

Claire continued her mute-like existence for two weeks, the sutures along her stomach beginning to itch and tingle. Soon it became possible for her to leave her bed, on brief sorties, padding to and from the nearest washroom. One day a nun she had never seen before came to her side wielding a pair of scissors and some tweezers. She lifted Claire's gown and methodically removed her stitches, smoothly drawing them out from her skin, one by one. That same day she was told, in reluctant, broken English, that she was now considered well enough to leave the hospital.

Claire gathered the few things she had, put on the dirty dress she'd worn to the doctor's office on the night of her operation, and signed her patient release form. She struggled with the spelling of the name O'Callaghan, two nuns standing close by, watching the end of her pen, the steadiness of her hand. Claire scribbled illegibly through the letters she wasn't sure of, and when she was finished, she looked up at the two nuns, who seemed to be waiting for her to say something. So, and mostly as a means of shunning their critical glares, she did.

She asked about the money that had been attached to her when she was found in the reception. She understood that there had been enough cash to pay for up to three weeks of care, which meant there should be almost a third of the money remaining. As she spoke in English, she was unbearably aware of her francophone accent, and the more she strained to conceal it, the more it spilled out, nakedly, into the open.

When she was finished, neither of the women moved. Finally, one of them said in a low, discreet tone, *"Mademoiselle O'Callaghan, tire pas sur la ficelle."* Do not push your luck, young lady. Then, reaching forward to gently remove the pen from Claire's fingers, the nuns bade her good day.

With that, Claire turned and lumbered away, only later realizing that her having apparently understood what the nun had said was, in a way, an admission of guilt, a loosely incriminating act of its own. But at the time it slipped her mind, and she simply ambled down the hall, through the front doors, and out into the blinding sunshine of the morning.

She squinted, a hand held out to shelter her eyes. Light splashed and sloshed through the snowy cityscape, bouncing from everything that could reflect it, pouring out of windows, piercing every mirror. There was a taxi close by, as if waiting there just for her, and with a hand on the black ragtop, she got into it with agonizing slowness, only to brace herself as the driver pulled away as if from a starting gate, painfully bouncing along the icy streets, sliding in and out of the deep ruts that the thin-spoked wheels carved into the packed snow.

When they pulled up to her apartment, Claire confessed that she didn't have a penny, and the driver, who still hadn't met her eyes, or even stolen a glance at her in the rear-view mirror, said that he would wait right there while she went inside to get the money. Claire had a few cents in her flat, in a chipped saucer on her dresser, so, clicking her tongue at the man, she said she'd be right back. It took her five long minutes to make the trip inside and back out again, leaning heavily on the staircase rails. The cabbie, still not looking at her, took a dime from Claire's palm, tossed a cigarette butt onto the snow at her feet, adjusted his hat, and sped away.

Inching her way back up to her apartment, Claire was thankful that the neighbours had shovelled the wooden planks of the stairs, even though they hadn't gotten around to salting the slick layer of ice that glazed them. Keeping tense for balance was painful. She stopped at her landing, where her mailbox was bulging with letters, sun-dyed paper fanning out from the lid, and laboured to pull the wad free without using her stomach muscles. Back inside, she was happy to discover that the air in her apartment had been kept more or less warm by the neighbour's wood stove below, dry heat slipping up through the loose-tooth gaps in the tongue-and-groove. She would only have to stoke a small fire, which worked out well, since she was running low on coal.

Claire slowly arranged a few things around her apartment, cleaning out the putrid remnants in the dried and crusted bedpan, digging out some fresh, though old and tatty, blankets (her nicest ones having been lost somewhere between her apartment and the hospital), and emptying out the few vegetables that had been in her icebox, which were now blue-furred and unrecognizable.

Easing onto the only chair she owned, she sorted through her mail, tossing the bills to one side and opening Cécile's

letters before folding them back into their respective envelopes. As a welcome surprise, the most recent correspondence
contained a cheque from her father, who was certainly making
a sacrifice with the amount he'd enclosed, even if he'd been
doubtful that she would cash it. For Claire, who was in desperate need of money, this was no time for pride or disdain. The
sum would be enough to cover her rent and some basic groceries until she could get back to the club, work a few shifts, and
start fending for herself again.

She wasted no time acting on the godsend, telephoning the
general store at the corner of her block, where she often paid
on credit, and asking for a few things to be delivered: milk,
butter, jam, oranges, pears. All things she could eat (once she
purchased some bread from the bread man the following day,
anyway) without having to cook. Claire, for some reason,
hated cooking, and had no idea how Cécile had grown to love
it as much as she had. It was such a stereotypical homemaker
thing to do. For Claire a baguette, some butter, and a dollop
of honey gave just as much satisfaction as an elaborate meal.

A knock came at the door and Claire shuffled across the
floor to answer it. The green-eyed, rosy-cheeked son of the
grocer put the paper bag of merchandise on the floor beside
him, dangerously close to some snow that had sloughed off
his boots. He took out a pad of receipts and pointed out that
Claire hadn't paid anything on her credit in weeks, and that
his father insisted he return with some kind of payment or he
would have to return with the groceries. At this point Claire
could have explained herself, could have shown him the cheque
and made him feel ashamed at the fact that she'd just returned
from the hospital and was in no condition to fight through the

city's snowdrifts to cash it. But none of that was necessary. Instead, she stepped close, held on to his arm, and blinked. She assured him that she would come in and straighten out her bill the following week. The roses of the boy's cheeks suddenly beaded with moisture from his hike, and he assented, and scurried back out the door, fumbling with the handle to close it. He waved a bashful smile through the window as he made his way around the bend in the staircase.

This was what she had hoped would happen with the cabbie as well. Men, thought Claire, gingerly lifting the bag of groceries, were somewhat sad creatures. They were pliable, predictable, and weak. Though, to be fair, most of the time she felt the same way about women.

Until her seventh year of schooling, Claire had been raised in entirely segregated conditions. From her education at a convent (from kindergarten to her sixth year) to dance classes to Sunday school, boys and girls were kept stringently cordoned off from each other. The one exception to this was in the streets, where francophone boys and girls swarmed the neighbourhoods together during the summer months, playing games with English names — branchy branch, run sheep run — or in winter, when they skated together near the local fire station, where the firemen hosed down a field to make a rink, or sledded together down the length of Hogan Street, the steep road lined with snowbanks and mittened children towing their toboggans back to the top to run down it again.

The girls at the École de Danse Lacasse-Morenoff talked giddily (stupidly, as far as Claire was concerned) about boys, with puppyish sniggers and cutesy affectations. Disappointed, Claire felt they were shamefully distracted from what they were all there to do, what they loved. Her classmates were losing their focus, too easily reshuffling their priorities, and it was maddening.

It was in grade seven, when she entered a school of twelve-to-sixteen-year-olds, that everything really changed. Claire was not prepared for how exasperating she would find the halls of a coed school that was pulsating with teenagers. It was as if, overnight, both the sexes had dramatically transformed, and the alterations were ludicrous. Girls whom she knew to be cruel and competitive and unforgiving were suddenly living out a kind of sham. They had instantly, and falsely, become frail and timid. What she found strangest of all was how they would out-and-out lie to make themselves appear stupid, even dull. The girls had become a pathetic charade. At the same time, they forgave the even more outlandish falsehoods being perpetrated by the boys, who were, in their own way, lying to make themselves appear fiercer, brutish, as if they cared forty times less than they actually did. It was baffling and, for Claire, a dismal turn of events.

After a year of Claire's friends (even Cécile) confessing, with an air of great secrecy, their consuming crushes and yearnings for these utterly feral creatures that were the opposite sex, Claire began to wonder if she was normal, if there wasn't something wrong with her. Even if she happened to doubt there was. If anything, the sensations her classmates were feeling — this irrational, fantasy-invading want — was something that she already understood better than most. Claire was well acquainted with infatuation; but more than that, she had come to know something beyond it, a kind of rare, sustaining, constantly maturing kinship. Only it was with dance, not boys. With dance she nurtured a relationship that was, even now, there for her, accepting her unconditionally in her daily moods, teaching her patiently about tenacity, resilience, art, subtlety, grace, beauty, and her body. Could a snivelling teenage boy really hope to compete with that?

Claire decided to ask her grandmother whether she would ever feel as strongly about boys as she did about dance. Afraid of giving herself away at the outset, she asked simply about love, in the most abstract sense of the word. It was a winter evening, and they were alone in the boudoir, listening to Vivaldi on the gramophone, and once the discussion began, her grandmother looked as though she'd just been asked to walk a thousand miles. She told Claire that a person only had enough room inside her body for love to occur — and she stopped to specify that she was talking here about the most real, rawest, most precarious kind of love — once in her lifetime. And if it happened at all, it almost always took place, she said, when a person was very young, at a stage when they were still foolhardy in their generosity, when they gave and gave away, unsustainably.

Claire, beaming with validation, hesitated for a moment at a discrepancy in her grandmother's statement. "But . . . I thought you moved to Montreal when you were twenty-one, from a small town up north, and *then* married Grandpapa, who died two years later." Twenty-one didn't seem young to Claire.

And by the looks of it, that wasn't quite the age her grandmother had in mind either. The woman's expression seemed to wade back to the tiny village in northern Quebec where she'd grown up, returning to some hidden secret there, among the dark spruce trees or loon-haunted lakes. Her grandmother didn't answer. Instead, she kissed Claire on the forehead and said, "Why don't you show me that new dance you've been practising."

As Claire danced, she thought of how lucky she was; how, as a fourteen-year-old, she had already come to understand, had already experienced, something that scores of married women didn't even know, and never would. What she felt for — and would give to — dance was obsessive. She already felt it eating up her world, taking on a life of its own. It seemed capable of consuming whatever she threw at it, and using it as fuel. Her desire to dance was ravenous, and it was growing stronger.

Medium: Gelatin silver print
Description: Women strolling, Palácio de Cristal
Location: Oporto, Portugal
Date: 1925

℘

The sky is boiling. Billows of shaded cumulus flex in the backdrop like the close-up of a cauliflower in negative. Its bulbs of dark expanding, distending.

The setting is a public place, on an apparently very public day. A dense crowd of people are passing through the frame, from left to right. Women in full dresses, men in full suits, tightly packed between the high stalks of trees and the low ruffles of bushes.

The branches of one of the trees, silhouetted in the mid-ground against the sky, are almost bare. Three leaves dangle so loose and low that they seem to be reaching out to the garden floor, as if wanting to join the others of their kind there, let go, surrender to gravity's tug at last.

Two young women, dressed in white, are in the foreground, and of the multitude of dense figures in the picture, they are the only ones looking at the photographer. Though it is much more like peering, focusing deep into the lens as if trying to decipher something through it — the one who is slightly taller in particular, who seems fixed, almost cross. Much like the sky, her expression toes the line between anger and delight. Much like the sky, it appears, both light and lifting, but heavy with warning.

8

S unday was not a day of rest for Serafim. There was
church to go to, and after the service (before the public
at large retired to their social clubs and private din-
ners for the evening) most of the population would spend an
hour or two promenading through the pruned grounds of
the Palácio de Cristal, a florid garden situated at one of the
highest points in the area, overlooking the city of Oporto and
the banks of the Douro, where they parted from each other
and folded out into the open sea. At times the massive and
ornate gardens would be so crowded that people had to shuffle through with elbow room alone, brushing against women
with their piquantly sweet perfumes and the contrast of their
white dresses and black shawls, the fabric fluttering like doves
taking flight at their feet as they walked, while above, a knot of
swan necks seemed to emerge through the dark embroidery at
their shoulders and peck at the height of their elaborate hats.
Men stepped smoothly in their Sunday best, elegantly poised,
bow-tied, and pulling the gold chains of their pocket watches
just to make sure that, indeed, all the time in the world was
still theirs. For a photographer, the opportunities were endless.

One late October day, Serafim, attracted by the looming drapery of the clouds tethered above, paid a visit to the gardens. Some of the trees had already lost their leaves, which added an intriguing contrast as the crowds fluxed between them with all the pomp of spring flowers. He had found a bare branch and a position — near a wall fountain made up of a face with a wide-open mouth that was drooling a tongue of moss and algae — where he was low enough to frame the sky as a backdrop to the people walking by.

Crouching there, he waited for everyone's gaze to become accustomed to his peculiar position; waited to fade into the surroundings, become static in their periphery. As people cast suspicious glances his way — a few of them even whispering and pointing him out — he wasn't yet free to take the Leica out of his pocket. Instead, he picked a fallen leaf from the ground and twirled it slowly between his fingers, as if he were an amateur botanist trying to key the specimen. While he did this, he thought about the settings he would need for the shot. Being backlit, it was going to be tricky. He would have no choice but to overexpose the sky and underexpose his subjects, hopefully finding the middle ground between the two, and then correct it in the darkroom by way of a technique known as dodging, and burning-in.

So Serafim wasn't ready for any shot, let alone one of the most important he would ever take. He had looked up from the violet leaf in his fingers and met a woman's eyes, suddenly overcome by a surge of self-consciousness.

She was walking arm in arm with another young woman, who had much the same bone structure, though without enough of a likeness to be her sister — a relative, perhaps. Their intimacy hinted towards this as well, as they leaned into each other, their faces bowing low to hear the other's murmur and whisper. They chortled giddily, walked with confidence. The woman was striking. And she kept glancing at Serafim as he crouched on the ground, dumbly twirling a leaf and forgetting what he was there to do. He had almost lost the shot completely when he remembered the Leica in his pocket. He tossed the leaf aside, fumbled madly for the camera in his jacket pocket, quickly turned the dial to advance the film, and held it, straight-armed, out in front of his face. It was enough movement for both of the women to inquisitively turn his way. He released the shutter.

To his horror, the taller woman was affronted, and stepped closer to his shrunken frame to speak, towing her relative along with her. The fountain wagged its green tongue beside him. "Excuse me, sir. Did you just take our photograph?"

Serafim paused, thinking of how best to answer this query, schools of diplomatic words swimming through his mind, delicate euphemisms to be used in place of that one callous word. "Yes," he said flatly.

"But we weren't ready!" The two girls laughed. "What kind of picture will that be? Besides, shouldn't you have asked our permission first, sir, at the very least?"

Serafim was playing with the settings on his camera, still crouching. He stammered in reply, "Well . . . n . . . you . . ." He cleared his throat. "You . . . you have to see . . . that the picture will be an excellent one *because* you weren't ready." Finally, it occurred to him to stand up. "In the same way that its value lies in the fact that I did not ask your permission."

The beautiful woman's mouth fell open. The other woman covered her lips and twittered, crumpling against her companion's side. "So you're saying that you knowingly steal that which is of most value to people?"

At long last Serafim was calm. He could agree with that more than anyone. "Yes."

The relative laughed again, while the woman with the dark eyes gave a teasing smirk. "You, sir, are diabolical."

"Perhaps." Serafim turned the Leica over in his hands and reset the shutter speed.

With a closing volley of laughter, the ladies turned and rejoined the promenading bodies weaving between the trees. But before the two of them completely disappeared into the crowd, the beautiful woman cast a final glance his way. Dark, stirring clouds.

Serafim began to breathe again. He needed to find out who the mysterious woman was, so he put the camera back in his jacket pocket and made his way to the small lake, where people paddled little boats beneath an artificial cave, water birds scattering to avoid them, blushing with their own astounding colours and the humiliation of their clipped wings. He found the man he was looking for within minutes, his station at the epicentre of all things public as reliable as the North Star, where he held a steady watch over the social constellations around him. For some reason, literature had people consulting fortune tellers and oracles for their critical information, when all one really needed to do was find the resident gossipmonger.

Serafim shook the man's hand, gave him some news about his uncle's bid for the tourism board commission coming up in the spring, and got right to the point. Who was that woman strolling, he asked, right — over — *there*? And how, please, could he possibly meet her? The man grumbled discouragingly, taking out a handkerchief to clean the monocle that dangled from a chain fixed to his vest. She was the oldest daughter of Mr. Sá, one of the more distinguished brokers at the Oporto stock exchange. A very well-to-do family. Word had it she was about to be presented as eligible, as well, at one of the standard balls for such things, held by the Portuense, the social club of choice for that echelon of society. It will, of course, be by invitation only, he added. So then, Serafim speculated aloud, if he could become a member of this club, he too would be invited to the ball — was that correct? Yes, but it is Mr. Araújo, who runs the club, and who owns, as you know, the most popular theatre in the city, and two of its most exclusive cafés, who alone decides the eligibility of its members. You would have to talk to him. And, Serafim interrogated without pause, could this Mr. Araújo be found anywhere today? Sure, mingling, as he always does on Sunday afternoons, in Café Majestic. Serafim had already begun to turn away but stopped to ask one last question: her name.

Inês. Inês Sá.

Before setting off, Serafim made sure to give the man a weighty thank you. To which the gentleman did not respond, but turned slowly back to the artificial lake, with its tranquil rowboats and frantic water birds, still trying to flee the confines of their own clipped wings.

Serafim left the throngs in the garden and walked into a street that was all but empty. A tram's massive electric engine was winding itself down to a halt nearby, but he opted to walk instead, wanting to clear his mind, prepare himself for the high-stakes meeting he was about to have with Mr. Araújo. He turned down a different street, where he heard an old woman singing a melancholic folk song through an open window. The volume of her lament rose as he approached and receded as he passed. Serafim began to feel the low drum of his pulse on his temples, thrumming an insistent pressure in his ears.

Inês Sá, he was thinking to himself. The name was undoubtedly a beautiful one, even if it was laden with tragedy owing to the well-known history of a Portuguese queen out of the fourteenth century, Inês de Castro. He found himself thinking of her ancient story instead of the urgency of his own. Her tale went like this:

The king at the time had his son marry for political reasons, namely to keep the nobles of Portugal bound tightly to each other in their collective wealth. But when the new bride arrived with her entourage, she brought with her a stunning lady-in-waiting named Inês de Castro, with whom the prince soon fell incurably in love. Their affair brought with it many complications, not the least of which was that she was Spanish, not Portuguese, and had given birth to healthy, vibrant children fathered by the prince. Meanwhile, he'd only produced one legitimate heir with his actual wife, the princess, a boy who was sickly and frail. Eventually the neglected princess died, and the king demanded that the prince marry another political interest. The prince, however, refused; he would marry Inês or no one. So the king thought he would solve the problem once and for all by having Inês banished, but the prince quickly found a way to live with her, in secret, in her place of exile. The king then found out that the prince had begun to appoint Inês's brothers to important positions at court. Fearing that his throne would fall into Spanish hands upon his death, he summoned three assassins and gave them orders. They descended upon the monastery where Inês lived in exile, and drew their swords. The prince, enraged at her murder, and knowing that the order had come from the king, organized an uprising and rebelled against his father's reign. It took a year for the revolt to be quelled and for things to return to normal, the prince back at court and in his seat, silent. But when the king died and the prince succeeded to the throne, he surprised everyone. He had the remains of Inês exhumed and adorned in royal robes and jewels, and he told the gathered court that he had married her in secret, and that she was in fact the rightful queen of Portugal. He had her skeleton crowned, and had the entire court kneel before her and one by one kiss her decomposed hand. Then he sought out her assassins. One escaped in transport, but the other two he had brought before him, where he cut into their torsos and dug out their hearts with his bare hands. He then commissioned two tombs to be built in the country's largest church so he and Inês could be buried facing each other. That way, on the day of the Last Judgement, when all the souls of the world rise from the grave, the first thing they would see was each other.

Serafim reached the café where he'd been told he would find Mr. Araújo, but he wasn't quite ready to storm inside. He stood on the walkway, smoking a cigarette, thinking that he was going to have to tackle this in precisely the same way he had other matters that had stoked his obsession. He would have to isolate the crucial steps and surmount each one individually. He would have to act as obdurately as the most extreme icons of his country's folklore. And if he committed to such action, little, he believed, could stand in his way. He removed his cap, wrapped his fingers around the café's brass door handle, the chandeliers glistening through the glass on the other side, and while he wanted to thrust the door wide open, he eased it ajar instead.

He approached the first waiter he saw — trim white jacket, gold-coloured buttons and shoulder boards. "I'm looking for Mr. Araújo, please." The waiter looked him over, then pointed to the back. As he walked between the rows of tables — conversations subdued, cups clinking, the smell of coffee, cinnamon sticks, and pastries in the air — Serafim crumpled his hat in his hands like a peasant. The white rococo ceiling towered high above with mouldings in blues, pinks, and gold, while the ornamental mirrors on the walls followed him as he made his way to the back of the room. He asked again at the bar in the rear and was pointed towards a low-lit backroom, where Mr. Araújo sat reading a newspaper, hunched over a desk between two kerosene lamps.

Instead of sitting up, Mr. Araújo simply peered over his glasses. "Yes?"

"Mr. Araújo, I understand that the Club Portuense doesn't currently have a club photographer, and I find it . . ." Serafim scurried through his thoughts for the word, the phrase having come out more combative than he'd intended. ". . . a shame. A pity."

"A pity?" Mr. Araújo settled back into the embrace of his leather chair. "A shame?"

"Yes, sir. I would imagine a club of such stature should have its own photographer . . . is all I am saying."

"And you, Mr. . . ."

"Vieira."

"You would no doubt like to remedy this deficiency of ours?"

"Yes, sir."

"I see. At what expense?"

Serafim hadn't thought of this. He swallowed. "At my own."

Mr. Araújo took his glasses off, nibbled on the end of one of the arms, and remained silent for some time. The café murmured behind them. A bathroom door closed. "Fine, Mr. Vieira. Post me your address and I will put you on our invitation list. You may come to the first three or four functions to take these" — he waved a flippant hand — "*photographs*, and demonstrate for me your product, what your services can do for us. Then we will talk." He put his glasses back on and hinged forward over his paper again. "Now, good day."

The first invitation was not to a debutantes' ball but to a horticultural exhibition at the Palácio de Cristal. Serafim dutifully attended and took pictures, slipping invisibly through the crowd, snapping the frames of a number of unfolding stories: An argument between two upstanding gentlemen, their exchange taut with overstrung niceties and nuanced slights, expressive gestures agitating the invisible venom between them. A boy being stiffly disciplined for playing. A lone woman straggling on the periphery of the room, caught in a pensive moment, looking into the dark of her gloved hands.

He attended another event the following month, a meet for horse enthusiasts with a small parade and a few races, and wormed his way imperceptibly through the flanks of onlookers. This time he found himself eavesdropping more, becoming aware of the distinctions in speech among the privileged classes. He paid close attention to what the men were wearing, to the latest styles of suits and hats, the colours and patterns of their ties, the shapes and tones of their shoes.

The third invitation was the one he'd been waiting for.

He had already developed the photograph of Inês strolling in the park several times. But he'd been right about it needing a lot of technical attention in the darkroom, and he hadn't quite struck the perfect balance yet, of burning-in the sky and its wildly textured clouds while still maintaining the crisp emphasis on the two women in the foreground. He was getting close, though.

His uncle stepped into the darkroom one morning to watch him work, standing around as if something were weighing heavily on his mind. Serafim was busy dipping two more prints out of the fixer and hanging them up to dry under careful inspection, the smell of sulphur radiating through the air. He sighed, knowing he would have to discard these ones as well, and looked over at his uncle, who in the saturated green light had a set of uncommon creases etched into his forehead.

"Serafim," his uncle began.

"Yes?" While the settings and timing for the new exposure were still fresh in his mind, Serafim placed another sheet of photographic paper in the easel beneath the enlarger and made some minor adjustments.

"I'm not . . . sure" — his uncle shifted his weight from one leg to the other — "that you have enough money."

Serafim, puzzled, looked at the number of sheets in the rubbish bin, then thought of the new clothes he'd just bought, the price of the tie, slacks, and jacket. He gave a factual nod. "Yes, I do."

His uncle seemed to want to say something more, fidgeted in the dimness while Serafim readied the equipment for another attempt. After a while his uncle slipped, wordlessly, back out the door.

On the night of the ball, Serafim was quite confident he would vomit. He was feverish with anticipation, cold sweat in his armpits, his stomach gnawing away at its own lining. A classical ensemble was playing music Serafim had never heard before. There were high chandeliers, red carpets, long velvet drapery hung in showy bows and columns of gentle folds. The men were self-assured and handsome. The women were beautiful, wearing white dresses embellished with elegant embroidery, their hair up, delicate necks strung with pearls.

Serafim couldn't dance to save his life, so he had to hover out of the way, taking pictures, trying to get as close to Inês as he could. He was discouraged to see that he wasn't the only one. Her attention was being sought by what seemed like the entire room, including other women. Serafim was beginning to lose faith, the night quickly drawing to a close, when she finally spotted him and approached as confidently as she had in the gardens. Part of Serafim wanted to turn and run from her, while the rest of him just froze.

"I see you have that devilish camera again. Stealing more photos, I presume."

"I . . . have been commissioned to be the . . . club's photographer."

"Really?"

"Yes. And I've brought something for you." Serafim jerked round and dug into the leather satchel that was hanging from his shoulder. He pulled out a piece of folded cardboard, in which he had mounted the photo, and handed it to her. As Inês opened it, she drew in a quick breath. "Now do you see how, had you prepared for the picture, carefully posed for it, the image would never have captured your ... *essence* the way this one does? Can you see that now?"

Her voice was far away, weakened. "Perhaps."

"Well, it is yours to keep. And ponder, if you like."

"Thank you, Mr. . . . ?"

"Vieira. Serafim."

"Sá. Inês." She offered her hand, which he leaned in to kiss, planting his lips on the tops of her fingers as if they were the sacred bones of an undisclosed queen.

It was a moment Serafim replayed in his mind much more, he supposed, than was healthy. Lying in his bed, his feet pressed tight against the wooden footboard, he was tense and agitated with a wanting so raw it corroded every one of his thoughts, infiltrated his every activity. He could scream at the injustices of courting rituals in Portugal. Every last humiliation and precarious manoeuvre was the onus of the man and the man alone. In direct contrast to the women, men had to lay bare their most private, physical desires for all of society to speculate upon. Serafim thought it ironic how the word for passion in Portuguese, *paixão*, had a braid of disparate meanings that somehow amounted to the same thing. Not only did it signify a corporal yearning, but it was also the word for fire, flame, the process of combustion, smoke trailing from a flare-up and dissipating into the dull sky; as well as being the word for the ordeal of Christ on the Cross. The sum total of all these meanings was how Serafim felt: strung up and naked for the world to see, his frailties exposed while his body slowly burned into a sorry heap of tepid ash. Unnerved, his hands would sink below the covers to tug out a grossly inadequate substitution that at least released him into a shallow and restless sleep.

Two weeks after the ball, at the beginning of the day's *sesta*, a quarter after twelve, Monday, February 8, 1926 (Serafim would later recall with precision), he received an invitation by post, cordially inviting him to a dinner party at the Sá residence. In the art of hosting such evenings, the note read, one must strive to strike a perfect balance of company, of common-grained views and dispositions; and no evening would be complete without at least one aspiring artist. RSVP. Yours, Mr. Abilio Sá.

That Wednesday, Álvaro left for Lisbon.

On Friday, the day before the dinner party, Serafim had a single flower sent to Inês's house. He had spoken with the florist for quite some time to find the proper symbolism for the sentiment he wanted to convey, finally settling on a gardenia, which stood for purity. It was a delicate flower of the richest, most lavish white, but when touched, it turned an acrid yellow wherever a person's fingers had been. Sullied, tarnished, stained. Women, Serafim had been told, valued their own purity as much as men desired it.

Ma tendre et douce petite sœur,

I'm so glad to have told you. Though it was ridiculous that, just to meet for a coffee, you had to skip your dance classes; while you tell me it's a miracle they've agreed to let you out for them at all, that your contract stipulates you can only leave their house two days a year. I honestly don't know what Maman was thinking when she signed you on. A little extra money for the family in exchange for a daughter in shackles is how I see it.

At any rate, now you know. Though I didn't tell you that I'd intended to end it with him, once I actually got around to marrying Gilles, once his familial chaperones would finally let us be. But the truth of the matter is that, though Gilles certainly pleases me in many, many ways, lasciviously, he could not begin to compare. They were in two different cities, two separate realities, which I soon found afforded me the possibility of being two women: one, a wife, who was upright and proper, and the other, whenever back for a brief visit in Montreal, who was suggestive and daring, and could balk at our inane and staid traditions.

So I know well what you are playing with. I urge you, only, to be prudent. Utilize your bit of freedom to keep a supply from the pharmacy. I use both cocoa butter and quinine before, and vinegar after, secrets I only came across by working with the wayward women who come to the YWCA for help; and who have taught me that our bodies and the concept of virtue are not inextricably bound. I believe there is more to us than that.

Un gros câlin pour toi, petite sœur,
Cécile

9

When Cécile finished her public schooling, she had great ambitions to go on to university, but both financially and as a French-Canadian woman, the only feasible option was to sit in on lectures and classes as an unregistered pupil. This was what she settled for in the end, and she was soon coming home with new ideas that she'd managed to pluck out of the most old-boy setting imaginable.

She would describe to Claire in great detail how, as the only woman in a room that was stuffy with suited men, everything she did was constantly observed, as if she were a bizarre imposter from some distant planet, brazenly infiltrating their ranks in broad classroom light. She would sit strong and straight, and try to appear oblivious to their non-stop, dumbstruck gawking, focusing on the professor, who would also pause to observe each minuscule change in her manner — when she re-folded her hands, or opened her books, turned their pages, dabbed the tip of her pen into her inkwell. It all, somehow, proved endlessly riveting to them, as if they were all motherless, had never seen a female before in their lives. And it was astounding to think, Cécile would say, that this very herd of oxen would be running the country in a few short years.

Though the possibility that might be changing did appear to be drawing closer. Alberta, Manitoba, and Saskatchewan had just granted women the right to vote in provincial elections, and much work was under way to win the right nationally. There was even ardent lobbying for women to be able to run in politics, and the notion was gaining surprising ground. Caught up in the momentum, Cécile volunteered most of her free time to the Fédération nationale St-Jean-Baptiste, one of the only francophone organizations bent on furthering women's rights in the city. And, as she was still living at home, she would report every success and bit of progress to her grandmother — who would, in response, give a single elated clap, or lightly thump the arm of her chair with her palm, as if it were the anvil at the closing remarks of some righteous proceeding — Cécile reading *La Bonne Parole* aloud to her in the boudoir, a magazine written not only for women but by them.

Cécile met a man at a suffragist rally who had come all the way from Quebec City to participate. He was mild and calm, but stood his ground with firm integrity. A bank manager who dabbled in politics, Gilles Taillefer had made his affections known to Cécile in a timely and respectable manner, and they were soon travelling between the cities to visit each other, in the reputable ways one might expect of a banker dabbling in politics. At an assembly near the end of 1918, in the midst of a crowd gathered to celebrate the announcement of not only the national vote being granted to women but the passing of an act that permitted them to run in federal elections, he got down on one knee and asked for her hand in marriage. She assented, on the condition that he continue to support her while she fought to win women's suffrage in Quebec's provincial vote, as well as a few other provisos. He agreed, and they were married early the next year, with Cécile moving to his modest townhouse in Quebec City.

Claire, who had just finished school, was the only child left in the household. She hadn't really been fazed by all this excitable suffragist rhetoric that had quivered through the house, having been much more absorbed in her classes at the École de Danse Lacasse-Morenoff. She eagerly mastered the dances they taught her — traditional and folk dances, ballroom, some exotic Spanish steps, the hop-trot, one-step Peabody, and even a little rudimentary ballet — warming up on the barre in front of the admiring mirrors that climbed the high walls with their reflections, stretching clear up to the ceiling with flattery.

When she was fifteen, through a friend from her classes, she landed a contract to work weekends at one of the city's cinemas — even if it was one of the more out-of-the-way and shabby ones — as an adagio dancer, part of a troupe that entertained in front of the screen between short movies, or when the reels were being changed for a feature film. Many of the girls were younger than Claire, most of them thirteen, and together they made up an eye-catching line of sixteen showgirls, dancing in unison to lively ragtime. It was the first applause she had ever received that wasn't coming from a family member or someone she knew, and she noticed how the clapping sounded all the more raucous and sincere because of it. Sometimes, looking out beyond the blaring lights into the darkness of the audience, she wondered how many people had come just for the dancers, whose act was always disappointingly interrupted by the moving pictures. The piano and trumpet players who helped them to entertain often told them at the end of the day how spectacular they'd been, sensational really, their hands brushing the small of the girls' waists as they filed out the back door to return to their unsequined civilian lives and another dusty week of school.

The limits of how evocative things could be onstage were just beginning to be tested in earnest by the cabarets and revues, the burlesque theatres, vaudeville, and musical comedies, all of which were nudging the envelope forward. Claire's parents had been to see two of her acts when she first got the job as an adagio dancer, and had reluctantly agreed to let her continue, glad of the extra revenue added to the household. But the moment she was finished school, sixteen years old and eager to move up and on from her inconsequential cinema job, they went to see her again, this time unannounced, and sat near the back of the theatre. In only one year, things had changed significantly. To their befuddled dismay, what they saw was their daughter, undeniably a young woman now, in a costume that revealed her legs in their entirety, as well as the white spans of her arms, and even a hint of her cleavage, all while she danced back and forth on the stage in what was (as chance would have it) the most risqué number she had ever performed. They left hushed and affronted.

A week later, her mother gave her the good news: she had found a real job for Claire. It was a job in which she could contribute, decently, to the family's income, and to her grandmother's burgeoning medical bills in particular. It had come from one of the well-dressed men who sometimes sauntered in from the opulent English-speaking wards, to walk the length of a working-class francophone street — Montcalm, Wolfe, Visitation — just to recruit a *jeune fille* for some affluent household to the west. A *jeune fille* was a kind of live-in maid, a position that offered an (often welcome) elimination of freedom for the teenage girl involved while paying entirely for her (assumed) lavish room and board, as well as sending a dependable cheque for her services directly to the family's mailbox every month, for between eight and twenty dollars. Claire's mother was elated to tell her that she'd been hired out for seventeen dollars. Just think of the way Claire would be helping her grandmother, she'd said.

A showy touring car picked Claire up and drove her across town, to the other side of the Main, into another world, one where people spoke another language entirely, held other customs, and had very different expectations. They pulled up in front of a stout brick mansion on Sherbrooke Street with classical white columns and a tight shield of lawn. She was given a brief tour of the interior, massive salons with oriental rugs and posh furniture, many of the rooms guarded by the low and swirling citadels of marble fireplaces. She was then led to a small room in the basement, her very own, next to the laundry facilities. It smelled of bleached mildew. That first evening, the woman of the house came down to make sure she was settling in all right. She was excessively cordial, and before bidding her a "simply splendid, magnificent first sleep," she handed Claire a welcome gift. A textbook on advanced English from France.

Claire spent the next days being schooled in her duties and responsibilities, straining to understand the exhaustive instructions in English. The woman was patient with Claire,

and tirelessly repeated herself. Eventually, Claire knew enough
to be left on her own to work, though the tasks were much
harder than she'd imagined. She was barred from contact
with people, cleaning unused rooms to a sheen, passing carpet
sweepers over the endless rugs, lathering expensive clothes
across a washboard. In the first forty-eight hours she thought
of running away several times, but on top of letting her father
and grandmother down, she knew several girls her own age,
other adagio dancers, who had run away from home and were
now struggling to make it on their own in an unforgiving city,
joining the ranks of the desperate and impoverished majority.
These girls tended to show up to work less and dance less, as
their obligations to establishments in *le Red Light* persistently
increased. Claire reasoned that, while working as a *jeune fille*
was only temporary, before she left her post she would have to
have at least some kind of plan or assurance in place. Besides,
she reasoned, at least she still had her Wednesday evening
dance classes to look forward to.

That Wednesday, after washing the dishes and eating her
dinner (at her station, on a stool at the kitchen counter), she
changed her clothes and asked for something she thought was
quite reasonable, a dime for a return trip on the tram that ran
the length of Sherbrooke Street, to where her dance school
was located in the east end. She stood before the couple, in her
clothes for going out, a small bag containing her dance attire
on her shoulder. The man and woman looked at each other,
shocked. Finally the woman, stuttering to start off, explained
that no, Claire could not leave the house on Wednesday evenings, or ever, really, except for the twelve hours on Easter and
on Christmas Day that had been agreed to in the contract.

As this sank in, Claire's mouth dropped open. Her bag fell from her shoulder. With water welling in her eyes, she cupped her hands over her nose and tried to hold back the wave of hysteria that was surging through her. She was visibly shaking, convulsing now with voluble sobs, gripping onto her hair in fists, buckling at the waist.

It wasn't the woman who went to Claire but her husband, a mild and relatively soft-spoken man. But when she saw him approaching, Claire screamed into his face, *"Me touche pas!"* Then her hands, as if of their own volition, were suddenly out in front of her, towing her body to one of the marble fireplaces, where she grabbed a hefty candlestick from the mantel, spun round, and hurled it at the wide-eyed man, whom it narrowly missed as he dropped to the ground on all fours. The silver candlestick clanged onto the floor behind him, rolling into a wall, and when it stopped, Claire scurried back down to her quarters and collapsed on her bed to weep.

She cried for quite some time, and when she suddenly stopped, she turned and faced the ceiling with solid resolution. She would not be defeated, not be denied. She would get to her dance classes because she willed it to happen. She willed it so forcefully that she wondered if something might transpire to get her there that evening. Her only problem in achieving her aim was that she didn't have any allies, didn't have anyone who actually understood her plight. This, she strategized, was the only thing she required. So, then, all that was left was to will this to happen. Claire clamped her eyes shut, stiffened her body, and bent all her concentration and strength and focus on this one thing. An ally. An ally now. Now. Now.

There was a timid knock on the door. She breathed a soundless sigh, and propped herself up on her elbow. "You can enter, please."

It was the husband again, his wife being apparently a little weak in the knees after such an outburst of emotion. "I . . . I would like very much to apologize, miss. I do believe the gentleman with whom I made the arrangement wasn't entirely forthcoming as to some of the details of the contract. And I —"

"Please, sir," Claire interrupted, "please come in. I wish for you to understand something."

The man hesitated, cast a glance at the open door behind him, and then sheepishly stepped forward, towards the bed. She grabbed onto his wrist and pulled it up to her chest, opened his hand and placed it flat on her bosom. Her heart was thumping to a measure he could clearly feel in the bones of his hand.

"Look at me. Please," asked Claire, waiting until he did so. "Now. I. *Need*. To dance." She drew a heaving breath into her lungs. "If not. I will die."

The husband searched her expression. "I . . . I see . . ." he murmured, clearing his throat. "Well, I . . . I will . . . discuss this with my wife and —"

Claire shook her head. "No. I don't want you to discuss it. I want you to say to me, now, promise, that I can dance."

"I . . ." The man tried to pull his hand away from her grip, but she wrestled it back into place, onto the centre of her chest. Finally, "Okay. All right, I promise, you can . . . next Wednesday — and every . . . Wednesday — you can . . . you can dance."

Claire closed her eyes in gratitude. "Thank you. Thank you. Much." But when she opened them, she wasn't quite met with an expression that mirrored her own clear and steadfast resolve. It occurred to her that she might have to give something in return. Yes, now that she was calm enough to think, surely, in exchange for a long-term ally, *something* would be expected. Such things weren't acquired for free.

Claire reached a hesitant hand out to his neck, her cold fingers sliding into his collar. She paused, tugged him closer, waiting for him to pull back and resist. He did not. With his face close to hers, there was nothing else to do but kiss him, at first with a closed pucker, but soon with a teary, open-mouthed softness, until she'd begun a slow and brave exploration with her tongue. Their breathing swelled. She moved his hand from the centre of her chest and into her dress's collar, then down, to cup one of her breasts. They leaned farther back, tipping onto the bed.

There was the sound of a drawer upstairs, closing louder than it needed to, and with that, the husband sprang back, stood up from the bed, straightened his tie, wiped his lips, and smoothed his neatly parted hair. As he was leaving the room, Claire called his name. He paused in the doorway, his back to her, and turned his head just enough to take her in out of the corner of his eye. "I thank you again," said Claire, having sat up on her bed, posture perfect. The man gave a feeble smile, nodded, and left.

The next Wednesday, as promised, Claire attended her dance class, as she did every dance class after that, for almost an entire year. Dancing made her weeks more bearable. The couple, who were from old money in England, eventually understood this necessity of hers, each of them having their own set of much-needed diversions and pastimes. For the woman, it was her rigid weekly schedule of tea with friends, an evening of cards, shopping downtown on Fridays, and an operetta or orchestra concert "at the weekend." Her husband had his own English pursuits, institutions that had been exported and adapted to fit a new, Canadian setting: golf, rowing, lawn bowling, even well-organized fox hunts — packs of hounds and terriers, men in trim red coats and teams of horses, bugles and hunting horns, all bearing down on a single rusty canine as it fled madly, and in vain, through a pre-scouted forest on the outskirts of the city.

The couple's predictable lives and schedules meant there were foreseeable slots of time when the husband and Claire would be in the house alone together, and he visited her room whenever he could. At first, for Claire, it was quite enticing, a kind of learning curve of increasing satisfaction, but then she realized she could use it to leverage more than just dance classes. With a bit of advice from the girls at the École, Claire learned that she could also insist on his giving her pleasure exclusively. To Claire, this was incredible. It was as if his desire for her was capable of completely blinding him — to consequences, to his own absurdity, his own folly. Sometimes, just to see if she could accurately forecast his behaviour, she would deny him, and then watch him, just as she'd expected, back out of her room, holding up his hands as if she were pointing a gun at him, his demeanour half embarrassed, wholly awkward, and slink away like some cowering vermin. Then, as simple as elementary arithmetic, the next time he knocked, his desire would be twofold.

This meant that, by careful degrees, and learning as she went along, she asked him for more things. First, to pay for her dance classes. Then, a couple of months later, for some new clothes, dresses (she lied) for dancing. Then, a few months after that, a gramophone, just for her, and some records, in order, she said, to practise. These requests would take place, unfailingly, just before lovemaking, during the frantic buildup, as his hands began to slide more firmly over her body but at a point when he could still pause to speak. He granted every request immediately, almost without hesitation. She made sure to remind him he had done so afterwards as well, just before he left the room. "Right," he would say, as if distantly recalling it, "of course. Of course, yes."

Eleven months later, when she asked for permission to go out on both a Thursday and a Friday morning for an audition at one of the city's premiere vaudeville houses, the man finally voiced some reservations. Claire begged him, though even if he'd said no, she would have found some way to go. It was a great opportunity for her, one a friend from her dance school (whom she'd known for years) had set up for her. The girl was one of the few people Claire knew who was actually making a living at dance, working the vaudeville scene. She was even living in an apartment with two other dancers, and hinted that there was room enough for one more. And, just as Claire had willed it to happen, after the second long morning of auditions, she was offered the job.

That weekend, she told him about the changes he could be expecting, in her schedule and availability. They were alone in her room, Claire's back to the door, while he was on the edge of the bed, taking off his shoes and dress socks, loosening his tie. His wife was downtown, springtime window-shopping with friends.

"I have news! I got this job I told to you." Claire was smiling, euphoric.

He looked up at her, frozen, thumb in the ankle of his left sock.

"So," she continued, "I will need to go and practise each Monday for all the morning, and I will need to go and dance five nights in the week. But I will still do all my jobs here. I think it is okay."

"I ... You ... No. No, it is not okay." He stopped taking his sock off. "I'm ... afraid that you cannot." He stood up from the bed, stepping towards her. "I am sorry. But you *will* not."

Claire had expected him to say this. She nodded, grinning dangerously. "Yes. I am. You will let me. If you do not, I will tell your wife." She watched the colour drain from his face. "And I will tell your neighbours." She straightened, her hand on the doorknob at her back. "I will tell everyone about your visits in my room."

While Claire had prepared herself for things to go wrong, it was surprising to her how quickly it all unravelled. His voice deepened, became sinister. "Why, you conniving little ..." He lunged forward and clamped his hands around her throat. Grabbing onto his wrists, she kneed his groin with a well-trained, highly athletic kick, and as he folded onto the floor, she dashed from the room.

Rushing into the laundry room, she bolted its heavy wooden door behind her and, calming herself, turned on the gramophone that she'd placed on the floor there, just prior to his visit. She slipped her oldest and baggiest dress over her head, grabbed the valise that she'd already packed, and climbed her way out of the coal chute. He was pounding on the laundry room door, his shouts and threats to open it resonating through the wood. She wiped the dusting of coal that was on her hands against the sides of her old dress, pulled it over her head, and threw it down the chute. Then, without shutting the trap door, the neighbours already opening windows at the commotion emanating from the chute, she walked away, striding buoyantly along Sherbrooke Street, making her way to her friend's house. Claire was going to take her up on her offer to become a roommate after all.

That night, a Saturday, Claire went out as an unchaperoned, unhindered adult for the first time in her life. She and her friend went to a cabaret where one of the dancers who lived in the apartment was performing, and when she was finished, she joined them at their table, five young women together, all of them independent and unquestionably sovereign. Claire was astounded at how many people came up to the table to praise the girl who had performed, telling her how she'd stolen the show. Drinks were bought for them and placed on the table in the midst of an endless stream of flatteries and advances.

Well after midnight, two young men, proud McGill University students, came in, surveyed the room, and were soon shuffling onto a bench in the intimate corner where Claire and her friend were sitting. They confessed straight away that one of them had stolen his father's car for the night, and that they'd just finished steeping its furnace with coal. "What! A steam-powered motor car?" Claire laughed. "Impossible!" But they swore it was true, and even offered to take them out for a drive around town inside it, if they wanted. The two girls exchanged a daring look, and agreed.

Sure enough, the car was just as they'd said it was, a Stanley Steamer, as one of them called it. It was an open-air cabriolet, and with a right-hand drive, it was unlike any vehicle they'd ever seen. They climbed in, Claire in the front with the driver, who asked which direction they should head in first. Claire said she needed to deliver a few letters, and now was as good a time as any. Wanting only to joyride, the driver wasn't all that interested in running errands. He suggested an alternative route, reaching down on his right to give the brass horn two quick squeezes.

"No," Claire said in her innocent accent, "you don't understand, this is special." She hooked her arm into his, leaned closer. "Because . . . I need you to protect me."

The young man required all of one and a half seconds to think this over before agreeing, though with considerable reluctance. "All right, where is it, then? Sherbrooke? Okay, sure. Right, is everyone holding on back there? Because here — we — go!" There was a gradual hissing acceleration, then the night wind picked up, a sea-breeze whisper at first, which surged stronger and was soon whooshing through their hats, until they had to hold on to them, palms pinning them down to keep them from taking flight, the tree-lined streets soaring past on either side like a stratospheric tunnel of green clouds.

When they pulled up to the English couple's house, Claire and the young driver, with exaggerated stealth and stifled chuckles, stole across the lawn and eased onto the regal portico. Claire slipped an impeaching and scandalous letter into the mailbox without the slightest hesitation, knowing that it was his wife who collected the post every morning. Claire wondered how splendid and magnificent she would think her husband upon reading the letter. The two of them then delivered the same letter (Claire had written it out five times in all) to the two adjacent neighbours, and then, for good measure, to the two manors across the street as well. After that, they returned to the ol' Stanley Steamer, climbing into it on the weightless rungs of teenage laughter. Then, with a sudden valve release and burst of vapour from the exhaust pipe, the vehicle began to creep forward, inching gradually into higher speeds. There were random whoops and yippees shouted from the cab and into the early summer air as they drove off.

When they could feel the wind again, Claire turned around to face her friend and new roommate, who was nestled in the leather of the open back seat, holding on to her hat once more. Claire giggled at her, the mansions of Sherbrooke Street now dwindling in the distance; and as they receded, so did the possibility, in Claire's mind, that the thing she had just done would ever be able to follow her. Her friend, like a champagne bottle foaming over with jubilation, suddenly threw back her head and laughed, one of her arms spilling out over the back seat, flailing into the night behind them. She and Claire laughed up at the stars and into the long pearl boulevard of the Milky Way.

It was the beginning of summer 1920. They were seventeen. And the times — you could feel it — were changing.

Medium: Gelatin silver print
Description: Joan Forsyth, candid portrait
Location: Lamego, Portugal
Date: 1925

ↄ

Pencilled onto the rear of the print is a note, dated March 1926, which, in Portuguese, reads:

> *In regards to our discussion, the exposure I spoke of, and for which I was recompensed. To you, with my deepest and most heartfelt affections, S.*

It is a photo of a young girl wearing an ornate and formal dress, the kind not likely permitted to be worn while playing, even if that is precisely what the girl appears to be doing. It is unclear whether her palpable sense of mischief stems from this rebellion or from the fact that she is digging for something, through the plants, with her right hand. She is tiptoeing to reach into a decorative planter with ornamental leaves that spout from its centre; she is dwarfed by its foliage fountain, its splashing froth of flowers.

The fist of her left hand is clasped onto the rounded cement lip of this planter, pulling her higher to explore the secret world between the stems of the undergrowth. She is looking over into the lens of the camera, at exactly the moment her hand seems to have finally come across the object she has been searching for — her reward for winning a difficult game. Her expression also conveys that the object she has just discovered is not quite equal to the accumulation of all the anticipation and coaxing that has led her to this hiding spot. But her eyes still dance. At least she has found it. And for now, it is hers. All hers.

10

Serafim thought very carefully about what time he should arrive for the dinner party at the Sá residence. If he went too early, he would risk giving himself away as eager to the point of maladroit fixation, which was of course the case, so, cunningly, he opted to be fashionably late. As it turned out, however, his timing was less fashionable and more just plain late. He was given a formal, if cold, reception at the door from Mrs. Sá, and then a dismissive introduction to the rest of the guests by Mr. Sá in the drawing room. Serafim gradually inched himself into a corner, at first to inspect a framed photograph and then to lean on a column and sip his aperitif, listening to the static wash of overly polite banter and the profane distortion of a gramophone crackling from an adjoining salon.

The conversation had already sculpted the room with its niches and bas-reliefs, the company standing and sitting in their chairs at angles to listen to the most intriguing and charismatic of the guests, the spotlights already set fast for the diorama, radiating with flair. It was evident that every male guest who had been invited was there for the courting and the courting alone, seizing this sliver of an opportunity to make a festering impression. After assessing the competition, and disheartened by what he saw, Serafim found himself cataloguing the articles on display in the room — the plush carpets, wrought-iron light fixtures, untouched finger food laid out in silver serving dishes on the tables, and convoluted trays with decanters and carafes of Scotch, brandy, and port.

Inês was nowhere to be seen.

Then, as if out of thin air, she materialized right beside him, in the shadowed alcove of his retreat. She spoke to him in a hushed tone, so as not to become the centre of the room's attention just yet. "Do tell me. Would they make for a good photo, sitting as they are right now, not ready to be photographed?" She gestured at the company.

Luckily, Serafim had assessed the shot long before she'd asked, and answered with factual automation. "No. The lighting is in all the wrong places. I would need a tripod, and there is, frankly, not much of a story to be captured at the moment." Serafim turned to reassess the scene, shocked at how relaxed he'd sounded, even confident. "Though," he reconsidered, "if I could get closer to that well-dressed man who's speaking . . . who *is* quite animated . . . and had a great deal more direct light on his face . . ."

"So do you see everything in life as if you were viewing it through a camera lens?"

"Yes."

"And don't you find that at all peculiar?"

"No. I think we all see our world through the filters of our own obses —" Serafim checked himself "— of our keen interests. In fact, I would hope that everyone alive has, in some way, some kind of burning . . . fascination. Yourself?"

Inês inspected her hands with a quiet smile then leaned forward, close enough that Serafim could smell the soft sea of her skin beneath the citrus of her perfume. "In truth, I do — though I've been told it's a rather unbecoming curiosity for me. Cuisine. In fact, I was just now in the kitchen, with the cooks and servants, wearing a common apron, whilst everyone scolded me for treating this like every other meal they've made. Since I was very young, I have loved being in the kitchen with the maids. Such smells and colours. And do you know, every, every last recipe has a secret to it? Out of tradition or chemistry or folklore. Every one."

"Really." Serafim's voice sounded mildly sedated. "Like what?"

She leaned in even closer, as if to whisper, but would not be given the chance.

"Why, Inês!" the well-dressed gentleman called out. "There you are. You make such a stranger of yourself! Come out from the dark there and join the discussion. We're speaking of the American fashions making their brutish way to Europe." A burst of agreeing laughter followed his declaration.

Serafim's chance to speak with Inês alone, or with any kind of intimacy, was over. She would be monopolized for the rest of the evening; while Serafim would eventually become the reluctant focus of the spotlight.

It happened during the dessert, after Serafim had sat quietly through every other course, revelling in the thought of Inês's fingers and secrets pinching salt into the various dishes he forked between his lips with slow artisanal appreciation. There was talk of where everyone would gather after the dessert, when tea was served; and if any of the young women present wanted to show their talents at the piano, or bring out their paintings or sketches. The mere mention of art made a well-dressed gentleman's eyes, which had scarcely seemed to notice Serafim before, hone in on him with all the iris flame of a hawk. Serafim's fork paused, protruding from his mouth, waiting for the man to speak.

"I understand that you have taken to dabbling in photography, Mr. Vieira?"

Serafim removed the fork, swallowed. "Yes."

"I, too, have a camera, a Kodak Brownie, and take pictures on all my travels in the countryside, sending my films away to be developed three times a year. So what do you make of this debate, that photography is art?"

"I don't think there is a debate. It simply is."

"You should read more, Mr. Vieira. There is quite a debate. It is interesting to consider that, if you're right, then I too am an artist. I must confess, I've been quite unaware of it until now." Laughter.

Another gentleman broke in. "Have you read any Baudelaire, Mr. Vieira?"

"No."

The man appeared to find this fact amusing. "Well, Baudelaire, an exemplary critic of the arts, believed photography to be useless, incapable of depicting what he called 'the monsters of his fantasy.' In fact, he saw the photographic calling as the lot of failed painters. But I think that photographers such as yourself have moved forward from this initial criticism, and now make a conscious effort to arrange people and props in your studios in as artistic a way as you can, and it is there, I believe, that the art comes in — in the deft orchestration of the composition. Is that not the case?"

"No. I would consider none of my studio work art. However, I *would* consider the photos I take, which are entirely spontaneous and candid, to be exactly that: art. The orchestration you speak of is then in your positioning, your timing."

"And your luck," the gentleman who had begun the conversation added.

"Yes," Serafim conceded, watching the same well-dressed gentleman look away from him, dismissively moving on to something else, "and your luck."

"Have you ever sold one of these 'art' photographs?" asked the Baudelaire proponent.

"Yes. One."

"One," he confirmed, deadpan.

There was a dense quiet. Inês gave Serafim a reticent smile. Inês's mother placed her dessert fork soundlessly onto her plate.

Mr. Sá gave his hands a sudden clap. "Why don't we serve tea back in the drawing room."

The company moved into the other room and Serafim sat in an out-of-the-way chair near an end table. His hands fussed over each other in his lap, and he was glad not to have a hat to scrunch like a peasant. He politely refused a cup of tea, and after everyone had been served, Inês, quite unexpectedly, approached him. Walking gracefully, floating over the floor along the hem of her dress, she asked, "Are you sure you wouldn't like a cup of tea, Mr. Vieira?"

Serafim stumbled into thoughts of the secrets she kept. "You know, I think I would."

"Let me get it for you." Everyone in the room watched her out of the corners of their eyes, everyone waiting for her father to insist that this was a task for the maids to do, not the feature aristocrat's daughter; it was almost laughable. Indeed, her father cleared his throat in disapproval, but Inês wilfully dismissed proper decorum and left the room to fetch Serafim some tea. She returned with a tray, beautiful and defiant, and poured a cup of caramel-coloured liquid that swelled to the lip of the whitest porcelain. "Sugar?"

Serafim preferred his tea with nothing in it, plain and bitter. "Yes. Please."

She didn't ask how many teaspoons, as if she knew. He watched her long fingers, the creases and folds of her wrist as it swayed and lifted, the downy hint of hair climbing into the dark of her sleeve.

"Milk?"

"Yes," he answered, whispering. As she was pouring the dab of milk, one hand on the handle of the carafe, the other on the lid, he felt a kind of disorderly, irrepressible urge to simply lean in and put her hands into his mouth, suck back all the luscious flavours and salts of her skin. He wanted to run his lips over each knuckle, nail, and furrow. Inês lifted a spoon and stirred the honey-coloured mixture, the rhythmic, swirling scrape of metal against the bottom of the cup. Serafim felt a kind of darkness descending over him. He felt his control and restraint slipping off the sides of his body like the skin of a snake squirming free of a cumbersome moult. He bent his shaky head closer to the cup, his mouth falling open as it neared her hands.

"There you are." Inês tapped the rim of the cup with the spoon and placed it at a reckless angle on the saucer, before lifting the tray and turning on her heel to walk back to the centre of the room. Serafim, somehow spent, slumped back into the chair.

Later, Serafim wouldn't remember drinking the tea, the taste of it, or how warm or heavy the cup felt in his hand, but he did remember its image, with precision. Serafim memorized the cup of tea, his head cocked at an angle, staring at it unflinchingly, taking in every shade, glint, curve, and bend of light, until he could feel it burning into the glossy film of his mind's eye.

The next afternoon, he asked his aunt for a cup of tea, taking milk and sugar for only the second time in his life. He would get used to the new taste, but never quite used to how shocking and implicit was the sullied spoon that lay sated on the saucer afterwards, its only purpose, the only point of its existence, served. And sometimes he wondered if these constant flights of fancy were healthy. Sometimes he thought they weren't.

His obsession drove him to find out what church she went to, and he would attend, sitting near the back just to watch her in her veil, with only the fine rim of her face showing when she turned from the altar after Communion. Above her, the rococo nave was blazoned in gold and leafed out from the ceiling like ten thousand gilded springtimes, cherubs grinning mischievously, as if dwelling upon the naughtiest of divine intimacies. Then one day she looked up at him, smiled, and flashed an encouraging, even flirtatious, look. It had been five weeks since he'd dined under her roof, and this, he deemed, was a signal, the cue for him to act or be forgotten.

He had, of course, already sent her several gifts, flowers, chocolates, photos — including the one candid portraiture he'd been remunerated for, with a note on the back indicating such — but for this particular correspondence he chose to send only a brief note, four lines in his quavering penmanship, asking for her hand in marriage. He posted it immediately.

He imagined he would receive a response the following day, Tuesday, or Wednesday at the latest, but when Thursday's sun had also climbed and descended the walls, he reasoned that she must be taking a thoughtful, dispassionate approach to her reply. Serafim's patience held its breath for days, then a week, then two, as he maniacally and repeatedly checked the mail. The one day that his aunt beat him to the postbox, she told him, as Serafim walked through the door, that there was a letter for him on the table, the address printed in an elegant hand. He rushed into the dining room, held the letter up to his nose, and opened it. It was not from the Sá residence, and his disappointment was so apparent that his aunt made a point never to take his post from the mailbox again. Small amendments provide immeasurable mercy. The letter on the table turned out to be from Mr. Araújo, who was asking to see some of the pictures that Serafim, his probationary and so-called "club photographer," had taken.

The darkroom work required to supply Mr. Araújo with the photographs gave Serafim some needed distraction. He devoted himself wholly to the task, arranging his photos in a stylish album with an attention to detail that he hoped would impress. The photographs, thought Serafim, also happened to be some of the strongest he'd ever shot.

He met Mr. Araújo in the backroom at Café Majestic on a Sunday, after he'd received another, rather cryptic glance from Inês at church. Mr. Araújo shook his hand this time, then returned to the other side of his desk to sit down. "I'm interested to see these photos, Mr. Vieira. By all accounts no one recalls even *seeing* a photographer at the last few events, let alone posing for one."

"I prefer shots that are a little more natural, sir." Serafim placed the album proudly on Mr. Araújo's desk, who then tugged it towards himself and flipped through its pages with all the skepticism of someone reading over the fine print of a business contract.

When Mr. Araújo finally spoke, Serafim's back was turned, as he squinted at a map on the wall.

"I . . . I don't know what to say," Mr. Araújo stuttered. Serafim beamed, rocked on his heels. "It is . . . It's insolence. Impertinence."

"I'm sorry? Sir?"

Mr. Araújo opened the album and spun it around for Serafim to see. "These two men — they hate each other. I know them both very well. And in this picture, you can see it. Clearly. Unmistakably. And that is what I'm saying: This isn't a photograph. It's a mockery."

Serafim dangled in the middle of the room from a thread of disbelief. "What . . . could it possibly be mocking if it accurately depicts what you yourself have said is the truth?"

Mr. Araújo's expression melted into one of scorn. "Mr. Vieira, you have wantonly wasted my time." He closed the album and slid it back across his desk with revulsion. "You will not be given a single escudo from me. Now or ever. Take yourself and your photographs out of my office, and do not come back."

Serafim walked home with the album under his arm, feeling neither dejected nor miserable. Instead, he was busy mulling over the enigmatic glance that Inês had given him at church earlier that morning. That was all that mattered to him anymore. It was the only thing.

Then, a week later, it hit him. He had come out of the studio and was waiting at a street corner to get to the other side, having to time his crossing with the horse carriages, ox carts, and trams, as well as the few automobiles that puttered and weaved through all of it, startling the animals, enraging the tram engineers. At his feet, the sun was slicking the tread-worn paving stones, and a motor car whisked by on top of them, swerving onto both sides of the road. Like the burst of air he felt as it passed, an idea suddenly planted itself firmly in his head. It wasn't a belief or conviction as much as a pinprick knowledge, a kind of obscure though patent fact: Inês was going to accept his proposal. She was going to marry him. He was, suddenly, certain.

This changed everything — the way he saw his day-to-day life, the way he thought of the future. He felt lighter, nimble, and began considering where they would live, what their lives would look like, even when and where they would have the wedding. He wasn't embarrassed to say it, either, to his aunt, his uncle, even to people he spoke to throughout the day, clients at the studio, lottery vendors, his butcher, tailor. He would be the man to marry Inês Sá, and he knew it. He just, unerringly, knew it.

Another two weeks passed. His aunt complained that he wasn't eating enough, was looking gaunt and washed out. This was incongruous with the uncharacteristically hot mid-May weather, the sun having the same sharp feeling on the skin as it did in midsummer. People were already using umbrellas to shield themselves. It was a Wednesday, after the *sesta*, and Serafim was returning to the studio and had stopped to buy a newspaper.

The man behind the newspaper stand looked self-satisfied for some reason, smugly adjusting the arm band on his shirt before digging for Serafim's change. "I understand Inês Sá has finally accepted an offer of marriage," he said.

Serafim froze, grew colder in his stillness.

"Gustavo Barbosa. Works in the stock market with her father. Fine-looking man. Thirty centavos your change. Next! What can I get for you, ma'am?"

Serafim found himself walking aimlessly for some time, stopping at a corner to realize that his palm was still cupping thirty centavos. He turned his hand slowly around and dropped them on the ground. Above him, seagulls were agitating the rusty hinges of their calls. His feet turned and marched off in another direction, wandering rudderless through the streets of Oporto, wanting only numbness, an escape from the cold twisting at his centre, the sad fibre of his being wrung with a fist of disillusionment at one end and humiliation at the other. Finally, on a street he was convinced he'd never walked down in his life, he spotted an ill-kept and sun-faded sign over an entrance to a grimy commoners' tavern. He ambled towards it, stepping listlessly from the glaring sun into the dark of the entranceway. Once his eyes had adjusted to the gloom and he was sure there was actually a barman on duty, he approached the man behind the zinc counter, who was running a grey rag over a milky tumbler.

"I would" — Serafim cleared his throat — "like a glass of *bagaço*. Please."

Ville de Québec, le 26 juin 1920

Chère et adorable sœur,

It is so exciting to hear you are living from your love of dance, performing like some famous star of the moving pictures, out there on your own in the big city. My baby sister, how quickly you have grown up! I wish I could have experienced the same thing, if only for a few months, when I was your age. I am quite excited to hear of your adventures.

For me, life in Quebec City is quiet and tame. We went to the St-Jean-Baptiste parade two days ago, and to be honest, it was so mild and conservative I could have screamed. It struck me for the first time — with everyone waving their Carillon-Sacré-Coeur flags, watching the floats go by in the same themes as last year, celebrating the arts of spinning and baking, the sanctity of Church and an unwaveringly traditional home — how great the barriers are that we will have to break down before any real progress can take place. I am beginning to think we see this devout sentimentalism of ours as a strength, not a weakness.

On the other hand, walking around this city, I feel for the first time that I'm at home in the land of my own mother tongue, where everyday commerce and ad boards and tram stops, everything, is spoken and written in French. It is so reassuring somehow. As is the newspaper here, Le Soleil, which is quite progressive. The paper even had the mettle to criticize the Church's constant electoral interference (and was shut down for it).

I might see you soon. I'm travelling to Montreal next month — for the risk.

Mille baisers,
Cécile

117

11

Plunged into an intensive showbiz immersion, Claire quickly learned the ropes, though she couldn't have picked a more demanding, animated, and hectic scene to start off in. Vaudeville was made up of a dizzying ensemble of acts that had to be sequenced seamlessly then run through in rapid-fire succession. Mixed in with the always indispensable dancers were quirky musicians, minstrels, comedians, celebrity lectures, animals with zany tricks, magicians with much the same, two-man acrobatic routines, contortionists, strongmen, female and male impersonators, even small sets of actors staging pungent one-act plays. All of the performers had their own props and costumes and makeup, which was amassed and competing for space in the cramped warren of backrooms and passageways, pinched corridors, and dwarfed ceilings. Being a dancer without any props, Claire was usually jockeyed into one of the farthest corners with a few other dancers, who often had to sit on the three tiers of a toilet, one on the ground, one on the seat, and one on the tank, all of them bent over their hand mirrors applying their eyeliner, unperturbed as people passed the doorway in garish period costumes, thumping the door with their crinolines; or gingerly duckwalking by, trying to keep their monstrous headdresses from peeling off their scalps just before they stepped into the limelight. The stale smell of fabric saturated in sweat; spouts of perfume haze squeezed from vaporizers; mists of talcum powder swirling the cheap lights that filled the backstage area.

Among these dancers, there was less of a feeling of sorority than Claire had always expected. It soon became clear that she wasn't the only one with a dream of attaining sweeping adoration, success, and glory through dance. Though this really only served to reinforce her conviction that an unshakable fixation was the only method of attaining success. If she were to waver for just a moment in her drive and resolve, someone else, she thought, would simply slide into line ahead of her. In fact, she performed with women who would outwardly discourage her while at the same time (and in the sweetest voices) offering her all kinds of advice, on dance, show business, management, love, life. It soon became clear that their motivation for doing so was corrupt, that they saw her as just another rival, another obstacle that they now had to work around. What they really wished was for her to fail as quickly as possible, fall by the wayside, and forever be forgotten there, making their own path that much clearer.

In this slough of underhanded niceties there were men as well, playing their part. Claire had quickly sussed out that the dance world was a very steep hill to climb, the top of which loomed with positions and venues that were highly respectable, legitimate, even prestigious, while the bottom, where gravity constantly tugged and drew, was a sinkhole of a much seedier nature. There were always offers of roles in seamy

theatres that were much better paid, but which required performers to go on "dates" with patrons in private backrooms
after the production was over. Other proposals of more profit-
able work, which ranged from dabbling on the fringes of the
Red Light to delving right into its midst, were made almost
nightly.

On a more personal level, the same thing played itself
out at the tables and taverns after every show. Hovering men,
most with still-moist, tender white bands of skin on their ring
fingers, supplied a deluge of drinks, presents, and promises
whispered into young girls' ears that sounded too good to be
true. The number of dancers who fell for them was stunning
to Claire, who, while never once believing a word these men
said, would often indulge in an alluring tryst herself, accrue a
week of gifts — flowers, jewellery, furs — as well as, potentially, a few evenings of adequate pleasure amidst a more than
adequate standard of bedding. Surprisingly, from time to time
a true story *would* circulate, of one of these elderly men actually following through with his pledges and assurances, and a
run-of-the-mill affair would lead to a scandalous divorce and
remarriage.

It was in this way that Claire believed Cécile when she said
that men and women were exactly, precisely, equal. They were
equal in absurdity, contradiction, inadequacy. These character-
istics manifested themselves in different areas, of course, but
their sum totals came more or less to the same. As an example, Claire was convinced that, for every man who bent his
integrity, continuously lying to have an affair with some young
and impressionable girl, there was a woman out there who
was doling out the same amount of deception, only lying to

herself, bending *her* integrity, just for unlimited access to the wealth and power of some flabbily old and impressionable man.

Perhaps the most surprising aspect of dancing profession-ally, Claire had to admit, was that there were actually times when it felt like just another job. There were days when she would dutifully perform her steps and routines, keep time to the music, and go through the motions without giving much of anything to her audience. On such days, she would count the money she'd made and reason that every penny was needed to just barely pay for her rent and food. Sometimes the need to eat meant simply punching a clock, even if, before, this was something she would have considered herself above.

But at least, with dancing, there was always the potential for banality to be interrupted, unexpectedly, by the sublime. For Claire, there were still moments onstage that were noth-ing short of extraordinary, moments that could outshine even an eternity of ordinary ones; and it was amazing to think that almost no other career in the world could render or evoke them. These were the times when the musicians managed to play beyond themselves; and the audience, as if sensing some-thing in the air, would let go in order to follow them, rise from their dreary inhibitions and egos, leave themselves behind, and watch as Claire lifted and soared on the updrafts of the ineffable, channelling their adoration and awe, dancing fault-lessly, with a precision and grace akin to a swallow in flight. When she was finished and the audience could again catch its breath, she would watch them leap to their feet beyond the glare of the spotlight, a flower sometimes thrown into its white beam in a high, soft arc, landing on the stage without a sound, the applause deafening. She would bend low to pick it up and kiss it, then kiss her hand, flicking the moisture of her lips out at the adoring crowd, who clapped all the louder, shouting encore, *encore*, encore!

It was enough to sustain her. She worked in the vaudeville scene, dancing, shifting from one venue to the next, ascending in slow, incremental steps up the ladder of the entertainment industry, for four years. It was then, gradually, that she began to feel she was missing something, that it was time to set her sights on something bigger, more advanced, grandiose. She began auditioning for things that were a little further away from her zone of expertise, asking a friend to coach her with her singing, though she had always known that, while she could hit almost any note nearly spot-on, her voice was neither particularly beautiful nor winningly unique. So the failure she met with in singing parts was no surprise. Her failure in auditions as an actress/dancer, however, came as a complete shock.

Claire had always assumed that acting was the easiest (and involved the least talent) of all the arts. It was, after all, just people convincingly pretending to be something they were not; which, to some degree — in most situations, at least — every one of us did anyway. It was almost criminal that people were paid for it. Claire was told, however, repeatedly, discouragingly, that acting was certainly not her forte, and that she should leave behind any and all attempts at making it such.

Dusting herself off from the criticism, she concluded that she would just have to find some kind of illustrious venue that featured dance alone, a Broadway show about the life of a dancer, for example. In search of such a prospect, she went to every performance (usually on the spare-no-expense arm of her most recent tryst) that featured dance alone. She saw an American musical called *Aphrodite*, which had intricate dance sequences created by the world-famous ballet choreographer Michel Fokine and a cast of three hundred. The poster for the show, which featured a testing-the-waters image of a loosely robed Greek goddess, was pasted around Montreal, and overnight it caused such a controversy among the puritanical elite of the city that the theatre's staff ended up rushing around the streets with glue and scraps of paper to censor the images. For Claire, the show was promising, but in the production itself she was disappointed to find that there was no single dancer who acted as the focal point, carrying the work in the way that she pictured herself doing someday. (The production also featured elaborate tableaux, which Claire found futile and irritating, dancers frozen in stop-motion poses, a kind of anti-dance, making up an image that was void of movement and life, that was as pointless and dead, thought Claire, as a photograph.)

She began to wonder if her way out of the vaudeville scene might come in a less deliberate and calculated way, and arise as something more spontaneous and glamorous. Anything was possible in this business. It might simply be a matter of impressing the right person at the right time, dazzling someone in some high-up place, who would then back her, vouch for her, believe in her. Big breaks, after all, were not unheard of in Montreal.

Claire had worked with her dance teacher's son, Maurice Lacasse, the heir of the École de Danse Lacasse-Morenoff. She had landed several supporting roles from him, and had been called back on more than one occasion, dancing at a couple of private concerts in Westmount, a few gigs at the

Palace Theatre, and a weekend at the Clarendon Hotel in Quebec City. In 1924, he told Claire about an audition for an eminent part in a Russian ballet, which was just then passing through Montreal and looking for a bit of local colour and flavour to add to their mix. The ballet was set to tour extensively throughout the Unites States. Claire trained and rehearsed for it relentlessly, and spent an entire evening willing herself to win the part. She showed up at the audition at the majestic Capitol Theatre an hour early, just to sit and focus all her thoughts and pining on the artistic director's decision. Claire was rejected. But Maurice was not. And he and his wife, Carmen, were whisked away to a ballet school in Toronto, and within months, when the feature Russian couple of the company fell sick, they stepped up to replace them, and were instantly launched to stardom.

After this setback, Claire was finally given the break she'd been waiting for, her ticket out of the vaudeville scene. She landed a contract at Midway, a successful burlesque theatre on St. Catherine Street, and was ecstatic about it. In America at the time, burlesque was synonymous with scandal, but the French-Canadian version was much less salacious. It was still lowbrow and ribald entertainment, but it was much less explicitly sexual, having yet to delve into the risqué striptease that was ruffling feathers in the United States. Instead, the French-Canadian way focused more on trendy choreographed dance. It was performed in both French and English, and had become a form of entertainment that was positively flourishing in Montreal.

The director at Midway was taken with the idea of having his dancers perform to "black jazz" — which at the time was being stiffly emulated by white musicians, playing with anaesthetized smiles — in hopes of giving the club a more exotic flair. It allowed their club's patrons to feel "less threatened" than if they were to go to one of the authentic black jazz clubs on St. Antoine Street. The director, who appreciated Claire's energy and commitment, also decided to give her several pieces to choreograph, with complete artistic freedom. What she came up with were temptingly racy numbers, as impressive as they were suggestive, and her work soon became the most successful acts of the night.

Feeling she had reached a sort of high in her career, Claire told her parents about it during a Sunday lunch at their place. As the years had gone by, her mother and father had asked fewer and fewer questions about her work, or what she did with all her time; and whenever she offered information freely, in passing, they seemed tense and discomforted, which baffled Claire. When she told them the news about her choreography work in burlesque, while her father passed a plate of boiled potatoes over the Sunday table, the air suddenly congealed, as if she'd told them she had a terminal illness. Even her grandmother was incapable of grasping the significance. Affronted, Claire promised herself never again to mention her achievements to her parents. They had been growing in opposite directions for some time, but Claire felt they were now so far away from each other — like land masses drifting apart until they'd blurred out of range — that they could no longer decipher what the other's world even looked like.

The following Thursday, she was shocked to see them after her final act, sitting small and pale at a table near the back. She approached them elatedly. "Maman, Papa! What are you doing here! And what did you think of my act?" She kissed her hellos and pulled up a chair. Her parents didn't answer. Instead, they lowered their gazes, studied the surface of the table. "Is . . . is everything okay?" asked Claire.

Finally, her mother looked up, lips atremble. "Well . . . it's no wonder we don't see you in church anymore. I think . . ." She pressed a fist into her mouth, as if physically muscling her tears back into her throat. "You know, I think . . . that we don't know our little girl anymore. I think our daughter . . . I think she's lost." Her tears began to stream.

Claire's eyes darkened, deepened, a slow smirk crossing her face. "*Exactly*, Maman. Your daughter is lost. Which is where she was designed to be. Where she belongs. And if you don't know that, I really don't think you know her."

Her mother, crying audibly now, stood up from her chair, tugging on her husband to do the same. "Let's go. I will not sit here with some woman I do not know, with some . . . some common prostitute." She pulled at Claire's father and together they turned, taking several steps towards the door before her mother paused, spinning round impulsively, and declared, "And nor will I allow such a woman into our home. She is not welcome." As they left, Claire's father looked back at her as he tried to keep up with his wife. And tried not to.

As soon as they were out of sight, Claire slumped in her chair. The music was bouncy and upbeat. A passing waitress paused to see if she wanted anything to drink, but she hesitated before asking, looking Claire over. She decided against it, and continued on her rounds. Claire eventually lifted herself from the table and took a taxi home, where she crawled into bed, her body on the mattress feeling as heavy as limestone. Like sediment, she sank into sleep.

When she woke in the morning, however, it was with certainty and vigour. She interlocked her fingers over her stomach, pointed her toes. She didn't need her parents. She didn't need them or their petty judgements, their antiquated views and conventions. What she needed was to be precisely where she was, and further, always moving further along, pushing the envelope of her success. Nothing would deter her. Not even her own blood, who happened, she thought sadly, to be too simple and ordinary to see how their duty was to encourage her dreams, not deflate them. One day she would become someone on whom they would deeply regret having turned their backs. One day.

She was sure of it.

(TWO)
VENTURING OUT

Medium: Gelatin silver print
Description: Man standing in marina at night
Location: Oporto, Portugal
Date: 1926

◌

A man stands alone on the paving stones of an embankment, between two overexposed street lanterns. Massive ropes stretch into the frame as if reaching out at the subject and, slacking, tired with the effort, moor themselves instead to cleats and bollards that can just be seen in the dark of the foreground, a few metres in front of the man.

His posture is strong, as if he is heaving with a deep breath. His body is not squared to the camera but askew, thoughtfully angled, while his head is turned to look directly into the lens. He is wearing a dark suit, and his collar, framing a light-coloured tie, is the only white object in the frame, and appears to be shining, providing a glow that illuminates his facial expression.

It is a contemplative look, seemingly tight-lipped beneath the man's bushy moustache. His eyes gleam moist. It is as if he is trying to communicate something to the photographer. Something where words will almost certainly fall short. Or already have.

Coming from the anchored boats in the night around him — one of which, it appears, the shot was taken from — one can almost hear the single, lonely clink of a bell. Other than that, the scene appears to be perfectly quiet.

A fog looks to be brewing, swarming the lanterns as if with wispy insects, while a thin film coats the dark space between the cameraman and his subject, like an opaque curtain, drawing closed.

12

Serafim opened his eyes to an unfamiliar room that was almost completely dark. He could detect a few unidentifiable shapes and angles but could not quite recognize his surroundings. His muscles were stiff from the fetal position he'd fallen asleep in. His head smarted. He clenched his hair, moaned, and sat up to look around, sorting through the shadows. Then he remembered, leaned forward, and buried his head in his hands.

Floating on the unseen floor at Serafim's feet was a choice he knew he had to make, because there was only a very small amount of courage left in his veins to make it, the brave conviction that had burned in his chest only hours ago depleting rapidly, fading, as is the nature of cinders. If he were going to take this merchant acquaintance of his up on his offer, he would have to do so in the next hour. Or never. He closed his eyes and let out a long sigh that stunk of hunger and alcohol.

Serafim stood up and began fumbling towards the noise of the quay outside, which was still bustling at night. Opening a doorway in front of him framed by artificial light, he flinched at the brightness of a gas lamp nearby. The soapy smell of the

Douro made him queasy, and as he stood, grimacing, a man passed the doorway and looked him over with disapproval. Confused, Serafim inspected himself. His vest and jacket were still unbuttoned, his clothes creased, a shoe untied. He patted the top of his head to discover tufts of unruly hair sticking up in the back. He'd apparently lost his hat somewhere along the way.

The mast of a ship in front of him swayed on the river, pointing rigidly into the night. He heard the shout of a man in the distance, asking if there was room enough for one last box, the reply to which was unintelligible, muffled, swallowed by the dark. On a street nearby, an automobile cranked into life, accelerated, shifted gears.

With a sudden, invigorating certainty, Serafim knew what he had to do, his decision made. He set off as quickly as his headache would allow towards his uncle's house, back to his room and his things. He would need to gather them up quickly. He stepped into the apartment, thinking about eating, and realized that he'd missed supper without finding a way of letting his aunt know, which was inconsiderate and something he hadn't done once in the ten years he'd lived there. The smell of warm food was hours old, and as he passed the dining room, he saw no place setting ready for him. This meant they'd heard the news and knew that he had probably taken it hard. He found his uncle and aunt in the sitting room, waiting anxiously.

Serafim stood in front of them with a hand on his forehead. "I'm sorry I missed dinner. I am leaving Oporto. Do we have any aspirin?"

His aunt and uncle exchanged a look, reluctant to respond. Finally his aunt spoke up. "In the bathroom cabinet, on the right."

"Thank you."

Serafim swallowed six aspirin and pocketed another hand-ful in case he needed more, then went to his room and began rifling through his belongings. In his closet was the trunk he'd packed his clothes in when he had moved from his father's house. He hoisted it onto the bed and hinged it wide open with a creak. Folding pants, shirts, ties, pinching pairs of shoes together, he began to fill it. Looking over his shoulder, he noticed his uncle in the doorway, leaning against the frame.

"Are you heading to Lisbon, to join Álvaro?"

Serafim halted in the middle of the room for a moment, a heap of socks in his hands. Interesting — he hadn't even thought of that as an option. "No. I'm heading onto a boat."

"I see. Bound for where?"

Serafim himself was surprised to hear the words. "I...don't know." He was sorting through his underwear now, dividing the new from the old and uncomfortable. "I think it's going to France."

His uncle stood quietly for quite some time, his eyes follow-ing Serafim back and forth through the room. "Serafim, ..." He paused to bite his lower lip. "I am not...sure this is the kind of thing you can run from."

Serafim slowed his movements, a shirt in his hands hover-ing over the open trunk. "You know" — he flipped the shirt over, lifted the collar, frowned — "I've always hated this shirt. I'm not bringing it." He carried it to the closet and hung it back up.

"And when does this boat leave?"

"Before daybreak. I'm expected to sleep on board tonight." Serafim put two more articles of clothing into the trunk and turned to see why his uncle hadn't responded to him, but he was gone.

His uncle returned when Serafim had just closed the latches on his trunk and had stepped away from it, admiring his packing job with no small degree of satisfaction. He realized that he could fit his entire life into one small box. It was incredible somehow. People, he thought, could be so much less encumbered than they imagined themselves to be.

His uncle interrupted Serafim's thoughts, suddenly standing beside him with a thick envelope in his hands. "I have been to see Mr. Moreira downstairs." Mr. Moreira, Serafim knew, was a businessman who lent money as an aside to his regular trade. "Because ... I have known you all your life, Serafim, and luck is something, you must understand, that is not on your side. You will need this where you are going." He handed Serafim the envelope. When Serafim saw how much money was there, he refused, and tried to give it back. But his uncle held up a stiff palm, not willing to budge. "You will need it where you are going."

With a reluctant hand, Serafim put the envelope in his pocket. "Thank you. Now I have to get this trunk to the ship."

"I'll help you carry it. That way we can stop off at the studio and you can retrieve any archival film you'd like to keep, and that lens for the enlarger you saved up for, which you need for that thirty-five-millimetre film you use. I suspect the use of the moving-picture format for still photography is a passing fad, so you're best to take that enlarger lens wherever you go, just to be able to develop what you shoot."

"Of course," Serafim said, somewhat aghast. He hadn't thought of any of these things. What else was he forgetting? It was such an impetuous act that there were bound to be things he was forgetting. But the thought of stopping to compile a list or go through a set of priorities petrified him. If he hesitated for even a moment, his bravery would slip away forever. In the same way that it was slipping away right at this moment, making him want to sit down, eat a warm meal, and rest his throbbing head. He turned to the bed and grabbed hold of the handle on one end of the trunk. "Then we should get moving."

He said goodbye to his aunt, who insisted he take several *pastéis de bacalhau*, wrapping the salt-cod cakes in layers of serviettes, their oil bleeding out to form transparent stains in the tissue. He and his uncle dropped by the studio, added a few more items to the trunk, and made their way to the quay. As they walked silently, words formed on Serafim's lips that felt so empty and thin that they eventually just evaporated. They passed a tavern where Portuguese guitar was plucking out a plaintive tune, a fado singer joining midway through, a coarse female voice singing a doleful melody.

At the quay, they ascended the long plank into the boat and were greeted by a shipman hustling to meet them, presuming they were mistaken. "Is there something I can do for you?"

"Yes, my name's Serafim Vieira. I believe I have a room on board."

The sailor looked amused. "You mean a berth. It's that hatch, first door on the right, top bunk." He hurried away.

When they'd placed the trunk in the room, Serafim accompanied his uncle back outside, where they stood awkwardly on the cobblestones facing each other, again not knowing what to say. Finally Serafim offered, "I imagine I'll be back in a year or two."

"Of course." His uncle gave a perfunctory nod. "Of course."

Serafim took his uncle's hand and shook it. "Well, wish me luck."

His uncle smiled as if with a dull pain in his abdomen. "Take very good care of yourself," he said, then embraced him, speaking over Serafim's shoulder and towards the river that flowed out to the sea. "*Adeus.*"

Serafim walked up the gangplank, pinching his throat that ached with tears he refused to let fall. He turned on the deck to see that his uncle was still watching him, standing between two of the gas lamps on the quay. Not knowing what else to do, he took his Leica out, rested it on the ship's railing, set the shutter speed to Z — which he'd read stood for *zeit*, "time" in German — and released the shutter. He kept it open for a second or two and pressed it again to close it. Then he waved at his uncle and went below deck, knowing, as he took another four aspirins and settled onto his berth, that in this life anyway, he wouldn't see his uncle again. The aspirin slowly lulled him into a numb and welcome sleep.

He awoke to the ubiquitous growl of a steam engine, the ship, having already embarked, swaying gently from side to side. Feeling strangely panicked, Serafim sprang from his berth and climbed the stairs to the early dawn above. There was a river fog, as there often is during the mornings in Oporto, shrouding the city that was already well behind them, hazing the last of the bridges, which they'd already passed beneath. A few straggling fishermen could be seen casting their lines out from the banks of the Douro, baskets on the ground beside them, wicker mouths open wide and waiting. They passed the final tributary as well, feeding into the river where it began to splay into the delta, a siege of herons standing in the water at its entrance, statuesque and inspecting their own reflections, seeing through them and to the life on the other side. Above the boat and fog, seabirds pencilled their shapes into the sky, V-notching every layer of the horizon out to sea. As the ship headed north, the smoke from the stubby stack dragged parallel with the undulations of the waves.

Farther up the coast, Serafim could hear music as they passed a fishing boat, and he went to the tip of the bow, as far from the engine drone as he could, to listen. Men were hauling nets over the gunnels, singing a rhythmic song in a minor key to keep the task synchronized, fluid, and efficient. Watching and hearing them, he found himself holding on to the railing and squeezing it. What he felt was both a consummate adoration for his homeland and a consummate loathing, both so powerful and simultaneous that each pierced the skin of the other, making them bleed into each other, become muddled and murky. On the hunch of his slouched back, he waited to be lifted by the inspiration that he felt was owed to him. He wanted to feel the wings of freedom and adventure, the release of his burdens and disgrace, the quickening air of his plunge from the treetop. But all he really felt was the cold of the metal in his hands, and the clothes on his back.

Ville de Québec, le 8 octobre 1926

Ma douce, ma sœur,

Thank you for being so patient with me on the phone. I've been thinking about your question and why it infuriates me so. I think the reason lies in how utterly powerless I am to criticize Maman, to step in on Grand-maman's behalf. My hands have never felt so tied, Claire.

Everything she is doing ostensibly for Grand-maman is exactly as Dr. Bertrand had suggested. After her stroke last month, he insisted she have plenty of fresh air, and that she have as much human inter-action and stimulus as possible. So, then, how could I have the audac-ity to disapprove of her wheeling Grand-maman to church? Oh, Claire, but you should see the way she sits there, parked at the front of the congregation, slumped to the side and gripping the wood and wicker of her mobile chair. If she could speak, I am convinced she would curse us all to hell and back. Instead, she can only quiver and grimace in the clothes and hats Maman has dressed her in. There are tears smearing her cheeks at times, and I am weak with the thought that they might be of the truest kind, that they have nothing at all to do with the dryness in the air.

Maman, who still will not speak of you, seems determined to have the last word on how our inimitable Grand-maman will be seen and spoken of in this world. Between you and me, I wonder if she would not find death at her own hand more dignified.

Tu me manques, Claire,

Cécile

13

The autumn that Claire's parents effectively disowned her was a rainy one. Red, wet leaves tongued the windows, rusted foliage slicked the cobblestones, and the gutters overflowed. While Claire's normally animated nature felt just as dampened as the weather, her shoulders hung as if with the weight of a woollen, drizzle-drenched sweater.

By the winter, she was returning to her normal self. She rang in the new year of 1926 by raising a volley of champagne glasses, and stepping through the snow in high heels to climb the steps of another club for more after-hours dancing.

She continued her work in burlesque and was given more freedom and say at Midway. She felt increasingly appreciated there, though at the same time understood that she was in no position to make demands, that she could be both instantly and easily replaced. At any given moment there was an elaborate queue of potential dancers, each of them as young, attractive, and talented as the next, biding their impatient time just behind her.

Dance had certainly come into its own in the city. In terms of artistic merit and importance, it had become such a high priority that the government had adopted an immigration law that gave dancers the same title, status, and priority as specialized workers. Lithe and limber Europeans now punctuated the competitive mix, and stood out with their distinctive dress and styles.

Throughout the year, and for the first time in her life, Claire prided herself on staying one step ahead of fashion. As it became more in vogue for women to smoke with cigarette holders, she took to smoking hers like a casual man; when hemlines rose above the mid-calf, Claire's encroached upon her knees; as hairstyles shortened in length, she had her own cropped into a bob so high she could barely use the new "bobby pins" designed just for that coif; while the highly desired boyish figure had her, unlike many women, actually binding her breasts tight to her ribs.

It was also the year that her grandmother had a stroke, and Claire struggled with wanting to go and see her and needing to acknowledge her parents in order to do so. She was made doubly indignant by the fact that they hadn't even bothered to let her know it had happened. In fact, if it weren't for Cécile's correspondence, she would have been left entirely in the dark as to her immediate (and extended) family's existence. Claire felt that her father, in some nameless and obscure way, was betraying her, betraying a kind of unspoken trust and alliance they'd once shared. The shiniest of steel attachments appeared to have corroded overnight.

The trend of trying to hold her chin up high above the gloom of bad news continued the following winter when, before the confetti of the new year's festivities had even settled, the city was struck by a horrifying disaster. Claire was out shopping the Sunday it happened, January 9, when she heard the first sirens and commotion on St. Catherine Street. She followed a team of horses that had careened past in a thunder of hooves, firemen at the reins on their way to a blaze, hauling a massive steam pump. A coal truck to fuel it was in pursuit right behind, carving through the streetscape of stilled trams and vehicles, dumbstruck drivers huddled on the snowy curbs. Claire followed the smoke and panic, both towering in the distance.

She eventually approached the Laurier Palace Theatre, where grey-brown fumes rippled and ballooned from the upper windows. Ladders were clumsily being assembled to reach them. Most of the sounds, however, were coming from below, where it soon became apparent there were children trapped inside, blocked at a door that should have opened out onto the street but had been hinged backwards so that the harder they pushed, the harder the door sealed itself. The door bulged with the crushing weight but would not give way. Frantically men tried to break it down and pry it open. Others fumbled to get water to spout from limp hoses. Nothing seemed to be working as it should. The pounding of little fists grew fainter as time went on. The muffled moans, screams, wails, and coughing grew quiet. Horses stood staring forward, adjusting their ears, shifting anxiously.

Finally, the door was broken in, but in lieu of a scurrying confusion of children's legs escaping, only smoke and silence poured out. A man finally leapt into the fumes, only to re-emerge dragging a small body that he would momentarily learn was his son. Other tiny bodies were tugged onto the sidewalk, flaccid and quickly piling up. Claire watched, removing her cloche hat and holding it against her mouth, her knees threatening to give way. In her other hand she held the strings of a paper bag, a new pair of shoes (with button-fastening Mary Jane ankle straps that she'd bought for a steal) inside. A large sign on the adjoining building continued to boldly advertise Rex Cigarettes.

Clambering over the hoses, blackened snow, and splintered window frames on the ground, Claire saw two photographers, one taking pictures of the bodies as they mounted — there would be seventy-eight in all — another taking shots of the crowd as they watched it all unfold, quickly winding and adjusting a tiny camera in front of his chest before each new exposure. Claire felt a wave of disdain for such photographers, people who, in place of helping, seemed bent on archiving their own vile curiosity instead. When the photographer taking pictures of the onlookers caught sight of Claire, he slowly lowered his camera from his eye and looked at her, singling her out with even greater focus. Disgusted, Claire turned and hurried away from the chaotic scene, from the hysterical fathers and mothers screaming and moaning in grief, leaving it all behind.

A few months later, Claire had a conversation that would shake her, and eventually jar her into action. She'd been sitting beside the radio, that vital organ at the centre of every dwelling's life, where people gathered, sat, and stared into the middle distance while listening to their daily broadcasts. The radio where Claire lived was always tuned to CKAC, which catered more to a French-Canadian audience and, like every station in Montreal, was hosted by agile bilingual broadcasters, such as J. Arthur Dupont and Phil Lalonde, who could suavely switch between French and English at every introduction, advertisement, and commentary. Claire was listening to an interview with a famous Canadian actress who was touring Montreal at the time before returning to Hollywood. The host's voice was soft, his questions flattering and flirtatious.

A new roommate — a young girl who was already showbiz hardened and smart-alecky — came into the room and flopped herself down on the coffee-stained sofa across from Claire. She listened for a few seconds. "Bea Lillie? Pfff. I could act her off the stage." She waved a contemptuous hand at the speaker. "Really, I could."

"Then I would get to it if I were you," said Claire. "Can't make it any bigger. Surely beats a two-minute vaudeville routine in some mislaid theatre."

Snubbed and spiteful, the girl didn't hesitate to respond in kind. "You know, you'd be surprised the things I learn there. Why, just the other day this woman enlightened me with a hard-and-fast rule that I didn't know about: if a girl waiting around to make it big hasn't done so by twenty-five, she never, ever, will. So I got to thinking about exceptions to that rule, looking for them in my head and in the papers, on the radio, and I just couldn't find a single one." She stood up. "Such a shame," she said, leaving the room, not waiting for Claire to answer the question that she left trailing behind her. "Say, how old are you again?"

Claire was twenty-four; in just over half a year she would be twenty-five. While it was something she hadn't thought about for quite some time, she knew, had always known, that the girl was right. In fact, now that she mentioned it — Claire's eyes darting around the room — at twenty-four she was the oldest woman in the house, as she had been in the last three apartments. And she was without a doubt the oldest dancer at Midway. Claire sank deeper into her chair. Come to think of it, she was the oldest dancer she knew of, anywhere. How had she let this happen, so quietly, so invisibly? While being convinced that she was always progressing, on to bigger, more prestigious venues, she'd actually, slowly, settled herself into a complacent niche, becoming gradually indolent. If this tried-and-true rule held water (and everyone knew it did), there were really only six months remaining for her to rise to the kind of starlit fame she'd always imagined herself basking in for the rest of her days.

That afternoon, she started getting ready for her evening performance at Midway hours before she needed to, adding the final details to her makeup — generous dabs of ivory face powder, eyes lined and the points of her brows extended with kohl, tiny pucker of lipstick in oxblood red — long before she had to leave the house. She stood around the apartment for a few minutes, turning in front of her mirror. Then she left, taking a tram along St. Catherine Street and getting off at St. Urbain, just in front of the Gayety Theatre.

Of the three or four burlesque venues in the city, the Gayety was undoubtedly the most prestigious. Most of its shows came direct from New York, and it was an integral part of the Columbia Amusement circuit, with open ties to Broadway, even Hollywood. It was seen by Montreal dancers as more or less off limits, as its performers were of the touring variety, always imported from afar and passing through without even so much as a perfunctory wink at the local talent. Claire had never heard of anyone breaking through its elitist barriers. But on this particular September day, with only eight months left before she turned twenty-five, and having long ago exhausted every other prospect she could think of to access industry bigwigs, Claire calculated that she had little to lose in giving it a shot. She crossed the street, paused at the threshold, and stepped through the hallowed door.

It was a Friday, four o'clock, and the night's preparations were just getting under way. Claire stood on her toes to ask a man behind the bar, who was on his knees and stocking the liquor onto shelves, if she could speak to the manager. He reluctantly got to his feet and returned with a short man walking briskly behind him. Everything the short man did appeared agitated, quick, and jittery. He hiked up his pants, looked at the empty door behind her, then at the stage, back at Claire, then hopped on his toes and started towards her. "What are you, doll, late or early? Sorry, got no time to punch the bag right now. Did we talk on the phone?" He stopped in front of her, shot a glance to his right, offered her a cigarette, lit it, then steadied the match to the tip of his own. "I call you?"

Claire smiled. "I am" — she drew in a long breath of smoke — "a great dancer," she said, blowing a stream of grey over his head.

"Fine, fine. Called a few of ya. So the act's a lead-in to our Harlem dancers. World-class, they are — and how! So it's gotta be hot, 'kay? Let's get Stanley play ya a ditty and see whatcha got." He turned and gave a whistle and holler to beckon Stanley as if he were a German shepherd, and the piano player emerged from a backroom and waited for his orders. The manager motioned for him to play something and turned back to Claire. "Was a car wreck busted her leg. Is who I need a stand-in for, you see. Up there on the stage, and make your way towards me with the goods."

In truth, Claire missed most of what he was saying, but she managed to catch the general drift that she'd stumbled into the right place at the right time, and that she now needed to impress him. And she did. When she was finished, both he and the pianist wiped their brows and shook their heads. The manager whisked her into a dressing room and explained that she would be hired for the night, and that he would see how things went from there. In the dressing room, she was introduced to the other dancer she would be performing with. It was explained that she would be one of two dancers flanking a well-known feature performer at centre stage, all three of them moving to hot jazz over a ten-minute routine. The act would come after a ventriloquist, and would nicely set the tone for the famed Harlem dancers to follow, with their patchwork of bright tassels and sequins barely covering their caramel skin, swinging legs and arms with a rhythm and skill that was legendary.

Claire had to steady herself with all the excitement she felt. It wasn't only the performers and musicians she rehearsed with that were more professional, more elevated than she was used to, but the theatre itself. It was lavishly decorated, with designer lights, crisp linen, and exclusive wooden trim. During the first act, when Claire peeked at the audience through a slat in the plush curtains, she realized that these were likely the very people who lived at the foot of Mount Royal, in the Golden Square Mile. They were some of the wealthiest people in the nation, upper-class anglophones out for an evening of leisure after having supped at the nearby Hôtel d'Italie, or the chic and exclusive La Corona, or some other luxurious and pricey restaurant in the city. Any one of them might be her ticket to the big time, providing the finger flick that would finally get the ball of her career unstoppably rolling.

Onstage, Claire stood out like never before, to the point of upstaging the feature performer whom she was supposed to be supporting. She felt her limbs moving like supple willow branches, wafts of music shuddering through her frame. When their act came to an end, she saw several elegant and jewel-bedecked wives elbowing their husbands for clapping too raucously. In the powder room afterwards, the feature dancer wouldn't speak to her. Claire wasn't particularly bothered by this because after the show, and in lieu of that feature dancer, it was Claire who was called over to the manager's table for a drink.

Standing tall and commanding in front of the table, dwarfing the stunted manager, she was introduced to a semicircle of powerful men — theatre executives, producers, agents, directors — and was heartily congratulated on her performance, the rims of champagne flutes clinking at the centre of the table like transparent oohs of adoration, foaming at the mouth. Not knowing what else to do, Claire simply giggled through all the English slang she didn't understand, words such as *milquetoast*, *flivver*, *rubes*, and *hooey*. By the end of the evening she'd managed to win them over enough to be invited out, and continued dancing well into the night.

She was ushered from club to club in a motorcade of luxury cars — Rolls-Royces, Cadillacs, limousines — storming in and out of establishments at will. Claire watched as her smartly suited chaperones slipped effortless bills into the hands of everyone who might possibly stand in their way. Small bribes were offered for everything: to quickly get in, out, ready the cars at the front doors, have someone go ahead to chill the champagne, musicians to keep playing, clubs to stay open, police to ignore curfews and bylaws, the lights to be dimmed, private rooms to be cleared, tables to be pulled together. Tiny bribes everywhere, for everything.

Well into the morning hours, Claire stopped kissing the manager long enough to ask him about the following night, the Saturday. Could she perform again? Of course, of course, the manager promised, leaning into her once more, his hand on the skin of her knee, hurriedly exploring farther into her dress. Claire helped his fingers along, and by the time the sky began to pale with the light of morning, she was inside his sophisticated mansion, throwing her clothes over his elegant furniture, gripping tight to the silken sheets of his bed, and laughing at the high ceiling above him.

When they woke several hours later, he pulled back the blankets, groaned, and held his head. He made his way out of the room, telling her she could find her own way out. Before he left, he mumbled that he would see her again that night, as promised, for another performance at the Gayety. A Saturday night, the theatre's biggest.

Late that afternoon, while Claire was rehearsing before the show, it occurred to her that in the sweep and swirl of the previous day's events, she hadn't even thought to call her old club to let them know she wouldn't be showing up. It was the kind of thing that was almost sure to get a dancer fired, at least the first time it happened; it would unquestionably get her fired the second time. Claire was amazed at the fact that she didn't really care about this. What was a razed bridge if you didn't even want the *choice* of crossing back over it?

While she rehearsed with the other two dancers that afternoon, the feature dancer was curt and condescending with her, exchanging scathing glances with Claire at every turn and in the glimmer of every mirror that tilted in her rival's direction. Claire simply ignored her. She was too busy willing herself to exceed expectations. She felt invincible.

Medium:	Gelatin silver print
Description:	*Il fascio*; Italians on pier
Location:	Le Havre, France
Date:	1926

❧

Three men in black shirts — sleeves rolled up, and one or two buttons undone from the collar — are smiling, elated, in what appears to be morning sun, in springtime or summer.

Two of them are wearing flat caps; the other bares a head of dense, wavy black hair. Both hats are not on straight, as if they've only just been donned, hurriedly, for the picture; or have been continuously removed and replaced as a part of the men's reverie.

Each of them is looking in a different direction, away from the camera; the man in the middle looks as if he is about to drop his hands from the flanking men's shoulders. Their faces are carved with archetypal Roman features, like three busts in an Etruscan museum.

Behind them looms the hull of a leviathan steamship, rectangular sheets of metal stitched together in a patchwork of seams and rivets, stalwart industrial needlework.

The man on the right is turning away dramatically, gazing slightly over his shoulder, stepping away from his companions, looking back at something that is out of the frame. One couldn't guess what he sees, but there is a strain in his expression that seems to indicate there is a whole lot more to smile about. And a whole lot less.

14

Serafim stood on a wharf in northern France, deafened by what sounded like all the languages in Europe trying to drown each other out. The quayside roiled and churned around him, men and women carrying trunks for short distances before putting them down again; children crying, wide-eyed and snivelling, clinging to their parents, brothers, sisters; men brushing close to Serafim and giving him half-aggressive nudges, likely because he was the only one in the knotted crowd who wasn't in a hurry.

The ship from Oporto had landed the night before, and it was the morning of disembarkation. Minutes earlier, Serafim's merchant friend had given him a few direct, seaman-type orders. He had one day to unload merchandise. If Serafim wanted, he could sleep on the ship again that evening, but they would set sail the following day at noon, so he would have to have all his belongings off the boat by then. Good luck, *adeus*, a firm handshake, and his friend was off into the swelling confusion, bent on making sense of at least his part in it. Which was more than could be said for Serafim.

He was quiet in the bedlam, thinking how strange it was that his new-found freedom felt so terrifying. He wondered if complete freedom was one of those things people aspired to but secretly held themselves back from attaining. Serafim now had the liberty to go anywhere in the world, do anything. He had no land, no ties, no home to return to. He was unbound, floating illimitable; yet he had never felt so burdened in his life. What if we *choose* confinement, he contemplated; what if we actually *seek* to settle into the security of some type of bondage? A person certainly never has to worry about their bearings, or who and what they are, when held in place by a few simple, even token, chains. Rendering oneself a captive liberates one from all the squeamish dilemmas of free will.

Serafim shouldered his way to the outer edge of the mob and began sauntering down the quayside, waiting for some idea of what to do with his day, as well as the rest of his life. He wanted an idea to spring from the chaos, pin him down, muscle his head in some direction, set his sights on something. He contemplated making his way to a train station and heedlessly getting on the first train that stopped in front of him, letting it pull him out to some waylaid village, or anonymous university city, or bourgeois suburb of Paris.

A man bumped into him from behind. *"Je m'excuse! Désole, hein?"* Flashing a set of palms, backing away. Serafim told him it was nothing, in Portuguese, which either fell on deaf ears or was devoured by the flurry of moving bodies around them. Serafim passed the next ship along the pier, being loaded with burlap sacks and wooden barrels, the workers' vision tunnelled onto the queues leading up the boat ramps and onto the deck. He waited for a break in the lines to weave through them, excusing himself as he scurried by. He passed another massive steamboat, which had fewer people in front of it, and by the time he was approaching the one after that, the crowd had become sparse enough for him to look around, observe his surroundings in a little more detail, come out of his shoulder-hunched self. As he did so, he heard music nearby.

A group of men in black shirts, Italians, milling about in front of a steamship, had broken into sudden song with the greatest animation and bravado, several of them conducting the lyrics with clenched forearms held high, two of them with hands on their chests, swaying their heads, all of them smiling. *"Dell'Italia nei confini / Son rifatti gli italiani / Li ha rifatti Mussolini / Per la guerra di domani ..."* It continued, finally reaching a crescendo with a collective hooray, which found them laughing and splintering off into smaller groups of natural conversation that became, in their own way, even more animated than the singing. The photographic potential was ideal, and Serafim lingered on the sidelines, waiting for them to get used to his presence, dawdling in hopes of becoming socially invisible. But before that could happen, one of them, crouching over a makeshift stove and brewing what appeared to be coffee, gestured for him to come over and join them.

It was in fact coffee, or at least some kind of shockingly bitter syrup that resembled it, Serafim thought, wincing and swallowing it down like aspirin. He crouched in the midst of the men as they nodded welcoming hellos in his direction — *ciao, buon giorno, salve*. The man who'd given him the tiny cup of coffee felt the need to explain the song, their black shirts, the insignias on some of their things (an axe bound to a bundle of sticks with several twines of rope). Had Serafim heard of Il Duce yet? In the papers, yes, Serafim intimated, he had.

"I am happy to hear," replied the man, "because Benito Mussolini, he is a good, good man. He is bringing back, how do you say, *restoring* (you understand? — *bene*) restoring the dignity, the international dignity, of Italy. We" — the man made a giant, inclusive circle with his hands, encompassing the ship behind them as well — "we, all of us, are *il fascio* (how do you say?) — *fascistas*. Yes, Mussolini, he is going to change the world, *amico mio*. The world. You understand?"

And Serafim, radiating with understanding, seemed to grasp the depth and import of the message better than the messenger himself. He pulled out his Leica, inspired, and asked if he could take pictures of these proud fascists. Of course, of course! A floppy hand flicked him out into the dynamic throng, granting him free passage to whatever intimacy he came across. Serafim moved from small group to group, the men often posing together, hands on each other's shoulders, dragging other people into the frame, while Serafim pretended to release the shutter at the predictable moment and then, holding the camera at his chest, waited for the better shots to unfold, snapping them deviously, imperceptibly. Instead of this window of opportunity closing itself in the fleeting way it usually did, the exposures only got better the more used to him they became, until he was completely out of film. Intending to return once he'd replenished the film, he then thought of doing something even more active, more committed. Painted on the side of the hull that towered above them were white letters stencilled onto a low-gloss blue, the ship's name, *Resolute*,

which, he noticed, was also printed on a manned booth opposite the ship — presumably the ticket vendor.

Serafim approached the man, struggling in his grade-
school French. "I would like to know . . . how much is . . . a
ticket for your boat?"

"You can speak in Portuguese," the man said, recognizing Serafim's accent, in the way people do when they share a
mother tongue.

"Oh," Serafim said, relieved, "you're from Portugal?"

"Yes, but working for this shipping company, English
owned, most of my life." The connection required little more
explanation. "It sounds like you are from Oporto."

Serafim faltered, self-conscious. The Oporto accent wasn't
known for its refinement or beauty. "Yes, I . . . was — but now
would like to get on board the *Resolute*."

"Of course." The man opened a book, procured a pad of
receipts. "What will your final destination be, Mr. . . ."

"Vieira. Well, to be honest, it depends on where those men
are going, the Italians."

"Montreal."

"They're going to America?"

"Well, Quebec, Canada, but the city is only kilometres
from the United States, yes."

"I see." Serafim turned to take a look at them again, his
eyes pinpointing the insignias of what was almost sure to
become a vital political movement, the men's expressions,
telling postures, wildly whirling arms and gesticulations,
the limitless potential for photos in that one moment alone.
"Montreal it is, then." He turned back to the vendor and
showed him his camera, "I thought we might come to some

kind of arrangement. I imagine you need up-to-date photographs of your ship, for advertisements, et cetera?"

The man cocked his head, "Perhaps." Then, unhurriedly, he left the booth and entered a building nearby, returning a few minutes later to rearrange the book and pad of receipts in front of him. "Have you been commissioned for commercial photography before — for shipping, commerce?"

"Yes."

The man smirked. "A businessman, Mr. Vieira, must know the nuances of when and how to lie. You are not much of a businessman, are you?"

Serafim's face warmed. "No. But I am a sound photographer."

This time the man laughed, readying a pen and turning over a new receipt. "Tell you what. I'll have you pay me, upfront, the second-lowest fare we offer to Montreal, one above steerage. At the end of the voyage, you show me the pictures that might be of use to us, and if we take any of them, I'll deduct their worth from your initial fare and give you a refund. Sound fair to an Oporto businessman such as yourself?"

Serafim smiled, shrugged, held out his hand. "Fair enough."

The following afternoon, grey plumes mushroomed from the smokestacks of the *Resolute*. Billows of steam, rich, slightly sweet-smelling, began first to slant then to drag behind the boat, impelling it forward, out into the open Atlantic, to carve colossal through the dark swells. Serafim had no one to wave to back on land, but he found himself waving anyway.

His third-class cabin was deep in the ship, and was shared with three other men, two of whom snored throughout the rolling hours of the night, barrels of sound wheeling from one side of the room to the other with each sway of the vessel. The one who slept silently had yet to address Serafim, but by the way he spoke to the other two in the cabin Serafim could tell the man was coarse and abrasive. He was a man, Serafim noticed while strolling around on deck, whose sharp words either commanded respect or deeply annoyed, even enraged people. Serafim was feeling lighter and more excited than he ever had in his life, and he made a point of avoiding the man, keeping even the tight-quarters interactions in their cabin as limited as possible. Until three days into the trip.

Serafim had been taking pictures in an out-of-the-wind but well-lit part of the upper deck when a different man — an emotionless, bland-looking gentleman — called him over and asked him to take his picture. Not in any position to say no, Serafim obliged, surreptitiously catching a shot of him after he'd relaxed from his pose, and while he was giving a haunted look to someone standing nearby. The man then asked — and Serafim, who was catching more Italian by the day, was sure he misunderstood him at first — for the picture Serafim had just taken, wondering when he would actually have it in his hands. Serafim explained that he would have to develop it in a darkroom, enlarge it in order to make a single copy, so to speak, once they arrived in Montreal. The man became perceptibly anxious, wanting to know if it was possible for Serafim to make, say, a million copies of this photo if he so wished. A million copies that might be kept for years, and handed out at any time, to anyone, such as the authorities, or one's enemies, people who might be looking for you?

"Well, sure," Serafim answered, "once the film is developed, that is possible, yes."

"In that case," the man commanded vehemently, "I want one photo, *and* this thing, this film of my photo, that a person can make copies from."

It was hard to believe he wasn't joking, but Serafim felt the quiet, pressing need to agree to this.

"Good," said the man, "good. So, you will give me the photo and this film the day we arrive in Montreal." It was not a question.

"Sure," Serafim agreed, and eased himself away from the man, stepping backwards, and in the process bumped into his controversial cabinmate.

"Ah," the man who didn't snore said, "it is my neighbour. A gentleman who is clearly not Italian himself, but who, nevertheless, cannot stop taking photos of them." He looked to be about Serafim's age, early twenties, and, like him, wore a moustache and a flat cap.

"Yes," Serafim confessed, "I am interested in your political movement. And how animated you all appear. I am from Portugal, where people are guarded, reserved — probably *too* composed." Serafim spoke mostly in Portuguese, throwing in a few of the main verb differences he'd managed to pick up already. To his delight, the man seemed to understand perfectly. He calmly turned and they walked together along the deck, shoulder to shoulder.

"I see," he began. "Well, if you would like to understand something about our 'political movement,' as you say, you should understand first that it is the opportunistic exploitation of the *fessi*."

"What means *fessi*? Sorry."

"The imbeciles, idiots, the easily led. Eight, nine of these people out of every ten cannot read, write, inform themselves with any kind of critical speculation."

"Surely there are things one can understand without reading."

The young man pivoted on one of his heels, facing Serafim. "Yes. There are. Like understanding who that man you were just speaking with is, what he does, why he should be avoided at all costs. Or like the situation right now in the steerage class below us, the fetid conditions there, and what those conditions brew. Like the expendability of all these seasonal migrant workers around us, travelling ahead of their wives and children to make enough for their transport — you haven't noticed many women on board, have you? — all of whom will find employment agents waiting for them on the docks when they arrive, their own countrymen, shamelessly poised to take the fullest advantage of them. Like being able to recognize an idealistic Portuguese photographer who only sees in other people" — the man tapped Serafim's Leica — "the light that bounces off their skin."

Serafim swallowed.

The young man, seeing how serious Serafim had become, chuckled empathetically, held out his hand. "Antonino Spada."

"Uh ... Serafim Vieira. Pleased to meet you."

Later that evening, after the subpar meal in the third-class dining area, Serafim, unsettled and curious, was drawn down the set of stairs that led to the steerage class. As he descended into the murky, lamp-wavering dark, wafts of putrid smells rose to meet him: urine, vomit, rancid sweat, burnt pot scrapings, and flatulence (though it might have been feces). People coughed, moaned above the sounds of the steam engine deep in the ship's interior. It was almost entirely open and stuffed with bodies, black corners with people sleeping, some prostrate or sitting against walls, holding their heads in their hands. He didn't linger long, in sudden need of the fresh, clean, sea-salty air above. As he climbed out of steerage, he passed a guilty-looking man carrying two glass bottles, frosty and freshly filled with water. Men thieving water, he thought to himself, from the third-class section of the ship. Coming up into the open air was like surfacing in the Douro after diving down too deeply for a childhood dare. The halved-grapefruit horizon traced the last light of dusk on one side and the first pinpricks of stars on the other.

That night, antsy in his sheets, listening to the two men aside from Antonino Spada grunting and snorting — like the creaking commentators of their own banal dreams — he heard the strangest sound creeping up from the steerage class, and poked his head out into the gangway to investigate. It was two young women (of the mere handful he'd seen on board), one of them supporting the other, who was weeping silently, inconsolably, leaning heavily against her companion, clutching the fabric of her dress between her legs.

He closed the door before they could see him and made his way back to his bunk. He spent hours fighting his way towards sleep, restlessly scanning the slats of wood on the cabin's ceiling as if they were text, until he realized that there were things to read there between the lines.

Ville de Québec, le 8 novembre 1927

Ma sœur adorée,

I hope this letter finds you still in very high spirits. I was obviously elated to hear of your recent success in that renowned theatre (of which I believe even I have heard). As you say, there is no telling where such elite connections will take you. As I haven't heard from you in weeks, I wonder if it's already begun.

I wish I had a success story to swap. For the first time, I feel that the women's organizations here in the city are moving in very disparate directions, that the only thing that binds us is the fact that we all happen to be female. From the Church-oriented vice squads to remnant prohibitionists, I feel our force in this province as a whole is both angrier than ever and increasingly diluted. While outside Quebec the struggle is focused on winning the right for women to sit in the Senate, we, here, remain the last sad pocket (seemingly anywhere) that has still to attain even provincial suffrage. Again the Legislative Assembly voted against it, with a full eighty percent opposed. At times I feel we've become a laughingstock, a stronghold of antiquity where inequality is preached from the pulpit, and adhered to by a domesticated flock all too eager to keep itself penned in.

In the meantime, I continue to be engaged at the YWCA. Much of our work is in education, like helping girls find domestic employment in the city, or teaching them to read. We also give courses for women seeking citizenship, wherein, ironically, we're often confronted with immigrants coming from countries that have more rights than we've ever known. It is not an easy situation, Claire. At times, I envy you, in your personal aims.

Je m'ennuie beaucoup de toi,

Cécile

15

Claire stepped onto the stage bristling with charisma, the musicians watching her, smoothing their rhythm over, giving her time. She had the full attention of the theatre from the start. When the feature dancer entered the stage on cue, strutting down its centre, Claire was prepared to upstage her throughout the entire act, secretly sure that she would soon become the woman's replacement anyway. In fact, she was paying the feature performer such little notice that she hadn't even caught on that the routine she was performing was about to change.

The lead dancer stopped just behind Claire, removed a heavy scarf from around her neck, winked at the audience, and with an audible cracking sound whipped the side of Claire's buttock. Claire wheeled around, affronted, breaking out of character. The audience, having paid to see slapstick comedy at some point during the evening, roared with laughter. Then the feature dancer, ignoring Claire's stupefied reaction, turned to whip the buttocks of the dancer on her other side. The other dancer's reaction was timed and deliberate, rehearsed, her eyes widening, hands on her mouth, a quick naughty-girl stance before she continued gracefully on with her steps, the two conspirators in perfect time with each other, seamlessly moving away from the debacle, leaving Claire behind to wallow in it alone. Uneasily, the audience laughed again.

The routine continued, only Claire, the undisputed brunt of the joke, was now shaken, watching out of the corner of her eye for some other rehearsed gag to be conjured without warning, and aimed solely at her ridicule. Her steps felt stiff and contrived, clumsily following the other dancers' lead, lagging behind, trying to catch up, and she strained to keep the smile on her face from wilting sour. Embarrassed for her, all eyes mercifully returned to the feature dancer. When the act finished, every pair of hands in the theatre clapped exclusively for the restored favourite, back at centre stage, arms outstretched.

Claire, afraid of what she might do to the other two dancers, didn't return to the powder room as she had the previous night, but went straight out into the theatre instead and looked around for the manager. Knowing that her window of grandiose opportunity had instantly narrowed (and was likely about to clamp shut), she had the feeling that, if she were going to slip through it at all, she would have to do something quickly, and on the sly.

She found the manager and sat next to him, ordering a cocktail. Seeing the disappointment in her posture, he reached across and sympathetically patted her hand, lit another cigarette, and forgot all about her. She hovered there beside him, making herself small, having senseless little conversations with some of the powerful men she'd met the night before, her words placed on the tablecloth like cute and quiet artifacts lined up for a child's amusement. By the end of the night she was still close by, and managed to shuffle into the confusion of cars in a motorcade, on its way to an after-hours party.

Claire's heart skipped a beat as the Cadillac she was in pulled up to a massive house on Sherbrooke Street that was, of all places in Montreal, directly across from the mansion she had left as a rebellious *jeune fille* eight years earlier. Seeing the expression on her face, someone in the cab asked if she was all right. Yes, of course, fine, really — shouldn't we go inside now? Sure, sure, filing out into the autumn night, her high heels digging into the grass that she'd once furtively stolen across to deliver a ruinous letter.

In the house, Claire recognized the sights and smells as those belonging to an echelon of society she'd first come to know from the outside looking in: the gilded picture frames that she'd once dusted, the opulent rugs she'd swept, the gleaming silverware she'd polished. Just then a maid appeared with a silver tray listing with champagne glasses. As the woman lowered it to the circle of guests, hands shot in to snag a flute each, fingers raising them high to clink-clink. The maid was ignored, though excused herself anyway, mumbling in a French-Canadian accent and scurrying off to fill more glasses, to keep all the late night visitors cheerful and serviced.

As Claire watched the maid disappear into the kitchen, she wondered if she recognized the woman — only it was Claire herself who would be recognized.

"Wait a minute," an older gentleman said. He had joined the group and was suddenly pointing into Claire's chest. "Didn't . . . think . . . no, I'm *sure* . . . you used to work just across the street, years back, at the Applebys'. Did you not? Yes, I'm sure of it. You sent us that diabolical letter upon leaving their residence." He chuckled. "That's right. Is it not?"

Claire felt herself growing very small. She feigned confusion, tried to be dismissive. "*Non.* No-no. I don't know what you mean. Honest." She shook her head, sipped from her glass, watched him above its tight rim.

"But I am *sure* of it. In fact, let me get my wife, see if she recognizes you too. Just a moment." He left the circle as more people filed through the front door, fanning out into the open spaces and dark wood of the manor like spilt milk. A band swept into the party and, after tuning their instruments, began to play. The people who had been standing around mingling were slowly drawn towards the music.

Claire, suddenly alone, looked at the front door, then looked around for the manager of the Gayety, whom she spotted talking to a young girl at the top of a curving, red-carpeted staircase. Meanwhile, the owner of the house had found his wife and the couple were now making their way towards her, the husband explaining his conviction as they shouldered through the crowd, which was just starting to snap its fingers, women's hips beginning to sway.

Claire's window of opportunity had diminished to a sliver of light. She had one simple decision to make: engage or retreat. Claire took a deep breath, placed her champagne glass on a small table at her side, and tucked a strand of hair further beneath her cloche hat. Then she slipped into the salon, out of sight, and re-emerged near the red-carpeted staircase, which she quickly climbed, directly towards the manager. She grabbed him by the hand and dragged him to the first door that she could reach.

She pulled him inside, closed the door behind them, and began kissing him, fighting to pin him against the wall as he initially tried to free himself, laughing uncomfortably. He looked around the dark of the room, which appeared to be a guest bedroom. Claire loosened his tie, unbuttoned his shirt, kissed his chest, eased onto her knees, and unfastened his belt.

They locked the door and eventually made their way to the bed, where the sex was abrupt and assertive, on top of the sheets. The manager pinned her arms above her head and thrusted with sickly wheezes, baring his cigarette-yellowed teeth. When he was finished, he rolled off her, caught his breath, and made his way to his clothes.

"Listen," Claire whispered as he picked his pants up off the floor, "I think we should go. Back to your place. Right now."

The manager was already buttoning his shirt. "Gotta better idea, doll. Back in a jiffy."

Claire strained to give him a teasing smile as he straightened his bow tie and opened the door. "I will wait right here, then," she said, running a hand along her bare thigh.

He paused, taking her in, giving his head a shake. "Bearcat!" Then he left.

When the door opened again, he wasn't alone. He'd brought two of the other executives she'd been talking to earlier, both of them with crooked smiles, slicked hair, and empty eyes. Claire turned onto her stomach, covering herself and trying to giggle, though trying harder to work out just exactly what was expected of her. The door was locked and both of the new men began to undress, watching her as they did so, exchanging mischievous glances.

The manager sat on the edge of the bed beside Claire and produced a small brown bottle with a wide mouth and stubby glass stopper. "Little present for you, doll."

Claire looked at it doubtfully. "Whiskey?"

"Cream sherry, only hopped up, and how!" He removed the stopper and licked its rim. "Mmm, mmm, *mmm*, he says!" He dipped his pointer finger deep into the bottle and held it out in front of Claire's mouth, waiting for her to suck it. She did as expected, sure that the taste was going to be bitter, some sour concoction, but instead found it to be sweet, nutty, velvety. She suggestively sucked on his finger for a long while, until she'd licked the last of the residue from the skin of his knuckles. As she removed his finger from her mouth, her lips and tongue began to go numb and tingle, an easing wave of calm washed over her, her body felt like a weight that was growing heavy, sinking into dark water, as her head nodded down onto the mattress, her body submerging, drawing her further into a floating quietude.

In the drifting of this slow oblivion, she was aware of two distant facts. Her body seemed to be having sex incessantly, with man after man, numberless dry hands squeezing at her breasts and buttocks, while a finger with the same sweet liquid kept wetting her lips, kept dabbing her farther and farther into the dark.

When she awoke in the same strange bedroom, it was noon of the following day. She heard church bells tolling in the distance. Claire, cold and unclothed on top of the covers, rolled around to gather sheets closer to her skin, coiling herself into a ball and moaning. Her sounds, however, beckoned a set of quick footsteps, and the door was suddenly flung open.

"What in the...Just...who...Why, goodness! Would you please leave at once!" It was the same wife who had been summoned (and eluded) the night before. By the looks of it, she had finally succeeded in recognizing Claire.

Claire scrambled out of the bed and yanked her clothes on, while the woman, clearly disgusted, watched, her narrow eyes seething, arms across her chest. Claire's hand slid down the wooden banister and she was quickly out in the bright Sunday light. The couple gawped at her from the porch, scandalized again.

As she walked, Claire became aware of just how sore she was between her thighs, and how sensitive her eyes had become to the hard autumn sun. She cupped her brows with her hands, and a block later waved down a taxi. She went directly to the manager's house, opened his door as if she'd been living there for years, and found him reading the paper at his kitchen table, in his housecoat and slippers, clearly not happy to see her. "Got something against knocking, doll? Am a little busy today."

Claire took a deep breath and used the very last of her patience and energy to give him an easygoing smile. "I didn't have a chance to talk to you last night, about my career."

The manager looked regrettably into his coffee cup, put it down, and lit a cigarette. "Well, I don't need you to stand in anymore, if that's what you mean. Gotta real floorflusher on her way up from New York right now. She'll get in this afternoon. I'll pay you what we agreed, though, even throw in a little bonus for ya." He gave her a wink, took a swig of coffee.

"*Non.* No, I'm not talking of this small part. I'm talking about my career. Of Broadway, Hollywood. You can help me."

He sighed, slumped in his chair. "Look, we established ya can't act, can't sing, butcha can dance."

"So a Broadway show, of a *dancer*! Can't you see it?"

He scowled, shook his head. "No. No, I can't see it. Look, doll, I'll tell it to yuh straight. You're a looker, a real tight tomato, and you can dance, no question. You're good. But you're not great, and surely not prodigious. With only a couple years before you dry up, you got it good here, in this town, right where you are." He butted out his freshly lit cigarette. "Sorry, doll. That's how it goes. Now, be on your way." He waved her back towards his front door. "Your cheque'll be ready to pick up next week. So, if you'll excuse me." He lifted his newspaper, folded it in his lap.

Claire stood in his kitchen, staring at the sunlight on the floor. She could hear children playing nearby, their muffled shouts of mock terror and elation. She was shaking, weak, and wanted to cry, but she wanted more to simply smash something, feel it break in her hands, and then inspect the millions of tiny pieces in her palms. She looked to her left and saw a series of envelopes, the tops of which were ripped and frayed, a copper letter opener resting beside them. She snatched it, making a fist, its handle in her grip, and stepped towards the manager. He stood up, eyes wide, hands open, displaying his complete submission and readiness to co-operate. "Now just ... now just calm down there."

Claire held the knife against his neck, his Adam's apple rising and falling around the tip, which was pressing a dimple into the soft skin of his throat. He took a few steps back, and she took a few steps forward to compensate, until he had backed himself into a corner.

At that point, Claire glanced down at his feet, and with sudden clarity commanded that he kick off his slippers and slide them across the floor. He complied. Then, holding the knife out at him still, she slowly backed away, towards his kitchen cupboards, where her reaching hand seized upon a wineglass. She hurled it in his general direction, and it smashed against the wall to his left, shards splaying onto the floor around his bare feet. He flinched, cursed, and tried to take a step towards safety, quickly realizing his inability to escape.

Seeming to grasp what was coming next, he slowly crouched into a tight ball, tucked himself into the corner, and placed his hands over his head. The next glass shattered just above his crumpled form, slightly to his right. It was hard for Claire to believe how satisfying these sounds and sensations were. She grabbed another glass. Wineglass after snifter after tumbler after flute were pitched against the white walls of the kitchen, exploding into crystalline splinters that further constricted his movements until he could no longer even rock onto the sides of his feet to shift his weight, and every last glass in his kitchen had been obliterated. As she left towards the front door, he lifted his head to watch her go, shards in his hair and on his shoulders tinkling to the floor. Moving very carefully, he said nothing.

That same afternoon, Claire learned, officially, that she'd lost her job at Midway. She spent the following week soaking her pillow with tears, but eventually she left the house to visit the only two other burlesque theatres in town, Starland and the King Edward. She knew she was going to run out of money soon. But the news of her madcap stunt against the manager of the Gayety had fanned out across the city's entertainment world like windy fire through parched grass, and neither of the theatres wanted anything to do with her. The same went for every other reputable establishment. This more than pleased the other dancers Claire was rooming with, who vehemently demanded she pay her late rent, knowing she must be nearing the limits of her means.

Claire moved out and found a minuscule and incredibly cheap apartment where she could be alone and free from their smug remarks. She got a job at an off-the-map cabaret in the east end, which only just managed to cover her expenses, eating scraps of food she was meant to be clearing from patrons' plates, as well as the secret packages of leftovers that her flirtations with the plump and sweaty cook afforded her.

Convinced that things couldn't possibly get worse, she then missed her monthly cycle. She would close her eyes at night, willing her next one to come along with the new moon, as it always had before. Soon she began waking at dawn with an irrepressible need to vomit. Claire took steps to force herself to miscarry, but they didn't work. By the time she'd missed her third month, she was beginning to show, and started asking other waitresses and dancers at her scruffy cabaret if they knew of a place where she could be "treated for a suppression of her cycles." One of them did, and not only gave her the address but lent her the substantial sum she would need to have the procedure performed.

Meanwhile, the wind had turned icy and the streets were full of dirty snowdrifts. Claire's appointment was at night, and while she'd noticed that the address was in the Red Light district, she'd never thought to consider that it might actually be inside a brothel. A madam answered the door. Confused,

Claire handed her the slip of paper she'd been given, with the address on it and the name of a man. The madam told her to stop looking so sheepish and out of place.

She led Claire by the arm through a tiny common room where a piano player was jumpily pounding at the keys. He gave them a missing-tooth smile and leaned further into the ragtime song he was playing as they passed behind him. Claire was pointed to the top of a staircase and told to go to the last door on the right. No one was in the room, but it smelled of sex, the bed ruffled, creased, and moist. Moans and grunts of women's pleasure, clearly exaggerated for their patrons' bene-fit, pulsed through the walls on all sides. Somewhere, someone was laughing uncontrollably.

The door burst open and a thin and awkwardly tall man stepped in with a case, from which he produced a bottle of rye whiskey and a knitting needle. After she'd handed him the agreed-upon fee, he handed her the bottle of rye, adding that she should drink at least three-quarters of it, as fast as she could. Claire did as she was told.

The moment she was feeling drunk, he asked her to swal-low one last shot before he began. He then had her lie on the bed, hike up her skirt, and take off her underclothes. He pro-duced a small wooden spoon, had her clamp it in her mouth, and inserted the long knitting needle between her legs, soon finding the spot where it would continue much farther. The pain was instant and intense. She bit into the wood. The man then applied pressure down, up, from side to side, as a means of dilating her cervix. Claire almost lost consciousness twice from the pain. But with the spoon in her mouth, her muf-fled shrieks blended readily into the medley of noises in the brothel. After several minutes of this, he stood up and nodded. Now, he said, he could begin.

That was when the piano abruptly stopped in the middle of a Scott Joplin tune. There was the sound of scuffling downstairs, then a door slamming shut, someone whistling, followed by the thunder of footsteps both climbing and descending stairs. The man hustled to the window, peered down into the street. *"Câlice . . . Tabarnak!"* He scurried out of the room, though in all the confusion it was hard to distinguish which of the footsteps were his. Claire, drunk, maudlin, draped her hands over her face and began to whimper.

He returned a few minutes later, locked the door, and stood at the end of the bed, Claire's legs opening out at him, while he explained that there was a police raid in the brothel directly opposite, and that the police had already been paid off and were more than satisfied with the sum. That said, they would still have to fill their paddy wagons, a question of quota, before setting off back to the station. The raids themselves were only token, a reliable source of revenue, filling both the city's coffers and the sergeants' pockets with bribes and the five-dollar fees everyone arrested had to pay in order for their names to vanish from the books the following day. The police would start in the other brothels and end at the one they were in. He had time, he assured her, but would have to move faster.

He propped her head up in order for Claire to down the last of the cheap rye, replaced the spoon in her mouth, and crouched at the foot of the bed again, disappearing behind her skirts. Then he began to forcefully scrape away at Claire's insides, gouging long lines against the tissue at her most tender centre. Claire let out muffled screams into the wood between her teeth, held her hair in her fists, eyes rolling, even spiralling out of consciousness once, though managing to cartwheel back into it again.

There was a knock at the door, as if in Morse, clearly coded to mean something, and the man instantly straightened up, pulled the knitting needle out of her, tugged the spoon from her mouth, threw everything into his bag, shoved it under the bed, and, as he scurried to leave the room, whispered over his shoulder that the job was done, and that, should she ever mention his name to the authorities, he had friends who could get at her anywhere. Just so she knew. Good evening to you, *mademoiselle*. Bowing slightly, he quietly shut the door behind him.

Claire rolled onto her side, heaving breath, exhausted from the pain, and spinning drunk. She felt the aching at her core gradually begin to subside. An unknown amount of time passed. Suddenly the madam opened the door, put her face in the gap, and commanded Claire to lock herself in, quickly, with the latches on the inside, and not open up for anyone. She then reminded Claire that, unlike everyone else on the block, if she were caught, she'd be going to jail for a very long time. Now, lock it, she recommended. The madam eased the door closed and hurried away.

Claire managed to get to the door, and to put on her underclothes and a Kotex, which she was happy she'd thought to bring along. Then, before returning to bed, she went to the window and looked down into the street. The paddy wagons were near bursting, the very last of the arrested men and women squeezing into their boxes. One of them, a moustached man, looked up at Claire in the lit window and locked eyes with her. She felt as if she recognized him, in some distant way; it was clear that he recognized her. He had to be shoved by a policemen to break his gaze, and with that, Claire turned from the window, shut off the lights, and slept until morning.

She returned to her apartment, still sore, and was interrupted by instants of intense pain in her lower abdomen. The ejection of clotted matter seemed logical enough, but the way the bleeding didn't let up was somewhat worrying. Days passed without improvement. She kept to her tiny apartment, called in sick to work, and began spending all her time in bed, playing her favourite song on the gramophone, imagining how she would choreograph a dance to it.

After several more days, a fever lit up in her bones. She began to think she might be in real trouble, particularly as this was an illness that she could not, under any circumstances, call a doctor about. The fever slid her towards delirium. She listened to her song again, and again. In her most coherent moments she would think of ways she could approach her family doctor, ways in which he would be forced to help her, and keep mum at the same time. It began to snow, which quickly turned into a blizzard. The cold from outside permeated the windows and seeped through her skin.

She lost track of time. Until the moment she realized that, if she wanted to live, she would have to act now. She replaced the needle on the gramophone, grabbed the telephone, and listened to the song while sitting on the floor against the coal stove, heat leaching through all the blankets she'd swaddled herself in. The song came to an end. Snow tapped against the windowpane. Shivering, and straining not to fall back asleep, Claire lifted the receiver from the telephone stand.

"Code and number, please."

"Uhm . . . Lorimier. Zero. Four. One-seven."

On the fourth ring, Dr. Bertrand answered, his voice sleepy, checking the hour. She had once heard him say — in a tavern during the false armistice — that brave acts were, at times, done merely out of weakness. And that, thought Claire distantly, would have to do. She told him she would be heading out to his office immediately. Then hung up.

Claire struggled to her feet. The wind outside chattered its teeth. The naked light bulb over her head flickered. She made her way to the door.

Medium: Gelatin silver print
Description: Italian immigrant, candid portrait
Location: Aboard the *Resolute* (transatlantic)
Date: 1926

༄

A man sits on a long bench, his back against the steel bulwarks of a ship. One imagines the metal against his spine to be cold, dusty, coarse.

He is young, likely in his early twenties, though his face holds the distance of hard experience, draining away the boyishness that one might normally associate with such youthfully plump cheeks.

There is an ink-blot mole on his temple, island on a milky map.

He is wearing a fedora and looking out of the frame, to the left; his hat is tipped down but only manages to shade one of his eyes from the harsh sun. The unshielded eye is squinting, folding into velvet creases, which will only claw deeper as he ages, eventually cinching into crow's feet.

His level gaze is contentious and cool; its ferocity reined in, taut, and anchored.

It is a look that no one would want to be the recipient of. His sunlit iris stained with a dull, unnameable poison.

16

For the remainder of the voyage, Serafim spent much of his time with Antonino Spada, smoking cigarettes and chatting, leaning out over one of the railings, the dark water sliding past at a remarkable speed while the steamship sliced its sluggish weight through the waves. They flicked their cigarette butts into the distant water, stroked their moustaches, adjusted their caps in the salt spray, and pulled them tight onto their brows.

Serafim marvelled at the way such different people could sometimes be drawn to each other. Outwardly the two men had little in common — Antonino with his endlessly outspoken opinions, and Serafim with his quiet views and paltry knowledge on most everything scholarly and intellectual. Which was probably why it worked: Serafim suddenly had quite a few questions about the world in which he was now a castaway, and its politics, including the new land both of them were moving to and its machinations. Antonino had a vigorous answer for every one of Serafim's questions.

Antonino was also a man, Serafim noticed, who didn't have a lot of friends. Other passengers would whisper disparaging remarks in his direction, especially when Antonino was with a few of his other acquaintances on board. Serafim heard the group of them referred to as *cani sperduti*, stray dogs, which he found confusing. Unlike an opportunistic mongrel, and just below his abrasive growl and bark, Antonino was, undeniably, a humanitarian. He seemed uniquely concerned with both the issues and the people that no one else gave any weight or importance to, the kind of people who didn't have the clout or voice to speak up for themselves.

Antonino and Serafim were talking about photography when they spotted land for the first time, the ship soon entering the St. Lawrence River, whose shores constricted throughout the day into a tightening gullet. Below them, clusters of whale spouts could be seen coughing out geysers of mist before being swallowed up again by the placid surface.

The next morning they woke to a lurch, signalling that they'd arrived at the port of Montreal. Serafim sat up in his berth, rubbed his eyes, and kicked himself for making such complicated promises to both the intimidating immigrant whom Antonino had advised him to steer clear of and the ship's operators, both of whom he'd assured would receive photos the moment he arrived in Montreal. While everyone else on board would be busy finding lodging and comfort, Serafim was going to have to run around a city he wasn't acquainted with, looking for a darkroom to rent or borrow for a couple of hours. (Though, he knew, the money he was going to save would come in handy, given that he had to set himself up in a new country. This was the kind of shrewd frugality that paid off in the long term.) He put only the money he imagined might be asked to rent a darkroom into his wallet, worrying about pickpockets, and placed the rest in his trunk, which he then locked and slid as far under his bunk as he could. He patted his jacket before leaving his quarters: his camera, the film to develop, the lens for the enlarger, the key to his trunk. He had everything he needed.

Serafim found Antonino amidst the chaos of disembarkation, shook his hand, wished him luck. Then Serafim made arrangements with the immigrant whose photo and film he would deliver. He pointed out a place on the pier where they agreed to meet in about three hours. Then Serafim made his way down the gangplank. He had his papers stamped and made his way onto the busy quay.

There were new sights and smells for Serafim. A vendor roasting nuts; a gentleman jauntily walking with a chrome-handled cane and a threadbare top hat; workers with white cloth aprons loading a horse carriage; a bicycle with a wooden box strapped to the back and a *woman*, with short hair no less, riding it. She smiled at Serafim while he gawked and watched her pass.

Serafim, unconsciously following her, worked his way to the left, through tight streets, and finally approached a man in front of a burring machine shop. He took out his camera and began fumbling in French through a query as to whether there was a photography studio nearby. Serafim struggled with the man's impossibly strange accent for half a minute before realizing that it was actually English he was speaking, though with a liquid cadence he'd never heard before. The man, like every male he'd seen so far, was clean-shaven, and had a slightly too-large hat that flopped and folded to a slant on his head. He pointed Serafim to the next street down.

It was a tiny studio, on a corner, a single wedding photo propped up against the shop window. Serafim went in and, on a whim, addressed the proprietor, who appeared from the gloomy back, in English. "I wonder if I can ask of you a favour."

The man nodded, resting his hands on the counter. "Go on, then."

After he'd explained himself as best he could, the man appeared hesitant, and it was then that Serafim offered to pay for the use of the darkroom. The man spoke in dollars, so Serafim had to show him that he only had escudos. The man walked over to a phone, lifted the receiver, cranked its side, and called out a word and four numbers. It was apparently a bank, and they told him that, considering the exchange rate, the transaction would require all the escudos that Serafim had on him.

"That is . . . rather expensive."

"Well," the man countered, "you're free to try to find another studio that'll agree to such a request."

Serafim looked at the time on the man's wristwatch, scratched his neck, and emptied his wallet onto the counter.

The darkroom was much more spacious than the storefront, and the proprietor sat on a high stool inside, watching Serafim work, and talked idly about photography in the city, while listening for the tinkle of the bell that sounded when someone entered his shop. As the film was drying, Serafim fitted his special lens into the enlarger, asking over his shoulder, out of curiosity, if the man was from England.

"I should hope not. Irish. Like everyone used to be here in Griffintown. But that's changing." Serafim turned to him, perplexed, and the man explained, beginning with a chuckle. "It's not *only* French Canadians in Montreal, you know. Mostly, of course. And they're a good lot, fine Catholics. But they're in the east. You see, we all have our little enclaves, our own churches and hospitals. Jews, Italians, Chinamen, Negroes. While the English, par for the course, are set up in their mansions downtown and up towards the mountain, where they lord it over us all."

"I see. Of course."

"And yourself? Spanish?"

"Portuguese."

"You don't say. Never met one. So tell us, what brings you to the frozen land?"

"I am following an important political movement, as a photographer."

"By the sounds of it, you already have plenty of shenanigans of the sort in your own country, what with the *coup d'état* that just passed."

Serafim spun round. *"Coup d'état?"*

"Sure. Read it in the papers. Still have it if you'd like." He left the room and returned with a journal, pointed to an article, and handed it to Serafim, who held the newspaper up to the dull yellowish light in the darkroom.

"Portugal's now run by a military dictator. A big improvement, by all accounts. So," the man continued, "if it was politics you were after, I'm guessing you would've been better to stay home."

"Meaning the anarchists . . . they're . . . It is over?" Serafim said into the newspaper.

"Couldn't tell you."

There was a chime as someone entered the studio, and Serafim was left alone with his thoughts, thoughts about where Álvaro would go, and what he would do now. Thoughts of the country he'd left behind, and what he might have captured there, at that critical moment when the republic crumbled and — just as Álvaro had predicted — something bold and brave had swept in to take its place.

After the proprietor had served his customer, he busied himself with something else, and only returned to the darkroom just before Serafim was ready to leave. Serafim had developed four large sheets of photographic paper, the one photo of the Italian immigrant and three contact sheets in order to show the ship's operators every shot he'd taken, allowing them to pick just the ones they wanted him to develop for them.

The studio owner bent over the photo of the Italian immigrant and clicked his tongue. "Shame you were a second late. It would have been a great portrait."

"Yes, well, thank you for your time and equipment." Serafim shook the man's hand and took the four sheets, which weren't completely dry yet, and put two in each hand in a way that would minimize his fingerprints and maximize the sheets' exposure to the passing air as he walked, drying them as he returned to the wharves. Passing through the streets, brooding over his decision to leave Portugal, his determination suddenly limping, white sheets spread at the ends of his draping arms like the exhausted wings of an angel that has gone astray.

Serafim was a little late, but he found the Italian immigrant exactly where they had agreed to meet, his hands deep in his pockets, standing over his baggage. As Serafim approached, the man was so eager to see the photo that he let his manners slip, plucking the picture from Serafim's hand before they'd even greeted each other. The photo was apparently larger than he was expecting it to be, and less like a professional portrait than he'd hoped, but he was satisfied enough with the finished product to open one of his valises and slide it into a wide pocket. Then, without hesitation, he asked for the film, or more precisely "the thing that anyone could use to make copies of this." Serafim, who was quite happy with the shot, had thought about telling the man a harmless lie, giving him a tiny cut-out of the contact sheet, for example; he certainly wouldn't have known the difference. But in the end he'd decided to give in entirely to the man's obtuse idiosyncrasies, and handed him a tiny fold of paper with the exposure in it. The man unfolded it and held the rectangular piece of film up to the grey sky and smiled. Gesturing that he was satisfied, he took out his wallet (which had Serafim thinking he might be remunerated for the peculiar favour), slid the film into the note sleeve, and replaced the wallet in his pocket.

"What is your name?" the man asked as he picked up one of his suitcases. When Serafim told him, he paused as if to consider it for a good few seconds, then nodded. "It's good," he said in Italian. "I will remember this name." Then he shook Serafim's hand, picked up his other large suitcase, and walked away. Serafim watched him disappear into the throng of the port, thinking him entirely eccentric. Shaking his head, he continued to the boat.

Having to show his ticket to get back on board, he explained to one of the crew that he'd been commissioned to take photos of the ship and the people it transported. He was soon escorted into a small room where the same Portuguese gentleman with whom he'd made the ticket arrangements was noting something in a ledger. The man looked up from his work. "Why, Mr. Vieira, I see you've brought me some photos to look at."

"Well, not photos exactly, but a way for you to see the shots I've taken. I can develop any of the frames on these three pages that interest you."

The gentleman put the sheets on top of his book and bent in to inspect them. "So," he said offhandedly, "did you hear of the coup?"

"Yes. What do you know of the details?"

"Little. But I sense good change in the air. The republic was a deplorable sham."

"Yes. Something a close friend of mine always said."

"And he was right. I . . ." The man flipped to the second sheet, then the third. "Mr. Vieira, what have you been taking pictures of all this time?"

"Sir? The passengers, the ship, the everyday life on board."

An astounded pause, further inspection. "Mr. Vieira, I get the feeling that you didn't compose a single photograph on our ship in any kind of proven or conventional way. It's as if these people, who are *never* pictured in a charming pose, were not given warning that you would be taking their picture at all."

Serafim crossed his arms, stood firm. "And you would be exactly right in that, sir."

The gentleman looked up, flabbergasted, searching for words. Not finding them, he hurriedly gathered the three sheets from his ledger and handed them back to Serafim. "We will purchase none of these. Good day to you, sir."

Serafim, indignant, looked at the contact sheets. "Then I have no use for those, and will leave you to dispose of them yourself. Good day to you, sir." And he turned, left the room, and made his way to his cabin in the third-class section of the ship to get his things.

The ship was empty, and the rooms were stripped of their sheets and blankets. Serafim was glad to see that his trunk was in the centre of the room he'd stayed in, so he could tell it apart from the others. He sat heavily on one of the berths, feeling annoyed and doubtful.

Staring forward, he became aware of two things almost simultaneously: one, that his trunk had been moved from where he'd secured it; and two, that the lock had been jimmied open and was now warped and damaged.

"*Virgem Maria!*" he hissed, clumping onto his knees on the floor and wrenching the trunk open, his hand diving to the place where he'd left his every escudo in a bulging envelope, safe and sound. It was gone. So he emptied the trunk onto the floor to search more thoroughly, scattering his clothes on the ground, shaking them out, hoping for the envelope, plump and full (like a paper grub that might have wormed its way deeper into his wardrobe), to drop from one of his garments. It did not.

A man's voice hollered down a nearby gangway, calling out that no passengers should now be on board. Doors were being closed, rooms checked. So Serafim, arms moving limp and feeble, piled his clothes back into his trunk without folding them, closed the lid, latched it shut, took the key from his pocket, and tossed it, useless now, onto one of the berths. Then he left the ship.

He carried his trunk through the chaotic port, lumbering awkwardly, not knowing where he was going or why. He heard a group of Italians calling out at each other, angry shouts escalating, becoming incensed. Montrealers stopped, agape, waiting to see what would come of it, whether or not someone would be killed, but Serafim was already used to the Italians' dramatic antics, and knew that whatever it was, they would work it out before it ever came to blows. Nearby, he found a section of a jetty that was planked with wood, and which moored some of the smaller vessels in the port. He placed his trunk onto the boards there and sat on its lid, hunched over, watching the smaller boats oscillate and sway in the water around him, rocking themselves to sleep.

Oddly enough, he wasn't panicked. He was more numb than anything else. He thought how strange it was that, at the moments in our lives when we *should* be feeling the most, we almost always feel the least. He was in a dismal mess, with no money whatsoever, destitute in a foreign land, with no real plan of action coming to mind but to sit and watch a bevy of small boats list and bob in the water in front of him. Behind him, the Italians were winding down from their argument. Above him, a seagull floated by. Around him, gradually, the thought and image of Inês Sá began to coalesce from the water and its dizzy refractions, swirling into a daydream that was warm and inviting.

The daydream was a photograph in the flesh, a tableau of two actors, motionless: Inês lying in the sun, naked and shameless, her hair untied and cascading over her shoulders, her arms loosely cradling Serafim, who lay coiled on top of her, weak and tired, his hands confining her breasts like scallop shells cupping a mermaid. On the ground beside them was a cup of tea, a bucolic witness. Both within the daydream and without, Serafim grinned.

"*Serafimeh? Tutto bene?*" Antonino Spada tapped Serafim's trunk with his foot. "*Eh!*"

Serafim, startled, grabbed hold of the trunk's lid. "Antonino."

"Yes, ridiculous, but I am still here," Antonino said, looking back at the same group of men who had been in disagreement earlier. "These odious *banchieri*, the employment agents I told you of — and others — here to exploit their own ignorant countrymen, right off the boat, get their meathooks in early. But I tell you, just a few pointed questions, you can divide the con men from the genuine, send the former limping back to their brothels. And you, Serafimeh? What are you still doing here?"

"I was robbed" — Serafim bent round to finger the jimmied lock of his trunk — "of every escudo I had. I've not a centavo to my name now."

Antonino took his hat off, stamped the boards at his feet. "*Merda.*" He slapped the side of his leg with his hat. "*Cazzo!*" he belted out, conclusively. Then, with a long sigh, he put his hat back on. "And your camera, what you need to ply your trade, did they take this as well?"

"No, no, I still have my camera."

"A stroke of luck, then." Antonino craned his neck to size up a row of taxis waiting in a long black, vinyl-roofed queue on the other side of a railway track. "Why don't you come with me. Help me with your trunk. Come on, grab hold, I'm not going to carry it alone."

Serafim, with dull automation, did as he was told, and was carted from the port and into an Italian neighbourhood, then into a long and thin apartment that had twenty-two other people living inside it, *bordanti*, boarders who paid an Italian family three dollars a week for cooking, cleaning, laundry, and lodging. Antonino handed over his own money for both of them, reassuring Serafim that he would find a job soon enough and could pay him back then. Serafim thanked him quietly, and set his trunk in a corner of the apartment, where he was given a thin, straw-stuffed mattress on the floor and a blanket that smelled of horses.

That night, he and Antonino ate their meal, a plate of pasta, on their laps, out on the apartment's balcony, overlooking an impossibly long street that was lined and trembling with young trees. Serafim wasn't in the mood to speak, and spent his time listening to Antonino rant and bluster. Between each of his diatribes, Antonino would offer a few encouraging words, asserting that things were sure to go more Serafim's way in the coming weeks.

When they had finished their meal, Antonino lifted a small basket of bread from between their feet and broke a piece off to clean his plate, wiping it.to a porcelain shine. He offered some to Serafim, who shook his head. But Antonino insisted, ripping off a long chunk and tossing it onto his plate. Serafim looked down at it for a moment, then out at the street, up at the grey sky, and back down to his lap. Then he took the piece of crust and began wiping up the remnants of the sauce, daintily at first but with growing gusto, sponging every blot of tomato sauce that stretched with the sheen of olive oil, soaking it from the plate and into the dough, which then slipped from his fingers and melted in his mouth.

Serafim closed his eyes, tilted his head back, and rested on the red brick of the building, sated with a satisfaction that seemed to glide out from the terrace and over the trees. He wondered if every blessing was like this; like the weight of a songbird that had been trapped, fettered, and at last let go.

Ma chère Claire,

Having just gotten off the telephone with you, I will admit that I feel no small degree of frustration with our conversation; or, rather, your seemingly apathetic response to the horrible news, of which I am still shocked you heard for the first time from my lips, and not elsewhere. The fact that the Supreme Court has decided that the constitution does not recognize women as "qualified persons," and hence cannot be orchestrators in our own fate and station in this country, didn't appear, if I may say so, to affect you in the slightest. Claire, sometimes I could shake you!

This frustration got me thinking about our conversations of late, our letters, which reminded me of something. Claire, you know very well that I have never considered it my place to be critical of you or your choices, but to be perfectly forthcoming, I'm not sure that you are even aware of this: Do you know that I never hear you speak or express any degree of curiosity about anything outside your own epic journey towards becoming a famous dancer? Not so much as a whisper that alludes to even the existence of the plight or quandary of anyone outside your own being.

I promise this will not descend into a lecture. I guess it is more a question than anything else. Am I not right? And if I am, Claire, I cannot help but wonder, my dearest little sister: Does it not get lonely in that head of yours? Do you not miss, even once in a while, the reassuring company of other people's stories?

Avec toute mon affection,

Cécile

17

C laire was sitting on the only chair in her apartment, staring forward at nothing, the cracked and glued-together bowl on the table in front of her cupping three apples with fragile care; a still life of bread crumbs and blighted fruit, faithless offering to the light that filtered through her window from the streetscape outside.

For days now, in a murky and faraway consciousness, Claire had been busy dismissing her sister's insinuation that she had gradually become, for all intents and purposes, a narcissist. What her sister did not know was that, over the winter, Claire had accrued what felt like enough worries and concerns to fill more than a few lives. She was still working at the same scruffy cabaret in the east end, still failing to pay off her debt to the waitress who'd lent her the money for her "salvation," still hadn't succeeded in finding a job at any of the reputable establishments in the city, while in two days she would be turning twenty-five. But there was more. Since Claire had come home from the hospital, she had been waiting for her body to return to normal, to find its balance again. She religiously took a tea-spoon of cognac with a bit of milk at eleven each morning to build up her strength, while waiting for her menses to fall back in line with the new moon, like the clockwork it had been running on since she was thirteen. Yet three full months after her operation, there was still not a hint of this happening.

Claire didn't particularly want to see Dr. Bertrand to ask him about such matters, but she knew he was the one person who was already acquainted with the necessary details and could be trusted. Not turning Claire in to the authorities the very moment he'd learned she'd had an abortion made him just as much a criminal as she was. So she decided she would take a walk near his practice, saunter past his front doors, where, provided there were no other patients waiting to be seen, she would step inside and get his opinion.

It was the very beginning of May, when the arms of the trees were still grey, though the tips of their fingers were just starting to turn rubbery and brown with buds. It was the time when gangs of pick-and-shovel men, municipal workers, went out into the streets to chip and chisel ditches alongside the sidewalks, allowing for the accumulation of melting ice and snow to run off into the sewers. Claire listened to the music of the streets as she walked, the rhythmic swinging of the men's tools making hollow thunks in the ice that were followed by tinkling echoes. The returning crows watched from bare branches, offering a ragged chorus of caws and chortles, while the murmur of meltwater at her feet burbled through the ditches in rushing streams, disappearing into the cool black mouths of storm drains, which hummed as deep as gargling throats.

Claire happened to pass Dr. Bertrand's practice at a fortuitous moment. Not only were there no patients waiting, the doctor himself was standing in the entranceway, his winter-pale face soaking up the first of the year's sun, eyes closed.

Claire hesitated on the sidewalk, waiting for him to see her. "Dr. Bertrand?"

He opened his eyes. "Claire," he said, as if he'd been wishing for her to appear in front of him, as if he'd conjured her himself. "Follow me."

He led her into a room and closed the door behind them, gesturing for her to sit on a wooden examination table. He stood opposite her, arms across his chest, bushy eyebrows furrowed. He looked angry.

Claire smoothed her dress down, waiting for him to say something, and realized for the first time that he might actually expect her to pay him — for his services, as well as that of the hospital, which, after all, he'd footed the bill for. Aghast that she hadn't thought of this before, she tried hard to smile. "And how is Mrs. Bertrand these days? Keeping well?"

Dr. Bertrand stared her down for a few weighted seconds more before speaking. "Why did you not come to me, child? I would have done it. I would have done it for you myself, I swear. And in doing so, I would have put myself at considerably less risk than the position you forced me into, that of having to both remedy and cover up for some exploitative underworld butcher. Having seen his work first-hand, I happen to doubt the man was even a veterinarian."

Claire looked into her lap, at her hands gathered there, her voice retreating into a whisper. "I don't know, sir."

Dr. Bertrand emitted a long breath. "Well, let us have a look at how the sutures have healed over."

Claire lay back on the clothed-over table and lifted her dress. His warm hands pushed and manipulated her skin. "It is less pretty than I had hoped for, I must confess. But, all things considered . . ." He pulled her dress back down over her stomach, gestured that she could sit up again.

"The reason I came, doctor, is that, well, my cycles haven't yet returned to normal, and I should have thought that, by now . . ."

Dr. Bertrand shook his head. "No, Claire, I'm afraid you don't quite understand what has happened here. The intense scraping in your uterus left enough tissue damage to give way to an acute infection. The only way to keep you alive, to keep that infection from spreading into the rest of your system, was to remove, entirely, the contaminated organ. Meaning I have taken out your uterus. Your ovaries are still in place, so you will not know the symptoms of menopause until you're much older, but in terms of your cycles, and with that the possibility of children, you will never, can never, have that again. I am sorry. But again, given the circumstances, it was the only solution."

Claire looked around the room, her eyes eventually settling into one of its blank corners. She blinked. "I . . . Thank you, Dr. Bertrand. Now, I really must be going." Claire pushed off the examination table and rushed from the room, out into the springtime street, where she wandered the wet sidewalks of Montreal for hours, past gangs of men swinging their picks and adzes, workers chinking away troughs of slush and sluice. Icy water sloughing away in every direction around her.

Hiking along, she was filled with the sudden urge to be occupied, busy, tirelessly busy, and so she trudged the streets until it was time for her shift at the cabaret, where she then worked all night long, even going into the back and scrubbing dishes once the manager wanted to send her home. For the next two days she managed to keep herself almost completely active, frantic with tasks that were growing in both quantity and complexity. She worked until her eyelids were leaden with sleep.

However, during those two days, and even at her busiest moments, there were thoughts that managed to enter her mind for a few troubling seconds. Claire felt that she had become less free, confined to a future to which she hadn't given much consideration before. In fact, she had never once gotten around to picturing what her life might look like after twenty-five, hadn't imagined her existence beyond the stardom she was so sure she was going to attain. The threatening vertigo that she felt during these moments made her push the thoughts away and she would quickly find something else to do, something difficult, something in need of her undivided concentration.

On the night of her twenty-fifth birthday, she went out dancing, alone, and had all the men buy her drinks until her speech was slurred and almost every other reveller had gone home for the night. A single musician was at the piano, playing for Claire alone, a tune that was slow and sad. The pianist eyed her as she swayed her hips from side to side, her hands wrapped around her own torso as if they were the arms of a smitten lover.

As she danced alone on the hardwood floor, she heard her own voice in her head, speaking to her. Both detached and warmly reassuring, the voice told her: You have only ever done one thing. You only know how to *do* one thing. Without it, you are nothing. You must understand that you have not failed in your pursuit. Instead, will has failed *you*. You can continue, but you must do so on your own, compensating for the things that the force of will once provided you with. In order to rise above your station in life and the situation you have made for yourself, you'll need to be bolder than ever before, more daring and audacious. Time is not on your side. If you are going to make a move, you must do so now. Now.

Claire straightened and woozily turned round to take in the room. Besides the pianist and the bartender, there was only one man in the club, a grey-haired gentleman, watching her with bleary eyes and nursing what was likely his fourteenth tumbler of Scotch. She walked straight towards him, leaned on the bar. "It is my birthday. You should buy me a drink."

The man smiled the smile of a drunk. His suit was trendy, expensive, his shoes freshly shined. "Yeah? And how old are you, sweetie?"

"Twenty-four. I'll have what you're having."

The man snickered and gestured for the bartender to comply. Then he stood up. "Hafta visit the gents', doll, but'll be right back."

"I can't wait," said Claire, putting an arm around his waist, her hand slipping down to his buttock. She kissed him, slowly, then leaned away, letting him pass by her on his way to the urinals. Before disappearing through the doors at the back, he exchanged another lusty look with her, then stumbled inside.

Picking up her coat from a seat, Claire shoved the wallet she'd just stolen from the back of his trousers into one of her coat pockets and hurried outside, where she waved down a cab and headed home.

The next day, she went to one of the biggest cabarets in town, the Kit-Kat, on Stanley, and asked to speak to the manager. Unfortunately, he recognized her. "Wha'd'*you* want here?"

"A job. I can waitress, and dance. Both better than most."

"Not hiring, sorry." He turned to leave, but she caught his arm and forced a wad of bills into his palm.

"Please," she pleaded. "Just one shift, to start."

He stepped back, looked her over, then counted the bills, hesitating.

"Please," she repeated.

He sighed, buried the wad in his pocket. "So much as a blink of funny business and you're black and blue in the alley, hear?" He shook his head, as if at himself, as if he were wilfully ignoring a bad feeling that was worming around in the bottom of his gut. "Shift starts at five."

Caro Serafim,

How extravagantly unpredictable this world is! Travelling through Oporto last month, I learned that the calm and provincial plan you once had for your life has since turned itself into an ocean-going adventure. How I await news of the photography you see there, and wonder if it is as vibrant as in Paris.

Yes, Paris. With the dictatorship installing itself in Portugal, the anarchists' aims were forfeited, and so I began to ask every photographer I knew to point me in the direction of where the vanguards of our medium were gathering. The answer was either Berlin or Paris. I chose the latter because it was closer and cheaper to get to. But Serafim, what a decision it was!

I've set myself up in Montparnasse, which it would seem is the very hub of art on the planet. Writers, poets, painters, sculptors, photographers, as well as the models required for their work, meet and mingle at the Café du Dôme every morning and evening, in an air that is gentle and smells of coffee and warm brioches. The atmosphere is fluid and accepting, newcomers greeted as regulars, the boundaries of class and ethnicity lifted.

My first day here, a painter saw my camera and commissioned me to take shots for his studies. Later, in his studio, two young models called by, looking for work. He asked them to remove all their clothes and stand near the window. Would you believe that they did?! This, now, is what I photograph to pay my rent.

And you, my dear friend, how are you finding America? Your uncle seemed to hint that you had happened across a substantial sum before embarking, hence I've been imagining you in some lavish city skyscraper. Please, tell me, of your photos, your life.

As minhas mais sinceras saudações,

Álvaro

18

Serafim was soon swallowed into the folds and undulations of his brand new world. He lived as a boarder in the Italian neighbourhood at Coursol Street and Dominion, rooming with Antonino Spada for his first year. Just as Antonino had predicted, Serafim managed to find a job quickly, as a darkroom technician at a photography studio downtown. The studio was owned and operated by an old Scotsman, a man who was constantly smoking a pipe, and who spoke very little; sweet and silent clouds ribboning the bulb of Serafim's darkroom. While living in relative poverty, Serafim slowly and painstakingly scrimped together enough to pay Antonino back for his first weeks as a boarder. He made a point of reminding his new friend, on a daily basis, that he hadn't forgotten his debt, and that he was busy saving whatever he could to chip away at it. After what felt like an eternity, he finally handed Antonino the last of the money he owed, which freed him up to begin scraping together whatever he could to take and develop photos of his own again. He did this by saving chemicals and paper that would normally have been discarded in his regular darkroom work. The results of his photography were less than optimal, but, he reasoned, developing subpar photos was better than producing nothing new at all.

In the autumn, he showed some of his new images to Antonino, which had the instant effect of deepening their friendship. With the exception of Álvaro, Antonino was the only person to have ever expressed authentic appreciation of Serafim's talents, his eye, his aesthetic. He'd even — though unconsciously, without meaning to — referred to Serafim as an artist once or twice.

Antonino himself was staying in Canada on a student visa, studying at one of the city's universities. Within weeks of their arrival, his fiery discussions had burgeoned into polemics that, he was convinced, could no longer be contained. Action had become necessary. Antonino was most upset by how blindly supportive the Italian community was of Mussolini, and by two highly publicized trials of Italian immigrants, one unfolding in New York, the other in Montreal. The verdict in Montreal had already been meted out, with seven men sentenced to hang at the Bordeaux jail for robbery and murder. Four of them (three of whom were Italian born) had already been executed. During their trial, however, there had been countless allusions and references to kickbacks and protection money that had been systematically paid to the authorities, from beat-walking constables all the way to the police chief himself. Yet, Antonino pointed out to Serafim, it was only the lowly immigrant "dagos" whose heads were being bridled by a noose.

During the course of several drunken discussions, Serafim took pictures of Antonino's enraged gestures as his hands and arms swung out over oak barrel tops — barrels of beer that the matron of their boarding house purchased and served for extra income, the woman stoically filling steins as if deaf to the shouting around her. Antonino eventually decided that he would start an independent newspaper, and that he would call it *Il Risveglio Italiano*. It would be a journal that offered a refreshing perspective, though most importantly (and he swore this on his mother's soul) it would *not* be just another *boccheggiante*, something that paid lip service to the Church and prominent members of the Italian community.

When the first issue was printed, Antonino, bristling with contentment, tied a stack of the papers in hemp twine and brought them home, jauntily thumping the package onto the floor and soliciting Serafim's help in distributing them. He was sorry the antiquated press he'd procured could only print four pages of text and no photos; otherwise, he said, he would happily have printed one of Serafim's shots. Antonino gauged the newspaper's success by how entrenched and loyal his old friends were forced to become, as well as by the growing number of new enemies he was making. People shook their fists at him as he passed in the streets, cursing the same mother whose soul Antonino had sworn on to hell, or at times (and this was a complete mystery to Serafim) cursing him to Naples.

Throughout his first year, Serafim often asked people where he might find other Portuguese immigrants in the city. Constantly struggling in Italian, English, and French, and never feeling the words leave his mouth as they did in his native tongue — as effortless and weightless as breath — had him hankering for even the smallest small talk in Portuguese. What soon became apparent to Serafim was that there were very few, if any, Portuguese denizens in the city. Things had

substantially improved in Portugal and there was little reason
to leave, unless, like Serafim, you'd made a reason for yourself. And so, in his head, with an internal Portuguese voice that
spoke in soliloquies (and with no small degree of sentimentalism), Serafim catalogued the differences in the ways the sea-
sons changed, between his old land and his new.

First, he noted that the summer heat was less dry in Montreal than it was in Oporto, more oppressive. It stuck to his
skin like a damp cloth beneath his jacket, vest, and shirt. This
was followed by his perpetual shock at the colours of autumn,
which were vibrant and luminous hues that soaked and bled
into the streetscape, drew the eye up and out at the sky and
its grey-lacquered clouds. The leaves had tones that made
Serafim wish colour film had developed beyond either prohibitively expensive experiments or lengthy screen-plate processes
that rendered unconvincing results. He had long since trained
his eye to see in grey-scale, in degrees of contrast, recognizing the way light on objects would translate into the fields of
black and white. For the first time, however, he wanted to hold
and record the entire spectrum of colour. That is, until all the
leaves were gone.

Winters in Portugal had been, at worst, cool and gloomy. In
Quebec, Serafim discovered that the coolness in the air could
quickly reach a point where the air particles themselves felt
jagged, like teeth that could bite pinholes into his skin, despite
the layers and layers of clothing he wore. Serafim observed
oblong puddles from bitter rain begin to clamp shut overnight,
incisors of ice sealing themselves up into plate glass smiles,
cross-hatches of canines and molars maniacally clenched. He
sometimes wondered how people in the streets, slouching

with their collars high and going about their daily business, didn't die in great numbers.

When the first snowfall, sparse and icing-sugar soft, spiralled from the sky, Serafim photographed children running in circles on the sidewalk, giggling with their mouths open, chasing the flakes with the pink of their tongues. He had seen snow only one other time in his life, while on a train southeast of Oporto, where the mountains of the Serra da Estrela had risen as a pallid set of hills in the far distance. Until he moved to Montreal, the concept of snow had been remote and abstract. Now that he could see it up close, he was mostly preoccupied with brushing the flakes off his camera, worried about their possible effects on his equipment. When he woke the next day, most of the snow was gone, the cityscape dusted white, salted like cod. He imagined the rest of the winter would continue this same way, a few flakes here and there, which would then be gone by the following afternoon. Perhaps, he thought, winter was going to be manageable after all.

As the winter truly dug itself in, however, Serafim was astounded that a state of emergency was not being called. In fact, to all appearances, it was even the contrary. These people almost welcomed the cold and snow, revelled in the way it piled up, high, higher, banking the streets and drifting onto the storefronts. People shovelled it as if they were transporting boxes on moving day, simply, methodically, and as a matter of course, digging out cars, converting their horse-drawn vehicles into sleighs and cutters, and draping themselves in thick animal skins to ride outside in the freezing elements — mitts, woollen hats, fur gauntlets, and muskox robes. Kids skated at intersections or near fire stations, where the very people who were responsible for ensuring safety and security in the metropolis used their hoses to create massive rinks for wild children, who would then wield precariously hooked sticks and strap blades to their feet to shove a rubber disc and speed around after it. On the weekends, people took to the hill that stood at the centre of the city (which everyone referred to as "the mountain") to play in the arctic white — skiers in overcoats with sashes, snowshoers in short blanket coats or mackinaws, everyone sporting high boots, heavy knickers, sweaters, and woollen underwear. A lane for toboggans was fashioned on the mountain, with flares shooting violently into the night to beckon onlookers to a place where water had been poured on the hill, creating a straight-run luge track where math students with stopwatches calculated the tobogganers to be running at close to 90 miles an hour. These people, Serafim was increasingly convinced, were mad.

On the other hand, their print media was as conservative and lagging behind the times as it was in Portugal. Serafim had scanned everything that was printed in the city, looking for photographs that might stretch beyond the limits of the standard portrait mug shots of opulent proprietors and politicians. Sadly, there were virtually no exceptions to the conventional rule. Even though the technology existed almost everywhere to blanket journals and periodicals with every kind of photograph imaginable, the only cities experimenting with such possibilities were, according to reports from Álvaro, the illustrated news and travel magazines out of Paris and Berlin. Álvaro had sent Serafim a few pages from one of these magazines, published in Paris, called *Vu*. Serafim was astonished to see such creativity and openness in a popular publication: cutting-edge angles, candid shots, and experimental subjects and processes. Serafim was sure that the rest of the world was just about to catch on. It had to, he thought to himself (in an appeasing Portuguese voice). It had to.

He had approached a few of the newspapers with some of his candid photos, armed as well with the best of the glossy pages that Álvaro had sent from *Vu*, but it was all for naught. People, the editors argued, simply wouldn't be receptive to such abnormal pictures. They would be seen as untoward, unseemly. "Trust us. We've been in the business for a long time. But we do thank you all the same, and bid you a very fine day." The click of the door as it shut and sealed at Serafim's back. He was disheartened, to be sure, but not dissuaded, and continued spending every penny he could afford on taking candid shots in the streets.

One Sunday in January, he had again bundled himself up against the absurd temperature, fifteen below, and set out towards the larger buildings of downtown to take a few exposures. He was on St. Catherine Street, taking a break in a café, when he became aware, looking through the café's window, of a jarring shift in the way people were acting. Something was clearly wrong. He hustled to pay for his coffee and headed out the door to spot a crowd gathering around a theatre several blocks away. Smoke was being emitted from its upper floors in ever-greater plumes.

As Serafim got closer, it became evident that there were people trapped inside, and nearing the horses and firemen, he could hear the high-pitched screams of children. The following morning he would read that eight hundred of them had crammed into the theatre to watch a Sunday matinee, and that seventy-eight did not come out alive. Many of the children were crushed or asphyxiated in the confusion and architectural mistakes of the building. The silent film they had been watching was a comedy starring Stan Laurel, and the title was *Get 'Em Young*. The fire had been caused by a discarded cigarette, which had smouldered in a slat in the floorboards, its heat sponging into the wood, until a patient splay of embers eventually blossomed into flame.

Serafim, distressed and unnerved, simply stood around like everyone else, watching as the firemen raced and fumbled to save whatever lives they could. They laboured with a steam pump, shovelling coal into it from the back of a truck. Teams of white and bay horses that had hauled the pumps, ladders, and equipment twitched, muscular and motionless, the skids on the sleighs behind them resting heavily on the compacted snow. Eventually a door was broken in, and tiny bodies began to be yanked out, and were grimly piled onto the frozen side-walk, placed out of the way as rescuers continued searching for the living.

Needing to avert his eyes from the sight — youthful, char-coal-smeared cheeks, now lifeless — Serafim found himself focusing on the crowd that had gathered, noticing the looks on everyone's faces, depicting the depth of the tragedy. It occurred to him that these expressions had to be recorded, were themselves in need of being witnessed, documented. So he took his Leica from his coat pocket and began snapping photos of the bystanders. A man with a hand pressing firmly down on the top of his flat cap, agape, eyes wide and wet. A woman cupping her fingers over her nose and mouth, standing tall, still, statuesque. An older gentlemen with the handle of his cane lifted to his temple, the length of it dangling limp in the air at his side, his gaze as busy as a speed-reader's.

While he hadn't thought for a minute to approach any of the city's newspapers with what he'd captured, a photo of the event, taken by someone else, was in fact printed in *La Presse* the following day. It was the first explicitly candid shot he'd seen since he arrived.

As Serafim was taking pictures of the crowd that afternoon, he would swear on his mother's memory that he saw Inês Sá among the faces; or at the very least someone who bore a striking resemblance to her. The woman had the same features and jawline, the same thick head of auburn hair (though it was cropped quite short), the same dark-water irises. But just at the moment he'd noticed her, she vanished, and so he'd hurriedly snapped an exposure in the direction that she disappeared. When he developed the photo the next morning, however, all he could make out was a blur of tresses amid a cluster of horrified faces.

What might this mean, he wondered, seeing Inês thousands of miles away from where he knew she was? And why would this happen, of all moments, alongside a disaster that was so busy ushering seventy-eight innocent souls through the flames and up to their Maker? As Serafim developed the photo with varying settings, it was a question to which he dedicated a great deal of philosophical thought and time. Gradually, and with an irrefutable logic all its own, an unsettling answer began to emerge.

Medium: Gelatin silver print
Description: Vaudeville dancers
Location: The Blue Sky, Montreal
Date: 1922

ભ

Eight young women on a stage, posing in a chorus line, one leg out in front of the other, pointed toes, heels lifted daintily from the ground. A white plume arcs from each of their hats, curling back on itself like the gangly neck of a crane, furled and preening. Their faces are young, dark-lipsticked, powder-puff pale.

They are divided, four on each side, and have been arranged in descending height from the centre, carefully symmetrical, flanking each other in identical feather-ruffled costumes; the open wings of a colossal bird whose spine is aligned with the parting point of the curtains that loom behind them. The curtains rise to an unknowable height, out of the frame, climbing vertical folds up through the rafters, disappearing into the heights of cardboard clouds and stencilled stars.

Each of the girls is reaching down with one hand to lift the hem of her dress, revealing a white shin in its suggestive entirety, peaking close to the knee. Sleeveless arms and low-cut necks are milk-smooth, untainted. The smiles on their lips suggest a mischievous abandon, imply that at this moment they feel careless, lewd, bawdy.

One of the girls, however — on the far left, shorter — has a certain weight to her expression, an encumbrance. As if she knows something more than the others. As if she wished she did not.

19

Claire ended up keeping the job she'd underhandedly sidled into at the Kit-Kat Cabaret, though she was cautious never to take it for granted. She came to her shifts on time, when onstage danced with gusto, unglamorously served tables, washed glasses, and even managed not to react to the sneers and remarks that were audibly whispered by the other dancers — gossiping in the powder room about Claire's stunt with the manager at the Gayety, smashing glasses against the kitchen wall of an influential man, derailing her career. Claire was counting on the fact that there were other commanding individuals in the city, other opportunities that remained hidden, waiting to be teased out into the open.

She thought one of these opportunities might have arisen when a smartly suited gentleman came into the cabaret late one Thursday night, wanting to chat with some of the performers at his table after the show. He was unmistakably married, rich, prominent, but what wasn't quite clear, and something Claire only learned from one of the musicians in the band, was that he happened to be one of the five city councillors out of Westmount, the affluent and English-speaking powerhouse at the epicentre of the city. He'd only been voted in a year and a half earlier, in the 1927 election, in which the campaigning had been famously full of pomp and pageantry. Now he was there in front of them, and plainly looking for an anonymous and uncomplicated tryst. Female entertainers gaggled in around him, laughed at everything he said, and jockeyed for a position at his side.

Claire, however, wasn't quite feeling the part. Even if she had set out to seduce him, she doubted she would've been able to go through with it. She'd become acutely self-conscious about her serrated scar, that unsightly lightning bolt of pink that cascaded from her navel and pointed into her hairline. She imagined the disgusted sip of air that men would take in when first catching sight of it, their pause, and how naturally the questions would flow from there. This insecurity had her missing the one chance she would ever have of winning the favour of this gentleman, who would be the only city councillor ever to frequent the Kit-Kat. Instead, he made the obvious choice. Hours later, Claire saw him in one of the backrooms, naked and thrusting on top of the youngest dancer in the establishment, the two of them having pulled a three-piece oriental screen in front of a doorless frame, the lights on, radio playing, impish laughter. Claire scurried past their groans and sighs and took a tram home, completely unaware of how important the situation she had just seen would one day become.

Arriving back home, Claire found she couldn't sleep, lying in her bed, staring at the ceiling, the city noises colouring the darkness: tram bells dragging sparks over wires, hooves trotting past, the putter of automobiles shifting gears. Beneath the sheets, Claire ran her fingers along the scar of her abdomen, thinking again about her sister's insinuation that she had become entirely self-absorbed, that she'd been clinging so tightly to her own affairs for so long that she'd somehow lost the facility to grasp anyone else's. It was a possibility that conjured an unsettling memory for Claire. Knowing she wouldn't find sleep for hours to come, she got out of bed, turned on the lights, and rummaged through a drawer, looking for a scrapbook she kept that tracked her career. In it, unglued and sliding out from the pages, she found the photograph she'd been thinking about. She carefully brought it over to her only chair, sat back, crossed her legs, and inspected it.

It had been taken when she was nineteen and still working the vaudeville circuit, mostly at the Blue Sky (where the image had been captured). She remembered the portly photographer, how he'd stood below the dancers, right in front of the stage, his camera flush with the wood, encouraging Claire and the other dancers to pinch the fabric of their dresses just a little higher — yes, perfect, now, only a slight bit more, yes, yes, excellent, now, I wonder, if, yes, just a trifle higher — squinting through his viewfinder, sweaty brow sheening. What she remembered most about that day, however, was what happened when he left.

One of the dancers at the Blue Sky, Corrine, had been "unwell" for quite some time, having missed her shifts for more than two months, a kind of unofficial sick leave. Since she had both the face and the body that were likely to stir the most interest out of all the dancers, Corrine was ordered to show up for the promotional photo shoot. When she refused, she was threatened, then finally coaxed to come out with money. When she arrived, the reason for her previous absence became clear: she was pregnant, and was now showing. To solve this problem, all the dancers were instructed to wear the loosest costume they had, and told to lean slightly forward for the photo, arms in front of their stomachs to pull the hems of their dresses higher. After the photos were taken, Corrine was promptly fired, and told never to return.

Only it wasn't the last anyone saw of Corrine. Sniffling and hanging around just outside the club on St. Catherine Street, she met each of the other dancers as they left the cabaret either to head home or to go out on the town. She begged them to listen to her, to help her, insisting that things had dramatically changed for her, and that she suddenly found herself with nowhere to go and not a friend in the world. Claire was one of the last to wander out that evening, and was met with Corrine's intense and frantic pleas, asking for, at the very least, a place to stay for the night. Please, please — a prayer to the god of tightly pressed palms — please. Claire was actually on her way to meet her most recent (and soon to pass) fling, but thinking of Cécile and what she would do in the same circumstances, she decided to invite Corrine home. She had to admit that, in the tram at least, she felt rather virtuous. That was soon to fade.

They arrived at Claire's apartment, which at the time she was sharing with three other dancers, and the two young women settled in the cramped space of Claire's room, sitting on either end of her narrow bed, arms around their knees. Corrine told Claire her story, how she'd been dating a wealthy older man whose hair was streaked with grey. He worked in the Montreal Curb Market, bragged about having liquidated his house and other properties to place his every asset into the runaway stock exchange that he himself was helping to snowball, and boasted about tripling then quadrupling his net worth. He bought her pretty gifts. She suspected, however, that he bought his wife and children prettier ones.

Corrine swore she wasn't so naive as to think he'd actually leave his family and start another one with her, but she did allow herself to believe that they might come to some kind of agreement, that it might be possible, with the proceeds of all his investments, to live out a comfortable though secret existence, be given a modest apartment and humble grocery allowance for her and her future child, maybe even see her prosperous lover on the weekends, take brief holidays together in anonymous towns through New York State.

But the moment he found out what was growing in her belly, he threw her out of their hotel room and made it clear that if she ever so much as whispered a word about him to anyone, she and her bastard child would be made to quickly (and painfully) disappear, their faces suddenly shuffled into the neglected pages of the province's missing persons' list. After the confrontation she stayed home, weeping for her lot. She pawned his gifts until they ran out, then sold what she could of her own things, and only managed to be lured from her apartment by the cash carrot of posing in a promotional photograph for the Blue Sky — money which, once they saw her condition, and after the photos were shot, they refused to fork over anyway. Now she had nothing, had been kicked out of her flat for not paying the rent, and had no way of making cash so that she could disappear, in that age-old and proven way, long enough to have the child, give it up for adoption, and return looking much as she had before, ready to continue her life as if nothing had happened.

Claire listened and grew restless. There was obviously no solution here, because it was far too late to consider terminating the pregnancy. Claire wasn't about to offer her tiny room and income as a safe and secure haven for the next six months, either. Claire was yet to gain first-hand knowledge of how prone kind-hearted Catholic families were to disowning their wayward daughters, but she assumed that appealing to Corrine's parents was quite out of the question or she would have done so long ago. There was, of course, the highly selective assistance of the Church that might be sought, though every woman had heard rumours about the humiliation that option involved. No wonder Corrine found herself friendless, thought Claire. Her very existence imposed itself on everyone around her, required them either to take action to help her or to abandon her, which, whatever way you looked at it, was a bit much to ask a person on a light and breezy Saturday night. To Claire's shame, she began to feel a niggling regret at having invited Corrine into her apartment. How was she ever going to get her out again?

So Claire pressed her to think harder, to consider even the most distant of relatives who might be trusted to keep her secret, and could feed and house her for the few months necessary. Reluctantly, Corrine mentioned an aunt who lived in Three Rivers, who, while not exactly the sweetest or most tolerant individual, was a widow, lived alone, and presumably had the means. No sooner had she mentioned this than Claire grabbed her arm and whisked her to the telephone in the adjoining apartment, urging Corrine to make the call. After a great deal of persuasion and encouragement, she picked up the receiver, bared all, and tearily arranged to meet her aunt at Windsor Station the following afternoon. Claire spent the rest of that evening reassuring her that she'd made the right choice, and even carted Corrine off to the station the next day, pleased and satisfied to have been of service. She mentioned the deed in a letter to her sister a few weeks later, a righteous exploit, her very first stroke for the female cause. Predictably, Cécile lauded her efforts.

The event flitted from Claire's mind, and she had almost forgotten about it when, a little under a year later, there came a knock at the door. It was a shivery autumn day, raining and windy, so Claire only cracked the door open a bit to keep the warm air of the apartment from draining into the outdoors. It took her a long moment to recognize the tattered woman on the other side as Corrine.

"Hi," she said, stealing a look back over her shoulder, watching the bread man as he made his way down the street. She shuddered as the man slammed the wooden door of his carriage and, with a wicker basket heaped with loaves, trotted towards the next apartment on his route. "Hi," she repeated. "I didn't ... This is the only ... place I could think to come." Her words, Claire noted, were vaguely slurred, sluggish. She was filthy, blotches of oily stains on her dress and coat, and she smelled of body odour.

"Corrine? Are you all right?"

"Can I ..." She looked at her hands, the tips of her fingers frenetically rubbing against each other. "Can I come in?"

Claire hesitated, tactless. "Well ... yes, yes, of course, come in." She opened the door and, as Corrine passed, covered her nose.

"I ... Thank you."

Claire closed the door behind her. "So, the first thing we should do is run you a bath and get you some fresh clothes. Then we'll catch up. Okay?"

Corrine thought about this for a dull moment, then agreed with a drunken nod and anaesthetized grin.

Out of the bath and into an old but clean dress of Claire's, and with a warm cup of coffee in her hand, Corrine filled Claire in on what had happened since she'd left that same apartment eleven months earlier.

The aunt who had met her at the train station had apparently never once entertained the idea of taking Corrine back with her to Trois-Rivières, but ushered her instead into a taxi and headed straight for the Miséricorde, where her parents were waiting to register her stay. The Miséricorde was a Catholic institution in the middle of the city whose sole aim was to bring unwanted and illegitimate children into the world and give them up for adoption; where soon-to-be mothers could be placed in the concealed and competent care of nuns throughout their pregnancy, childbirth, and postnatal recuperation. Corrine's parents had quickly signed the papers, letting her know how disappointed they were in her. She was then deposited on the other side of a locked gate.

Generally speaking, the girls there were from the countryside and had been working as servants or *jeunes filles* in private homes, with English or Jewish families. Few of them were originally from Montreal, and none were anglophones, who (the Irish aside) would have the means to send their daughters off to private doctors and discreet residences in Boston, New York, Philadelphia, or Washington. The nuns were severe and unsympathetic. When a girl gave birth, she was kept from knowing the sex of her child, hence preventing her from form-ing an unnecessary attachment (or guessing which baby was actually hers). After they'd delivered, the women were charged with breastfeeding the infants in the institution, a chart being used to systematically swap babies and the breast that a woman was using for each feeding. The only way the women knew that a child had been given away was when the woman who had been breastfeeding the longest was suddenly released, and so conveyor-belted through the roster and back out onto the street.

Corrine returned to her parents' home to be placed under the severest of control. Forced piety and religious duty had her realizing she was being prepped for spinsterhood, the only path to redemption following such a disgraceful plunge. So she ran away, tried to get work as a dancer again, but her figure had taken a turn for the worse, and the only place she could find work — after several weeks of spending her nights in the abodes of the shiftiest, seediest men — was a venue where going on "private dates" with some of the higher-paying clien-tele was part of the unwritten contract. That was something her father, who was searching for her, soon caught wind of, and he asked a policeman (while licking a few dollars free from his billfold) to pick Corrine up at her place of work and drop her off at the reformatory.

The officer signed her in, and duly passed on the fact that she had a history of running away. Luckily, they knew just how to deal with such individuals. Corrine was processed — stripped, scrubbed down, her personal items confiscated — and was then given clothes that would be entirely unsuitable to escape in, should that bright idea even enter her mind. She was forced to don slippers and transparent gowns, her bare breasts and underclothes so visible that even the women in the reformatory couldn't help but stare. She was at first isolated from the others, made to clean long and dark hallways on her own, and every interaction she had with the staff was designed to illustrate and reinforce the fact that she was entirely power-less and vulnerable. It was explained to her once, by one of the women in charge, who was consoling Corrine through the grated window of her cell, that it honestly wasn't her fault; that somewhere along the way she, Corrine, had somehow adopted a disobedient nature, and that nature now had to be broken in order to make room for a more compliant and respectable one to replace it, which would then grow and flourish. Surely that much was understandable, was it not? Months passed before she was able to speak to anyone else, and when she was finally given the chance, she felt the last of her hope ebb away. Because the only thing anyone in the girls' reformatory could talk about was the burgeoning influence of the Montreal Local Council of Women.

The MLCW was a coalition of several women's groups in the area, primarily headed by Protestant anglophone wives, which, at the time, was bent on weeding out the sordid vice of prostitution from the city's streets. Together with local priests and other men of virtue — who were given the dastardly task of going undercover and staging stakeouts at dance halls, pool halls, and "disorderly houses," in order, of course, to analyze the goings-on there by way of the most rigorous scientific scrutiny — they reported their findings to allies who worked at upstanding newspapers and journals in the city, published brochures of their own, and disclosed their findings to stra-tegic men of the cloth to get their message blaring out from the pulpit as well. The aim was to appeal to the upstanding populace, to incite their moral outrage, provoke the radical change that was needed to clean up the misguided modern culture. Such efforts, it was often pointed out, had already successfully lobbied for prohibition in the United States and parts of Canada, bringing about marked and positive changes in society. However, what had really caught the attention of the women in the reformatories was that the MLCW had recently renewed its attempts to convince the provincial minister of justice of the need for reformatories to offer "indeterminate sentences for prostitutes." They felt that if a prostitute could not be reformed, if she was likely to re-engage in an amoral lifestyle once released, then society should be able to postpone her reintegration in perpetuity. Surely that much was understandable. Was it not?

Having heard this, Corrine's behaviour approached angelic. She was eventually released and returned to her family, where she lasted all of a month before choosing (over drowning herself) to run away again. She fled, was elbowed in the same direction of the seedy men she'd stayed with previously, and was soon given shelter by a "procurer," then some clothes, unwavering protection, even a bit of money. She tried to step out of the underworld several times, but with each job she found, from waiting tables to clerical work to labouring in the manufacturing sector, once her past as an occasional prostitute was discovered — and without fail it was — she was let go and told never to return.

The reason she'd come to Claire's apartment was that she just happened to be in the neighbourhood and she feared she was going to be beaten. She had blown off her old procurer for the slightly better offer of another one, and someone, she said, was going to be punished, very badly, and it wasn't yet clear if the fists would fall on her or one of the men — it was often hard to tell. She only needed to stay for the night, she promised. By morning, she would be gone.

Claire, however, watching Corrine scratch at the pinpricks in the crooks of both elbows, suspected there was more to the story than she was telling. Claire asked if she could help in any other way, besides a place to stay for the night.

Corrine eased onto her side of the bed, coiling into a ball on Claire's mattress, and folded the top cover back on itself to tug it over her shoulders. "No," she mumbled. "No, I've had your help before." Then she closed her eyes, her lids trembling tight, and pressed herself into a fidgety sleep.

Now, five years later, Claire held the photo with her and Corrine in it, standing in a chorus line on a vaudeville stage. Claire found herself wondering where she was, if she was safe, well; though she happened to doubt very much that she was. Isn't it strange, she thought, how she hadn't recalled this incident for ages, and how it could rise up out of nowhere and leave her with a more cumbersome feeling than before? She'd already felt hampered of late, as if she needed to slow down, stop, rest, and take stock. And she saw this recollection as yet another reason to fear what would happen when she finally did.

Paris, França; 25 de agosto de 1927

Estimado Serafim,

How fascinating to think that we were, almost certainly, both taking photos in the streets yesterday, capturing the riots in our respective cities, sparked by the same event. The wrongful execution of Sacco and Vanzetti has, or so I've read, incited protests the world over. Our planet, as the artists of Montparnasse are wont to say, is more interwoven than ever before. The riots here besieged the American embassy, and did appreciable damage to the Moulin Rouge. I've enclosed a contact sheet from one of the films I shot throughout. I would love to know what took place in Montreal — protests, unrest, arson? What of the anarchists there?

I have also included more pages of the illustrated magazine every photographer is striving to work for, which features, almost exclusively, candid photography. I know of several people who believe this to be our medium's future; though the camera of choice here seems mostly to be (unlike yours and mine) the Ermanox, for its high-resolution optics and ease of concealment. However, before you begin saving for a new model, you should also know that these are the same individuals who champion the photomontage, which I vigorously dislike.

Apart from photography, the design in Europe at the moment is all refreshingly modern. Art deco delineates every interior with geometric motifs and bold colours, while the surrealists are proclaiming this as their very own époque des sommeils.

What news of your fascists? Are all the Italian immigrants you told me of still standing so united?

Espero ansiosamente a tua resposta,
Álvaro

20

B y the following summer, Serafim felt he was making a steady-enough income to venture on from his life as a boarder in a congested Italian household, with its seasonal flux of migrant workers coughing and snoring — railwaymen, construction workers, miners — as well as the apartment's persistent smell of horse manure and hay that wafted in from the stable located in a nook behind the building. But since almost all the connections and acquaintances he'd made were Italian, he found a place in another, though older, Italian neighbourhood, at St. Timothée and St. Agathe, only a few blocks east of the Red Light. It was tight, as far as apartments went, and there was little movement of fresh air in the summer months, but (the real reason he'd taken it) there was an uncommonly large closet at its centre, which Serafim could convert into a makeshift darkroom to develop his personal photos. He also found a hidden storage space that was cool and dry, where he constructed a kind of drawer to store both his developed film and the large spools of unexposed thirty-five-millimetre motion-picture stock that he bought and cut into smaller sections for use in his Leica.

Serafim then purchased a second-hand set of dishes, as well as a few pots and pans, and tried his hand at cooking for the first time in his life. He failed miserably, convinced that he was missing out on those critical secrets which every recipe apparently hid, secrets that only the likes of Inês Sá discovered and hoarded. Though with scarcely enough money for food, he had little choice but to eat his culinary disasters, soaking up the blackened remains from his plate with a crust of bread.

Meanwhile, Antonino was increasingly becoming less a student and more a journalist. *Il Risveglio Italiano* had quickly gained a reputation as a voice of controversy and agitation, and with the few new friends this won him (friends with deeper pockets than Antonino enjoyed), the newspaper was able to expand to a print run of several thousand copies a week. At the same time, aside from his journalistic duties, Antonino was helping to organize three food co-operatives in the city, the most dynamic of which was in Ville Émard, where a hall, the Sala Mazzini, soon became the headquarters of the local anti-fascist movement.

While the anti-fascist group remained intensely unpopular, and continued to incite aggressive and even violent opposition, it did manage to win over several labour unions in its appeal. The swelling of its threadbare ranks, however, did not go unnoticed. Antonino not only received threats, but he began to have problems when dealing with any red tape that was even distantly connected to prominent members of the Italian community, inconveniences about which, he endlessly exclaimed, he "couldn't give a cabbage."

He sometimes invited Serafim along to take photos during planned altercations. A cluster of anti-fascists waving socialist red flags would descend upon a proud march celebrating Giovanni Caboto or Guglielmo Marconi, ranks of unyielding men in black shirts and women in charcoal skirts and white blouses parading along Sherbrooke Street with great fanfare, everyone bearing the fascist insignia. Serafim was astounded that people weren't actually killed. Ironically, the most violent confrontations erupted after Sunday Mass, when Antonino and his tiny clan would gather outside the Madonna della Difesa Parish. The curate there was the single most influential proponent of Mussolini in the city — the church a stronghold of fascist propaganda, and the chief co-ordinator of blackshirt parades — and the man would all but sic his churchgoers on them, a furious mob forming around Antonino's provocateurs, shoving, punching, kicking. Afterwards, the tattered group would walk away, limping and bruised, swabbing drops of blood from their nostrils, Antonino striding beside them with an air of accomplishment.

Lionel Groulx, an activist, Catholic priest, and historian, was immensely popular with French Canadians at the time, and was also a firm proponent of corporatism, which he believed would one day replace class struggle with class co-operation, an idea shared with Mussolini. Fascists, and indeed the majority of Montrealers, were not exactly great sympathizers of leftist causes or ideologies like anarchism, so the turnout of protesters to rally against the executions of Sacco and Vanzetti was a rather meagre one. It was so unimpressive, in fact, that Serafim had only snapped a few exposures throughout, and when he developed them, he couldn't find a single frame worth sending to Álvaro, who was used to seeing things of a much more dramatic and glamorous nature.

In the autumn, Antonino also moved, though only a few blocks away from the original boarding house where they'd roomed together for their first year. He had found two other aspiring journalists as flatmates, which meant the apartment was steeped in discussion. The three of them had taken to sitting on the stoop of their building in the Indian-summer heat, chatting, smoking the slow of the evenings away like a wick. All of them bought cigars from the Italian company Capuano & Pasquale, who divvied them out for a penny each. Serafim often joined the group, sitting on their periphery, watching them as they spoke while petting the neighbourhood dog that would inevitably drop by, a mongrel panting onto the men's leather shoes, the dog's shadow waiting beside Serafim, eager to amble away and seek out the children playing in the streets before they were called indoors for the night. Radio orchestras crooned through windows as they talked.

Whenever they were left alone, Antonino would encourage Serafim to analyze or intellectualize his photography, asking him unwieldy questions and patiently waiting until he answered. Serafim thought it a good exercise, sure that Álvaro was doing the same thing in Parisian cafés every day.

"But why is it the setting of the street that draws you so?" asked Antonino, bracing for the long pause he knew would follow.

It stretched out longer than both of them expected. "I think . . . that art's function is to depict life, the human experience. And life, real life, manifests itself in its most naked form on the street."

"You don't think that's done behind closed doors?"

"No. Well, yes. But what I mean is . . . the street is the place, for example, where our greatest victories are celebrated, our traditions, and sudden or dire circumstances like protests and riots and warfare and revolts. But . . . but that nakedness extends to peacetime as well, to people going about their daily errands, buying bread at the bakery, carrots at the grocer and such. We are never more genuine than we are in public life."

"Is that the right word, 'genuine'?"

"Yes. I mean the way we keep ourselves on guard, how we restrain and contain ourselves — that is what reveals us. I mean the cadence of our pace, or our fashion sense, posture, disposition, our confidence, how we react when we are bumped into, how we cope with everyday annoyances. That is who we really are: the person we are on the streets."

"But don't those things happen in private as well? At a private party, for instance."

"No, because a private party isn't changing constantly, the way the streets do. The streets are the most dynamic place we encounter. We must be in the mindset of a traveller there, moving through an exotic land, a land that changes anew, every day, every minute. The happenings on a street are jerky, with distinct occurrences right beside each other, with no connection, and no transition. Endless, random juxtapositions, a constant stream of unexpectedness. The street is graceless, like us. Which is precisely its grace, why it must be captured and depicted. Why photographs taken of it are art."

"Serafim," said Antonino, stretching out a hand to tap him gently on the back, "I think you should learn to organize your thoughts more coherently. But I think this is a good start."

The two of them continued to smoke, moving to easier subjects, until the neighbourhood was completely dark, moths drunkenly orbiting the few lampposts, the drone of masculine voices muttering in the shadows, pointing themselves out with the red tips of their cigars as they inhaled.

It was the same autumn that Serafim's unspoken suspicion about Inês and what had since happened to her began to take root. He soon lost patience developing the elusive exposure that he'd captured the day of the Laurier Palace Theatre fire, the day he saw that ghostly flicker of Inês's face in the street; which, in the darkroom, only yielded a blur of bobbed hair. So instead he reverted to developing the shot he'd taken of Inês at the Palácio de Cristal, a shot that was infinitely more gratifying to reproduce; so much so that he spent the majority of his free time over the next few months in his converted closet working on it. He'd long ago perfected the exposure's development, but now he knew how to refine it to an even greater degree, drawing out the features of her face, intensifying her expression, while burning-in the livid clouds that loomed in the background over her shoulders. The more satisfied Serafim was with these results, the more dissatisfied he became with his inadequate sexual life, which was still pathetically confined to furious bouts of auto-stimulation.

As the winter approached, Serafim — for photographic purposes only, to be sure — began venturing into the Red Light district, located only a few luring blocks away. There he would snap pictures of the various harlots, madams, pimps, and procurers as they solicited men who were passing by, stopping many of them to make what seemed to be secretive negotiations. He would wander down Gauchetière Street, where it was common to see young women buying cocaine and sniffing it out of tiny spoons in plain view, standing in a circle as if they were smoking casual cigarettes. They would often call him over, giggling, intimating for him to join in, or gesture to a nearby window where another mistress would be leaning out over the sill, waiting to render her services. His photos were poorly composed, often unfocused. Which in turn had him venturing back — in the interest, to be sure, of attaining better results.

Then, one December evening when it was too dark to take photos, he decided to take a stroll for some fresh air. He left his apartment without his Leica but with much more cash in his wallet than it was his custom to carry. He was soon moseying down a small and discreet avenue in the Red Light district, and when he was approached (as he had been countless times before) he did not, in keeping with his well-established habit, hold up a hand and shake his head, lower his gaze, and scuttle off in the direction he'd been heading. Instead, he listened to what a slick-haired man had to say. The man smelled of pungent cologne and shaving cream, and asked Serafim point-blank what kind of woman visited him in his dreams. Serafim hesitated at first, but then eagerly described her, and in likely more detail than the procurer had ever heard before. Amused, he led Serafim two blocks farther along, asked for five dollars, and handed him over to a madam standing at the entrance to a nondescript apartment, from which Serafim could hear a piano playing ragtime somewhere nearby.

Respectfully taking off his hat, he was led up a narrow staircase, having to step around an accordion player who was swaying to his own music and who gave Serafim a cordial nod in passing. At the top of the stairs the madam ushered him into a small bedroom and sealed him inside, alone with a not-unattractive brunette. Upon his entering, she had stood from the bed, placed the emery board she'd been so busily filing her nails with onto a bedside table, and pulled her dress over her head.

Serafim averted his eyes from her nudity. She laughed, settled herself in the centre of the mattress, and waved him over. Serafim scrunched his hat in his hands and made his sheepish way to the foot of the bed, blushing, unsure what to do. He undressed, folded his clothes, piled them on a chair, and stood there in front of her, covering his erection, awkward and gawky. The mistress had to physically reach forward and pull him onto her and guide him inside. Intensely excited, he didn't last long, and they were soon sharing a cigarette, lying side by side, Serafim desperately trying to think of things to say. He felt somehow unsatisfied; but also purged, released from a kind of nameless discredit. The act had been messier than he'd imagined, his stomach sweaty and both their fluids matting his pubic hair. In his drained calm he wondered if he should ask her what her name was, or where she grew up.

But before he could, there was commotion outside, the sounds of panicked movement throughout the building, a quick double knock at the door, the accordion player stopping abruptly and hustling away, the last wheezes of his instrument trailing behind him. The girl pounded a fist against the mattress, cursed, and rolled off the bed, throwing her dress on and stalling in front of the mirror to apply some quick makeup. Serafim looked at the door and heard the sound of bodies rushing and stomping on the other side of it. Then he looked over at the woman and waited for her to say something, to explain what was going on.

Unflustered, having clearly done this several times before, she muttered (her mouth stretched wide, applying mascara), "Police raid."

"Excuse me? Police?"

The door burst in. Serafim fumbled to cover himself, falling onto the floor, scrambling towards his clothes. The mistress put her mascara down and picked up her purse.

They were not handcuffed but brusquely guided down the stairs and out, single file, into the cool night air. Several paddy wagons — named for their customary function of loading up groups of revelling and combative Irish — were waiting for them in the street, men and women alike cramming into their boxes, mumbling lighthearted jokes. Girls were pinched, and frivolously slapped the men's shoulders in retaliation, fixed their hair and hats, and passed lipstick and compact mirrors to one another. Men tucked their shirts in, straightened their ties, and adjusted their cuffs and collars.

Serafim, beneath the clenching terror in his chest, felt his throat begin to swell and smart. He wanted to weep. Was there any harder luck in this world than to be sent to jail for losing one's virginity? Could there be a more lopsided justice than having his only time in a brothel be the one that sent him to prison?

The mistress that Serafim had been with noticed his expression and, sensing he was struggling with an unnecessary weight on his shoulders, shuffled closer. "Don't worry. Happens all the time." Her French was extremely colloquial, her accent garbled and nasal. "It's just for the *piastres*, the cash, sweetie. Tomorrow they'll write it all up in the papers, the pretty sum this raid won for the city's coffers, and that's it. Politics. Nothing more. Just don't go giving your real name or address. Make something up, pay your bail as soon as we get there, and disappear. They only want your five dollars. Whereas I'll likely have to give a little more." She winked, and stepped into the back of one of the paddy wagons.

Serafim, relieved, paused on the road behind the vehicle and, as if to follow the sudden sense of floating release he felt, found himself looking up into the grid of wires that draped across the side street, netting in the night sky and its plankton swirl of stars. It was then, as he was looking up, that it happened, again. A woman with a remarkable likeness to Inês Sá stepped into the frame of a lit window and looked down at him for a moment, with something like recognition. Unlike Inês, the woman appeared tired, worn, perhaps even in pain. Just then a policeman nudged Serafim towards the rear door of the nearest paddy wagon, and Serafim stepped inside, excusing himself for the crowding. The door slammed shut, and the paddy wagon was soon jostling down the avenue on its way to the police station, while Serafim's thoughts swam away in quite another direction.

Over the next two months, his initial suspicions matured, became more refined and intricate as they moved towards a kind of irrefutability. In Serafim's mind, the only way to approach these otherworldly phenomena was to use otherworldly logic. Inês Sá, it seemed clearer and clearer to him, was dead — an accident, sudden sickness, in childbirth, or a suicide. Anything was possible. And it would appear that the regret she'd been wrestling with, at not accepting Serafim's hand in marriage, had haunted her throughout her final days, and so her ghost was now haunting him in an attempt to make amends, to redeem herself, and stay true to the secret affections she'd so convincingly concealed.

On a cold February morning, Serafim's suspicions would become all but fact. He had spent the previous evening working in his private darkroom on the mysterious photo he'd taken during the Laurier Palace Theatre fire, until the light and chemicals had woven his concentration into a haze. He had a fitful sleep, twisting in his bed through fragmented dreams of Inês. When he woke the next morning, groggy, with a slight headache, pinching the gritty deposits from the corners of his eyes, he walked into the kitchen that he always kept fastidiously clear and clean, and froze in mid-stride. On the table in front of the chair where he always sat was a cup of tea, which had certainly not been there when he'd gone to bed. A teapot was soaking up the morning light beside it, as were a bowl of sugar and a carafe of cream from his icebox. The spoon used to stir the tea stained the saucer. The kettle was still on the range, though it was cold, so it must have boiled at some point in the middle of the night. The first thing Serafim touched was the match resting on the counter beside the stove, its tip a bulb of charcoal. Its tinder had burned along the shaft until, it seemed, some invisible pucker, breath of ice, had blown it out.

Medium:	Gelatin silver print
Description:	Aghast onlookers
Location:	St. Catherine Street, Montreal
Date:	January 1927

❧

A throng of people along a street are standing still, gaping in the direction of the camera. Though not into its lens; they are focused, intently, on something beyond it. Something that is palpably alarming, calamitous. Faces pale, brows creased.

They look like people who've been interrupted while going about the daily motions of life, their Sunday errands on pause. Bags dangle from their hands, twined parcels wrapped in butcher's paper cradled silently in their palms. The cane of an older gentleman has been lifted from the sidewalk and hangs forgotten, suspended somewhere out beside him, like the reality he has apparently just stepped out of.

While they are standing shoulder to shoulder, they're also harbouring their distance, not touching one another. Islands cordoned off in private despair; an archipelago of slender volcanoes, emitting shock and grief.

They are dressed for the cold. A stonework building spans the background, snow gathered in muffled rows and arrangements on the horizontal ledges and mouldings. Spilling from a dark recess, a sinewy icicle stretches out for the ground, its translucence frail.

In the centre of the photograph, between the tweed shoulders of two men in the mid-ground, a woman with bobbed though full-bodied hair is spinning to turn round, her curls unfocused, a mud-smoked smear. One can feel the urgency in her twist and step; her need to turn away — from whatever the scene is — and disappear.

21

Claire felt her charismatic momentum picking up, ploughing forward, and in many ways like it never had before. Toeing the line at the Kit-Kat Cabaret, she learned to keep her mouth shut and the jaws of her audience open, calls for encores to her acts becoming an almost nightly occurrence. She felt physically fitter than she had in years, working herself into a streaming sweat at every practice, pouring herself into new projects and choreography with an obsessive commitment reminiscent of her youth.

What was driving her, however, had changed. Claire had always known that genius wasn't born out of a gift or education or genetics. It was born, simply, out of love. When a person loved one thing and one thing only, they could give themselves to it, surrender themselves entirely, sacrifice blindly. Genius, as it turned out, wasn't a cause but an effect. It was something that followed almost naturally in the wake of the truest kind of love. What had shifted in Claire wasn't the intensity and conviction of that love, but what it was pinned to. For Claire it was no longer just about seamless movement, about physically channelling the music that was quivering in her bones; no longer, really, about great dance. It was about greatness itself. Claire was falling exclusively in love with the *idea* of success on a grand scale. And she was sure that genius would follow her there.

It was around this time that Claire began frequenting the Terminal Club. It was no secret that the entertainment scene, even the film industry — with the new "talkies" synchronizing a track of sound and music with the moving pictures for the first time — was incorporating more and more black entertainers into its mix. It was the future, and everyone knew it. Black jazz was all the rage, Harlem dancers the ticket act for every venue, the "Black Bottom Stomp" taking over from the Charleston. Even the Kit-Kat hired black musicians and entertainers, though it continued to insist on a Caucasian-only audience (ads in the newspapers specifying that, while the artists in their acts and revues might be coloured, the club itself "welcomes white patrons only").

The Terminal, located right across from Windsor Station, was the heart of Montreal's black community, where the bellhops, ushers, and porters of the city, who were almost exclusively black, gathered after their work shifts on the trains and at the downtown hotels at the end of the day. It was more of a joint than a club, with its minimum of trimmings, bare floors, pot-bellied stove, and lack of bathroom facilities. People had to head out into the alleyway during intermissions, where men stood in a line and urinated against brick walls, women in showy dresses and hats heading off in groups to squat behind refuse bins. Yet in spite of all this, it had become *the* after-hours locale, the place where talented musicians came to jam following their last act and the clientele could continue to party long after every uptown club had shut down for the night. It was a joint known for welcoming any colour that happened to love music, dance, and revelry.

It was there that Claire almost always found someone to dance with who, if they didn't end up teaching her a new step or two, could at least inspire with their impeccable rhythm and fluid feel for the new jazz, which was continuously replacing the old. Often they were women, Harlem dancers themselves, beautiful, flawless-figured performers in a rare moment off-stage, though still showing scandalous amounts of their bodies — sandals, bare arms and legs, their skin covered at times, it seemed, by mere patches of sequins and tassels, blurs of blue, red, and silver that accentuated their swings, slides, shuffles, and sways. Claire danced in their midst, and a group of three or four of them would quickly become a spectacle, everyone stepping back from them to ogle and clap.

While she was enjoying herself more than ever before, Claire's circle of acquaintants, and even her flirtations and trysts, were far too low on the societal ladder to be influential connections, to be the decision-making people who guarded the cloudy heights of the industry. As winter turned into spring, and her twenty-sixth birthday (that grave milepost of defeat) crept ever closer along the blocks of her calendar, it occurred to her for the first time that, if she could just obtain a substantial sum of money, actually have a wad of cash in hand, she could simply bribe her way to those powerful people, stra-tegically sliding bills into sleeves until she created her own break. And the more she thought about it, the more she realized that not only had this approach worked for her before, but it was the one thing that every powerful person she'd ever been around was sure to do on a daily, even hourly, basis. It was the way that other world worked. Money was the language they spoke.

She had done all she could do in terms of practice, skill, and perseverance; she was as prepared as she ever would be. Claire felt more capricious, more daring, and bolder than ever before. She was also *more* than ready to do things others might consider ethically dubious in order to win over this necessary wad of bills, although she didn't know what those things were, or even, for that matter, what they might look like. She hadn't trained her eyes to see opportunities the way a swindler or racketeer might. It stood to reason that there were, very possibly, opportunities all around her. Her ticket to the top might already be within her grasp, lying somewhere in her everyday life, just waiting for her decisive action of plucking it out and running with it.

It was an appealing thought, and one she was ruminating upon while walking to rehearsal on an early Monday afternoon in May, a week before her wretched birthday. It was a sunny day and Claire was walking along St. Catherine Street, and had stopped to inspect a few hats in a window, squinting at the prices on the other side of the glass. The refraction from the window was glaring, and her reflection was almost as distracting as if she were standing in front of a mirror. She checked herself over, and as she did so, she noticed a man with a flat cap and a moustache standing a few paces behind her. He had something small and metal in his hand, and had stopped on the sidewalk for seemingly no other reason than to stare at her back in a kind of stunned disbelief. She turned to him, waiting for politesse and decorum to break the spell. He didn't look away. Instead, he took on a demeanour of even greater shock.

He appeared dazed and shaken. Odd bird, thought Claire, then turned and continued along the street.

She looked back twice on her way to the Kit-Kat, and saw that he was following her, distantly, in a painfully unconvincing attempt to be furtive. When she glanced back, she caught him both times making adjustments to the tiny metal contraption he was carrying, just before he quickly held it up in front of his face for a brief instant. Claire reasoned that he must be taking photographs of her, a random woman walking down the sidewalk, which struck her as even more peculiar.

She arrived at the club, checked over her shoulder to see if he was still there (he was), and stepped inside. She walked straight over to Callum the bartender, intending to alert him so he could keep an eye on the door in case the suspicious character came in. She would hate to look out from the stage during practice and see him there.

But Callum was the first to speak. "Hey, doll, afraid your rehearsal's been postponed a spell."

Claire slumped her shoulders. "Why?"

Callum was slicing limes with a tiny knife on a thick wooden cutting board. "One of your fellow recitalists is presently indisposed, and will be for quite some time, I suspect. Her eminent furnisher's dropped by again."

It was not always easy for Claire to understand what Callum was saying. English was one thing, but his was something else entirely. Claire was too proud to make him explain and headed towards the back to change, where, apparently, she would find out for herself what was going on.

She heard the radio before anything else, a sleepy ballad by a big band. It was louder than it should have been, but as Claire got closer to the blaring doorway, blocked by a partitioned Chinese screen, she heard the illicit grunts and moans that the volume was intended to censor. She stopped in front of the doorway, unseen in the dark corridor, and stared in with a complete lack of discretion. It was the same Westmount councillor, atop the same dancer, the youngest and most attractive at the Kit-Kat. Again. In fact, this was the fourth time Claire had stood in that very same place, lingering for a moment in the murky hallway, peeking through the hinged slats of the screen with a feeling that was a mix of distaste, excitement, and contempt. Only on this day she experienced much, much more. She had an epiphany.

Suddenly breathless, she could barely keep herself from sprinting as she hurried back down the hallway, past Callum at the bar, out the front doors, and into the bright afternoon. She stood on the sidewalk and pivoted round, surveying the streetscape, searching for the strange man with the camera. She soon caught sight of him across the lane, standing in front of a shop as if he was waiting there for her to come out again. He was facing the club, and as soon as he saw her, he began to snap pictures again, his lens pointed in her direction.

Claire fixed herself in the centre of his viewfinder, along his line of sight, and stepped to the edge of the sidewalk, waiting for a horse-drawn cab to pass from the right and a motor car from the left. When she approached him, his camera was still in front of his face, obscuring it, while he repeatedly released the shutter, his blind fingers turning a dial to advance the film. She felt like a celebrity, her every motion hungrily captured by a camera.

As she stopped in front of him, he snapped a final shot then hesitated, as if he was scared to lower the contraption from his eye. Finally he did, slowly, and offered her an unsure smile.

Claire considered his moustache, the olive colour of his skin. "Do you speak French?" she asked in patois.

He nodded, looked down at his camera as if in shame, and delicately adjusted one of its dials.

Claire grinned, looked up and down the street. Then she leaned in close to him. "You and I, we need to talk."

(THREE)
SERAFIM AND CLAIRE

Adorado Serafim,

I must confess my complete astonishment at the inquiry in your last letter, of Inês Barbosa and the state of her health. Serafim, you are the closest that I have to a brother in this world, so I am confident you will forgive me for suggesting that, after a full two years have passed since her marriage to Gustavo Barbosa, perhaps it is time to banish her from your thoughts and compulsions. I will of course not let you down, and have already sent the requested inquiries, and upon their reply will duly pass on news of her well-being. Though I worry of your overlooking opportunities in Montreal in favour of that which is categorically unattainable elsewhere.

I have been desperately trying to break into the illustrated magazines that are commissioning candid photography, and have met with some, but mostly limited, success. It's often said at the Café du Dôme *that in photography right now it isn't enough to be a genius, you also have to be Hungarian. And it's true. All the names making headway in avant-garde photography are from Hungary: Stefan Lorant, László Moholy-Nagy, Kertész, Aigner, Brassaï. This doesn't leave much room for the rest of us, having to fit ourselves into our chosen medium's minuscule niche.*

This doesn't mean I'm not content. I have more than enough work on my hands, and plenty of time for private pursuits as well. Perhaps it is worthwhile to remind oneself that, no matter how devoted one is, there are some obstacles that one will never be able to surmount.

Os meus sinceros cumprimentos,

Álvaro

22

As the winter tarried, Serafim became accustomed to waking in the morning to find a cold cup of tea on his table, waiting for him in front of his usual seat. It didn't happen often (once every two months at most) and he was gradually becoming less alarmed by the phenomenon. He was no longer scared to be in the darkroom the following day, shivers climbing his back as he watched photographic paper in the pan of developer, portrait faces emerging like sceptres from a fog bank. He rounded the corner to his kitchen every morning, paused at the threshold, and sometimes even felt a pang of regret when he was greeted by an empty table. When he did see a cup of tea there, he would find himself carefully inspecting every artifact in the room with scientific scrutiny, as if looking for clues; though he didn't want so much to solve the mystery as simply to verify that he already held the solution.

He wanted to tell Antonino about the tea, but he was sure he wouldn't believe him. Besides, Antonino had his own issues to deal with. The Italian community was so industriously dedicated to silencing his anti-fascist views that they'd managed to wheedle and pull their strings all the way to the Canadian immigration office, which had put Antonino under investigation for staying in the country on a student visa while having apparently ceased his studies altogether. At the same time, Antonino had just managed to convince an attractive young woman he'd known in his native Sicilian city to marry him and join him in the hinterlands. He had barely scraped together the funds for her steamship ticket (Serafim was proud to be able to reciprocate the favour and lend him some money to do so), and she would be setting sail in a few months. He'd lied through his teeth about the weather.

Considering Antonino's plight — as well as that of Álvaro, who, like Serafim, hadn't exactly met with great success while following his passion — Serafim decided to ask Antonino's opinion on what he thought God wanted from people. (This was his way of touching on the topic of the ethereal, of the hereafter and providence.)

As they were sitting on the stoop sipping beer, Serafim finished his glass and placed it gently on the concrete between them. "Antonino, I wonder what you think of God's plans. When I hear of your visa story, of these powerful influences pitting themselves against you — and against anyone who marches out of line — at times it makes me wonder if God is taming us, if He would rather we be docile, like sheep. Maybe He flogs the ones who are more wild or inspired than the others, in the same way man does with a horse, who, after it's broken, is left without a will, surrendering his resolve and spirit entirely to his master. Isn't it possible that that is what God is trying to do with us, what He wants of us?"

Antonino squinted. "For starters, I don't believe in God. Instead, I think it is the complexity of the world, of man, that unthinkingly forces us, not in the direction of submission, but of modesty. All deities aside, the way people act on their own is more than enough to drive us towards humility. Couldn't one also see these endless defeats from the opposite side, as events that actually serve us? What if chaos is constantly pushing us into corners that somehow result in our betterment, oblige us to demonstrate the stuff we are made of? However, if you really must think of it as God, then why not take comfort in the fact that the Messiah, the saints, martyrs, they were all, every one of them, eccentrics, fanatics, revolutionaries. All of them were, as you say, marching out of line. Yet they were all eventually rewarded for it."

"Yes, but the reward was unknown, and usually followed a torturous death."

Antonino scratched his neck. "That is true." He repositioned his legs. "Your glass is empty. I'll pull you some more beer from the barrel."

Serafim handed him his glass, dried froth cobwebbing the rim. "Please."

That September, something happened that frightened Serafim no end. He received a letter from Álvaro stating that he'd heard back from his acquaintances in Oporto, and it was his duty to report that Inês was in perfect health, still married (to all appearances happily) to Gustavo Barbosa, who was still one of the most talented brokers at the Oporto stock exchange. What was more, they now had an infant, a son named Salvador, an apparently beautiful and animated baby.

Serafim was beside himself. None of this, nothing at all, added up. To make things even stranger, the day after he received the news, he woke up in the morning to find a cup of frigid tea on his tabletop. It crossed his mind to smash it in the sink. But in the end he didn't, washing it instead, the way he always did, tenderly, cradling it in the basin, a deliberate hand scooping soapy water over its surface as if it were the skin of some wide-mouthed and brittle-boned creature who, if dropped, would shatter with surprise at such a breach of trust.

Soon after, the autumn trees ignited with colours. The wind blew them out, doused them in the storm drains. And winter, Serafim's third, set in. Once every few moons, tea-pots continued to brew themselves in the dark of his kitchen. While about as often, Serafim would venture out on late night escapades to the Red Light district. He was once again caught in a police raid, but this time the prostitute he was with sug-gested he find the highest-ranking officer who was rounding everyone up and slip a handsome bill into his fingers, "in hopes of coming to some kind of understanding," and hence spare himself the ordeal and humiliation of having to go down-town, forge his name, and pay his coffer-filling bail furnishing. He was nervous when he was actually bribing the man, but was instantly released from custody, a shooing hand sending him on his merry way quicker than you could utter the word "crooked." On his way back to his apartment, Serafim smoked a thoughtful cigarette, his eyes perusing the deserted streets. He was astounded at how easy it had been, and by how unbur-dened he felt by that fact, less accountable, less confined. He stopped in front of his apartment before making his way up the icy staircase to his door, giving a mean flick to his cigarette butt, ignoring its bounce on a crusted ridge of snow.

A few months later, on a bright spring day, Serafim was walking along St. Catherine Street to a distributor to order some darkroom chemicals. He was thinking of nothing in particular when, out of nowhere, stepping from the sleepy fog, she was suddenly there, in the flesh, in front of him, and heading straight his way.

It was the woman who bore an uncanny likeness to Inês. She was dressed as a trendy flapper, with red lipstick, eyes lined with kohl, a loose mint green dress cut just below the knee, and a matching coat and cloche hat. Almost as soon as he spotted her, she stopped at a window to look at some hats on display. Serafim stopped on the sidewalk, peered round in disbelief, and began to approach her. He stood behind her, having unconsciously taken his Leica out of his pocket, hoping, reflexively, to snap a picture, to prove to himself that he wasn't just imagining her.

Then, as if sensing that he was standing there, she turned and looked directly at him, as though she was waiting for him to speak. Serafim, however, could not breathe, much less talk. Eventually she turned and continued on her way down the bustling sidewalk, passing between shoppers and businessmen. Serafim followed, determined not to lose sight of her. It occurred to him that he hadn't actually taken her picture when he was standing behind her, that he'd been too flustered when she'd turned round to face him. He adjusted his settings, guessed at her distance for focus, and managed to snap two shots of her looking back at him before she turned down Stanley Street and disappeared into an uptown cabaret.

Serafim, not having the courage to follow her inside, stationed himself on the opposite side of the street, intending to wait there until she came out again. Minutes later she did, and fixed her gaze on Serafim's presence on the opposite sidewalk.

She allowed some traffic to pass, then strode directly towards him.

Serafim was petrified, and hid behind his camera, snapping exposures, noting her likeness to Inês as she walked — the bone structure of her cheeks, her dark eyes, though her calves were more shapely than he would have imagined Inês's to be, more athletic. She appeared just as self-confident, perhaps even more so, and was relishing the attention of his lens. He took pictures until she was standing right in front of him, her body taking up more than the viewfinder could contain. He kept the camera held up in front of his face for one uncomfortable moment longer before reluctantly lowering it. He took off his hat, inspected his shoes.

After a quick exchange to elicit that he spoke French, they agreed to meet later that evening, to discuss, she insisted, something very important. She pointed out a pub close by, a tavern on the corner, and mentioned the time she would be there, adding that she hoped he wasn't the type to show up hours late with paltry excuses. Serafim shook his head no, nothing of the sort, eager to please, and with that, she returned into the dark of the cabaret that she'd emerged from.

Serafim was at the pub half an hour early, nervously nursing a pint of lager and watching the Monday evening flurry pass by on the other side of the window. Bootblacks, newsies, and organ grinders were the only points of stillness along St. Catherine Street, like river stones around which a froth of bodies streamed and eddied.

She entered the bar and walked up to his table. He hurriedly stood to greet her, though once on his feet he was speechless again. A clunking tram ratcheted past. She introduced herself.

Claire Audette, a lovely name, thought Serafim. And in one graceful movement she kissed her hellos, called to the server to order a Coca-Cola, and sat on her wooden chair as if it were a pillow of down.

What shocked Serafim the most about their ensuing conversation was that she wanted, almost exclusively, to know about him: where he was from, why he'd decided to immigrate, his passions, his beliefs, his hardships. He found himself telling her the truth, albeit a highly selective version of it. He noticed that she seemed particularly interested — straightening up in her chair, cheeks and eyes lighting up — in his *lack* of success with candid photography, asking him if he'd given up on it yet, if he was ready to admit defeat. He wasn't, he assured her, asserting that the industry would come round at some point, as a simple matter of course, and until then he had his own private darkroom where he continued his work in peace, away from critical guffaws and disparaging eyes.

Claire suddenly clapped her hands over her cola glass. "Your own personal darkroom," she gasped. "Well, now that is something I have to see for myself. So, when is that possible? When can I come over to your place? Tomorrow? The next day? What day would work best for you?"

Serafim was reeling to keep up with how forthcoming she was. "Well, Wednesday," he ventured, as if testing his own voice.

She slammed her hand onto the table. "Wednesday it is, then," she said, suddenly spinning round to the bartender. "Excuse me, sir," she called out, "would you happen to have a pencil and piece of paper? Just need something to scribble an address on is all. Thanks."

As they parted ways, she gave Serafim a tender kiss good-bye on the cheek. Sensing how he was perplexed by, even suspicious of, the ease of her affections, she offered a cursory explanation. "You must think me very forward. But you will see there is a reason. I have something to ask of you, and I don't yet know if I can trust you with it. But I have every intention of finding that out on Wednesday." She pointed at Serafim's address in her hand. "I will drop by around seven, then?"

Serafim managed to keep himself from stammering. "That would be fine, yes."

He watched her stroll away, meld into the streetscape. Another drop in the river.

Before heading off himself, he looked back through the window to see if her soda glass was still there, as if to verify he hadn't just imagined the whole thing. He then quickly took out his Leica, ensuring he had actually used up film taking pictures of her. Serafim, of all people, knew how a remnant drinking vessel could hardly stand as evidence for something real. Photographs, however, could.

Medium: Gelatin silver print
Description: Woman approaching
Location: Montreal, Quebec
Date: May 1929

౿

A young woman is crossing a cobblestone lane; caught in mid-stride, at its centre. She is stylishly dressed, the greyscale variance of her outfit suggesting that her ensemble is well matched and well considered. Her cloche is banded with a thick ribbon, which is darker than the bell of felt beneath it, and is adorned with a burst of delicate feathers in the same shade. The brim of the hat presses the curls of her dark hair tightly against the white of her cheeks.

She is stepping with confidence, an arm swinging naturally out in front of her. Her knee is brushing against the hemline of her dress, the mould of its silhouette creasing into the fabric.

In the mid-ground on the right, the back end of an automobile can be seen, dragging its blur out of the frame. The thin spokes of a spare tire, mounted onto the rear, create lines of elongation; claw itself out beyond the moment.

The woman is looking directly into the lens, her expression one of fortitude. She is wearing a smile that is slight, wry, though also somehow profound, as if it were being conjured from some deeper, darker place. At the instant of the exposure's capture, one can sense that this woman feels, unmistakably, beautiful. And one can sense her purpose woven even into that.

23

Claire rapped playfully on the door. She stood on the landing, surveying the neighbourhood, waiting for Serafim to answer. A cluster of newly returned songbirds huddled in a tree at the same height nearby, watching her silently. Evidence of the monumental moving day that always took place on the first of the month (the newspapers quoted it at fifty-two thousand families this year) could still be seen: a broken chair piled onto the skeleton of an armoire, splinters of wickerwork like spilled matches on the sidewalk.

The cluster of birds didn't fly off as the door flung open. "Mademoiselle Audette. I am very pleased you could make it."

"Call me Claire, please. Hope Serafim's okay for you, too." Claire peered around his body in the doorway. "Say, is that a last year's Philco?" She edged past him and into his apartment, directly over to the deluxe cherrywood radio, ran a hand across its sleek contours, switched it on, adjusted the volume.

"Well, I am not sure how new the model is. My employer gave it to me at Christmas, as a bonus. He had just bought a new one, and so I guess had no use for the old one."

Claire was listening more to the music than to what he was saying. She pointed at the speaker. "The Jack Denny Orchestra. Definitely. Sounds like a remote. On a Wednesday night, no less! Probably isn't being broadcast from the Normandie Roof."

Serafim gave a slow grimace, confused.

"Like on Saturdays," she clarified.

He nodded tentatively. "Of course."

"So! What does a girl have to do to get a drink in this place?"

Serafim faltered, appearing to give the question some serious deliberation. What *did* a girl have to do in order to get a drink in his place?

"A drink," she repeated. "Aren't you going to offer me a drink?"

He suddenly paled, mortified. "Oh. I . . . don't have any alcohol, I'm afraid . . . in the house. Right now."

Claire let him off with an easy laugh, removing her hat, shaking out her bob. "Well, I guess you'll just have to go and get some, then." She sat down in an armchair, crossed her legs. "What do you usually drink?"

"Uhm, normally beer, from the barrel, with a friend. Sometimes cognac. There is an *épicerie* on the corner where I can refill my bottles in the back. Bottles of cognac and molasses, I mean."

"I know. So it's settled, then. I'll wait here." She looked around the room. "Oh! Why don't you show me your darkroom before you go."

Serafim took a moment to steady his posture, drew in a deep breath. "Yes. I have prepared it for your arrival. I will ask you not to touch anything inside it. Please."

Claire gave a dismissive wave of her hand. "Of course, of course. So where is it?"

"Here." He pointed at a closet door. "I have also set some photographs aside, of mine, for you to look at. If you would like."

"I really just want to see the darkroom." Claire stood and opened the door that he'd pointed at. Serafim stepped into the dark behind her to plug in an orange lamp. "So," Claire ventured, "if I understand, you can take a picture anywhere, bring it here, and put it on a piece of paper, without anyone else ever seeing that picture throughout the process?"

He thought about the weightlessness of this question with considerable gravity. "Yes. That's correct." Serafim unplugged the light, escorted her out of the room, and closed the door. "I . . . should go and refill that cognac bottle. Please, excuse me."

While he was gone, Claire wandered through his apartment, moving her body to the song on the radio. His apartment, she noted, was clean, tiny, arranged with modest furnishings; the only thing modern or of value was the Philco in his sitting room. She returned there, to wait on his outmoded sofa, in front of which was a small coffee table with a photo album placed evenly at its centre. She leafed through it, distractedly tapping her foot.

What she found in its pages surprised her. She'd never seen photographs like these before. He clearly had an eye for choosing moments and creating compositions whose movements continued on, the life of his subjects still breathing. Claire closed the album, sat back on the sofa, and contemplated his poverty, his defeat, his just-out-of-reach aspirations, even his talent. This man, Serafim Vieira, was going to suit her ends like a tailor.

Serafim soon returned with the cognac and they drank into the night, laughter flitting through the room. Serafim lit a paraffin lamp, and Claire danced to the radio alone, swaying over the hardwood floor. He watched her, his tie loosened, collar button undone, with a stupor grin and his eyelids half closed. When Claire finished, she sat down next to him on the sofa, seductively close, and topped up both their cognacs. She smiled. Suddenly feeling guarded, Serafim wanted to know once and for all what her visit was all about, what she'd wanted to ask of him, what she wanted him to do.

Claire eyed the photo album he'd set out for her to see. "Well," she began, "sometimes people are born with a gift, a talent. They are designed to do something great. They have all the skill, determination, commitment — but something stands in their way. Something is blocking their path to greatness. Now, what they need is a little luck, but it isn't there, it doesn't come. This is the point where most people would give up, or wait for whatever that obstacle is to move. But what if there was another option? What if there was a way to jump over it? What if there was a way to help providence along, a way to create our own luck? Would that..." Claire reached a soft hand along the back of the sofa to touch Serafim's shoulder. "Tell me, would that interest you?"

Serafim nodded deeply. "You cannot know how much that would interest me."

"Good. Okay. Now. You know how corrupt the politicians are in this city. You know that they spend most of their time stealing, paying off the police, investing in the bootlegging over the border, all while employing people like us for pennies. And you know that, if they were made to hand over just a bit of their money, it would be a significant sum to us and an insignificant sum to them. Like the misplacement of one of their many fur coats. While for you and I, with but a trickle of their funds, just imagine the people we could convince to give us a break. It just so happens that I have an incredibly simple way to get at those funds. But I need your help. I need a photographer. That is what I want of you. Would you like to hear more?"

Serafim did. He wanted to hear it all. Down to the finest detail. When Claire had finished, Serafim gave her a look that suggested he had been waiting for someone like her to come along for a long, long while.

Claire shuffled closer. "I knew I would be able to trust you." She kissed him, slowly at first, but their breathing soon grew urgent and could be heard above the radio static. Buttons were unfastened, vests, shirts, dress removed. But before Claire took off her chemise, self-conscious of her scar, she blew out the lamp and led him to the bedroom. The sex was insistent, impatient, and afterwards he fell asleep on top of her, still inside, and only rolled off when she shifted his weight.

Claire had little rest. Serafim was a fretful sleeper, turning endlessly, stretching, plying his hands, muttering in Portuguese. Exhausted, she thought of leaving his apartment at one point, but in the end succeeded in calming him into stillness by lightly stroking the back of his neck for half an hour. There was something boyish about him, she thought. He was like a very serious child.

The twin bells of his alarm clock rang early — an untimely, unwelcome surprise. Claire rolled from the bed to find her chemise before he could see her. She put it on as he moaned, holding his head, hungover.

But the moment she'd left his bedroom, he called out at her in an assertive, almost angry tone. "Stop! Wait, please. I have to check the kitchen." He hustled out of bed, threw some pants on, and craned his neck through the kitchen door, presumably, thought Claire, looking for rats. He was outwardly relieved to find nothing there.

Claire put on the rest of her clothes and headed for the front door. "I think we should go out on Friday to discuss the specifics."

"Okay."

"Meet me at that same tavern, then, at seven again."

"Okay."

Claire put on her shoes, opened the door to leave.

"Wait," said Serafim. "I was wondering, do you . . . do you secretly love cooking?"

Claire snickered. "I secretly hate it. More than anything. See you Friday." She swung the door shut behind her, somewhat harder than she'd meant to, thinking already about which tramline would work best to get her home.

Querido Serafim,

I hope this letter finds you well. I wanted to let you know that, as per my inquiries into the health of Inês Barbosa, I have received replies from my acquaintances in Oporto. She is, apparently, in superb health, still joyfully wed, and has recently given birth to a boy, Salvador Sá Barbosa, by all accounts a robust and energetic child. I do trust that this news will aid you in putting your unhealthy quandaries, and her memory, to rest.

I have some wonderful news to share with you. I've begun selling photographs, more or less regularly, to a newspaper here in Paris. The pictures that interest them are nothing like the ones in the illustrated magazines, but at least they are, finally, running photos to supplement some of their news stories. Of course, they require most of the shots to be posed, but they do ask that the subjects be situated in the context of the adjoining article. This is doubtless new ground, which, as you can imagine, has me engaged in current events much more than before.

In this same vein, I read your letters and see your words becoming more socially aware than I ever remember them being. Why, just in a conversation yesterday, I cited something you wrote about "witnessing" in your last correspondence. It occurs to me that we may be on the same path, again, in more ways than one. Perhaps, my dear friend, following news stories and taking photographs for the journals will come to interest you as well. Even if it is merely a means of moving towards your greater goal. Regardless, the richness in this new thinking of yours seems as good a fortune as any.

As minhas maiores saudações,

Álvaro

24

That Friday, Serafim was early again. He'd imagined that he and Claire would stay for a drink at the tavern, and so had chosen to sit at the same table they'd occupied the day they met, same chair, even ordered the same drink. But when Claire came in, she had no sooner kissed her hellos than she was scanning the establishment and suggesting they leave, right then, take the number eleven tram to the top of the mountain, where they could have a stroll and discuss things without being overheard.

They were quiet throughout the jostling tram ride, sitting shoulder to shoulder, tight-lipped and opposite a sign exclaiming, Do Not Spit on the Floor! Once at the top of the mountain, they sauntered along well-kept paths, Claire's arm hooked through Serafim's, looking much like a serene married couple to passersby, uttering plans for racketeering and extortion instead of endearments.

The details were all ironed out: when the picture was to be taken (the following Tuesday), whether or not there would be enough light to snap it, and how Serafim would both enter and exit the back of the cabaret unnoticed. The more they went over it, the more impressed Serafim was. She had obviously thought everything through. She was clever and thorough. However, while her scheme was admittedly seamless, leaving nothing to chance, he wondered if there was something he wasn't seeing, some razor-thin element that could cause the entire thing to messily unravel. Serafim stole glances at Claire whenever he could, catching her unguarded expressions, trying to work out what she might be thinking, wishing that his memory worked in the same way film did. He still couldn't believe he'd managed to sleep with such an eye-catching woman without being made to pay for it.

They stopped at a viewpoint, looked out over the city and its many squiggles of smoke that rose like snags in a stonework carpet. The Montreal Harbour Bridge would be completed soon, and its two largest spans extended over a void of water, reaching out towards each other above the St. Lawrence River, girdered fingers stretching out to touch, an unseen spark of static threatening to link them.

Once they finished discussing their plans, their words faltered, trailed into blanks, and it seemed it was time to head off in their respective directions, something Serafim wished to postpone as long as possible. Suddenly, Claire suggested they go out on the town to celebrate her birthday.

"Why, I would be delighted," said Serafim. "How old are you, if you would permit me to ask?"

"Twenty-four. Should we go?"

"Sure," he said, stiffly taking her arm again. "You know, we're the same age."

"You don't say. I hope you dance."

"I . . . do not. But I enjoy watching."

"I'm sure you do. In the dance world, we have a word for people like you. Audience." She laughed easily. Serafim tried, but he didn't quite succeed in joining her.

They descended into the city again, starting out the evening in some of the uptown clubs. Claire confessed it had been ages since she'd had a Friday night off; it was one of the two busiest days of her workweek. Their conversation, at first stilted, grew easier as the night progressed and the alcohol flowed. Claire spent most of the night in the centre of the dance floor, while Serafim sat at a table, squishing folds of the tablecloth or taking pictures of couples as they whirled past in front of him. He felt that he was treading a fine line between enjoying himself and feeling unbearably jealous, watching Claire's intimacy and laughter with other men, many of whom moved their feet magically in time to the tunes being played, just like her. Occasionally, as she was dancing, she caught a glimpse of Serafim sitting in the dark of the periphery, and flung a wave and smile out in his direction, only to close her eyes soon after. She closed her eyes often while dancing, he noticed, as if it helped her listen to the music, as if she were dissecting the anatomy of its melodies with her movements.

At closing time, the band announced the last dance, and Serafim wondered if they would return to his place again, like a modern couple living in sin.

They stepped outside and he helped her with her coat, one gentlemanly sleeve at a time. "That was a lovely evening," he said.

Claire buttoned her jacket and flashed him a look of disbelief. "I hope you realize it's just begun. Taxi!" She rushed to a slate-black cab and opened the door, slid along the bench, and

patted the seat beside her. "Quick," she said, lighting a cigarette. Then, to the driver, in English, "Can you take us to the
Terminal, handsome?"

The Terminal Club was an experience Serafim was not
quite prepared for. Hearing black people on the radio was one
thing — or seeing them on record covers, as porters and bellhops, musicians, even as dancers — but having to drink a cocktail right beside them, share the same table, be the minority
among them, was another entirely. Serafim was intimidated
by their darkness, by the volume of their laughter, which he'd
never heard before. He followed Claire into the club, keeping close as they walked deeper into the bare-bulbed electric
light, where sweat, smoke, alcohol, and perfume washed over
them in a raucous wave that almost knocked Serafim back.
The music was more ardent and raw than in the other clubs,
with newly arrived musicians pulling bronze trumpets and sax-
ophones out of cases lined with purple velvet and shouldering
their way closer to the stage. To Serafim, it was bedlam. Claire,
on the other hand, fed on the chaos. She had begun to clap her
hands to the rhythm, fighting to get her coat off and drape it
over the back of a chair before hurrying onto the untreated
wooden floor, her body already creasing to the song.

Serafim ordered a drink and sat stiffly and uneasily in the
only free seat he could find, sipping his whiskey too quickly. A
waiter came by; he ordered another. Just then an older gentleman, his white beard a stark contrast to the shiny cinnamon
of his skin, leaned in towards Serafim to compliment his "fine
lady" and her sense of rhythm. "Yep," he said in English, "a
bona fide Oliver Twist she is, and a real Sheba too. Comes here
often, in fact." Serafim stalled, wondering what his meaning

was exactly, and waited for the old man to expand. He did not. Instead, the man began a long stream of monologues, which Serafim tuned in to and out of as one would a radio for the remainder of the night, listening at first with great anticipation and interest, and later with a kind of distant attention.

The old man got on to the topic of corruption, the Mafia, and the way it was in the city before Tony Frank was hanged in 1924. He leaned heavily across the table, closer to Serafim, to tell him all about Dandy Phil. "See, Dandy had run a nightclub in Montreal until he dreamt up an invention that landed him in a partnership with Costello, in New York City. It cannonballed him straight into the big time. Now Costello is a household name in the States, a man of *real* influence in the Big Apple down there. So the two of 'em team up to make a fortune with Dandy's new invention, see — call 'em one-armed bandits they do — candy-vending machines converted into gambling implements. Drop a nickel in a slot, push a combination for the buttons, and see if a whole load don't shower out at your shins! In the Big Apple it's said you find 'em everywhere — speakeasies, stationery stores, candy shops — and that all told they bring in a hundred thousand clams a day. Of course, with that kind of money, they also have an army of thugs collecting and reclaiming machines that is stolen (where there's money, there's muscle protecting it, and don't you forget!). Hell, I've heard these machines is so big with the tiny tots, those racketeers make little ladders available for to reach 'em!" The man wheezed with laughter, but seeing that Serafim wasn't joining him, he wondered if he'd lost him somewhere along the way. He asked Serafim if he knew what a racketeer was.

Serafim hesitated, looked around the blaring room as if it were quiet. "No, no, I don't know about racketeers. Why do you think I would know about racketeering?"

"Boy," the man wheezed in response, slapping the table and crumpling back into his chair, "you's one balled-up fella!"

As he recovered from his chuckle, Serafim ordered another drink from a passing waiter, and looked out at the dance floor for Claire. He managed to catch a glimpse of her, her head thrown back in laughter, hands gesturing like courting egrets, their motion fluid, a delicate rising and arcing in the air, only to see her disappear again, sinking smoothly into the boiling surf of misted foreheads.

"Now, you wanna hear a story" — the old man was suddenly pointing into Serafim's face — "about corruption, about politicians and Westmount, about the mayor hisself?" Serafim froze at the combination of these words and, as if being robbed at finger-point, sat still and attentive until the white-bearded man had finished.

The man recounted a story about a famous speaker for the Universal Negro Improvement Association who had been invited for a rally in the city only to be jailed and silenced by local politicians. He went on, tallying a long list of other misdeeds and double-dealings doled out incessantly by the monopolist class. He accented the end of each anecdote with a slap on the table and a wheezing laugh, then looked up at Serafim for an indication that he should carry on, implying that he had enough dirt to dish out for hours, there were that many injustices done in the city.

Serafim sipped his whiskey and listened carefully. So these were the people he was going to be taking money from, the obscenely rich and corrupt? It occurred to him that, sure, what he and Claire were setting out to do wasn't righteous by any stretch of the imagination, but for Serafim, with the help of such stories, their plan was slowly becoming somehow justified. It wasn't as if they were stealing from the virtuous or the poor. No, they were stealing from, at best, people who deserved it, and at worst, people who could afford it. It was a notion that Álvaro himself had brought up in a letter he had posted only two months earlier. Everything around Serafim was pointing in this same direction, like long grass in a windstorm.

The old man tapped Serafim's shoulder. "Boy," he said, standing up, "I gotta iron my shoelaces." After a moment of trying to figure out what he meant, it became clear to Serafim that the man was headed to the washroom, and since Serafim had to go himself, he followed. They exited the club and at once came up against a line of men urinating against one of the buildings in the alleyway. Serafim was inebriated enough to take it in stride, unzipping his pants in front of a brick wall and listening to the old man strike up a conversation with someone else.

Serafim stared up through the wires at the night sky. He felt a swimming pang of nostalgia, or, more precisely, of *saudade*, that untranslatable Portuguese concept, a sense of having lost things one might never have won in the first place. His existence in this new country was turning out to be more gritty and foreign than he'd ever imagined. As he looked up into the decidedly un-Portuguese night, this thought pleased him. Somewhere along the way his life had become adventurous, dangerous even.

He went back into the nightclub and found Claire sitting at the table he'd just left. She got up before he reached her, barely able to stop herself from moving. She watched the band from the edge of her seat, her spine arched as if the back of her chair were hot to the touch, jigging her legs to the beat of the song. It was clear to Serafim that all she really wanted in life was to jump to her feet and impel the world into evocative movement. In the same way that all Serafim wanted was to seek out evocative movement in this world and stop it, freeze it forever in a frame. Together, he contemplated, wobbly on his feet, they were going to make a great team.

Medium: Gelatin silver print
Description: Coitus
Location: Montreal, Quebec
Date: May 1929

ↄ

The room is small, confined. Folded backdrops and painted stage sets lean against the wall to one side. A lone sofa is keeping the accordion of these props tightly baffled, one of its arms pushing into the strata of plywood. A low coffee table hovers in front of the settee, an ashtray and radio resting on its surface, making the room into an impromptu lounge area for stage performers. Behind the settee, floral wallpaper blossoms and vines up and out of the frame, an overgrown two-dimensional Eden; while a couple, half unclothed, cover the sofa's cushions in a ravel of their limbs.

The woman — her face turned towards the camera, eyes closed, lipstick smeared, her features plump and girlish — is sprawled beneath the weight of a middle-aged man. Her dress is gathered in folds at her hips, her bare legs protruding from around the man's waist. Her right arm dangles over the coffee table, her lopsided breasts spilling in its direction. The wrist of her left hand is bent above her head and is clenched by the man, his grip squeezing white dents into the buttery texture of her skin, dimples shadowed.

His expression is semi-maniacal, biting down on his lower lip, eyes crazed, as he reaches out to the coffee table to adjust a dial on the radio, likely to conceal the sounds they are making. Obviously, one cannot hear the scratch of music from the speaker; though at the same time — in their expressions, the whisper of restless cloth, in the turn of his fingers — one can.

279

25

"There. A fancy Studebaker is slowing down, near the club. Yes, it's stopped. I think it's him." Claire was speaking quietly into the side of Serafim's face. "Now don't turn around. Keep your hands on my hips. Good. Kiss my neck. No, the other way, I can't see. Relax your legs, you're standing stiff. Try to look like you're enjoying yourself." Claire's back was against a brick wall, from which position, over Serafim's shoulder, she could see the front of the cabaret, down the street from where they stood.

"Okay, the driver has parked in the entrance of the alley-way. The councilman's out, hurrying to the door. He doesn't want to be seen, you can tell. Now he's inside. Okay. Oh — wait. The driver is still there, at the entrance to the alley. I guess he's going to stay. So you will have to access the alleyway down the block instead. Stay clear of his car. Remember the door in the back that I showed you? Wait there. I'll open it when the time is right. And remember: you'll only have a few seconds, so move fast but quiet. I'll meet you at your apartment later tonight. Are you ready?"

"I think so."

"Good. Let's go."

As they parted, Serafim wanted to kiss her goodbye, but she slid away from him, waving over her shoulder, as if they were a long-married couple parting for some errands.

It was Tuesday, and Claire crossed the street on her way to her early afternoon practice. She entered the darkness of the cabaret, walked over to Callum the bartender, who apparently hadn't even begun to think about working for the day, and stood slowly smoking a cigarette, watching the puffs feather and spread through the murky room.

"You all right then, doll?" he asked.

"I am just ducky. And you?"

"Likewise. Though I'm afraid your rehearsal'll be a tad late today. A certain magnate is, uh, gaining admittance again." He winked.

Claire had been expecting this but, as usual, missed the sense of his words. "Well, I will just start getting ready anyway," she said, making her way to the back.

"Hey, am I such a palooka you don't wanna wait here with me? S'that it? Come on. Pour ya a drink-avous."

"No, no. I really have to get ready. Thanks, though."

Callum smiled. "All right, all right, go on." He waved her off. "Who knows, 'f I'm feelin' real nice, might just bring you a jorum of skee for to sip back there." He winked again. "All by your lonesome."

Claire smiled coyly, not knowing how else to dissuade him, and continued on her way to the rooms in the back. She could see the light through the cracks, hear the radio and the young dancer, her easy giggles and flirtatious small talk, their clothes already coming off. She paused at the doorway, the unfolded

Chinese screen spread across it, and waited for them to become distracted by their foreplay before she risked passing through the hall, potentially giving away that someone was there.

She heard Callum get up from where he was sitting, and then the clink of glasses. She watched down the corridor, readying herself for the possibility that he might appear. He didn't.

As the laughter in the room increased and their breathing became heavier, she felt safe enough to tiptoe past. She made her way to the powder room farther down the corridor and eased the door open, wanting to make sure no one was inside.

"Hey, honey," a fellow dancer called out to her. She was conversing with Claire's reflection in the mirror in front of her. "Did you think I had a sugar daddy in here like the other one? Is that why you opened the door like a criminal?"

"No, I just was . . ." Claire pointed over her shoulder.

"So, looks like we'll be stalling a few minutes once more. Not counting how long Isabelle's usually late on top of that. Why don't you come have a seat, keep me company."

"No. I . . . have to talk to Callum about something."

"Suit yourself." She began to rummage through her cosmetics bag. Claire edged the door shut again.

She then made her way to the back door to unlock it as quietly as she could, which would take some time. It was a heavy metal door, with clanking bolts and hinges that whined and complained when touched. She wrestled the rusted bolts out of their sleeves, carefully freeing the plates, levers, and slots. She nudged it open to look outside and saw Serafim waiting against the opposite wall, looking guilty, holding his hat, squishing it nervously. For some reason Claire liked this little habit of his. She found it endearing in some way.

Leaving the door ajar, she crept back down the corridor to make sure Callum was still at the bar in the front and the dancer still in the powder room. The coast was clear. And by the sounds of it, the councilman and the young dancer were, if not already in the act, very close to it. She returned to the back door, pressed it open, and gestured to Serafim to come in.

Together they stole down the hall, Serafim readying his camera. They stopped just before the Chinese screen, crouching low, and Claire pointed to the spot where Serafim could achieve the best vantage point. Serafim, all business now, peeked through the gap, adjusted the distance settings on his camera, and held the lens up to the slat of light that pin-striped his face and torso in the dark of the corridor, ready to take the shot.

Which was when Callum appeared in the hallway, a grenadine-sweetened cocktail in a vodka glass pinched in his right hand.

Claire jumped to her feet in a flurry, silent as snowflakes, and hurried towards him, careful to keep her body between Callum's line of sight and Serafim, who was still squatting in the hall behind her.

"You are so sweet!" she said, stopping in front of Callum, his progress stalled. She scooped the drink out of his hand and took an audible swig. "Mmm. Thank you. Thank-you-thank-you. Thank. You."

Callum looked her over, perplexed.

"So good. So, so good. Really. Thank you." Claire suddenly pointed at the front window. "Wow, how ugly is that dress?"

Callum turned and she hooked her arm into his, leading him back towards the bar. "So. Can I tell you a secret?"

Callum didn't answer, just continued to observe her carefully, eyeing both her expression and the way her hand was stroking his arm.

"You just caught me. I confess — I was watching them. I have watched them before, too. I think it is ... erotic."

Having arrived at the bar, Callum took his place behind it, smiled, straightening his collar. "Oh, yeah? You ... you like to watch, you say?"

"Yes, I do. Now" — she took a long drink of her cocktail, placed it with conviction on the bar — "would you mind if I ... kept watching? You will not tell, I hope."

"No!" he insisted immediately. "No. Me? Hell no. Go on. Enjoy yourself." He winked at her for the third time that day.

Claire smiled, and in mock mischief tiptoed back towards the corridor.

As she neared Serafim, she was glad to see he hadn't stopped taking pictures. He might already have what they came for, she thought. He was busy snapping exposures, tilting the camera at different angles against the gap in the screen and making incremental adjustments to his settings. Someone on the other side of the screen turned up the radio, their groans and sighs swelling with the volume.

Then, just above the music, Claire heard the rusted wail of the back door opening, as a fan of daylight spread across the end of the hallway. She and Serafim exchanged a panicked glance, and Claire headed towards the back door, mouthing blasphemies through every shade of vulgarity.

The other dancer stood in the daylight, looking up at the clear sky. She noticed Claire behind her. "Hey, sweetie, someone left this open. You know some rummy out in the back could walk right on in here?"

"Really?" Claire paused, feigning shock. "My . . . God." She looked through the doorway. A tin garbage can on the other side of the alley, lying on its side, stared emptily back. "It must . . . I mean, maybe it has to do with, you know, what is going on in there."

"Oh." The other dancer considered this. "Maybe."

"But you know" — Claire pointed at her — "you know, I thought I just saw somebody in the backrooms who didn't belong. I mean, maybe some rummy *did* get in." She turned and scurried back into the dark, over to the Chinese screen. The councilman on the other side gave a climactic grunt and shudder, while Claire lifted Serafim by the arm and pushed him forward, towards the light of the back door, where the other dancer still held it open. At first Serafim resisted, but he soon surrendered to Claire's impulse, plodding along in the hope that she knew what she was doing.

"Now beat it! Filthy drunkard! Pervert!" She pushed Serafim out into the bright alleyway and fumbled to close the door behind him, as if he might try to dash back inside. The clang of metal, schlock of bolts sliding back into their sleeves.

In the sudden darkness, Claire felt her way to the powder room and opened the door, offering herself and the other dancer both light and safety. "I'm glad *that*'s over," she said.

"Yeah," her companion agreed, though she was still hesitantly working things out. "Did that guy . . . did he have a camera?"

"No . . . I don't think so. But I wanted to ask you, do you have any mascara I can use? I forgot mine at home, and I could really use some." Claire opened the door farther, an invitation for the other dancer to enter, move on, and forget what she might've just seen.

The dancer's posture relaxed, as if physically letting the incident slough off her shoulders, no longer her concern. "Yeah, of course, in my bag," she said, on her way to her seat in front of the mirror. Claire closed the door, sealing them both inside.

Later that evening, she rushed to Serafim's apartment and — too impatient to knock —barged in to find him smoking on his sofa. "And?" she asked him, glad to be speaking French again. "How did they turn out?"

He gave her a stern look.

"Now, don't tell me they didn't work. I thought you told me you were a professional."

"No, that's not it. It's the way you pushed me out, like you were going to call the police. Why did you do that? That woman saw me and my camera."

Claire laughed. "It was to save us! Pretending you were just a drunk who stumbled in through the back door was the best way of getting you out of there, with the photos and everything intact. Now you're just a drunkard in their minds, who was stumbling around in a place you weren't welcome. It happens all the time. No one suspects a thing. Promise."

Serafim thought this over, looking at his cigarette. "Well. Okay. The pictures are there." He gestured to a large envelope near the radio.

Claire rushed over and slid the photos out. Gasping, she spun round. "These are perfect! Perfect." She stared into the dreamy centre of the room. "By next weekend, we'll be rich."

"I hope you're right."

"I am. Nothing can go wrong now." She slipped off her shoes, removed her jacket and shawl, and dragged it suggestively across the back of her neck. "The hardest part is behind us," she said, already making her way towards him. "You'll see."

Paris, França; 7 de março de 1929

Estimado Serafim,

Thank you for sending me those last photos. I really enjoy the body language of the prostitutes and how readily they lend themselves to interpretation. The pictures got me thinking of a conversation I had the other week, about Lucien Aigner.

I'm not sure if you've heard of him yet, but he's well known here, primarily for his stunts. He carries a camera in his pocket (he swears by the same model you do, in fact), and once he's in the private settings of the notable, politicians and high society, he shoots them on the sly. "Caricatures, grimaces, the unaware moment, the pratfall, showing the mighty made human; in pyjamas if possible," he said in an interview. The resulting photo essays printed in Vu and some of the German picture magazines have damaged more than a few reputations.

This sparked the discussion I had. It comes so easy for us to take pictures of prostitutes, urchins, street people, because, I think, it costs them little to be photographed. They are already stripped down to a fundamental state, and as I've seen with the models I photograph, the simple act of having to stand nude tends to make one unashamed of one's form. This has me wondering, then, if we should not be concentrating more on the rich, on those whose baring of their true selves, whose being caught and seen as manifestly human, costs them so much more. They can, after all, afford it. If empathy is the end goal, shouldn't we actually be seeking not only moments of majesty in those whom, like prostitutes, society has torn down, but the moments of frailty in those whom society props up?

Abraços,
Álvaro

26

Serafim was feeling light, having just finished work for the day, and was walking through the streets of Antonino's neighbourhood, his eyes floating from one side of the lane to the other. It was a week after he and Claire had taken what was sure to become the most lucrative photograph Serafim had ever developed, and what was more, he had woken up that morning, again, with Claire sharing his mattress, and not a hint of steeped tea waiting for him on the table. Birds were returning in greater numbers. Tulips, teetering on their thin stalks, were blooming in gold and crimson. And the fateful letter to the councilman was ready to be sent to his office with an offer to exchange the incriminating film for money (all four thousand dollars of it) this coming Friday at noon.

He and Claire had agreed to continue in their routines and habits as if everything were completely normal, so that nothing might be seen as suspicious if ever looked back upon by those around them. Serafim was about to pay Antonino an unannounced visit, as he did at least once a week, though more often twice. Beneath his moustache, he was smiling as he approached Antonino's apartment. Then he became aware of sounds that were somehow wrong — scuffles, grumbles, the severity of grown men tussling. Now came the sound of Antonino's stomach being punched, his voice coughing out a winded rasp.

Serafim broke into a jog, holding his hat down on his head, and rounded the corner of a long row of townhouses, a carriage driveway leading to a courtyard stable. Three stout men were at its centre, surrounding Antonino, two of them holding his hands back, the other throwing hooks and jabs into his stomach. Serafim stopped, paralyzed. He was no fighter, and even if he had been, there were three of them, every one of them husky.

The one who was throwing the punches stopped to catch his breath. Hunched over, he spoke in Italian, taunting Antonino, who replied in a scratchy whisper. The man then reached into his pocket, unfolded a jackknife, and held it up in front of Antonino's face.

Serafim looked round, trying to think of a way to help his friend, and quickly realized he could do something that he'd learned to do just a week ago. He sprinted back the way he'd come, ran into the alley, and searched for the gated entrance he'd seen through the courtyard, which accessed the stable from the rear. Finding it, he rushed up to its tall bars, through which he could see the men still holding Antonino. The knife was being waved in front of his face. Seeing that the gate was chained shut, Serafim took out his camera, stuck it between the bars, took a quick shot, then yelled, "Hey!" He snapped another photo, then another. When the men realized what he was doing, they let go of Antonino and raced towards him. Serafim took yet another picture, keeping his face hidden behind the camera.

The men's bodies clanged against the gate, expecting it to swing open. Fortunately for Serafim, the chain held. They were incensed, pounding the metal, commanding him to stop taking their pictures, one of them shielding his face as if from a bright light. Serafim backed away, continuing to snap photos, and advanced the film without dropping the viewfinder from his eye. The men reached their arms through to grab at him, spat, threatened, cursed, until they were so enraged they spun on their heels and set out in the opposite direction, to catch him in the alley. He watched as they jumped over Antonino, who was now lying prostrate on the ground. Two of the men swept to the right of the driveway and another to the left. They were coming for him from both sides.

As Serafim was trapped, there was no time to make sure Antonino was all right. Thinking creatively, he pocketed his camera and jumped a fence into a tiny backyard where he heard children playing, assuming that the back door there would be unlocked. It was, and Serafim galloped through a stranger's kitchen and living room, coarse shouts following him. He left the front door open as he leapt over a few stairs to a gate, unlatched it, and kept running, this time up the street.

He continued for several blocks then doubled back, increasingly confident he'd lost them. He finally stepped into an *épicerie*, where he pretended to peruse the shelves, watching the shop's window for his pursuers, his pulse thumping in his throat. After a few minutes he asked to use the proprietor's phone in the back, so he could finally check on Antonino.

It turned out he was fine and had locked himself in his house, though he doubted the men would return. He added that Serafim should wait until dark to drop by (using the back entrance) so they could talk things over. Serafim agreed and, waiting out the sinking sun, found a shabby café where he sipped watered-down coffee for several hours, and continually checked over his shoulders while trying to read a newspaper. He set off for Antonino's apartment just after dusk, faces and shapes in the street coveting their details in velveteen blurs.

Serafim found Antonino alone at his table with a bottle of gin, the house quiet except for the creaks of wood shifting in the ceiling from the flat above. He shook Antonino's hand and, insisting the poor man stay seated, found himself a glass in one of the cupboards, poured himself some gin (which Serafim hated drinking straight), and sat at the table across from his friend. "Are you okay?" he ventured, after looking Antonino over for a moment.

"In truth, I am not so well," he said in a hushed tone. His eyes lagged slow and pensive, and judging by how much gin was left in the bottle, it wasn't the drink.

"Are you hurt? Should we get you to a hospital?"

"No, no. It's not that. It is . . . many things. All piling up at the same time."

"I see. May I ask why those men were beating you, what that was all about?"

"Oh" — Antonino flicked his wrist — "the fault was mine. I . . . received some bad news for the second day in a row, and was passing a stoop where those men — a few simpleton thugs really — were singing a *fascio* march. I wasn't thinking, and shouted at them, some ill-advised remark about that bastard son Mussolini. Insults were exchanged. They followed me to my doorstep, pulled me into the courtyard. It was for posturing purposes only, nothing more."

"How can you be so sure? They had a knife, Antonino. A knife, in your face."

"Well, yes. But it would have ended there." He paused, his gaze drifting. "Though, who knows? Maybe it would have gotten worse. Maybe I am a lucky man, and you saved my life. But I don't think so. What's more, I think it was unwise of you to intervene. First of all, there isn't a person you could show those photos to who wouldn't instantly burn them. The corruption in this city, and those who enforce it, is more endemic than you know. Those men are just brawn for hire, dimwits, but they can still work a few things out on their own. They could make the connection that it was you. They know you and what you look like. They know you're a photographer, and clearly a good friend of mine. I tell you, you shouldn't have intervened."

Serafim drank some gin, winced, and set his glass firmly on the table. "Well, I do not care what you think. If I saw the same thing this moment, I would do exactly as I did earlier. In spite of the danger — and your ingratitude."

Antonino laughed. "That is what you don't understand, Serafim. You would be introducing danger where, without such a reaction, there is none. I have been in situations like this before, you know. I happen to understand that I have . . . ways of getting out of them — proven ways, of turning things like this around."

Serafim crossed his arms over his chest. "Antonino, can you hear yourself? What could you possibly have that could turn that around? A Tommy gun?"

Antonino hesitated. "I happen to have a belief — and the deepest that a person can have — in humankind."

Serafim fought back a smirk. "You will forgive me for saying this, Antonino, but that is the only time I have known you to say something that I would call naive. I am confident that all the faith in humanity that exists couldn't stop a mindless brigand from doing what he wishes."

"You see, that is, perhaps, one of the reasons it works. Because I believe in those men, Serafim. And I *will* believe in them, no matter. Even if they do not stop. Even if they cut my throat like a butchered pig."

Serafim spat out an uncomfortable chuckle. "You are drunken, man. You are not making sense."

Antonino let out a long sigh and reluctantly leaned forward over the table. "Okay, I will explain it to you, if only for fear you may need it. Now, when I say I believe in humankind, it isn't the belief that human beings will do what is ultimately right or best or humane. As you know, it's often the contrary. Instead, what I believe is that inside every man, however far he lets himself fall, however depraved and brutal he lets himself become, there exists, at his core, a kind of nameless inclination, which is impelling him back in the direction he came from, in the direction of dignity."

"Ah, and you think you possess the ability to somehow *activate* this dignity?" Serafim said, acutely aware he was fighting back a smile.

"No. What I'm saying is, be it the most corrupt official, the most hardened beggar, the most desperate opiate addict, all of them simply *feel* this same indescribable tug, which is straining to lift them, return them to a place where they are more human. Of course, most of them lose the struggle daily. But my belief is only that that struggle is there, that it is present, always gently pulling at their centre, as quiet as gravity. Now, what has gotten me out of these difficult situations is that belief."

"How? Why weren't you busy *believing* the situation away when I came across you earlier?" Serafim uncrossed his arms, adjusted his glass of gin on the table.

"Well, had you not interfered and just watched, I would have. First, you see, I need to break the dynamic that automatically arises between those trying to assert their dominance and those trying to prove their submission — between the tyrant and the pleader for mercy. I have found that the only way to do this is by shocking them, saying something that stands completely outside the borders of that dynamic, outside what they would ever expect me to say or do. The moment I do that, I have their full and befuddled attention, I look at them in the most open way I can, and I communicate that belief to them, that whatever they do, I will understand, I will forgive it. They can do with me whatever they will, but I know — and, if they so choose, will go to my grave knowing — that at their centre was something nudging them, silently, subtly, to be more. Experience has proven to me that if they become aware that I hold this belief, they will stop what they're doing. Of course, they'll inevitably give a last kick or spit, to save face in their underworld, but it usually ends there."

Serafim considered this for some time before speaking. "I am still not convinced."

Antonino shook his head, smiled. "Serafim, I am not trying to convince you." He stood up gingerly, like an old man at twenty-eight, and made his way to the kitchen sink, where he leaned on its edge, his back to Serafim at the table. "I wonder,"

Antonino said, his voice unassuming, "if you have ever been in love. What I mean is that first, precarious, universe-swallowing kind of love."

Serafim's tone was confessional. "I have. Yes."

"So you know . . . how it changes you. That it pulls you apart, and when you put yourself back together again, you find that the pieces don't quite fit. Not the way they did before. For me, it was a girl in Floridia, my hometown, in Sicily. We were childhood companions first. That changed in adolescence. It was her that was coming to marry me. Only that she recently caught wind of my being in trouble with the authorities at immigration, and twice over at that.

"You see, when we met on the boat, Serafim, I wasn't emigrating but fleeing. I was the youngest child of five in my family, and the most promising in my neighbourhood, and so my parents had made great sacrifices in order for me to get an education. I was studying law at the University of Naples, and got involved as a journalist for the student paper. I wrote an anti-fascist article, a stunt I was warned never to repeat. I did — as many times as I could. A warrant was issued for my arrest. I had heard tales of worse than confinement, for those the police took away. So I took the money I had and hopped on a boat, changed my name from Antonio to Antonino, on my passport and birth certificate and everything else I've signed since. My family doesn't know my whereabouts, and doesn't want to, for fear the Italian government would have me deported from wherever I happen to be. The only one who knows I am in this country is this woman. When she heard I was in trouble with the immigration office *here* as well, it seemed all too clear to her that I was on my way to jail, or to becoming one of the disappeared. So she has accepted the hand of another.

"That was the news I received yesterday. Today I got another letter, from the deputy minister of immigration this time, granting me the right to stay in Canada, only on the condition that I cease publication of *Il Risveglio Italiano* immediately. As you see, I have no choice. I have been beaten. The game is up."

Serafim found himself thinking about the logistics more than anything else. "So, what will you do for a living?"

"I can bake bread. I might try to open a bakery. Sell coal, or cement work. I don't know. But I will find a way. I had hoped to save a little money with the paper and put it in a few stocks, like everyone else, but it seems my chance has run dry.

"You can see," he continued, "how all of this has got me thinking of something we once talked about, you and I, about whether or not the world (or God, as you put it) might be taming us, gradually turning us into beings who are more obedient, less wild and inspired. You talked about a horse. I seek solace in the idea that I might, right now, be like that horse, newly broken, compliant, apparently thoughtless. But tell me, in that creature, is there not still the potential to rear up, break away, run amok? And is that potential not always present there, inside him, trembling just beneath the surface, biding its time, waiting for the ripe moment to emerge again?"

Serafim sipped his gin. "You mean that it is there, even if it fails to manifest itself. Like dignity."

Antonino turned from the sink. "I am glad you understand, Serafim. Now leave me be. I am tired, and must sleep." He shuffled into his bedroom. "Good night to you."

Serafim sat in the quiet kitchen for some time before letting himself out, gently turning off the lights behind him. On
the long walk home he found himself watching the shadows
and looking into the parked cars for silhouettes of men lying
in wait. He arrived home without incident and was soon in
bed himself, though he couldn't quite get to sleep. He kept
thinking of what Antonino had said, about the politicians in
the city, and their network of corruption being more exten-
sive than Serafim knew; how, even if one were to possess
incriminating photos, there was no one to hand them to
who wouldn't instantly destroy them, or, worse, use them
for their own gain. There was the fault in the reasoning he
and Claire had adopted, and which he planned on bringing up
with her before Friday, before it was too late. But mostly he
was thinking about Antonino, and how alike their experiences
of affection had been, how they'd both had to leave behind
the women they'd first loved, women who had then chosen
another. Some other man, it was all too agonizing to think,
who was better.

Stirring up these thoughts of Inês, thinking back on how
he'd laboured in the darkroom for all those winter months,
working on the picture he'd taken of her in the gardens of
the Palácio de Cristal, the flexion of thunder implicit in the
clouds behind her, it was no real surprise to Serafim that, in
the morning, after accumulating what felt like only minutes
of sleep, he found a cup of tea on his kitchen table, waiting
for him. Though this time he noticed that three matches had
been struck while attempting to light the stove for the kettle.
He thought of what a distinct noise it made, and how, with
such a shallow sleep, he should have been able to hear it. Then,

standing with a spent match in his fingers, he recalled, in a remote and nebulous way, that he had in fact heard something the night before, something like that bright sulphur flare-up, at some point, somewhere nearby.

Medium: Gelatin silver print
Description: Three men attacking another
Location: Montreal, Quebec
Date: 1929

ᘓ

A narrow courtyard conceals itself; a finger of paving stones pointing the only way out, a driveway leading to a bright and overexposed street beyond, an outlying dreamscape of saturated light. The courtyard's high brick walls reach up and out of sight, blocking the sun. Metal railings are anchored into the masonry and spiral down, along a set of back entrances and wooden doors stacked three high. It is the kind of unseen urban corner where, one feels, flowers would not grow.

The paving stones in the foreground are flecked with strands of hay, spilling over from a stable close by, though out of the frame. Four men stand at the edge of this scattered feed, all of them wearing flat caps, which are crooked and tussled off centre. Two of the men are muscling back the arms of a third, exposing his belly to what one imagines to be punches given by the fourth, who is standing directly in front of the captured individual. The fists of this fourth man are not balled up. Instead, he is standing casually, hip cocked to the side, and holding a penknife as if it were a flashlight, shining its steel point into the dark of the captive's face.

One of the men holding the captive's arms is looking away, over his shoulder. The expression on his face suggests that he senses something worse is about to happen. Something more hurtful, more menacing, on its way.

27

Claire and Serafim were sitting on a bench overlooking the intersection of St. Catherine Street and St. Denis. It was noon and the streets were swarming with businessmen and restaurantgoers, vendors, hawkers, procurers, and shoppers. It was perfect.

"Why don't you just leave your hat on?" asked Claire. "Playing with it like that makes you look suspicious."

Serafim placed his hat back on his head, folded his hands in his lap, then refolded them. To calm him as much as she could, Claire shuffled closer on the bench, and with a hand over his shoulder she stroked the back of his neck, which had worked to mollify him once before. She was glad to see that it had the same effect now and she could get back to concentrating on scanning the faces of the passersby, looking for the councilman, who would be arriving any minute.

For what felt like weeks leading up to this noon hour, they had discussed ad nauseam the best way for the transaction to take place. The first option would have been to do it in a secure and private setting. But that felt like a risk for Claire and Serafim, because the councilman had — or could bring, if he so wished — people with guns, knives, and baseball bats. Things could go badly. So they decided on a busy intersection at a busy time. This way, the exchange could take place within seconds, surreptitiously, after which Claire and Serafim could simply disappear among the throng, heading in separate directions. They had already agreed upon who would carry the case, and where they would rendezvous afterwards.

Everything was set. The letter had been couriered anonymously to the councilman's desk on Thursday morning, with his cameo photograph and the promise of both the film and all enlargements ever developed from that film, to be exchanged for four thousand dollars in small bills. They had further stipulated that the bills should be carried in an attaché case with a small red ribbon tied to the handle, which would allow Serafim and Claire to spot it from a distance and make the trade as quickly as possible.

There were only two potential problems with their plan. The first was the point that Antonino had brought up. The councilman was sure to have friends in the highest places, in every influential position imaginable, people who would be willing to protect him if presented with evidence that might incriminate him. This was, after all, the very twine that bound the monopolists together and the reason corruption was so thorny a problem to uproot. But it was also a problem to which they could think of no solution. So they would just have to trust that nothing would go wrong with the transaction.

The second potential problem was a technicality. If they were to keep their word, and had both the film and every photo developed from that film contained inside a single envelope, what would happen if they lost the envelope or, God forbid, it was stolen en route? Where would they be then? So it was agreed that Serafim would process an extra photograph, and keep it hidden in the secret drawer that he'd installed in his apartment, where he stored all his archival stock and large reels of unexposed film. Just in case.

Claire took a deep breath of spring air, which smelled of horses, a bit of oil from the passing automobiles, and taffy and popcorn, a vendor of each positioned at opposing corners of the intersection. A concertina player weaved in and out of the pedestrians, followed by a young boy holding out a hat and soliciting coins for the performance. In years to come Claire would remember this moment as a time in her life when things were still simple. She fixed her gaze on a woman pedalling a bicycle, who had passed just in front of them, smiling at Serafim as she streamed by. Her dress sailed in the wind she was creating. Claire's eyes followed her through the intersection, admiring how gracefully she was moving her legs, and how straight and tall she sat on her bicycle seat. Then Claire's eyes stopped abruptly at the corner.

There was a man at a shop window, standing with his back to them, holding an attaché case with a tiny red ribbon tied to its handle.

Claire pointed. "That is him, there."

Serafim located the ribbon, inhaled deeply, and let out a slow breath. "As we discussed, you make the trade, bring the case to me, and I will slip away with it. Are you sure you are ready?"

"Entirely. We have nothing to worry about. I will be back in a moment." She put her hand on the large folded envelope concealed in her purse, stood up, and headed across the street, making her way through the traffic, flinching at the coarse-sounding car horn that bleated at a carriage on her right.

As she approached the man, she inspected the red ribbon, then noted his expensive shoes, suit, and hat, edging forward until she had sidled in directly beside him, where she ostensibly busied herself with peering into the window display as well, her free hand close to his case.

She took the envelope out of her purse. "I believe," she said in English, into the glass in front of her, "that I have something of yours."

To her surprise, the man was somewhat taken aback by this. "I . . . I'm sorry, madam?" He turned to face her.

Claire's lips parted. He was not the councilman. "I am sorry. I . . . thought that you were . . ." She shoved the envelope back into her purse. "I mean, I was . . . admiring your ribbon . . . there, on your case." She indicated it.

The man held it up. "Oh, yes, my daughter" — he shook his head in light paternal annoyance — "this morning, thought the drab old thing could use some livening up. Poor dear."

"Oh." Claire made a weak attempt at laughter. "I see."

"Well, madam" — he cordially tipped his hat to her — "a fine day to you." And with that, he stepped around the corner and disappeared into the bustle of passing people.

The concertina player ended his cheery tune.

Claire stood for a moment, looking around for anyone else nearby with a red ribbon tied to his case. There was no one. She crossed the street, perplexed, and returned to the bench, sitting beside Serafim, though at a distance.

"Claire, you . . . didn't get the case."

"Yes, I know. It wasn't him. It was someone else."

"I . . . That's impossible. What are the chances of such a coincidence? A man standing alone with the coded signal, at the very time that the signal was expected, at the very place?"

Claire shrugged. "I know. It is strange."

They looked at each other, the conclusion sliding towards them at breakneck speed. Their eyes widened. Suddenly, they understood what had happened. Without speaking, both of them pivoted to look out into the street, at the teeming array of faces situated at every point of the compass surrounding them. In a second-floor window, a man smoked a cigarette, intent on the bench where they sat. At one of the street corners, three men stood speaking to each other, one of them listening while staring at Claire. Across the street, another man was spying in their direction above his open newspaper. They had been outed. And as soon as they moved, they would be followed, pursued, and hunted. Until the photos, and the blackmailers who'd intended to use them, were gone.

"Oh my God," Claire whispered. "Oh my God."

"Okay, look," Serafim broke in, also whispering. "The photographs are what they want, and the most dangerous thing to be caught with. Let me have them."

Claire took the envelope out of her purse and slid it across to Serafim. He rolled it into a tube.

"Now," he continued, "we always had plans to split up. Each of us has already mapped out our own sort of escape route. I think we should use those, now."

"I'm scared."

"So am I. I will go first, so you can see if anyone follows me. Then you will know we are right. Then you should run, not walk. Understood?"

"Yes."

"Okay." He nodded to himself. "Okay. Goodbye." Serafim got to his feet and briskly headed down the road, cutting into an alley as soon as he could. Claire was petrified to see the men who amassed out of the woodwork and, like beads of water down a funnel, streamed in the precise direction that Serafim had set off in, many of them breaking into a quick trot.

"Oh my God," she whispered again, to no one. What was odd was that, knowing she now had to jump to her feet and sprint for her life, she found she couldn't move. She felt pinned to the bench, her knees already weak, her posture small. She looked around, trying to distinguish which men were charged with the task of apprehending her, which ones were waiting for her to move. She didn't stand a chance of outrunning them, or even outsmarting them in mid-pursuit. There were too many of them. It would be over before it began.

Then Claire saw a portly nun crossing the street, heading up St. Denis. Instinctively, she stood and hurried to catch up with the woman, slowing to a stroll just behind her, within reaching distance of her habit, stepping on her shadow as it floated over the cracks in the sidewalk. Claire felt like her heart had sunk into her stomach. She scratched her neck to look behind her, and it seemed as if the entire street were filing into a procession in her wake, men convening from every corner of the intersection. They were, however, still keeping their distance, not yet running.

Claire had only been ambling behind the nun for a minute or two before the woman began veering away from the street, towards one of the side doors of the church of St. Jacques. At a loss for what else to do, Claire followed. She looked behind and saw the men stopping, watching her, not even trying to hide the fact that they were in pursuit. Now that it appeared she was heading into a church, they weren't quite sure what to do. They exchanged glances and looked for direction, for someone to give them definitive orders.

Claire and the large woman climbed a set of eight stairs to a side door, and the nun opened it, turning to swing it wide, and in doing so, she was surprised to find Claire silently on her heels. *"Mademoiselle! Je vous prie!"* Perturbed, the woman stepped inside and tried to shut the door behind her.

Claire jammed her foot in the gap and in colloquial French implored the woman to please, please let her in, insisting that at that very moment she was in the gravest of danger, and that the consequences of her being shut out would very likely be lethal. Please, she begged, please have mercy.

There was a cold pause. "Mademoiselle O'Callaghan, I must say, your French has much improved recently."

"I'm sorry?"

The nun smiled, waiting for Claire to work it out on her own. So this was one of the many nuns who had cared for her at the Hôtel-Dieu, only fifteen months earlier. One of the women who, after spending almost three weeks with Claire in the most intimate of circumstances, had become convinced she was an imposter of some kind, for some unknown and sinister reason. Claire was just the kind of patient a nun would remember.

"I don't know what you're talking about."

"Well, I do, *mademoiselle*. Now, if you would please remove your foot from the door, lest I call for help." There were voices and movement inside the church, the sounds of people approaching.

Claire checked the street behind her. The men were growing in number, milling together. "Okay. Yes, you are right. I
was not who I said I was. I was lying. I lied to you all, every day
that I was there, in everything I did. Can you think of reasons
why a woman might do that?"

"I can, *mademoiselle*." Deadpan.

"Well . . . I was in trouble then, and you helped me regardless, and I thank you for that, very much. But you must understand that I am in much greater trouble now, and I am asking
you, I am begging you, for mercy. Please."

"By 'trouble,' you mean to say that you have done something against your fellow man, against the law, against God?
Again?"

Claire faltered. "Yes, all of them. Please. Open the door."

"So you would have us harbour a wanton criminal? Is that
it, Mademoiselle O'Callaghan?"

Claire's head fell softly against the wood of the door. "Yes."

The nun paused. "All right."

Relieved, Claire removed her foot and readied herself to
step inside. But the nun quickly shut the door and locked it
instead.

"No. No, no, no," Claire said, desperately listening for
movement on the other side, her face against the quiet of the
wood grain. With her body leaning against the door, Claire
gradually turned round. A car pulled up, its back seat empty,
intended for her. One of the men opened it, left it open, and
looked at her. Two other men set out towards her, quickly
taking the stairs. Claire covered her face with her hands.

She heard a click from the door at her back, and then it
opened, a hand pulled her inside, and the door was deadbolted

behind her. It was dark inside and smelled of stale incense. "Follow me," said the nun, "and not a word."

She led Claire to a backroom, down a set of stairs, and into a kind of kitchen area without appliances or cooking facilities, with yellow wallpaper and cold floors.

"Sit there." The nun pointed at a steel chair.

Claire sat down and hung her head. "Thank you."

"I don't need your thanks. I need you to understand that the most I can do for you is send for the police, who will collect you from the back of the building, through that door there. I will go and see if Father's busy, and if he will agree to make these arrangements. I imagine, if he has time, he will hear your confession. Now, wait here." She left.

Moments later, the door that she had indicated bumped open, and a man teetering with a heavy box stepped inside. He was fighting to fully enter the room, the door's tight springs conspiring against him. Claire stood up and held it open for him.

"Thank you, *madame*."

Looking outside, she read on the side of his coach that he was a deliveryman with the Canadian Pacific Express. As he was setting the box in a corner, Claire slipped outside, climbed into the back of his coach, and found a space to hide in a narrow slot behind a crate. She heard the horses blow and nicker. Seconds later, the canvas flaps that covered the back of the coach were draped shut, the driver mounted, and the coach jostled into motion, easing out into the dangerous streets, and passing, Claire imagined, a swarm of men watching and waiting for her to emerge from the church.

Perhaps a quarter of an hour later, the deliveryman made another stop, opened the flaps, and removed a box. Two deliveries after that, Claire climbed out while he was away and was back in the bright day without a clue as to where she was in the city. She hailed the first cab that passed, jumped into the back, lay down on the floor, and asked the driver to take her to her address in the east end as fast as he could. There was no curiosity from the driver about why she was on the floor.

When she arrived home, Claire locked herself in, closed the curtains, and tiptoed through the house, edging her way around corners. Once she was sure she was safe, she stood in the centre of the apartment, reached out to a stack of records placed beside the Victrola, lifted them high above her head, and slammed them onto the floor, letting out a scream that strained her throat, her fingers splayed wide at the ends of her arms. Then she collapsed into her only chair and into the stunned hush of the room.

As she sat there, she slowly realized that there was still a good chance they didn't know who she was. It wasn't as if she was famous. So long as she could change what she'd looked like the moment they'd seen her, there was still a chance this might all blow over.

In the bathroom, Claire cut her hair closer than the coif of a banker. She also drew extensions on either end of her eyebrows, and rouged different parts of her cheeks. She stopped to listen, makeup pencil hovering, whenever someone in her townhouse used the stairs, half expecting the door to be kicked in.

She knew she had no choice but to go to work that night. If someone on the staff were not to show up, it would seem suspicious, especially today. Knowing where the photo had been taken, the men were sure to be at the club. She felt sick to her stomach thinking of walking through the front doors of the cabaret, of having to perform in front of a horde of faces and searching eyes that might recognize her at any given moment.

When it came time for work, she felt as though she were walking the plank. She left through the back door, after ordering a taxi to pick her up in the alley. She lay down on the floor of the cab again, and got out on Stanley Street like a cached mistress, paying the cabbie without speaking. As she walked to the entrance of the Kit-Kat, she paused — much like a gambler might at a roulette table, before putting all his chips on red — then stepped inside.

Ciao Serafim,

I telephoned you multiple times today, but received no answer. I was in the neighbourhood so thought I would drop by to make sure everything was okay. Since you still haven't come home, I've scribbled this note for you to find when you do.

An acquaintance has heard whisperings in the wrongest of circles, of men who are searching for a surreptitious photographer. I discreetly inquired whether or not this might have to do with your taking photos of those men who were roughing me up the other day. I was assured, however, that it had nothing to do with that.

For some reason I fear that you have gotten yourself involved in something more dangerous than you know. These men of whom I speak, there is no telling what they're capable of.

If you could call to reassure me, I would be grateful.

Con affetto,

Antonino

28

With the photos and film in hand, Serafim stood up from the bench and set off at a good pace down the street, ducking into an alleyway the first chance he got.

With most of his attention focused behind him, trying to ascertain whether or not he was being followed, he didn't think of what lay ahead. Two men stood in the alleyway in front of him, shoulder to shoulder, straddling the shallow ruts in the concrete, waiting for him.

Behind him, Serafim was being followed by four or five men, who were right on his heels and hustling to catch up with him. He turned to face the alleyway, about to break into a run, but stopped in his tracks instead. Boxed in, he braced the rolled-up envelope, as if ready to wield the hollow paper column as a weapon.

He looked to his left, pocketed the envelope in his jacket, and leapt onto a fire escape ladder, quickly reaching a set of narrow stairs. He could hear the men below him, scampering over the metal in pursuit. Serafim tried every door as he climbed, each one of them locked, losing himself precious seconds. His last hope was that the fire escape would ascend all the way to the roof, where he might access other stairs or hatches to get back down to street level, but as he neared the final landing, he could see nothing that ascended beyond. It was over, and he stopped in front of the last door, an imposing barricade of painted steel and riveted sheet metal clamped tight. He tried the latch with a half-hearted tug, and to his astonishment it opened.

Serafim had just managed to get on the other side of it, slamming it shut and locking the bolt, when a rush of bodies clanged against it, with pounding fists and muffled curses. Their expletives were in Italian, he noted, backing away from the emergency exit. He continued down a hallway, as people poked their heads out of doors to see what all the commotion was about.

Descending a few sets of stairs, he found himself outside again, though he didn't dare risk crossing the street, knowing they would be racing to the front of the building at any moment. Instead, he walked as casually as he could along the storefronts, and just as he heard scuffling behind him, and people shoving through the crowds, he turned into a barber's shop. As the door closed behind him, the bell above his head tinkled a second time, startling him.

Serafim asked to sit in the chair farthest from the front window. He was trying hard to slow his breathing. The barber wasn't really inclined to use that particular chair, he admitted, but Serafim insisted, saying he would pay extra if the gentleman entertained his request.

"Fine, fine," the man finally agreed, draping a white cape around Serafim's body as soon as he sat down, cinching it snug around his neck. "What would you like done, sir?"

"A shave, please. Moustache and all."

"Very well." The barber clipped his moustache down to the skin then reclined Serafim's chair and smothered his face in a warm, wet cloth, only his nose protruding from its folds to breathe. It was then that the bells above the door rattled again and someone burst in, looked around, and dashed back out.

"Someone's in trouble," said the barber, removing the towel and straightening the chair, already working his brush into a lather.

"Well" — Serafim watched his own suspicious eyes in the mirror — "not our problem."

"No, sir," agreed the barber, beginning to daub shaving cream around Serafim's face. "Not our problem at all."

Before Serafim left, he stared out the front window for quite some time, hovering behind the coat stand, listening to the barber and another patron, a regular, as they chatted about each other's families. When neither of them was looking, Serafim took the envelope out of his dangling jacket, grabbed the other patron's blazer and hat (a fedora quite unlike his flat cap in shape and colour), put them on, and crossed the street, heading straight for a tram that was just about to set off. He kept his eyes on all the things he was least interested in focusing on, a trick he'd learned from street photography, which, he knew, made a person as invisible as any other bystander around him. He took a circuitous route home, making sure all the while that he wasn't being followed.

He arrived to find a disconcerting note from Antonino in his mailbox. He decided, however, not to call him back, sure that if his friend heard how rattled he was, he would ask questions that Serafim would have trouble answering.

That night, he spent a great deal of time peeking through a slat in his curtains, watching for strange vehicles hesitating near his address. Serafim had already unlocked the back door, having made sure the metal stairs and passageways were all clear and uncluttered, in case he had to make another off-the-cuff getaway. He was waiting to hear from Claire, sure she would phone the moment she finished work, which was when they had initially planned to rendezvous. He was still convinced she was fine, that no one had even thought of following her, since they saw the envelope physically change hands between them. He was doubtful there were enough people to have Claire followed as well.

As the night drained away, so did his confidence in this assumption. Surely she should have called by now, he thought, checking the time every three minutes. Surely her shift must be over. He busied himself with making certain the envelope was safely sealed with his film, inside the hidden drawer, and that the right amount of household paraphernalia was haphazardly leaning against it, looking neglected and natural. The only corner in his apartment that looked chaotic.

The phone rang, but when Serafim answered, the person on the other end didn't say hello, only breathed into the receiver. Finally he hung up, only to have the phone ring a second time, while his hand was still on it. It was Claire. She had called before as well, needing first to make sure that Serafim wasn't being held at knifepoint, thinking that if he had been caught, they might anticipate Claire's call and attempt to lure her close enough to nab her as well. Serafim sighed at this reasoning. It had all so quickly, so regrettably unravelled.

Claire explained that she had stayed for several drinks after her shift, trying to feel out whether or not anyone at the club had already been approached, and wanting to reinforce the few acquaintanceships she had, so that maybe her colleagues would keep their suspicions to themselves if asked. To her surprise, everything seemed to be okay. She increasingly had the feeling that they had both, somehow, managed to give their adversaries the slip. All she could hope was that it would end there.

They agreed that they shouldn't see each other for a while, and in the meantime they should just continue in their usual ways, exactly as they had before, as if nothing had happened, and as if they had never even met. For her part, Claire had every intention of heading to work at four the next afternoon, and would stop for the customary small talk with the bartender before continuing to the back to get changed, as she had a hundred times before. "I'm so sorry it turned out this way," she said before hanging up. "Take good care of yourself. Goodbye."

Serafim went to bed late, where he spent hours gazing at the ceiling, thinking of all he'd lost. He found the only image that gave him any consolation was the one he'd invented in a daydream the day he landed in Montreal, the day all his money had been stolen. The image was of him curled in a ball on top of Inês, her bare arms embracing him, holding him there, steady. Envisioning this was the only way he managed to fall asleep.

What Serafim woke to in the middle of the night was complete confusion, a bewilderment so profound that it would only become clear to him in time, and after scrupulous thought, what exactly had happened. He remembered hearing gruff voices just before a loud slamming noise. The bang was instantly followed by (what he would later figure out were) the rever berating coils of his bedsprings. They had overturned his bed, checking to see if he was hiding beneath it. He wasn't. Instead, Serafim was standing in the dark, in his sleeping clothes, in the middle of his kitchen, holding a kettle of boiling water.

He looked around, groggy. Through the entranceway of the kitchen, he saw that the lights were on elsewhere in the apartment. He heard the door to his closet-cum-darkroom thrown open, followed by a shout in Italian, inviting others to come and take a look. In a haze, Serafim turned, the kettle still in his hand, tiptoed to the back door, and silently let himself out. He stole down the stairs in his slippers. When he was at the bottom, his kitchen lights flickered on, and he heard the sound of a teacup and saucer being smashed on the floor.

Serafim was crouched behind a garbage can when the back door was finally flung open, a man standing on the landing, squinting into the dark, looking for movement before turning back into the apartment.

The men continued their search, overturning furniture, pulling out all the drawers, flinging his clothes over their shoulders, and tossing the prints they found in his darkroom around the sitting room, tiling the hardwood with their glossy pages. He heard the dying squiggles of static reception as the radio was smashed. Then the sound of his Leica, crushed under someone's heel.

Feeling the need to get farther away, Serafim retreated into the alley, where he found a large and filthy piece of cloth that someone had thrown away. He wrapped himself and his kettle inside it, and tucked himself between two garbage bins at a spot where he could still see the back door and the men moving around in his house, tossing aside everything that wasn't bolted down, looking for either clues to where he was or the film and pictures of the councilman.

Needless to say, hiding amid rubbish bins in the folds of a filthy mantle while watching paid thugs ransack his residence was a situation that inspired a bit of introspection in Serafim. He felt strangely detached from his current circumstances, removed from the sounds of shattered glass and toppling furniture, from the sight of his neighbours' lights being switched on then off again (thinking it better not to call the police, who, they rightly assumed, wouldn't respond to the complaint anyway).

So it had been him all along, he reflected. It was Serafim making tea in the middle of the night. Serafim Vieira was haunting himself. The idea was terrifying. The more he thought about it, the more he was sure he could trace the root of the phenomenon back to that insatiable hunger he always felt, festering at his core, no matter what he did. If he was honest with himself, it was there with him when he was in Claire's company, or when he was in Inês's, or Antonino's, or Álvaro's; it was there when he developed a perfect photograph in the darkroom; even there, lying on the damp sheets beside him, just after he'd made love. The constant presence of want, haunting him.

He thought it must be something he'd just grown used to, like an inextricable companion, or like family, something he assumed was supporting him, encouraging him to move forward, while discouraging him from growing complacent; a strength that was constantly compelling him towards the end goal of *not* being hungry, of not wanting anymore. The fuel of tenacity.

But now he wondered, what if the opposite was true? What if his wanting was the very thing that was holding him back, slowly poisoning him, insidiously leaching into his veins like mercury, making him gaunt and feverish? What if he had spent his whole life constructing, not ways of keeping himself safe from harm, but ways of blinding himself to the fact that he was the one who posed the greatest threat to himself? What then?

Unable to answer his own questions, Serafim stared through the open back door, where he saw one of the men now reaching into his kitchen cupboards and, with a sweep of his arm, pulling all the contents onto the floor in a cacophony of crashes. Serafim didn't flinch at the sound. Instead, he gathered a few folds of the dirty cloth he was shrouded in and nestled himself farther inside. It was going to be a long night.

À acheter pour chez Claire
— *Borax*
— *Lysol*
— *Babbitt's Cleanser*
— *Ammonia*
— *New, sharp scissors*

29

Claire stayed in bed most of the morning, the curtains drawn, the even light from the overcast Saturday seeping in around the edges of the window. Feeling drained, she lay and watched her arm extend from the covers, limp and heavy. She found it interesting that she didn't feel more disappointed by what had happened. True, her scheme had failed, and she wouldn't have the excess of money that she needed to bribe her way to stardom. But instead of disillusionment, she felt impatience. All she wanted was to know, with certainty, that she was never going to be implicated in the affair, that she was safe, and could go on with her unglamorous life much as before. And she wanted to know this now. She wanted release — if only to be granted the freedom to head back to the drawing board and try once more.

If she was honest with herself, she realized, her fatigue went even deeper than that, clawed further down, fastening her to the mattress. Claire felt she was growing weak, strangely enough, from always being strong, focused, and inspired. She found herself wishing for a rest from her own ambition. She wanted to just sit still and silent for once, without being bent on some greater aim that she was sure was waiting for her, somewhere out there in the dazzling world. There had been a time in her life when, she recalled, she felt less ambition, a time when things had been simpler, clearer. She wanted just a few moments of that time, now.

It was around noon when she finally pried herself from the bed, made a cup of black coffee, and drank it down while sitting in the curtain-drawn dark of her flat, a sanctuary with its own gloomy weather. She switched on the radio, turned up the volume, boiled some water, and poured a bath, where she spent a great deal of time shampooing the new, almost shaven feel of her scalp, finding clumps of hair where she hadn't cut quite close enough. During her bath, over the sound of the radio, she heard a muffled bump coming from one of the adjoining apartments. It was a fairly normal occurrence, and no cause for alarm. But when she was standing on her bath mat a few minutes later, drying herself off, wiping a bit of steam from the mirror, she noticed the space under the bathroom door behind her. The interior of her apartment was now swathed in natural light. Someone had opened the curtains.

Claire held the towel against her body, listening for movement over the drone of the radio. The floorboards creaked and an indistinct shadow passed along the light under the door.

Mouthing a curse, she looked round her cramped bathroom for something to defend herself with. There wasn't much. She wrapped the towel around her chest, tucked it tight, and grabbed hold of the only implement in the bathroom that she would be able to swing — a plunger. She raised it over her shoulder, a hand on the glass doorknob. Again she heard footsteps, which seemed to stop near the bathroom, listening. Terrified, Claire raised the plunger higher, nudged the door open — and was met with laughter.

"Do you mean to beat your sister to death with a plunger?" Cécile doubled over in hysterics. "Whatever are you doing? Look at yourself. You're preposterous."

"How . . . did you get in?"

Cécile, recovering, dried her eyes with the sides of her hands. "You wouldn't answer my knocks, and with the radio on I knew you were home, so I let myself in the back. The door was locked, but the window next to the latch was cracked open. And what a dreadful place it is!" She walked to the window, sliding it up. "I'm sure it hasn't been properly aired in months. And your kitchen sink is fetid. Revolting."

"How did you know where I live?"

"Darling, how many times do you think I write out your address every month? I practically know it better than mine. Though if I'd known such a warm welcome was awaiting me, I really would have come sooner."

Claire lowered the plunger. "I'm sorry. This . . . It's a bad time for me."

"Not anywhere near as bad as for me. That's why I dropped by, why I'm in Montreal. Something has happened and . . . in truth, I need your advice."

"Cécile, I really think I'm the last one you should listen to."

"Which is why I've come to you. So why don't you get dressed and I'll fix us some lunch from that wretched icebox of yours."

"Breakfast."

"My dearest sister, you're a disaster."

As Claire got dressed, she found herself annoyed by the clanks and bustle in the kitchen, by the presence of her competent sister, whose company she usually looked forward to but which now, given her current situation, only felt intrusive and inopportune. Claire wished to be alone. The very last thing she wanted was to be offering guidance or support to someone else.

While they ate, Claire pressed her for news of the family, trying to avoid delving into either her or Cécile's problems, asking instead about their parents, and how their grandmother was holding up. It turned out her grandmother wasn't doing so well; Cécile thought she didn't have long to live, though she saw this more as a mercy than a misfortune.

When they finished eating — one of them sitting on the only chair, the other on an end table they'd moved into the kitchen — Cécile cleared the plates away and returned to stand behind Claire, running her fingers through her new haircut. "This length looks good on you, but, if I may, it looks as if a gardener did it. Can I clean it up?"

"Please."

She found some paper scissors in a drawer and began to carefully snip the unevenness out of Claire's new haircut. After the first clip she clicked her tongue and walked over to a list she'd written out, of cleaning products Claire needed to buy. She added the words "New, sharp scissors" to it, underlining the word "sharp." As she put the pen down, she exchanged a glance with Claire that meant she intended this list less as a criticism and more as a simple, handy reminder. Claire returned a look that indicated she would likely just throw the scrap of paper away.

Cécile smiled and returned to stand behind her sister, dull scissors in hand. "So," she began, "I'm here in Montreal for the usual reason: to see him. You know, it's been going on for so long it's become quite comfortable for both of us. We have our hotel, our little rituals. He's married now, though still without children, like me. Neither of us (we've talked of it often) has ever felt the least bit guilty about it. Being true to oneself supersedes any vow of being true to another, is the way I see it, anyway." Snip. A light brush of her hand across Claire's shoulder.

"But late this morning," Cécile continued, "I was caught in a moment of incaution. I have almost never displayed any kind of affection for him in public, but when we were setting off today in our different directions, knowing we wouldn't see each other for at least a couple of months, I couldn't help but kiss him goodbye. It was a telling kiss. Right in front of a hotel we'd unmistakably just exited. So you can imagine my horror when I turned to head for the train station and ran straight into one of Gilles's colleagues. He is one of Gilles's up-and-coming opponents, a potential rival — the kind of man who might very well use this information in a damaging way." Snip, brush, pause. "And I am now at a complete loss as to what to do." Her voice was beginning to break, and Claire turned round to face her, touching the sides of her knees. "All I can think of is what *you* would do. You would do something bold."

"I would do something stupid," Claire countered.

Cécile crouched until they were face to face, holding the scissors by the blade now. "Exactly. You would do something stupid. But in doing so, you would provoke a significant change. You would put yourself in a situation that *forced* you to live with what you'd done. You'd make a mess, no doubt, but in your mess, at least the consequences that you had to assume would be clear."

"So you're thinking you should make a mess, like me?"

"Yes. I think I should ask Gilles for a divorce and live with the result, see my actions through to their end." Cécile began tearing up then began to cry in earnest, leaning against her sister. "I will ruin him, regardless."

Claire embraced her, and whispered lies into the side of her head. "No, you won't. Come, now."

At each of Claire's empty encouragements, Cécile chuckled through her tears. Eventually she pulled away, wiping her eyes.

"I told you," said Claire, "that this was a bad time for me as well. And while I don't want to get into it, I will say that for the first time I'm beginning to wonder if being bold is really the best way of getting what I want."

Cécile let out a teary laugh. "Of course it isn't. It's probably the worst. But it's the only way to bring about change on a dramatic scale; and change of that nature rarely has anything to do with getting what one wants. In my experience, the only people who get what they really want do so quietly."

"You must mean people who want to be pushed aside."

"No, I don't," Cécile said, standing up. She turned Claire around so she was facing forward again, took up the scissors by the handles once more, and combed her fingers through the hair above Claire's nape. "It might sound absurd to you, but I've seen it, again and again. It's like when Papa had that friend with the cutter, and in winter he would let you and me go for a ride to the top of the mountain with him. I remember there was just enough room for us to sit on either side of him, this bulky man with a deep voice, half buried under that heavy muskox pelt, the horse that was pulling us goliath in size to my twelve-year-old mind. All this brute strength and bravado, a commanding grip on the reins. But if you remember, it was our tiny requests that directed the sleigh. He only went where our little voices wanted him to, and avoided the places we didn't. Of course, if you'd asked him who was in control, there wouldn't be a doubt in his mind that it was him. But I wonder, was he really?

"This is something I see everywhere, in all the work I do. Even when it's just women dealing with women. There are these subtle pulls and sways that are always present, people who've installed themselves just *behind* the loudest voices, the brashest characters, exerting pressure by whispering from the sidelines. Sometimes I look at the network of organizations we've founded, and I think of the influence that women have already gained but which is unseen, unaccounted for, and which may not even be measurable by ballots or statistics.

"Or I think about the sermons we used to hear while growing up, all that preaching on how 'the meek shall inherit the earth.' Of course, one way to interpret it is that we should all just bow down in unquestionable obedience to the Church. But I think another way is, maybe, that we should strive, and keep striving, endlessly, but in the shrewdest of ways, by clever, strategic attrition. Sometimes I wonder if revolutions might even be won that way. Sometimes, Claire, I wonder if the meek have already inherited the earth, and the loud have no idea."

Claire didn't comment, but sat still and taciturn while Cécile finished clipping her hair, straightening the jagged lines around her cowlick. She found herself thinking about how much sense it all made. She promised herself that this was going to be the new way she would go about things — shrewdly and quietly. If she could somehow get away with her most brazen stunt to date, she swore, it would be her very last. If she could just manage to slip by unnoticed this once, she was going to change her tactics for good.

Claire checked the time on the clock that hung crooked on the wall. She still had a couple of hours before she had to head to work. She stared forward in her kitchen, listening to the squeak of the scissors, a rickety pendulum counting down to some near future that lay just ahead, as if in wait.

Medium: Gelatin silver print
Description: Woman emerging from Kit-Kat Cabaret
Location: Montreal, Quebec
Date: May 1929

ℭ

A young woman has just stepped out of a cabaret and is pausing on the sidewalk to look around, as if for something specific, a car she's waiting for or a person she knows to be nearby. There is something in her air and posture that suggests how comfortable she is with this particular doorway, as if she were standing on the stoop of her own home. She is stylishly dressed in a well-matched ensemble, her cloche hat tastefully feathered.

The photo has been crudely folded twice. The intersection of the creases that meet in the centre of the image is askew, dividing the photo into uneven quarters. The only care that has been taken in the folding seems to have been to ensure that the young woman's face and the signage of the cabaret were not obscured. Both of these elements hover safely at the centre of the upper quadrants.

On the back of the photo, the white paper exhibits several stains and blemishes: a smudge of what seems to be an orange paste, a faint coffee ring, and a dark green fleck with a small halo of oil swelling out from its centre. The stains suggest that at some point in the photograph's life it was discarded into a refuse bin.

30

While remaining hidden and huddled under the blanket he'd found in the alley, Serafim gradually began to realize what he had to do. Since the men were still waiting for him, lingering and smoking in and around his apartment in the pale light of morning, it seemed likely that they hadn't discovered his concealed drawer, hadn't yet found what they were looking for. So what Serafim intended to do was to show it to them; to hand it over as a kind of peace offering, as something, he rationalized, that would end this game. He would lay his harmless cards on the table, a bluff called and lost. It was also, he considered, the one way to ensure they wouldn't begin searching for Claire.

However, he wasn't about to saunter through the front door in his pyjamas and hand it to them. Instead, he would wait until the men left his apartment — even if it was just for a moment — rush inside, lay the envelope out for them to find in the most conspicuous place he could think of, gather a few of his clothes and things from the floor, and leave Montreal, maybe even Canada, for good. He wouldn't contact Claire or Antonino before he hopped on a train, in case he was being followed. After that, it was anyone's guess. Maybe he'd make his way to Paris and join Álvaro there.

The one problem with his plan was that the men in his apartment didn't seem all that eager to move. They continued to appear at his back door every few minutes and look around, blowing the smoke of their cigarettes up at the sky, where washes of watercolour had begun to stain the clouds with lilac and apricot. For Serafim, the daylight posed another predicament.

Considering they might very well be able to see him from his back door in the morning light, he needed to find a new location while it was still dark enough to do so. He would have to venture out through the alleys and streets in his sleeping clothes, where he was sure to be regarded as a madman. There was little other choice. He brought both the kettle and the blanket along with him, which he hugged tight in his arms, making himself appear even more unbalanced.

At a local tavern, a group of workers just coming off the graveyard shift snickered and elbowed each other as Serafim shuffled by. He was mortified by their pointing fingers, watching his slippered feet and cursing the absurd position he'd put himself in. He continued for a few more blocks, not lifting his chin until he found another forgotten corner in an alley to hide for a while.

The sun reared higher, and though it tried, it couldn't quite burn through the overcast ceiling. Serafim sat, dejected and awkward, until he heard a man in the distance, slowly making his way down the alleyway. The man was wailing as loud as he could, an eerie yowl that might have been weeping but which Serafim began to distinguish as words, something about searching for *chiffons*. Serafim left his corner to see what the noise was all about and spotted an old Jewish man pushing a handcart with a heap of rags and some potted plants inside. He was trading one of his plants for a handful of rags that a housewife had brought out to him.

When the man came closer, Serafim tried to barter his blanket, hoping to get something more suitable to wear in exchange, but the ragman offered him a frail seedling in return. So Serafim returned to his corner and brought out the kettle, which was undoubtedly of monetary value. The ragman wasn't interested, and offered him only a few more seedlings. It wasn't until Serafim made it clear that he had to find something suitable to wear on the streets, and would hand over his sleeping clothes as well, that the ragman reluctantly began to dig to the bottom of his cart, where, hidden under grimy rags, he kept the garments he'd amassed that were still intact. After a brief and humiliating moment of nudity in the alleyway, Serafim looked half presentable; or at least he looked like a grimy pauper, complete with a half-flattened bowler hat and pants that were too wide and long, and so covered his slippers. In any case, it was a step up from appearing to be a perfectly respectable gentleman who just happened to be walking around in his pyjamas. Seeming unsatisfied with the transaction, the ragman lifted the handles of his cart and continued on his way, his melancholic wail rising over the rooftops again, floating up and through the gnarled and extended branches of chimney smoke. Serafim headed the other way.

He decided to walk past the front of his apartment, to see if he could learn anything new. He made slow progress along the streets, trying to appear both stumblingly drunk and aimless. He kept his eyes mostly on the ground, leaning against a fence or tree from time to time, stealing glances of the world from just below the brim of his bowler hat. As he neared his apartment, he spied two suspicious cars parked together, one empty and one with a set of men inside, smoking cigarettes and checking the mirrors, tapping their ashes out of the windows. When Serafim made his way around the back again, he confirmed that there were still men inside his apartment, and concluded that the second, empty car belonged to them. He realized he would have to wait until the cars were gone.

He picked up an empty whiskey bottle from a garbage can to add to his charade and returned to the front of the building, where he found a place to sit at a safe distance from the vehicles to outwait these men. During the course of the day he was verbally abused twice more, this time by people passing by, once a group of municipal workers who shouted insults from the sidewalk they were repairing, and once a group of boys who had run by and then returned for an impromptu game of trying to be the first to hit Serafim's bowler hat with a pebble. Serafim let them, the pebbles bouncing off his shoulders, their giggles causing one of them to begin a strained-bladder dance. He found that appearing miserable was becoming less and less a feat of acting.

Towards the end of the afternoon, the men who had been waiting in his flat came outside and hunched over to speak to the men who were waiting in the car. After a brief exchange, they piled into the empty vehicle and drove away. The men in the parked car stayed behind, remaining in their sedan to guard the front door. While the situation was not ideal, at least for the time being his apartment was empty. Serafim stood up, his muscles stiff, and nervously headed into the alleyway.

He approached his back door at a painstaking pace. While still trying to look like a drunken vagrant, he also had to keep intensely sharp, listening for movement that might be coming from the apartment. Someone might be inside, waiting for just such an eventuality. And if not, someone from the car that was parked out front might enter at any moment, on any whim. He stopped at the landing, coughed into the open back door, pretending to swig the last of the whiskey from his empty bottle. There was no sound, no movement. He fought the urge to call out, "Hello?"

Serafim stepped inside, his slippers crushing shards of broken glass and ceramic pieces. Gently, he padded through his apartment and made his way into the sitting room. The place was in ruins. Clothes, shoes, photographs, ties, hats, sheets, furniture, everything he owned was splayed across the floor. Finally convinced that no one was waiting for him, he began rummaging through his things, assembling at least one suit that he could change into immediately. He threw off his beggar clothes and hurriedly donned his own, hobbling to the front window to peek at the car out front, wanting to make sure the men were still sitting inside it. From where he was, however, he couldn't see them.

He quickly checked to see if they'd discovered his hidden drawer. He had been right — they hadn't. He then found his Leica on the ground, damaged beyond repair. Without time to feel sorry for himself, he just left it there, and stepped into his darkroom.

Once inside, he felt as if the planet, for just an instant, had stopped revolving, had slipped and lagged into some kind of momentary standstill.

On the makeshift counter he'd made were a few of his prints, which he knew the men had found in a drawer just below. They were photos of Claire, the ones he'd shot on the day he followed her to her place of work. The photographs had been laid out in the sequence they'd been shot. Of the four pictures on the counter, three had been taken when she was walking towards the camera; the fourth he'd shot the moment she stepped out of her nightclub, the Kit-Kat, the name of which was clearly discernible in the frame. The first and second photos of the sequence were missing, the spots where they had originally been placed on the counter now empty. Serafim recalled exactly what the missing photos contained and what they gave away. He recalled the sense of familiarity she had then, the ease in her manners as she looked around for him, the way she stood in front of the cabaret as if she owned it herself. Serafim imagined they had easily recognized her as the woman who'd approached the phony councilman on the street. But now they also knew where she worked.

Serafim rushed back into the sitting room, where he remembered having come across his watch under a blanket. He found it, turned it over. It was ten to four. He might still be able to catch Claire, to warn her, before she left for her shift, where they would almost certainly be waiting for her. He dove into a corner of piled clothing, looking for his phone, tossing shirts and pillowcases over his shoulders, cursing in Portuguese. He finally found it, picked it up, manically clicking the switch hook to get the operator.

"Code and number please." A female voice, dry and sleepy.

"St. Louis one-eight-six-one. Please hurry."

"I'll connect you just as soon as I can, sir."

"Please."

As the phone was ringing, Serafim darted a look at the door. Someone was climbing the stairs to his landing. He held his breath. The phone continued to ring. It seemed unlikely anyone was home. The footsteps paused at his door.

The operator came back on the line. "I'm sorry, sir, no one's responding."

"Please," Serafim whispered. "Please, can you try again? I must get through." He watched the door.

"Fine, sir."

As Claire's telephone rang again, the footsteps continued to the next landing.

On the fifth ring, she picked up. "*Oui, allô?*"

"Oh, thank God you're still home," exclaimed Serafim in French. "Claire, they know who you are. They know who *we* are. Are you okay? Are you alone?"

"I am . . . sorry? May I ask who's speaking please?"

Serafim held the receiver away from his ear, staring at it in disbelief. He could hear a tiny voice still coming from the matrix of its pinholes.

"I'm afraid Claire just left for work. This is her sister speaking. Would you mind me asking if everything is all right? Is my sister in some kind of trouble? Hello? Hello?"

But Serafim had already dropped the phone and was running for the back door, down the stairs two at a time, through the alley and out onto the street, where he spotted a taxi in the far distance and began sprinting towards it, waving his arm, his palm unfurled like a white flag.

M. Villard,

I'm very sorry to let you know at such late notice, sir, but I'm afraid I won't be able to stay on and do my set tonight. Something happened and I'm feeling quite out of sorts, and won't be able to dance. Though I wanted you to know that I've called in Maude to take my place.

Also, just to help you out in terms of programming, you might want to have a replacement for Claire standing by as well.

I'm very sorry again. I look forward to seeing you for my shift next Thursday.

Vous remerciant d'avance de votre compréhension,

Mme Chantal Burgien

31

Before going into the nightclub, Claire hesitated on the sidewalk for a moment, looking around for no reason she could think of. Everything seemed normal. Down the street on her left, a couple were squabbling, the man holding the girl's arm, the girl squirming free and walking a few paces away before he caught up and held on to her again. Claire looked up the street, to her right, where a taxi was speeding around the corner, the cab tilting to its side, straining its leaf springs. She hated how taxis drove so recklessly downtown, careening through the pedestrians, buggies, and tramcars as if they were the only vehicles on the road. She clicked her tongue at the driver and stepped inside.

She heard the bartender, crouching out of sight, restocking his shelves for the night. "How are you doing, Callum?" she called over the counter.

Only it wasn't Callum who stood up. It was some other man, someone she'd never seen before. "Sorry?" he said, wiping his hands on the white of his freshly donned apron.

"Oh. Where's Callum?"

"Callum? Oh, other guy. Got hisself all black 'n' blue he did. Some beef with a couple torpedoes s'what I hear." He squatted down again, rattling bottles.

Claire faltered, looked towards the back, listening. Something was amiss, but she didn't really know what to do about it. She wondered if it was best to just keep acting as though there was nothing wrong, to cast less suspicion in her direction. That was, after all, what had worked for her so far. She continued to the back, bent on keeping her bearing perfectly normal.

She stopped at the door of the performers' change room, where she heard several voices on the other side, speaking softly. Claire knocked.

"Yes?" came the voice of the dancer who had almost caught her and Serafim the day they'd taken the pictures.

"Is everything okay in there?" asked Claire.

"Why, Claire! Yes, honey, everything's just ducky. Come on in."

At that same moment, Claire heard someone hurrying through the front doors of the cabaret and mumbling something to the bartender. She felt the need to close herself in, quietly lock herself into some safe place. She opened the door to the change room and saw the other dancer there, sitting alone.

The woman, who was wearing a wooden smile, tapped the chair next to her. "Come have a seat."

Trying to work out what her strained expression might signify, Claire closed the door, only to be startled by the sight of two moustached men hiding right behind it.

One of them gently and calmly took Claire by the arm and pulled her into the same seat the other dancer had been sitting in; while the woman stood up and, as if previously agreed, hurried out of the room, shutting the door behind her.

It was just Claire and the two men now. The room felt cold to her. Alarmed, she saw the events around her unfolding in a sluggish, inflexible way, the sounds that the men were making in the cramped space as brittle as icicles. One of them cracked the knuckle of his pinky.

The same man who'd led her to the chair crouched down to address her, speaking in French with a singsongy Italian accent. "I am sure you know why we are here. We are looking for some photographs, and we need to find them, tonight. You will help us." The two men exchanged a measured look. "Now, how painful you make this process is entirely up to you. So let me start by asking you plainly: Where are those photographs?"

"I honestly don't know." Claire swallowed. "Serafim has them." She looked at each of them individually. "But I can tell you where he lives. I can show you."

"That is not necessary. We know where he lives. The pictures are not there. Perhaps Mr. Vieira could help us. Do you know where he is?"

"No," Claire answered, sounding small, futile.

The man straightened up. "That is" — he let out a regretful sigh — "unfortunate for you."

The men traded another look, and the second man reached into his back pocket, from which he pulled a knife, unfolded it, and held it in a rather unthreatening way, as if playfully testing the weight of its blade.

There was a knock at the door. A man's voice, trying hard to whisper and not succeeding in the least, hissed through the wood, "Claire? Claire, I need to speak with you immediately."

The three of them looked at each other, as if seeking the one who knew what to do with this new turn of events.

It was the most unlikely of them who did. "Serafim, yes, I'm here. You can come in," said Claire.

The two men scurried back into the corner where they'd hidden before, and Serafim stepped inside. Claire, tangling her fingers in her lap, was surprised to see him without a moustache. "I am sorry," she said.

Before he could work out just what she was sorry for, the door closed behind him, revealing the two men. The second man was now wielding the knife in a firm fist, while the other had his hand in the inside pocket of his jacket, where, it was understood, he had a gun, though he didn't feel the need to pull it out because Serafim was the very model of surrender, his complexion a sickly white, his hands lifting in tired submission, without even the vigour to rise above his shoulders.

"Our lucky day," the first man said, still in his melodious French. "Now, we are going to get into a car together. It is parked in the back, just a few feet away. If either of you causes a fuss or tries to run, you will die. Do we understand each other?" Sombre nods. "Good. Then let us go."

They drove, mostly in silence, to the Italian neighbourhood near the commercial quarter of St. James Street. On the way, the man who seemed to be in charge, the only one to speak so far, turned to Serafim. "So, where are the film and photographs?"

"In my apartment," Serafim offered without wavering. Claire was relieved he was co-operating.

"No, they aren't. We searched the apartment."

"Yes, I know. I watched you. But they're in a hidden place."

"I see. Good. We will wait until after dark then go there together. You can show us."

"That's fine," Serafim agreed.

They pulled into another alley and Serafim and Claire were led into a shallow basement, the ceiling pressing down on them. The men pulled out two chairs and arranged them so they were facing away from each other, and Claire and Serafim were told to sit. The first man then produced a rope, and proceeded to have a conversation in Italian with the second, presumably, Claire gathered, about the best way to tie the two of them up.

To everyone's surprise, Serafim interjected, also speaking Italian. His tone was passive, reasonable. Claire worked out that he was saying such strict measures were unnecessary, that he and Claire would do nothing but comply, co-operate to the fullest. In reaction to this outburst, the two men paused, blinking. Then the second lurched forward and wrapped the thick rope around Serafim's head, tightening it over his mouth, gagging him. They had soon done the same with Claire. Then they bound their hands and feet. When the men were satisfied that the two of them would stay put, they left, locking them in and turning off the lights, leaving them with nothing but dark, mildew, and silence.

They settled themselves on their respective chairs, breathing through and around the ropes that barred their mouths. At one point Serafim tried to say something to Claire, but he failed, sucking back the spittle from the attempt. She felt him hang his head, defeated.

Claire found herself thinking about her sister, then of her parents, who hadn't entered her mind in what felt like years.

She recalled the way her father had indulged her, his warm words and effortless praise. The same could be said for her grandmother, and her sister. All of them, coaxing her towards something that, it was sickening to think, they might not themselves have believed she would ever become. Ironically, in the end, not doubting them for a second, she had left them all behind, on her way to that invented, extravagant place. In reality, where she had ended up was frightening. She couldn't stop herself from crying, tears and saliva collecting at the end of her chin, where they streamed onto her dress in long strings that she couldn't wipe clean.

She felt Serafim shifting around behind her. He managed to reach one of his thumbs to a point where it was in contact with her wrist. He gently stroked the skin he could touch there, and he didn't stop for hours, his thumb running back and forth in the quiet darkness, until the men returned and switched on the light.

They untied only their feet and dragged them back outside, where the sun had since fallen. They were pushed into the back of a different car this time, where the man with the knife, whom they had yet to hear speak, was waiting for them. Seated in the front were a driver and another man, both of whom Claire had never seen before. What was strange was that the man riding shotgun seemed to be well acquainted with Serafim.

He turned in his seat, smiled. "Serafimeh." He tipped up his hat. "*Come stai?*" Then he said something in Italian, which Claire took to mean, "Because I know you, I asked if I could come along. That way, we can get this over with as quickly and as smoothly as possible." He turned to face the front, while the man in the back gestured that they should crouch down, out of sight. As they complied, the driver started the car and pulled away, out into the Saturday night streets of Montreal, the sidewalks that ran on either side of them already mingling with revellers and clubgoers, all of them oblivious to what was passing them by.

Case No.:   L-3849
Article No.: 47
Description: Charred photo, recovered
Date: May 19, 1929

๛

Only a small corner is distinguishable as a photo, allowing the item to be identified as such. The picture must have been taken on the street, presumably in Montreal. Besides a line of pavement, one can just make out the back end of an automobile, dragging its blur out of the frame to the right.

From there, progressing to the left, the image becomes increasingly fire damaged. At first the picture is bubbled and mottled, whatever had been at the image's centre now obscured, stretching along the distortions that the paper made while flexing in flame.

Beyond that is a jagged rim of char, black feathers and flakes curling into dust, marking the place where the photographic paper as a medium of fuel was entirely consumed.

32

As they pulled up to the back of his apartment, Serafim was amazed at how calm he felt, even relieved. He was eager to get this over with, to give them what they wanted, offer his sincerest apology, and watch them leave, no harm done. This is how he'd imagined things unfolding; particularly now, as there was really only one man he felt he had to worry about, the smaller one, who had yet to speak. There was something about him that Serafim didn't trust, some glint in his expression that made him seem unpredictable.

The possibility of a peaceful parley, however, became doubtful when the smaller man retrieved a heavy canvas bag from the trunk and, much more roughly than was necessary, yanked Claire from the car and shoved her up towards the back door of Serafim's apartment. Also needlessly shoved, Serafim trailed closely behind them. The driver, he noted, stayed in the car, poised to flee.

Once they were inside, all of them stepping over the debris still scattered on the floor, things quickly turned sour. The smaller man, unshouldering the canvas bag, pulled Claire close to him and began sliding his hands over the fabric of her dress.

He was murmuring to her in Italian, as if speaking to a lover, his voice high-pitched and gentle. Claire looked away, the rope still in her mouth, hands still tied behind her back.

Then Serafim's head was jostled, and the rope between his teeth loosened, falling free. He stretched his lips wide, working out the numbness along the sides of his mouth, sweeping his chin across his shirt to clear the saliva that had gathered there. As soon as he'd recovered enough to speak, he addressed the smaller man, now squeezing his hands into Claire's buttocks as if kneading dough. "Excuse me," he said in Italian. "Please, this doesn't concern her. I am the one who knows where the prints and film are. I would ask you to please leave her alone. Please."

The smaller man, tilting his head at Serafim as if in sudden understanding and sympathy, took his hands off Claire right away. "Oh, I'm sorry," he said in Italian. He took a step back from her and paused as if apologetic for a moment, before swinging a wild fist and striking her in the face, knocking her to the ground, clumsily, onto her side, where she gasped for breath through the rope, writhing to overcome the pain and shock.

Serafim stood speechless as the same man then took a few soft steps towards him, only to mete out the same reprimand. Serafim was now also on the floor, squirming to recover. Tasting blood, he swallowed it down. Looking at his apartment horizontally, his ears still ringing from the blow, he became aware that the smaller man was now tying a piece of rope to one of Claire's ankles. Once he had done this, he dragged her across the floor, towards Serafim's bathroom, where he disappeared for a while, apparently tying the other end of the rope to something, maybe the toilet bowl. At the time, for Serafim, this made no sense whatsoever. Though he wasn't given long to think about it.

The second man squatted down near his face. He took off his hat and offered a warm grin. It was the man Antonino had warned him to steer clear of, the man Serafim had taken a picture of on the ship while crossing the Atlantic, and who had demanded he develop that picture as soon as they arrived in Montreal. Serafim had obliged, and had even given him the film to the exposure, a favour he was now glad to have done.

"So, where are those pictures, Serafim?"

Serafim twisted round, gesturing with his head at a corner of the room. "There. It's a false panel. That lower part pulls out as a drawer."

The man considered this for a moment before getting up and feeling around the cracks in the corner, kicking a few things out of his way on the ground. When he found it, he let out a childlike whistle of delight, then pulled the heavy drawer out until it crashed onto the floorboards. Tiny envelopes of Serafim's archival film fluttered in disarray, adding to the chaos already in the room. He soon found the large envelope and lifted it from the heap, looking back at Serafim. "Is this all of them?"

"No. I developed one extra picture, and placed it under those heavy canisters. It should be there somewhere."

Out of curiosity, the man lifted the lid of one of the bulky canisters, ruining the reel of unused film inside, before he located the extra picture. "Good, very good," he said, returning to crouch in front of Serafim.

He opened the envelope, slid the photos out, and looked them over, turning them around, viewing them at different angles. He raised his eyebrows, gave an impressed nod, and frowned. "You take good photos. I still have mine, you know. And I like it very much." He then threw the photos over Serafim, where they twirled like falling leaves and settled near the overturned drawer. Shaking the envelope until the film dropped out, he held one of the strips up to the light fixture. "Very good," he said in the same tone as before. "This is all very fine."

He then looked over his shoulder at the smaller man, who was standing above Claire's tied ankle, lying half in and half out of the bathroom. "But you know," he said, turning back to Serafim, "we have a problem. You once explained to me that with a film like this" — he wagged the strip in Serafim's face — "a person could make a million copies of a picture. Our problem is: How do we know this is the only film? How do we know there aren't more of these pictures, hidden out there in the city, waiting to resurface, waiting for someone else to try their hand at blackmailing people they should not? How do I know you haven't sold such pictures to others? You must understand, Serafim, I have a job to do here. My instructions are to make this problem, which you have created, go away forever. Now, how can I be sure that I've done my job?"

Serafim's voice betrayed his growing panic. "You . . . well, you have my word."

"So," the man confirmed, "to reassure me, you are offering the *word* of a scheming extortionist?"

"Please." Serafim rested his head on the ground. "I swear to you, on my mother's soul, I am telling you the truth."

The man dropped the strip of film. "You know, instead, I want you to tell me what you think. Do you *think* a professional dancer needs both her feet?"

Serafim lifted his head. "What?"

The bathroom door slammed shut, Claire's ankle preventing the heavy wood from making contact with the frame. She let out a muffled cry, curled in pain. The small man slammed it again. Again. Again. Huffing for breath, his eyes white and frenzied. Inhuman thud after thud, the sound changing as the bones in her ankle broke and so began to absorb the force more readily, in the way that soft flesh might.

Serafim yelled for him to stop, please stop, but it wasn't until Claire ceased making noise and seemed on the brink of losing consciousness that he did.

There was a strange quiet. Claire whimpering, the smaller man catching his breath, hands on his knees, inspecting the details of his work. The pulped skin of Claire's ankle had broken in several places, her calf flecked with red.

Serafim was also squirming, looking back and forth between the two men, not knowing whom to plead with. "Please, please stop this. I promise you, there are no other pictures, no other film. You have my *word*. Please."

The second man was still calmly crouched in front of him. "Yes. You've already told us that, Serafim. What we would like is to know something new."

"But I have nothing new to give you!"

Grimly, the man shrugged and turned to his colleague. More slams. Three, four.

"Stop!" To make an emphatic sound, Serafim pounded his head against the floor, dizzying himself. "Stop!"

The smaller man did, and once he had caught his breath again, he looked as though he agreed with Serafim, that it was time to end this, and he bent down to untie Claire's ankle. But Serafim knew it wasn't over, and watched him closely, powerlessly.

Having untied her ankle, he grabbed the knot of rope that was still fastened behind her head to gag her and dragged her over to Serafim, until she was only a few feet from where he was lying on the floor. The man straightened Claire into a sitting position, embracing her from behind. Her head flopped to the side, exhausted but conscious. He then wormed his fingers into her collar and ripped open her dress and chemise, exposing her breasts.

"I am begging you. Please. Please don't do this," implored Serafim.

The man produced the same knife they'd seen earlier, and unfolded it, watching Serafim's reaction. Cupping one of Claire's breasts, he held the blade just beneath it and, with a smile, spoke for the first time. "These are such fine teats. You know, I think I'm going to bring one home with me. What do you think? Do you think I should bring one home with me?"

Both men turned to Serafim, as if solemnly interested in his answer. But Serafim was descending into himself, digging deep, focusing. He took in a long breath, leisurely let it out. They waited for him to reply.

"Yes," he said. "Yes, I think you should."

The smaller man's smile faded.

Serafim looked at the man he'd met on the ship. "I think you should do whatever you feel you have to."

Serafim then struggled to turn himself over, to turn away from the man holding Claire. He just managed to, and spoke to the empty room that was now in front of him. "I have told you the truth, and have nothing more to give. I understand that you're just doing what you have been told to do. I hold nothing against either of you. Take whatever you will. I accept."

There was a baffled stillness behind him, then the shuffling of clothing.

The man he'd met on the ship eventually walked around to be in Serafim's view again. He didn't crouch this time. He put his hands in his pockets, looked around the room. "Okay." From one of his pockets he pulled a pack of cigarettes, "Okay." He traded a quick look with the other man, and gestured at the pictures and film that were scattered on the floor.

Serafim heard the smaller man let go of Claire and make his way to the canvas bag, where he retrieved something that sounded both tinny and liquid at the same time. He appeared in Serafim's sight carrying a jerry can. He unscrewed the spout and began pouring dirty water over the pictures and film that were spread out on the floor. Serafim's first thought was that water would do nothing to damage the prints or film; they would just need to be dried again. He was thinking of telling them this when the smell of gasoline washed over him, an ice-bath realization.

With an unlit cigarette dangling from his mouth, the man he'd met on the ship sauntered around to the back of Serafim and began untying his hands, talking through the butt clamped between his lips. "I want you to know," he said, "it would have been easier to kill you both. Consider this a mercy. But if I hear so much as a whisper of you taking blackmail photos again, I will come back and do it right. Do we understand each other?"

Serafim's hands came free. "Yes."

"Good," he said, standing up and making his way to the back door.

The smaller man emptied the last of the jerry can's contents on the pictures and Serafim's archival film and tossed it into a corner. He then looked at the door, looked at Serafim, and decided that before leaving he would run over and give him a quick, stout kick in the stomach, winding him. Once he had, he spat onto Serafim's neck and hurried outside, his footsteps clambering down the stairs.

Serafim was still sipping air into his lungs, rolling from side to side, when the other man finally lit his cigarette. He held the match out in front of him for a moment, waiting for Serafim to look his way. Serafim did. "It's not as if she can run," he said. "You'd best get moving." And with that, he tossed the match.

In mid-scramble to get up, Serafim was knocked over by the thunderous *whoomp* and burst of heat that lit up the room. He rolled back onto his feet and, with no time to think of how best to get Claire out, grabbed hold of the same knot that the smaller man had used to drag her with and did the same, sliding her across the floor through the islands of his scattered clothes, towards the front door, the flames madly climbing the walls and ceiling behind them, keeping up with their flight. He opened the door, stumbled onto the landing. He heard a window break. Then his neighbour began yelling fire, fire, *fire*. From the landing above, people were already streaming down the stairway, carrying toddlers in pyjamas, wide-eyed or crying, hurrying grandparents along.

He doubled over to help himself breathe, untied Claire's hands and the rope that was gagging her. Another window shattered from the heat, smoke billowing out his front door like the stack of a steam engine. Serafim stopped one of the last people to come down the stairs, a wiry young man, and asked him for help. Together they carried Claire to safety, lumbering with her limp weight down the stairs and across the street, where they put her down on a patch of new grass. Serafim slumped on the ground behind her, still taking in air like an asthmatic, and covered the rip in her dress with his hands. The howl of emergency horns already swelling, galloping teams of horses in the distance, their bells like delirious tambourines.

In front of them, the fire blossomed and bloated. The rhythm of its crackles accelerating, crescendo of some frantic tempo, losing time; the growl of its baseline distending, deepening. The flames danced higher, ever higher, climbing invisible stairs into the night, ginger hips rolling, arms swaying, reaching ecstatic, while reeling embers from their fingertips up into the sky, sparks that lifted and soared through the updrafts, only to vanish abruptly into skeletons of miniature parachutes, snuffed out and drifting, already forgotten, like the fanciful dreams of children.

(FOUR)
A NEW ERA

Medium:	Gelatin silver print
Description:	Woman staring
Location:	Montreal, Quebec
Date:	1930

ℭℰ

A woman lies on a low mattress. Folds of the duvet she's wrapped inside gather themselves and collect at her chest, her unseen fists like an arachnid clutching at the centre of a cloth web. Her cheeks do not appear to be flushed with fever, giving one the feeling that she isn't holding this material against her body because the room around her is cold, but that the inclement temperatures are, some-how, coming from within.

There is a bedside table at the head of the mattress. On it is a full glass of water that looks to have been sitting there for some time, minuscule bubbles lining its sides, frog eggs in a stagnant pond. A book rests in front of the glass, a limp marker of ribbon bowing over to touch the wood, inserted in what seems to be the book's title page.

She is young, likely in her late twenties, and is lying mostly on her stomach, staring at some vague and distant part of the room, perhaps into the rainy hills of a wallpapered landscape. Her hair looks unclean, oily, knotted into tufts and bristles. Her head, as if having unknowingly slid down the slope of her pillow, has sunk into the white sheet below it, a ragged weight abandoned in the snow.

The woman's face is devoid of expression, her facial muscles lax. Her eyes appear hazy, like a swirling nighttime pool, misted over.

33

Claire was whisked to a hospital, where a doctor inspected a blurry X-ray of her ankle, lowered it from the light, and shook his head. He set it as best he could, applying an ungainly plaster-of-Paris splint to the entire lower part of her leg, and sent her home only after Serafim had covered the cost. For almost two months she lay in bed, dozed and slept, her leg elevated, staring vacantly out the window of her tiny apartment. She had little appetite for the simple food that Serafim brought her, and more than anything she just wanted to be left alone, to sit in silence and look through her window at nothing in particular. Sometimes, still staring through it, she would distractedly scratch at the outside of her cast, never seeming to realize that she couldn't reach the damp itch below.

After seven weeks, the cast was removed, only to reveal how disfigured her ankle was, and would always be. She had lost a lot of muscle as well, which made it look even worse. The doctor doubted it would ever heal to the point where she would be able to walk without a pronounced limp. He didn't bother offering any predictions about dance. Recovery would be slow, he warned, stressing the importance of doing exercises to increase the ankle's mobility. She was given crutches, and told to begin gradually putting weight on it over the coming weeks, in slow increments. But all Claire really used the crutches for was getting to and from bed. Like an infant, she spent her time either in tears, nibbling food, or sleeping.

In the meantime, Serafim had moved in, both because it would allow him to care for her at most hours of the day and because he had nothing and nowhere else to live. He thoroughly cleaned the house and put his few things in a single drawer. Sensing that he wasn't particularly wanted in the apartment, and with Antonino busy wooing a new woman he'd met at an Italian-hall dance, Serafim took to working extra shifts at two of the other studios in the city. He was trying to save as much as he could over the summer, hoping to buy another Leica, to profit from the booming times.

And booming times they were. The main studio he worked in was undergoing massive renovations and expansion, and there was talk of Serafim being promoted out of the darkroom to become a first assistant, someone who helped control the lighting and props, and managed the enormous box cameras and lenses. By mid-October he'd finally saved enough to make his purchase, and he spent every dollar of his savings on the transaction. It put him in such a financial bind that he took to working shifts even at night, just to make enough to cover their rent for the month. He found himself eating as little as Claire.

On the last weekend of October, the newspapers reported that there was a potential financial crisis brewing. The following Monday and Tuesday saw investors fleeing the market en masse. The value of stocks and shares dropped like the blade of a guillotine. It was a catastrophe, to be sure, but thankfully it was one the critics, contributors, and columnists agreed would soon blow over. If there was something the previous decade had taught them, it was that one should never underestimate the robust power and vitality of unfettered capitalism.

By early winter, Claire was hobbling around the flat in her nightgown, shuffling in her slippers to keep the coal stove well stoked and eating apples while curled in bed, her pillow ceaselessly damp. At the same time the analysts and newspapermen were beginning to sound a little less sure of themselves. The lineup of patrons and families in the city who wanted their portraits taken dwindled to nothing. The small bank that had lent the money to the main studio where Serafim worked found itself scrambling to survive. They began hounding the Scotsman who owned it to pay back the substantial loan he'd taken out on his renovations. But the Scotsman had lost big in the collapse, and so had no choice but to file for bankruptcy, forcing Serafim to scrape by on the few supplemental ventures he'd managed to find while saving for his Leica. The work in those studios, however, was also diminishing.

Then, in December, kneeling next to the bed where Claire was still holding vigil over the blank window of her apartment, Serafim said, "I have some wonderful news." She didn't ask what the news was. "Last night, I accompanied Antonino to serenade this new lover of his. He can't sing so well — but he is getting married."

Claire's eyes moved from the window down to Serafim for a slow second, then back to the window. "That's nice."

"Would you . . . like to come? It might be good to get out."

"No, thank you."

But Claire would find that marriage was to become a topic of discussion the whole of that long winter. First, Cécile, inspired by Claire's impetuosity, asked Gilles for a divorce. As she'd anticipated, he was devastated. And he refused her, coldly citing the upcoming election and the fact that a divorce would cost him precious votes. If he lost, he told her, all his efforts would be for naught anyway, and with nothing left, he would gladly grant her the divorce she sought; if he won, however, he would ask her to stay with him at least until midway through his term. As it happened, he won. Their home became unbearable. Cécile urged him to lash out, to ruin her reputation and expose her as an adulteress, but he refused. Such a reaction had not been in her plans. Nevertheless, she wrote Claire a letter outlining the success she felt in her brief experimentation with rashness, telling her that she was now committed to getting to his mid-term and their inevitable separation, as well as looking forward to living in Montreal again, where she would be closer to Claire and where they would be able to see each other every week if they wished. Claire didn't respond to the letter.

The next talk of marriage came from Serafim. Encouraged by how easy the process had been for Antonino, he confessed his concerns about him and Claire living in sin.

"Wouldn't it be nice — better — if we were married?" he asked her one frigid Saturday morning.

Claire stared through the window, ignoring him.

"Well? What do you think?"

Finally, she looked over at him, as if distracted from some enthralling spectacle. "What are you talking about?"

"Marriage. I am talking about you and me getting married."

Claire was incredulous. For the first time, she felt the urge to ask him to go away, to leave her apartment and life forever. She had no idea how she would get by, but she didn't care. "Come here." Serafim eagerly crouched near her bed, where she took his hand and pulled it under the sheets, guiding it beneath her nightgown and onto the scar of her stomach. She ran his fingers down the length of it. "Do you know what this means?"

Serafim's face tensed up. "No."

"It means I can never have children. You would be marrying a broken woman. Is that what you want?"

Serafim pulled his hand away, stood up, and took a measured step back.

"I didn't think so." She returned her gaze to the window.

Without saying anything, Serafim put on his coat, hat, scarf, and gloves, and went out for a long walk in the snow. Claire half expected him never to return, and she was surprised that this possibility didn't bother her in the least.

But several hours later Serafim did come back, stamping his feet clear of snow on the landing, hanging his scarf with staid determination on the coat stand. He walked into the room and squatted beside her again.

"You are right. It's not quite . . . how I imagined my future. Not what I've always had in mind, I mean. But I'd still like to marry you, broken or not."

Claire shook her head as if at a bird that had just spent a great deal of effort learning how to pick its lock only to gain access to an adjoining cage. "Fine," she sighed. "But just you and I, and at some small, out-of-the-way church. Those are my conditions."

Serafim gave a single, serious nod. "Fine."

"Now," she said, burying herself farther beneath the covers, "would you be a dear and put some more coal in the stove? It's freezing in here."

They were married on a Monday evening, in a side chapel, a precarious crack serrating the ceiling above them. Serafim found the rings in a pawnshop, and Claire wore the most modest dress she owned. It was blue. Cécile and Antonino were asked to be the witnesses, and after the quick ceremony they decided to go out for a drink. It was one of the first times Claire had tried walking without crutches, and their progress from the chapel to the closest tavern was slow. When they finished their second beverage, Antonino, trying to heighten everyone's mood, gauchely suggested they find a place to go dancing. The table cringed at the mistake, panning over at Claire, who simply looked into her glass. Soon afterwards, Antonino and Cécile were deep in a discussion (which was on the cusp of an argument) about Lionel Groulx and his encouraging views on corporatism, something of which Mussolini was also a proponent and therefore Antonino felt he had to outwardly despise.

As their tones became more ardent, Serafim reached a hand over to Claire's. "Thank you," he whispered.

She gave him a sad grin. "You're welcome."

Soon afterwards, the two of them had formed a morning ritual, whereby Serafim would get out of bed, refuel the stove, and, while it warmed the room, brew some strong coffee in the percolator, turn on the radio, hand Claire a cup in bed, and sit on a chair next to her, both of them sipping away while listening to the morning news. She had initially taken him to be a tea man, but it seemed she was wrong on that count. They kept no tea in their cupboards whatsoever.

It was during one of these mornings, near the end of February 1930, that Claire shot up in bed and pointed at the radio's speaker. "Are you hearing this?"

Serafim, taken aback, wasn't used to seeing her animated in any way. "Yes. No. What?"

She grabbed onto his arm. "Would you be able to buy a newspaper on your way home today?"

"Of course," he agreed. He was so glad to see her inspired, or interested in anything at all, that he brought home virtually every paper published in the city, including the two major English journals. The effort paid off. Claire spent her days poring over every one of them, maniacally following what would come to be known as the *Phi-Phi* Affair.

Phi-Phi was a French musical comedy that had been playing in the city for some time. With the turn of the economic tide, the Catholic and Protestant "vice crusaders" found themselves newly frustrated and with much time on their hands. The musical comedy in question, which had opened in Paris at the end of the Great War and had been playing and touring throughout the world ever since, had salacious lyrics and revealing young chorus girls, and it dealt with the horrifying theme of adultery "flippantly." The righteous-minded flooded the main francophone newspaper, *Le Devoir*, with letters of moral outrage. Though the musical was already in its seventh showing in Montreal, the police chief now felt obliged to respond to the outcry. Just before the curtain went up, he had his officers storm the building and arrest seventeen members of the cast for "participating in an immoral production." The affronted performers were released on bail shortly thereafter and the French troupe returned to Paris, swearing they would never set foot in such a backwards land again. The morality squads patted themselves on the back.

Less than a month later, *Jazz Time*, an American burlesque revue, was also censored by the police, this time at the Gayety Theatre. While Claire was smug with the knowledge that the manager of the Gayety was in hot water, it was only the performers who were arrested, sixteen this time, all of them American. The dancers were again released on bail and quickly returned to their country, with a shaking-fist oath never to come back. In a single axe swing, the city's long-running ties to Broadway and Hollywood were severed.

Soon after, an official municipal theatre censor was appointed, and a law was passed requiring all traditional and musical productions to submit their scripts and lyrics for approval. The censor, like the one put in place for films, pledged to prohibit all productions that did not contain "respectable morality and family values."

On top of this, and for the first time, the movie industry could boast both sound and undreamt-of budgets, allowing ritzy musicals to be filmed once then screened countless times at nickelodeon theatres everywhere. Before, the only way to see Al Jolson in Montreal had been with the purchase of a prohibitively expensive ticket for the balconies at the Princess Theatre, when he happened to be passing through the city on one of his brief off-Broadway tours (aboard his private ten-car train). Now he could be seen any time, for pennies, at a commoners' cinema. The once-thriving musical stage in Montreal was in its death throes, and as soon as Claire was sure of this, she stopped asking for papers and returned to her bed.

As the spring fringed their apartment's window with green, Serafim was determined to get Claire outside. He saved his nickels for weeks to buy two tram tickets for one of the "golden chariot" lines, streetcars that were designed much like bleachers in a stadium, in successive tiers that sloped to the front, offering optimum sightseeing potential, the open wind in everyone's face. They went on a Sunday to Stoney Point in Lachine, and meandered through the countryside on a lone tramcar, coveys of birds that had been feeding in the long grass beside the tracks exploding into flight as they passed. Serafim caught Claire smiling, twice.

He would also go into record shops and, stealing processing time and chemicals from his odd jobs in darkrooms around the city, trade *carte de visite* portraits of the workers there for used 78-rpm vinyls, having no choice but to take their word on what was the newest and trendiest in jazz. He would wrap the records in the nicest newspaper pages he could find — usually illustrated fashion spreads of stick-thin women with modernist-sketched faces — and present them to Claire in her bed with great ceremony. Judging by her reaction when he eased the gramophone needle down onto them, however, the vendors were seldom telling him the truth.

Helping Antonino out with his increasingly important food co-operatives around the city, Serafim sometimes lent a hand picking dandelion leaves, which the Italians used as a pungent addition to salads. He would then bring home the modest yellow flowers and put them in a glass jar on Claire's bedside table, where they would smoulder in the corner for a short spell before drooping and fading away.

But of all these efforts to bring her round, none was as promising as what he stumbled upon one regular afternoon in August. He had been working at a studio with one of the more important francophone photographers of the day, though he had been demoted from doing even lowly darkroom work (in order to make room for someone in the photographer's family) and was simply there to sweep and clean, offering patrons beverages between shoots.

He reeled through the door with the news. "You will never guess who I met today," he proclaimed, flinging off his shoes and traipsing to where Claire was sitting on a chair near the window. "Two famous dancers, a young couple, who posed for their shots in impressive acrobatic lifts. They have apparently been dancing their way through America for some time now, touring with very big acts. They were originally from Montreal, and have returned to take over a dance studio that the man's father has run for years but can't anymore, on account of his health. L'École de Danse Lacasse-Morenoff is what it used to be called — now Le Studio de Danse Moderne. Anyway, when I was refilling their waterglasses, I took the opportunity to mention that I too knew a talented dancer, and one who might be able to help them in some way at their studio. They asked your name (just to be polite, you could tell), but it turns out they know you, said they danced with you when you were younger. And they would like very much to see you, to speak with you about, maybe, teaching lessons or something of the sort. Can you think of better news than that?"

Claire felt suddenly and inexplicably drained. "And what do you think a cripple could possibly offer them?" The question wasn't meant to be answered, and she returned to her bed as if amazed at herself for ever having had the gall to emerge from it.

The autumn came and went. Antonino's wife, who had gotten pregnant only four months after their wedding, had a child, a boy, in November. Serafim tactfully waited for the couple to invite him over after the delivery, not wanting to impose at such an intimate time. Antonino called him five days later — in a voice that seemed bent on not waking the baby — and asked him to drop by, and to bring his camera along with him. Serafim put his Leica in a shoulder bag and set off, having just splurged on two mid-range cigars.

He returned a few hours later to find Claire lying in bed, in the same position she'd been in when he left. She didn't notice his mood, or that he'd taken a seat across from her and was toying with his camera; she simply continued staring through the window. He took a picture of her, which in turn had her snapping a cross look back at him, as she knew she certainly wasn't looking her best. He hadn't taken a photo of her in well over a year.

She narrowed her eyes. "You *must* have something better to do than sit around here, taking my photograph. There are more interesting things, I'm sure."

He was in a peculiar mood, and didn't look away from her. "Yes, there are. But I had a single exposure remaining in this film. I used the others to take photos of Antonino's newborn." Serafim laid the camera in his lap, adjusted its weight, still watching her. "His son is dead. Antonino just asked me over to record what he looked like, to help him remember. The boy died of jaundice two days ago. He's still yellow. They don't have the money to bury him. I've lent him what I can, but he needs more. The child will have to stay in the basement until they scrape together enough to pay for the funeral. They're trying to get through it gracefully. I'm not sure they will."

Serafim retired into the kitchen to rummage up some food, leaving Claire in bed, still looking for words to say. And while he might already have made a point — by including her on a film whose every other exposure captured a child who had passed — he further emphasized it by bringing her a copy of her photograph several days later. He left it on the table just before setting out for one of his loose-end jobs. Claire sat down in front of the picture and was soon bent over it as if studying from a book. The photo was so lifeless, so dull, that she held it ever closer to her face, searching for hints of a spark somewhere, deep, hidden behind her expression. She could find nothing.

After she'd inspected the picture for quite a while, she crumpled it and got up from the table to throw it away and pour herself a bath. When she got out, she stood in the centre of the main room, straightened the simple dress she'd put on, and tried to stand on her toes, one of the exercises the doctor had given her to increase mobility in her ankle. It was soon sore and fatigued, and she spent another long while painfully stretching it out, straining to pull it back and push it forward, then wincing at the tenderness as she rolled it from side to side. It soon became an everyday ritual, her ankle continuously aching, though finally getting stronger. She also began going for walks around the block, three times a day, until the snow fell. Then, afraid she would lose all the progress she'd made, she went out late one afternoon in December to talk with the Morenoffs.

After theatrically kissing their long-lost hellos, her ankle was one of the first things they asked about. She made something up on the spot, which became the story she would use for the rest of her life: she was in a vehicle, driving too fast, and something went terribly wrong. To her amazement, the couple mistakenly assumed this was a recent event, and that Claire was still on the mend, that her walking, and dancing for that matter, would be returning to normal at some point in the near future. She didn't correct them, her confidence stepping up a notch in that one moment alone, filling the voids that reality had so eagerly kept empty.

It turned out they had a proposition for her. They didn't need instructors per se, as both of them were more motivated than ever and keen on doing all the teaching themselves. They did, however, have a few students who had managed to pay the full price in these hard times but who were lacking in either training or talent, or both, and to a degree that they were holding back some of the ambitious projects the school had on the go. They wondered if she might offer these girls some extra tutorship and guidance, revisit the fundamentals with them. The school, like every other in existence, was now mostly concentrating on the "black-influenced" dances, the Charleston, black bottom, varsity drag, the lindy eight and lindy six. Was she familiar with these? Danced at the Terminal you say? Well, then, you're probably better versed than we are. Though we would also expect some of the standards as well, warm-ups on the barre, a bit of tap, the buck time, waltz clog, maybe a few soft-shoe routines. You don't say? Well, you sound like just the woman we need. They pointed out that such an arrangement would also help keep her in shape while she worked that ankle of hers towards a speedy recovery. She'd be back into the (admittedly floundering) circuit by springtime.

Unfortunately, they added, the way things looked, it was doubtful they would be able to pay her — to start with, anyway. Money was tight. But it wasn't as if such hard times could possibly draw themselves out for years, decades. Just as soon as it was financially viable to pay her, they would, they promised. Even if, as a primary motivation, something like this shouldn't really be done for the money, should it? they asked. Claire smiled. No, she agreed, it should not.

They provided her with a small space in the building of the original dance studio, where Claire had spent the better part of her childhood. The grim fact was that there had been a terrible mishap with the elevator there, which saw two young girls plummet to a gory demise at the rebarred bottom of the shaft. The lift had since been dismantled, but still, no one wanted to buy, or even rent, the space that had been liberated in its stead. This space they were now stuck with adjoined a storage room where the studio kept its obsolete props, in case they might one day be salvaged or reused. It wasn't much, but it was all they had to work with. So, if it was all right with Claire, she could start the very next week.

Claire took the keys from them and dropped by on her way home. Outside, the winter sun was sinking, yellowing the building to the colour of aged newspaper, elongating its shadows like the slender letters of an art deco font. Inside, the place was cold and cheerless. It would need some work. A gramophone, a metronome, plenty of coal for the stove. She moved one of the backdrops to clear up more space, dusted her hands off afterwards, and scowled at the bare bulb that dangled from the ceiling.

The first student she had was a clumsy girl of thirteen who seemed, for all intents and purposes, hopeless. Claire had her tapping her toe to a waltz for an entire session until, at long last, she began to feel its three/four rhythm in her foot. Then another girl was added, and another — all of them faltering and insecure, shoulders pushed forward, heads hung low, hiding behind the smallness of their voices. Claire had them shouting, together now, louder. Now clap, *harder*, she encouraged, partly laughing with them but mostly commanding with sober necessity.

Both before and after each lesson, Claire would use the space herself to practise, figuring out steps, turns, and kicks that she could perform using her left foot only, while carefully planning her other movements to rely on her right foot as little as possible. She had soon developed a repertoire around her handicap, which would fool no one professionally but would at least make her seem like an authority to the few tatty students who frequented "the basement," as it became known. For Claire, it was increasingly important to impress this bedraggled set of girls. And likewise for them. Their teacher, they had learned, was the type of woman who gave compliments only when they were rightfully deserved. Her pupils were respectful enough to return the favour.

Caro Serafim,

The only thing the few photographers left in Paris can talk about is the exhibition showing at the Julien Levy Gallery in New York. It's said that it'll change everything. And this, with the kind of photos we've been dabbling in all along. Have you heard of Henri Cartier-Bresson? I met him once at the Café Cyrano *in '27. He was just a frustrated painting student then. Now they say he's set to definitively "legitimize our art."*

I know I've been complaining about it in every letter, but the exodus of talent continues to flee Paris for the U.S.A. Everything is suffering: the visual arts, literary, performance. One can actually feel the spirit in Europe changing, nationalism rearing its divisive head in every corner. Have you been following the exploits of Germany's new chancellor, arresting or killing off his Communist opposition? And sadly, this Hitler fellow isn't alone in his paramilitarism and hysterical propaganda.

Of course, Salazar's new constitution in March was welcomed as a harbinger of stability, but there's much in his Estado Novo that worries me. I certainly don't believe Portugal needs "saving" from the moral decay of modernism; and even if it did, I doubt that patriotic fervour and Catholicism would be the things to save it. Between you and me, Serafim, I have a terrible feeling that our homeland is opening its arms to precisely that which it should be rising up against: a military that looks just like Mussolini's, the strictest of state censorship, and a secret police already shipping dissidents off to unseen prisons in Cape Verde.

Who knows? Maybe I'll be heading your way soon enough. I envy you there, in Quebec. Though, the way I see it, you've always had a knack for being at the right place, the right time.

O teu amigo,

Álvaro

34

Hope that better financial times were just over the horizon soon spindrifted away like the last of the precious topsoil. The price of wheat plunged, and kept plunging, until it was only a third of what it had been before the Crash. The construction industry came to a standstill, with the lowly builders having to swallow many of the unpaid contracts from bankruptcies further up the ladder. Close to a quarter of the population of Montreal became dependent on relief, channelled through denominational agencies — Catholic, Protestant, Jewish. The Catholics, being the poorest, saw many of their parishioners switch to the English-backed Protestant faith, just for the better handouts. (The Jewish associations were known for not being charitable to fakes.)

Housing became a pressing problem, with sleeping stations set up in now-vacant office spaces. Single men and women banded together in scruffy apartments, four or five of them lying side by side on a mattress, others below them on the floor, flicking off cockroaches through the night. Only a select few of the elderly were fortunate enough to have pensions, and the winter months saw homeless seniors forced to seek refuge in jail.

With no money for gasoline, new vehicles appeared on the streets: automobiles towed by horses, dubbed "Bennett buggies" after the millionaire prime minister who lived in a posh suite at the Château Laurier in Ottawa, and who believed that in a free enterprise system governments had no place intervening in the public's affairs or hardships. The exceptionally rich found solace in the lowered prices of exclusive goods, the newest fashions from Paris were still being imported, and the opera was still running.

Radical "solutions" and political movements ebbed and flowed ineffectually. Work camps were initiated outside the city, providing single men with slavish employment and lodging in bunkhouses, but they were run at best like prisons for delinquents, and at worst like totalitarian regimes. They proved both unpopular and unsuccessful. Soup kitchens and breadlines were established. The streets saw strikes, marches, demonstrations, riots. Immigrants who had the audacity to ask for relief, and whose papers had only been stamped within recent years, were deported.

By 1933, Antonino had failed in turn as a coal merchant, a cement contractor, and a baker. Along with many other Italians in the city, he had moved north, along the Main and near the Mile End train station, where property was cheaper and there were still fields nearby in which French Canadians (for reasons no one could fathom) weren't using to grow their own vegetables. Antonino's wife had had a second child, who survived. She spent her days caring for the baby and preparing whatever Antonino brought in from the different green patches he was squatting on; making *conserva* from sliced tomatoes laid out on wooden boards in the sun; roasting peppers to store in jars; frying beans in olive oil and garlic; rolling homemade pasta to trade for large containers of tuna or a leg of salted ham that could be whittled from throughout the darkest months of winter.

Antonino's being deprived and in debt didn't mean he was any less politically engaged, however. The food co-operatives he'd set up had become more important than ever, while the spare hands needed to cultivate, organize, and transport the provisions were never more eager or easier to come by. In addition to this, and despite stern warnings from the Department of Immigration about his anti-fascist activities, he continued to do everything in his power short of founding another newspaper.

In the middle of July that year, one of the most eminent fascists alive was on his way to Montreal. General Italo Balbo was travelling with the Italian air force, and was setting out to make aviation history. He intended on crossing the Atlantic via the treacherous east-west route — something that had only barely been accomplished by a few solitary aircraft — and he was attempting it in a massive twenty-four-seaplane formation. Everyone knew that such a venture could only end in tragedy — or triumph. And as news arrived that it was likely to be the latter, Antonino and his friends began to organize as best they could.

Antonino's sole aim was simple: to keep the vainglorious fascists from being honoured, or even received, by any of the local politicians. To do this, he had thought of writing and printing copies of a persuasive diatribe and handing them out at city hall, but he was afraid of the potential back-lash from something so overt. It was Serafim who suggested a more subtle tactic. Why not just print photographs of some prominent people Balbo's fascists had assassinated and hand those out instead? Serafim proposed that the photographs might even be without captions, hence inciting people to talk about them more, become curious, exchange information on who they thought these people were and why they were being handed their photos, for free, on this day in particular. Antonino had given Serafim a hearty slap on the back, pro-duced a photo of a well-known and well-liked priest whom Balbo had ordered one of his fascist squads to kill, and sent Serafim on his way with it, across town to a friend's printing press. Fifteen thousand copies were run.

On the day the fleet of planes landed near the waterfront in Montreal, Antonino and his friends, eight carloads full, distrib-uted the photographs to officials, as well as to everyone in and around the Mount Royal Hotel, where the airmen were stay-ing. The protest was a success in that Balbo was received by no one in the local political sphere. He was escorted around with as much pomp as the local blackshirts could afford, phalanxes of men who punched and pushed reporters out of the way, over-rode the authority of the official security (the Quebec Provin-cial Police), and lined up at the entrance of every building Balbo walked into and out of, to raise their arms in a fascist salute.

The following day, Serafim and Antonino went down to the harbourfront to watch the seaplanes take off, each of them having to confess how exhilarating the sight was. They had both, it turned out, had a childhood fascination with flying machines.

Two months later, a painting was completed on the dome of the Madonna della Difesa, the principal Italian church in the city. Its fresco depicted Mussolini on horseback with several of his distinguished minions gathered around him, General Balbo among them. In a sermon soon after, the priest pointed up at the painting and repeated what Balbo had been quoted as saying to an ecstatic Mass celebrated by Italian Americans in Madison Square Garden: "Be proud you are Italians. Mussolini has ended the era of humiliations."

It was mid-October, and Serafim had stopped by Antonino's house. As he usually did while visiting, he was lending a hand in one of the small gardens for the food co-operatives. Neither of them were inherent green thumbs, both of them hating the feel of earth as it crammed and pried beneath their fingernails. But food in exchange for some sweat, backaches, and dirty knees was a fair trade, and one that others had little access to. They talked disjointedly, pulling weeds and picking vegetables that were overripe and needed eating as soon as possible: eggplants whose skin had grown tough and dull, carrots diverging into coarse knuckles, onions with layers slicking caramel.

At one point in the afternoon, a group of boys passed by and called out from the other side of an adjoining fence, begging for food. Antonino stood up, slowly ratcheting his spine straight. Sure, he said, but they would have to do a bit of work for it. They weren't afraid of work, were they? The boys were shaking their heads as they scrambled to get over the fence. Once on the other side, the men could see they didn't own any shoes (or if they did, they were so worn out as to be reserved for winter use alone), their feet blackened and callused from the long urban summer. Antonino showed them how to dig for potatoes, marking off a small patch for them to mine, telling them they could keep half of whatever they found beneath. They dove into the task with the enthusiasm of panners for gold, digging and sifting through the soil, holding every treasure they came across up to the sun, cleaning the dirt from the nugget before tossing it onto a frayed cloth that had been laid on the ground beside them.

When they were finished, the two men returned to Antonino's townhouse, each of them with one hand on the heaped wicker basket of vegetables that swung between them. They washed their hands in a bucket of rainwater outside, and Antonino stepped in to say hello to his wife and child before returning with some glasses of water and cigarettes. He'd opened a window near the stoop so they could hear the gramophone he'd put on — *Nabucco*, his favourite opera. Serafim knew that when Antonino's favourite song, "Va pensiero," came on, he would lose his friend for a few moments, his eyes fixed on some distant place in the bushes nearby as the first stanza was sung in Italian: *Fly, thought, on wings of gold; settle upon the slopes and hills, where, soft and mild, the sweet airs of our native land smell fragrant.* But for the time being they both lit cigarettes, settled until they were comfortable on the wood of the front steps, elbows resting on the stair at their backs, legs splayed out in front, diagonal in the autumn sun. The neighbourhood sleepy, windless, the leaves rusting dry in the trees.

After a short silence, Serafim mentioned the letter he'd just received from Álvaro, which led them into politics, from the growing unrest in Spain to Roosevelt's "New Deal" and whether they thought his ambitious economic programs would work. They agreed it was doubtful. This led Antonino to the topic of the local fascist groups again, whose most recent solution to the difficult times in Montreal was to organize and facilitate immigration back out of Montreal, to Libya.

As Antonino and Serafim were each lighting a third cigarette, a man walked past, giving a wave. Suddenly Antonino was gesturing for him to come towards them, calling out in his faltering French, a language Serafim seldom heard him speak. "*Approchez, gentilhomme, approchez!*"

The man stopped in front of the stairs, shaking hands with each of them. Antonino introduced Serafim with unaccustomed formality. "Yves, I would like very much for you to meet Serafim Vieira. This is the photographer we spoke of, whose album of pictures you were so impressed with."

"Why, of course. How do you do, Mr. Vieira?" said Yves.

"How do you do?" responded Serafim, before looking over at Antonino. "I'm sorry, what album of pictures?"

"The pictures you've given me over the years — I've put them all in an album. Yves here works at *La Presse*, and he was particularly impressed with some of the photographs you'd taken in the streets."

"Yes, they were good, if I recall," said Yves. "Made you feel for the people they depicted. Actually, I have a story I'm writing tomorrow, about the workers striking downtown. We might be able to use such pictures for the article. We've been told to incorporate more pertinent photographs with our stories. I can't make any guarantees, least of all about pay, but if you can head down there at some point and take a few shots, we might be able to work something out. I might be able to use them."

"Sounds fair enough. I'll see what I can do," Serafim agreed.

Yves tipped his hat. "Well, I best be moving. Enjoy the rest of your day, gentlemen. One of the last warm ones, I fear," he prophesied, setting off into the languid afternoon.

"Good," Antonino said after some time. "I have a good feeling about it. I think things will work out for you, with this *La Presse* thing."

"Yes, well, we'll see. I know by now not to get too excited."

"Of course, of course — times are difficult. What I meant was, if there is anyone whom something like this would work out for, it is you."

Serafim cocked his head to the side. "I'm not sure I understand."

"I just mean to say that I think of you as someone whom luck smiles upon."

Serafim leaned forward. "Really? Álvaro mentioned something similar in his last letter. I really must confess, Antonino, I've never quite seen it that way myself."

"I know you haven't. But that is the remarkable thing about luck: it doesn't care how we see it." Antonino butted out his cigarette. "Which reminds me, I have something for you." He stood up and gestured for Serafim to follow. The men passed through the house, Serafim kissing a quick hello to Antonino's wife, and were soon out in the backyard, where they stopped in front of a table covered with odd and bulky shapes wrapped in butcher paper.

"What are these?" asked Serafim.

"Well, a friend of a friend who works in transport hit a deer on the road last week. He brought the poor mangled thing over, thinking of the food co-operatives and not wanting to waste the meat. So I had a butcher friend volunteer to gut and divide it. Apparently skinning it would've taken too long, so the hide still has to be removed from several portions." Antonino picked up a medium-sized bundle and handed it to Serafim, "Why don't you take this. I think it's a shoulder."

Serafim held it up, turned it over. "Yes, but I haven't a clue how to dress it. There's an actual leg sticking out of this."

"I'm sure you'll figure it out. When is the last time you ate meat?"

"A fair point, yes. Well, thank you."

"Every little bit helps, said the man pissing into the sea. Why don't we get you some vegetables while we're at it."

Serafim soon filled the wooden crate he'd mounted on the back of his bicycle (whose patch-ridden tires had a wobble that prevented him from advancing along the streets with any real speed or efficiency). Antonino, not wanting to be accused of favouritism to his friends when handing out food from the co-operative, made sure to give Serafim only the most unsightly of the produce they'd picked: yellowed lettuce with slug-emp-tied holes, blighted potatoes, the softest of the onions. The two men shook hands and Serafim cinched his hat down tight, hopped on his bike, and wove away down the street.

Twenty minutes later, he had gotten off in order to cross a set of streetcar tracks that had no cobblestones between them, and had taken the opportunity to check his watch. He was a tad early and so decided to walk his bicycle the rest of the way. Claire had asked him to keep away from the house that afternoon, stipulating that he could come back any time after four, though when he did, he was to knock and wait for her to answer before entering. To many, such a request would be highly suspicious, but it was an arrangement Serafim had been agreeing to for years.

The first time she'd asked him, she had plainly stated that she needed to do something secret but it was the kind of thing that needed to be done and it wasn't hurting anyone. Serafim had told her he understood but he didn't really, and while he'd made himself scarce as agreed, he wasn't so trusting as to leave the neighbourhood. Instead, he kept close and watched the front door of their apartment. Soon after he left, a middle-aged gentleman showed up touting a heavy bag, his other hand pulling on the railing as he laboured up the stairs. Minutes later, a young woman — who, Serafim assumed, was enrolled in the dance classes Claire volunteered her time to every week — sheepishly climbed the stairs after him. About an hour later, the man with the heavy bag left, while the young woman didn't reappear for quite some time. When she finally did, Claire left the house with her, accompanying her to the nearest tram stop. Since then, this was an occurrence that repeated itself every two or three months, never the same girl twice but always the same official-looking man. It was something Serafim had simply learned not to ask for details about, especially considering how easily embarrassed he was with Claire's candidness when talking about "women's matters." He was confident she wasn't having an affair; beyond that, he felt it wise to leave well enough alone.

On this particular day, he came across Claire outside, just as she was leaving a new girl at the tram stop nearest their apartment. When she saw him, she lifted her arm to wave, already heading towards him, and they were soon walking together, one on either side of the bicycle. Claire had grown her hair out and no longer hid it beneath a hat when she left the house, and Serafim watched as the sun's rays ran through the length of it, auburn bands of iridescence oscillating as she stepped. The limp in her stride was pronounced but natural, something she'd grown accustomed to. She had learned to walk with an air that was graceful again, in a gait that was not.

Serafim, not wanting to refer to how her afternoon had been, waited for her to begin speaking. It didn't take long. "And how's Antonino? Wow, so much food! What's in the wrapped parcel?"

"Antonino is fine. And that, I am proud to announce, is meat."

"That's an odd description. What kind of meat exactly? And honestly, what does Antonino *do* to these vegetables? Have you seen sadder lettuce in all your days?" She reached back to finger a withered head of the stuff, its yellowed leaves flopping to the side as if trying to avoid her criticism.

"Might be the way he picks them. The meat is . . . what is the word in French? *Veado* in Portuguese. An animal from the forest."

Claire raised her eyebrows. "Oh my."

Serafim nodded. "I know. The hair is still on it. And there are thick bones. It was killed by a motor car."

"Oh my."

They'd reached the stairs leading up to the apartment and began unloading the small crate. The impediment of Claire's ankle was never more pronounced than when she climbed stairs. It took her some time. Inside, they put the things in the kitchen, a room Serafim kept clean and fastidiously organized. There was a place for everything, and he was always putting things back into those rightful places after Claire had spent any time there, leaving surfaces crumb-strewn and in disarray behind her. Never having set aside a place for meat in such a form as this, and with no idea how to begin preparing it, Serafim just dropped the entire parcel into the sink.

"Are you hungry?" he asked.

"Famished," said Claire, already reaching for a knife and cutting board and stationing herself beside the kitchen sink, her preferred place when they ventured to fumble through a bit of cooking together. Sometimes it felt as if they were improving, making culinary headway of some sort. Sometimes not.

Either way, the vegetables were a godsend. There was little food in the house, and no ice in the icebox to keep it fresh even if there was. Serafim hadn't worked for weeks, and they were behind on their rent again, like everyone else in the building. Their landlord was so tired of fruitlessly hounding people that he'd stopped even bothering.

"Today, Antonino introduced me to a journalist from *La Presse*. He would like me to take photos of the strike downtown tomorrow."

Claire spun round from the sink, the green top of a carrot sprouting from her hand. "Why, that's fantastic!"

"I know. There's no mention of money yet, but Antonino said he has a good feeling about it."

Claire shook her head. "Great news." She suddenly slammed the carrot and knife onto the cutting board. "Music — we need music." She left the room, the familiar sounds of her uneven footfalls across the hardwood to the gramophone, followed by the scratch of the needle as it settled onto the vinyl, the swell of blurry song. Bing Crosby, an orchestra lamenting just behind him.

By the time she came back, Serafim had seated himself at the table with a smaller cutting board and was slicing away the rotten and inedible parts of each vegetable, washing the salvageable pieces in a bowl of water and placing them on a plate for Claire to chop later.

Meanwhile, Claire had finished cutting the carrots (into wildly uneven pieces) and was now unwrapping the meat. "How do we get the fur . . . How do we do this?" she asked with her back to him.

"Well, I . . . was hoping you knew."

Claire sighed, took a knife from the cutting board, and began to poke at the venison in the sink as if it might still be alive. Serafim watched her. The last of the day's sunlight shafted through the kitchen window, brushing the tops of the plants they had tried, and failed, to grow on the sill above the sink, the sickly pale of their leaves straggled and thin but now glowing.

Impulsively, he dried his hands on a tea towel and slipped out of the room to get his Leica. He returned to where he'd been sitting, advanced the film, adjusted his settings, and waited for Claire to turn round. The song on the record ended and a new one began. Claire put the knife down, at a loss how to continue. She paused, still fixed on the quandary, still trying to work it out.

As she did so, waiting with his camera poised, Serafim found himself thinking about what Álvaro had written, about what Antonino had said to him earlier that afternoon. He grinned. Luck, he thought to himself, was indeed a strange thing.

When Claire turned, Serafim released the shutter.

Montréal, le 15 septembre 1933

Salutations ma belle,

A letter for you, like old times! You and Serafim were both out when I dropped by, so I thought I'd sit at a café and scribble a note to slip under your door. What with our living a half-hour walk away from each other, there's really little reason to write anymore, and I find I miss it at times. Peculiar.

Anyway, I called by to talk to you, about the meal this coming Sunday. I want you to know that just because we could sit down with Maman and Papa and seem like a regular family the day we buried Grand-maman doesn't mean it'll work outside that context. I guess I just don't want you to expect too much.

I thought a lot about what was said that day, and what was not. There was no reference made to my divorce, or Gilles, which I think is understandable. But if you recall, there was also not a mention of your life in dance, between the time you left the "care" of our parents and the car accident that ended your career. As if your life as a dancer were a thing to be ashamed of.

Claire, for me it's simple: either Maman stretches the confines of her pious mentality to a point where she can weigh your experiences as things of value, or her world is simply too small and petty for us to fit inside. We will always have each other. I would rather be motherless than have to pretend disgrace just for the benefit of someone else's ego and distorted principles.

At any rate, we'll see how it goes on Sunday. Till then, ma belle.
Grosses bises,
Cécile

35

As soon as her divorce was final, Cécile moved back to Montreal. Gilles — whose political career had, as predicted, been somewhat damaged by the scandal — found some way to plod along, and within a year he had married again, this time a wide-eyed girl of nineteen who was shy and laughed easily. Cécile, on the other hand, was content to remain single for the time being. Before moving to Montreal she had already been in contact with the network of suffragist contemporaries in the city for years, and so when she arrived, she had help finding an apartment and a job, and plenty of work the moment she was settled. Aside from Mexico, Quebec was the last remaining state or province in North America that had not yet granted its women the right to vote. There was work to be done beyond this as well, in terms of other rights, support, and programs. What was more, Cécile was now working directly alongside the iconic women of the province whom she had so long revered, such as Idola Saint-Jean, Marie Lacoste Gérin-Lajoie, and Thérèse Casgrain. She was also happy to see that Claire, while never becoming outwardly active herself, was at least more interested in what Cécile had to say than before. She had become more of a listener.

Their mother's obsession with saving the pagan soul of their grandmother before she passed away had reached an extreme. The old woman was wheeled to Mass twice a day, and later stationed in front of shrines and lit candles to "pray" for long periods of time, her glassy eyes staring at nothing in the flickering dark. On her deathbed the priest was sent for, and the last rites administered, three times before she finally succumbed.

When she died, it had been eight years since Claire's mother or father had spoken to her directly, without Cécile as an intermediary. Her father phoned her up to invite her to the funeral, speaking as if they had just seen each other the week before. Claire agreed that she would go to pay her respects, and afterwards, though it was never her intention, she and Cécile (who was now equally out of favour on account of her divorce) went together to the wake, where they sat in a corner as a cohesive team. Daniel, their obedient brother, kept his distance from them. A few of their relatives cautiously approached, asking Claire how she'd been, and what *ever* had happened to her ankle. It was criminal, they'd declared, how dangerous the roads had become.

Again quite unintentionally, everyone had suddenly left the house except for the immediate family, who found themselves together and in the same apartment the children had grown up in. So it was natural that they were all invited to stay for a meal, which went surprisingly well. Admittedly, the conversation was contrived, awkward, and careful, but Claire sensed a degree of warmth — in place of hostility — buried just beneath it all. When the three children left, it was with a tentative invitation to have a proper Sunday meal sometime in the near future. Though what exactly "proper" meant, with so little means to buy food, was questionable.

The fateful Sunday arrived, and this time it wasn't all smiles and niceties. Cécile made a point of asking about Claire's days as a performer, the people she'd met, the different shows she'd been involved in. Their mother wore a tense grin and tried to change the subject, but Cécile kept returning to it. Daniel watched his fork and moved food around on his plate. As soon as their father began to express valid interest and acceptance, Cécile boldly ventured onto her own forbidden ground, talking about Gilles, their divorce, and then — flabbergasting everyone at the table — the affair she'd had that led to it. The kitchen clock counted out the seconds of quiet afterwards. "Well," their mother finally said, lacklustre, "anyone for dessert?"

They left with the feeling that such meals were not about to become a weekly occurrence, but that the two girls weren't going to be banished from the apartment's devout and hallowed walls either. On the street outside, Claire argued with Cécile about her tactics. "I just don't think they need to be forced to accept *every* aspect of who we are, especially when I can't offer the same in return. Besides, there are things, you know, that I *want* to keep to myself."

"Yes, of course, but not whole spans of your life, Claire. Not things you don't think of as mistakes, things you're proud of."

Claire looked out into the neighbourhood, which was holding the night lightly in its arms. "I just think that not everything has to be said. What would we be without our secrets?"

Cécile laughed, embraced her. "Empty. Though I hope you don't mean to say there are things you keep even from me?"

Claire kissed her goodbye. "Don't be ridiculous. Of course there are!"

On her way home, limping fluidly along the sidewalk, Claire found herself cataloguing those secrets she kept. One of them Cécile of all people would be extremely supportive of, even proud of her for; yet it was something she'd decided to keep exclusively to herself.

It had begun in the spring of 1932. Over the years Claire had come to take her unpaid responsibilities as a dance instructor with increasing earnestness, and it had gotten to the point where she dedicated most of her waking hours to the task. What surprised her was that the bulk of this time and energy was spent in her head, as she tried to figure out ways of getting each of her pupils to reach his or her (often hidden) potential. Somewhere along the way, Claire made what felt like a fascinating discovery: each of her students was receptive to a different set of methods, techniques, and training regimens; and at times their progress and improvement depended entirely on Claire's ability to reinvent her approach. Every apprentice became a separate puzzle to solve, and the gratification of finding an individual solution, and then seeing sudden and rapid improvements as a result, became the fulfilling reward she was after. She found that the more undivided her attention, the more her students flourished, often letting it slip that they preferred learning in "the basement" more than anywhere else in the city. She would never have imagined herself as a good teacher, but that is what it seemed she'd become. At the same time, the trust her students placed in her sometimes spilled over and outside the realm of dance.

In the spring of 1932, one of her pupils was having a rough day. She was a fidgety girl of fifteen, who at the best of times was ill at ease and lumbering but who was now so unfocused that she was becoming a hazard. Claire asked her to stay for some extra practice afterwards, and the moment the two of them were alone the girl broke down. When she'd calmed herself enough to speak, she confided that she had wanted to talk to Claire alone for quite some time. She was in trouble. Unimaginable trouble. Claire discovered that she was pregnant, and asked if she knew who the father was. Yes, the girl wept. Which had Claire asking if she had been violated. The girl shook her head no. Well then, marriage, Claire suggested, might yet be an avenue. You don't understand, the girl exclaimed, breaking down again. After a long while and a lot of coaxing, it came out that the future child was her brother's.

As the girl sobbed into her side, Claire thought long and hard about what to do, even if it was more or less obvious to her. She finally told the girl to come back the next day and in the meantime not to look for any "guaranteed solution" from some Red Light charlatan. Claire happened to know of a safe way out.

With no one able to afford his services, Dr. Bertrand wasn't busy when she arrived at his office.

"Why, Claire, what a pleasure. Come in, come in. What happened to your leg?"

"An accident, automobile."

"Cursed things. Would you like me to take a look at it?"

"No, thank you." Claire hesitated, trying to size the man up. "What I would like ... is for you to keep your word, to keep a promise you once gave me."

Dr. Bertrand straightened, put his hands in his pockets. "And what was that?"

"I need a ... fetal expulsion."

He held very still for a moment. "Claire, that's impossible."

"It's not for me, but for a young girl I know who's in serious trouble. It's her brother's, and I suspect she'll get it done regardless of whether it's someone who knows what he's doing or not."

Dr. Bertrand pinched some sleep from his eyes. "Sadly, the Church has grown watchful these last years. Do you know what could happen to me? To you? Her? And I needn't even bother asking if this would be paid ..." He turned his back to her, playing with some papers on a table. "These are hard times, Claire."

"Harder for some than for others, Dr. Bertrand. I'm pleading with you. Remember that I barely made it through, and even then not wholly intact."

His shoulders dropped. *"Merde,"* he mumbled. "Fine. But not here. It will have to be at some local address, have to look just like a house call. And this girl, she should never know my name."

"Agreed." Claire rocked on the heel of her left foot. "Thank you. Thank you, Dr. Bertrand. This means much to me."

They set up the appointment and decided to use Claire's apartment, where she would be able to stay with the girl afterwards. There was the risk of Serafim discovering them, but she could find a way around that easily enough. Taking advantage of his traditional and prudish views, she insinuated that she needed to be left alone for "women's reasons," reasons about which he was more than free to ask, though he was sure to be mortified if given the answer. As predicted, he kept a sufficient distance and his misgivings to himself.

The arrangement was supposed to be a one-off, an isolated rescue attempt, but within a few months careful confidants and discreet inquiries had led another young woman to "the basement," where she waited outside to catch Claire as she left for the day. It was imperative, the girl said, that she speak with Claire right away. To Claire, every story she heard seemed more desperate than the last, until she simply stopped asking for them, as did Dr. Bertrand. The circumstances that these girls (and sometimes older women) found themselves in became less important than their obvious need and powerlessness.

Claire sometimes wondered why she kept this from Cécile. Oddly enough, it occurred to her that it was *because* Cécile would praise her efforts, commend her. Claire wasn't doing what she was doing for Cécile, or her approval. Neither was she doing it for herself. Like her dance classes, she was acting on impulse, and from motives that she'd never really imagined were in her. In many ways, the more silent it all was, the more valuable.

It was late autumn, and Claire had just walked the latest of these girls to a tram stop near their apartment. As she turned to head home she saw Serafim making his way down the street. Perfect timing, she thought, waving and setting off towards him.

Serafim hadn't been able to find work for the last several weeks, and something that amazed Claire was that, even with so much time on their hands, they still managed to inhabit such close quarters without getting on each other's nerves. She suspected that one of the ways they accomplished this was by reading, both of them settling in corners of the studio, hunched over tomes in their laps. And seeing as they only read illicit literature, it made for intriguing conversation afterwards as well.

Both Cécile and Antonino had their hands in the dissident underworld of banned books, which had been censored by the Catholic Church and were often smuggled in by mail — Trotsky, Balzac, Huxley. Sometimes Serafim's friend Álvaro would send a few additional blacklisted authors from Paris — Descartes, Flaubert, Hugo — and if he was feeling unusually nostalgic he might throw in a record of Portuguese music as well, something that was easier to come by in France than in Canada. They were records whose melancholic harmonies Claire often enjoyed more than Serafim, who had never been as taken with music as she was.

It was among the last warm days of the year, a clear October afternoon, not a breath of wind, and it looked as if Serafim had been gardening with Antonino again. She soon caught up with him, and they walked on either side of his bicycle. "And, how's Antonino? Wow, so much food! What's in the wrapped parcel?"

"Antonino is fine. And that, I am proud to announce, is meat," he declared.

They hadn't eaten meat for what felt like months, though it was probably only weeks. They brought the groceries into the apartment, and with both of them hungry, they decided to get cooking right away. It was true that neither of them were artists in the kitchen, but Claire felt that they bumbled along well enough, and that they were making improvements all the time. While the vegetables he'd picked weren't superior by any standard, with a bit of cutting away and cleaning up one could get to something salvageable, even fresh, just beneath. The meat, however, was another thing. It was apparently venison, killed by a motor car, and one of its sides was still matted with fur. Claire had no idea how to begin cutting it, and happened to doubt that even a trained butcher would know. But once she had finished chopping a few carrots, she could feel that the job was falling to her, that Serafim was waiting for her to at least give it a shot. She prodded the meat with circumspection, trying to work out the best way to proceed.

As she did so, Claire heard Serafim get up from the table behind her and return with his camera, adjusting the settings in that highly concentrated way of his. He had just given her news that he might have some work tomorrow, taking pictures for one of the city's major newspapers. Something to celebrate, to be sure. Claire put the knife she was holding down on the cutting board beside her, rinsed her hands.

Yes, she contemplated, they both had so much. Which was probably what he wanted to capture, considered Claire, probably why he had just slipped out of the kitchen and returned with his camera, why he was waiting for her to pivot round and face him.

Claire smiled, quietly, and turned.

Medium: Gelatin silver print
Description: Woman standing at a sink
Location: Montreal, Quebec
Date: 1933

ॐ

A woman, wearing a simple and modest dress, stands before the sink in a small kitchen. Her hands are wet. One of them is reaching slightly behind her, clasped onto the porcelain lip of the basin, near a wooden cutting board that balances pieces of a carrot, unevenly sliced. The other hand she doesn't quite seem to know what to do with (likely on account of its glistening with water) and so is holding it at her sternum, as if for the interim, where it cups its own shadow.

She is smiling, the few lines drawn onto the left side of her mouth, in the shape of brackets, parenthesizing an intimacy she has with the person holding the camera. Her hair, dense and dark, falls in loose curls to just below her shoulders. The right side of these tresses is rimmed with light, which draws the eye up and into the background, where a small window hovers.

The window is overexposed, though the coarse grain of its brightness suggests that the pane of glass is somewhat dirty. Despite this, the sliver of a cathedral shaft filters through, folding into the leaves of a potted plant on the sill. There, luminescence, balling up like melted glass, drips from the sill into the washbasin, a soldering flare. This light lands just behind her, fanning out and settling into depressions and corners, as soundless as embers. And as incandescent.

ACKNOWLEDGEMENTS

The research required to write historical fiction puts one in touch with remarkable people, and I owe immense gratitude to many of them, for their time and their passion. Though I wish to begin with two people in particular: Maria Teresa Veloso Alves Rocha Resende de Almeida was an Oporto archivist who went to great lengths to ensure I understood the complexity of her city as it was in the 1920s, which included exposing me to different sights, neighbourhoods, archives, and restaurants while in Oporto. And Armida Spada-McDougall gave me treasured information on her father, Antonino Spada, who was at first just another vivid detail of the era that kept cropping up in my research, but who soon became nothing short of a hero figure in my mind. At some point, I decided to incorporate his real character, and many of his actual stories and struggles, into this work of fiction. The information that his daughter provided to this end was invaluable.

I received guidance concerning the openings and closings of the letters, as well as ideas on names and other historical facts, from Jean-François Millette, Genevieve Côté, Sophie Wertheimer, Inês Lopes, and Salvador Maria Simões de Carvalho. Isabelle Perreault provided insight into the early years of the Quebec feminist movement. Joyce Gilmour generously gave her time to proofreading an early draft. And a place to live and write most of the book was provided by Julian and Anne Whitlock in Brittany, and Patrick Andrivet and Kathy Coit in Paris.

Archivists who went above and beyond to help out with information were:

Marie-Josée Lecours at the Bibliothèque de la Danse.

Theresa Rowat, who also helped with dance history in Montreal.

Lyne Champagne at the City of Westmount.

Nicol Huber at the Musée des Hospitalières de l'Hôtel-Dieu de Montréal.

Jean-François Courtemanche for incredibly detailed information on the Laurier Palace Theatre fire and other firefighting realities of the day.

Marielle Lavertu and Audrey Saint-Jean, who helped me find early street photographs from the massive collection of photos at the Bibliothèque et Archives Nationales du Québec.

Paula Alexandra Lages de Oliveira and Rosa Maria Teixeira at the Biblioteca Pública Municipal do Porto.

And Helena Parente at the Centro Português de Fotografia.

ა

Of the heap of books I read, scanned, and photocopied, three stand out as exceptionally important:

Bystander, a History of Street Photography, by Colin Westerbeck and Joel Meyerowitz (Bulfinch, 1994)

Montréal de vive mémoire, 1900–1939, by Marcelle Brisson and Suzanne Côté-Gauthier (Triptyque, 1997)

Fascism and the Italians of Montreal, an Oral History: 1922–1945, by Filippo Salvatore (Guernica, 1998)

೮ನ

Of the fourteen theses I read, three were both instrumental and an absolute joy to read, namely Master's work by Karen Herland, Marc Charpentier and Tamara Myers.

೮ನ

Thanks also to the wonderful editors Jared Bland and Janice Zawerbny, who I am convinced loved and understood these characters as much as I did; and to Sarah MacLachlan and all the immensely talented folks at Anansi.

೮ನ

And thanks, finally, to Lauren, for listening so carefully.

ABOUT THE AUTHOR

Mark Lavorato is the author of two novels, *Veracity* and *Believing Cedric*, and a collection of poems, *Wayworn Wooden Floors*, which was a finalist for the Raymond Souster Award. He lives in Montreal, Quebec.